James Lee Burke is the author of thirty-one novels and two collections of short stories. He won the Edgar Award in 1998 for *Cimarron Rose*, while *Black Cherry Blues* won the Edgar in 1990 and *Sunset Limited* was awarded the CWA Gold Dagger in 1998. In 2009, the Mystery Writers of America presented him with the Grand Master Award. He lives with his wife, Pearl, in Missoula, Montana. Visit his website at www.jamesleeburke.com

JAMES LEE BURKE
CRUSADER'S CROSS

An Orion paperback

First published in Great Britain in 2005
by Orion
This new paperback edition published in 2013
by Orion Books,
an imprint of The Orion Publishing Group Ltd,
Orion House, 5 Upper St Martin's Lane,
London WC2H 9EA

An Hachette UK company

9 10

A CIP catalogue record for this book
is available from the British Library.

ISBN 978-0-7538-2093-3

Printed in Great Britain by Clays Ltd, St Ives plc

The Orion Publishing Group's policy is to use papers
that are natural, renewable and recyclable products and
made from wood grown in sustainable forests. The logging
and manufacturing processes are expected to conform to
the environmental regulations of the country of origin.

www.orionbooks.co.uk

For Linda and Roger Grainger

acknowledgements

I would like to thank George Schiro and the other staff members at the Acadiana Crime Lab in New Iberia, Louisiana, and also Jim Hutchison, Judi Hoffman, Annalivia Harris, Bahne Klietz, Maureen Kocisko, and Debbie Lewis at the Montana State Crime Lab in Missoula for their patience and kind assistance over the years.

Thanks also to David Rosenthal, Michael Korda, and Chuck Adams for their support and editorial help.

My thanks again to Patricia Mulcahy and my agent Philip G. Spitzer and his assistant Lukas Ortiz for their loyalty and friendship and goodwill.

Lastly, I wish to acknowledge those who have been with me for the long haul – my wife, Pearl, and our children, James L. Burke, Jr., Andree Walsh, Pamela McDavid, and Alafair Burke.

God bless all creatures and things, large and small.

Crusader's Cross

chapter one

It was the end of an era, one that I suspect historians may look upon as the last decade of American innocence. It was a time we remember in terms of images and sounds rather than historical events – pink Cadillacs, drive-in movies, stylized street hoods, rock 'n' roll, Hank and Lefty on the jukebox, the dirty bop, daylight baseball, chopped-down '32 Fords with Merc engines drag-racing in a roar of thunder past drive-in restaurants, all of it backdropped by palm trees, a curling surf, and a purple sky that had obviously been created as a cinematic tribute to our youth.

The season seemed eternal, not subject to the laws of mutability. At best, it was improbable that the spring of our graduation year would ever be stained by the tannic smell of winter. If we experienced visions of mortality, we needed only to look into one another's faces to reassure ourselves that none of us would ever die, that rumors of distant wars had nothing to do with our own lives.

My half brother was Jimmie Robicheaux. He was a hothead, an idealist, and a ferocious fistfighter in a beer-glass brawl, but often vulnerable and badly used by those who knew how to take advantage of his basic goodness. In 1958, he and I worked ten days on and five days off for what was called a doodlebug outfit, or seismograph crew,

1

laying out rubber cable and seismic jugs in bays and swamps all along the Louisiana-Texas coastline. During the off-hitch, when we were back on land, we hung out at Galveston Island, fishing at night on the jetties, swimming in the morning, eating fried shrimp in a café on the amusement pier where the seagulls fluttered and squeaked just outside the open windows.

The Fourth of July that year was a peculiar day. The barometer dropped and the sky turned a chemical green, and the breakers were full of sand and dead baitfish when they smacked on the beach. The swells were smooth-surfaced and rain-dented between the waves, but down below, the undertow was terrific, almost like steel cable around the thighs, the sand rushing out from under our feet as the waves sucked back upon themselves.

Most swimmers got out of the water. Perhaps because of our youth or the fact Jimmie and I had drunk too much beer, we swam far out from the beach, to the third sandbar, the last one that provided a barrier between the island itself and the precipitous descent off the edge of the continental shelf. But the sandbar was hard-packed, the crest only two feet below the surface, which allowed the swimmer to sit safely above the tidal current and enjoy a panoramic view of both the southern horizon and the lights that were going on all over the island.

The sun broke through the thunderheads in the west, just above the earth's rim, like liquid fire pooled up inside the clouds. For the first time that day we could see our shadows on the water's surface. Then we realized we were not alone.

Thirty yards out a shark fin, steel-gray, triangular in shape, cut across the swell, then disappeared under a wave. Jimmie and I stood up on the sandbar, our hearts beating, and waited for the fin to resurface. Behind us we could hear the crackle of lightning in the clouds.

'It's probably a sand shark,' Jimmie said.

But we both knew that most sand sharks were small, yellowish in hue, and didn't cruise at sunset on the outer shelf. We stared at the water for a long time, then saw a school of baitfish scatter in panic across the surface. The baitfish seemed to sink like silver coins into the depths, then the swell became smooth-surfaced and dark green again, wrinkling slightly when the wind gusted. I could hear Jimmie breathing as though he had labored up a hill.

'You want to swim for it?' I asked.

'They think people are sea turtles. They look up and see a silhouette and see our arms and legs splashing around and think we're turtles,' he said.

It wasn't cold, but his skin looked hard and prickled in the wind.

'Let's wait him out,' I said.

I saw Jimmie take a deep breath and his mouth form a cone, as though a sliver of dry ice were evaporating on his tongue. Then his face turned gray and his eyes looked into mine.

'What?' I said.

Jimmie pointed southward, at two o'clock from where we stood. A fin, larger than the first one, sliced diagonally across a swell and cut through a cresting wave. Then we saw the shark's back break the surface, a skein of water sliding off skin that was the color of scorched pewter.

There was nothing for it. The sun was setting, like a molten planet descending into its own smoke. In a half hour the tide would be coming in, lifting us off the sandbar, giving us no option except to swim for the beach, our bodies in stark silhouette against the evening sky.

We could hear music and the popping of fireworks on the amusement pier and see rockets and star shells exploding above the line of old U.S. Army officers' quarters along the beachfront. A wave slid across my chest, and inside it I saw the pinkish blue air sac and long tendril-like stingers of a Portuguese man-of-war. It

3

drifted away, then another one, and another fell out of a wave and twisted in an eddy like half-inflated balloons.

It was going to be a long haul to the beach.

'There's sharks in the water! Didn't you fellers see the lifeguard's flag?' a voice called.

I didn't know where the girl had come from. She sat astride an inner tube that was roped to two others, a short wood paddle in her hands. She wore a one-piece black swimsuit and had sandy reddish hair, and her shoulders glowed with sunburn. Behind her, in the distance, I could see the tip of a rock jetty that jutted far out into the breakers.

She paddled her makeshift raft until it had floated directly above the sandbar and we could wade to it.

'Where did you come from?' Jimmie said.

'Who cares? Better jump on. Those jellyfish can sting the daylights out of you,' she said.

She was tall and slight of build and not much older than we were, her accent hard-core East Texas. A wave broke against my back, pushing me off balance. 'Are you fellers deaf? Y'all sure don't act like you care somebody is trying to hep you out of the big mess you got yourself into,' she said.

'We're coming!' Jimmie said, and climbed onto one of the inner tubes.

Waves knocked us over twice and it took us almost a half hour to cross the trough between the third and second sandbars. I thought I saw a fin break the surface and slide across the sun's afterglow, and, once, a hard-bodied object bumped against my leg, like a dull-witted bully pushing past you on a crowded bus. But after we floated past the second sandbar, we entered another environment, one connected to predictability where we could touch bottom with the ends of our toes and smell smoke from meat fires and hear children playing tag in the darkness.

4

We told ourselves a seascape that could contain predators and the visitation of arbitrary violence upon the unsuspecting no longer held any sway in our lives. As we emerged from the surf the wind was as sweet as a woman's kiss against the skin.

The girl said her name was Ida Durbin and she had seen us through binoculars from the jetty and paddled after us because a shark had already attacked a child farther up the beach. 'You'd do that for anybody?' Jimmie said.

'There's always some folks who need looking after, at least those who haven't figured out sharks live in deep water,' she said.

Jimmie and I owned a 1946 canary-yellow Ford convertible, with whitewall tires and twin Hollywood mufflers. We drove Ida back to the jetty, where she retrieved her beach bag and used a cabana to change into a sundress and sandals. Then we went to a beer garden that also sold watermelon and fried shrimp. The palm trees in the garden were strung with tiny white lights, and we sat under the palms and ate shrimp and watched the fireworks explode over the water.

'Are y'all twins?' she asked.

'I'm eighteen months older,' I said.

She looked at both of us. 'Y'all sure favor for brothers who aren't twins. Maybe your mama just liked the way y'all looked and decided she'd use just one face,' she said. She smiled at her own joke, then looked away and studied the tops of her hands when Jimmie's eyes tried to hold hers.

'Where you live, Ida?' he asked.

'Over yonder,' she said, nodding vaguely up the main drag.

'You work here in Galveston?' he said.

'For a little while, I am. I got to go now,' she replied.

'We'll drive you,' he said.

5

'I'll take a cab. I do it all the time. It's only fifty cents,' she said.

Jimmie started to protest. But she got up and brushed crumbs of fried shrimp off her dress. 'You boys don't get in no more trouble,' she said.

'Boys?' Jimmie said, after she was gone.

Galveston Island was a strange place back in those days. The town was blue-collar, the beaches segregated, the Jax brewery its most prominent industry, the old Victorian homes salt-bitten and peeling. It was a vacation spot for the poor and the marginal and a cultural enclave where the hard-shell Baptist traditions of Texas had little application. Every beer joint on the beach featured slot and racehorse machines. For more serious gamblers, usually oil people from Houston, there were supper clubs that offered blackjack, craps, and roulette. One Sicilian family ran it all. Several of their minions moved out to Vegas in '47 with Benjamin Siegel. One of them, in fact, built the Sands.

But nonetheless there was an air of both trust and innocence about the island. The roller coaster in the amusement park had been officially condemned by the Texas Department of Public Safety, the notice of condemnation nailed on a post hard by the ticket booth. But every night during the summer, vacationers packed the open cars that plummeted down warped tracks and around wooden turns whose spars and rusted bolts vibrated like a junkyard.

Churchgoing families filled the bingo parlors and ate boiled crabs that sometimes had black oil inside the shells. At daybreak, huge garbage scows sailed southward for the horizon, gulls creaking overhead, to dump tons of untreated waste that somehow, in the mind's eye, were refined into inert molecules of harmless matter.

But inland from the carnival rides, the fishing jetties,

6

and the beachfront beer joints and seafood restaurants, there was another Galveston, and another industry, that made no pretense to innocence.

During the next two days we didn't see Ida Durbin on the main drag or on the amusement pier or on any of the jetties, and we had no idea where she lived, either. Then, on Saturday morning, while we were in a barbershop a block from the beach, we saw her walk past the window, wearing a floppy straw hat and a print dress, with a lavender Mexican frill around the hem, a drawstring bag slung from her shoulder.

Jimmie was out the door like a shot.

She told him she had to buy a money order for her grandmother in Northeast Texas, that she had to pick up her mail at the post office, that she had to buy sunburn lotion for her back, that she was tied up all day and evening.

'Tomorrow is Sunday. Everything is closed. What are you doing then?' he said, grinning.

She looked quizzically at nothing, her mouth squeezed into a button. 'I reckon I could fix some sandwiches and meet y'all at the amusement pier,' she said.

'We'll pick you up,' he said.

'No, you won't,' she replied.

The next day we discovered a picnic with Ida Durbin meant Vienna sausage sandwiches, sliced carrots, a jar of sun tea, and three Milky Way bars.

'Some folks don't like Viennas,' she said, and she pronounced the word 'Vy-ennas.' 'But with lettuce and mayonnaise, I think they're real good.'

'Yeah, these are a treat. Aren't they, Dave?' Jimmie said.

'You bet,' I said, trying to wash down a piece of simulated sausage that was like a chunk of rubber.

We were on the amusement pier, sitting on a wood bench in the shade of a huge outdoor movie screen. In the background I could hear pinball machines and popping sounds from a shooting gallery. Ida wore a pink skirt and a white blouse with lace on the collar; her arms and the top of her chest were powdered with strawberry freckles.

'Dave and I go back on the quarter boat in the morning,' Jimmie said.

She chewed on the end of a carrot stick, her eyes staring blankly at the beach and the surf sliding up on the sand.

'We'll be back on land in ten days,' Jimmie said.

'That's good. Maybe I'll see y'all again,' she said.

But if there was any conviction in her voice, I did not hear it. Down below, a huge wave crashed against the pilings, shuddering the planks under our feet.

chapter two

After the next hitch we went back to the motel where our cousin, the manager, who was confined to a wheelchair, let us stay free in return for running a few errands. For the next five days Jimmie had nothing on his mind except seeing Ida. We cruised the main drag in our convertible, night-fished on the jetties, went to a street dance in a Mexican neighborhood, and played shuffleboard in a couple of beer joints on the beach, but nobody we talked to had ever heard of Ida Durbin.

'It's my fault. I should have given her the motel number,' he said.

'She's older than us, Jimmie.'

'So what?' he said.

'That's the way girls are when they're older. They don't want to hurt our feelings, but they got their own lives to live, like they want to be around older men, know what I mean? It's a put-down for them to be seen with young guys,' I said.

Wrong choice.

'I don't believe that at all. She wouldn't have made sandwiches for us. You calling her a hypocrite or something?' he said.

We went back on the quarter boat and worked a job south of Beaumont, stringing rubber cable and seismic jugs through a swamp, stepping over cottonmouths and swatting at mosquitoes that hung as thick as black gauze inside the shade. When we came off the hitch we were sick with sunburn and insect bites and spoiled food the cooks had served after the refrigeration system had failed. But as soon as we got to our motel, Jimmie showered and changed into fresh clothes and started looking for Ida again.

'I found her,' he said our second day back. 'She's at a music store. She was piddling around with a mandolin, *plink, plink, plink,* then she started singing, with just me and the owner there. She sounds like Kitty Wells. She promised she'd wait. Come on, Dave.'

'Why'd you come back to the motel?'

'To get my wallet. I'm gonna buy us all a meal.'

Jimmie had said she was waiting in a music store. It was actually a pawnshop, a dirt-smudged orange building sandwiched between a pool hall and a bar on the edge of the black district. She was sitting on a bench, under the canvas awning, twisting a peg on a Gibson mandolin that rested in her lap. Most of the finish below the sound hole had been worn away by years of plectrum strokes across the wood.

The street was hot, full of noise and dust and smoke from junker cars. 'Oh, hi, fellers,' she said, looking up from under her straw hat. 'I thought you weren't coming back. I was just fixing to leave.'

'Did you buy the mandolin?' Jimmie asked.

'It's already mine. I pay the interest on it so Mr. Pearl doesn't have to sell it. He lets me come in and play it whenever I want.'

She returned the mandolin to the pawnshop owner, then came outside again. 'Well, I'd better get going,' she said.

'I'm taking us to lunch,' Jimmie said.

'That's nice, Jimmie, but I got to get ready for work,' she said.

'Where you work?' he asked.

She smiled, her eyes green and empty in the sunlight, her attention drifting to a car backfiring in the street.

'This time we'll drive you,' I said.

'My bus stops right on the corner. See, there it comes now, right on time,' she said, and started walking toward the intersection. A throwaway shopper's magazine was tucked under her arm. She looked back over her shoulder. 'I've got your phone number now. I'll call you. I promise.'

Jimmie stared after her. 'You should have heard her sing,' he said.

When the bus pulled away from the curb, Ida was sitting up front, in the whites-only section, totally absorbed with her magazine.

Just as we got into our convertible, the owner of the pawnshop came out on the sidewalk. He was a tall, white-haired man with a sloping girth and big hands and cigars stuffed in his shirt pocket. 'Hey, you two,' he said.

'Sir?' I said.

'That girl has enough trouble in her life. Don't you be adding to it,' the owner said.

Jimmie's hands were on top of the steering wheel, his head bent forward. 'What the hell are you talking about?' he said.

'Sass me again and I'll explain it to you,' the owner said.

'Screw that. What do you mean she's got trouble?' Jimmie said.

But the pawnshop owner only turned and went back inside his building.

The next night Jimmie came in drunk and fell down in the tin shower stall. He pushed me away when I tried to help him up, his muscular body beaded with water, a rivulet of blood running from his hairline.

'What happened?' I said.

'Nothing,' he replied.

'Is this about Ida Durbin?'

'That's not what they call her,' he said.

'What?'

'Shut up about Ida,' he said.

The next morning he was gone before I woke up, but our car was still in the carport. I crossed Seawall Boulevard to the beach and saw him sitting on the sand, shirtless and barefoot, surrounded by the collapsed air sacs of jellyfish.

'They call her Connie where she works. They don't have last names there,' he said.

The previous afternoon Ida had called him at the motel and told him that he was a nice fellow, that she knew he would do well in college, and maybe years from now they'd see one another again when he was a rich and successful man. But in the meantime this was good-bye and he mustn't get her confused in his mind with the girl who was right for him.

After she rang off, Jimmie went straight to the pawnshop and told the owner he wanted to buy Ida's mandolin.

'It's not for sale,' the owner said.

'I'm going to give it to Ida as a present. Now, how much is it?' Jimmie said.

'What do you think you're gonna get out of this, son?' he said.

'Get out of what?'

The owner clicked his fingers on the glass display case. 'It's thirty-five dollars on the loan, two dollars for the closing charge.'

Jimmie counted out the money from his billfold. The owner placed the mandolin in a double paper sack and set it on the display case.

'Can you tell me where she works or lives?' Jimmie asked.

The owner looked at him as though a lunatic had walked into his shop.

'Thought you were a put-on, boy, but I guess you're for real. She lives and works in the same place. On Post Office Street. You figured it out by now?'

The paint on the two-story houses was blistered, the dirt yards weedless and hard-packed, the bedsheets on the clotheslines flapping in a hot wind. Jimmie parked the convertible and looked uncertainly at the houses, the neck of the mandolin clutched in one hand. A city police car passed by, with two uniformed officers in the front seat. They were talking to one another and neither paid attention to his presence on the street. 'I'm looking for Ida Durbin,' Jimmie said to a black girl who was hanging wash in a side yard.

The girl was frail and wore a dusty yellow blouse with loops of sweat in the armpits. Her forearms were wrapped with a mottled pink and white discoloration, as though her natural color had been leached out of the skin. She shook her head.

'She has freckles and sandy red hair. Her name is Ida,' Jimmie said.

'This is a colored house. White mens don't come in the daytime,' she said. The wind flapped a sheet that was gray from washing across her face, but she seemed not to notice.

Jimmie stepped closer to her. 'Listen, if this girl works in a place for white people, where would I –' he began.

Then Jimmie felt rather than saw a presence at the window behind him. The black girl picked up her basket of wash and walked quickly away. 'You don't look like the gas man,' the man in the window said.

He was white, with small ears, sunken cheeks, and hair that was as black and shiny as patent leather, oiled and combed into a slight curl on the neck.

'I'm looking for Ida Durbin,' Jimmie said.

The man leaned on the sill and thought about it. He wore a creamy cowboy shirt with stitched pockets and chains of roses sewn on the shoulders. 'Four doors down. Ask for Connie. Tell you what, I'll walk you there,' he said.

'That's all right,' Jimmie said.

'I'm here to serve,' the man said.

On the way down the street, the man extended his hand. It was small and hard, the knuckles pronounced. 'I'm Lou Kale. Connie's your heartthrob?' he said.

'The girl I'm looking for is named Ida.'

'On this street, nobody uses their own name. That is, except me,' Lou Kale said, and winked. 'I was gonna call her Ida Red, after the girl in the song. Except she didn't think that was respectful, so she made up her own name. What's *your* name?'

Jimmie hesitated, touching his bottom lip with his tongue.

'See what I mean?' Lou Kale said. 'Soon as people set foot on Post Office Street, their names fly away.'

Lou Kale escorted Jimmie through the front door of a two-story Victorian house with hollow wood pillars on the gallery and a veranda on the second floor. The shades were drawn in the living room to keep out the dust, and the air inside the heated walls was stifling. The couches and straight-back chairs were empty; the only color in the room came from the plastic casing of a Wurlitzer jukebox plugged into the far wall. Lou Kale told a heavyset white woman in the kitchen that Connie had a caller.

The woman labored up a stairs that groaned with her weight and shouted down a hallway.

'Look at me, kid,' Lou Kale said. He seemed to lose his train of thought. He touched at his nostril with one knuckle, then huffed air out his nose, perhaps reorganizing his words. He was shorter than Jimmie, firmly built, flat-stomached, with thick veins in his arms, his dark jeans belted high on his hips. His face seemed full of play now. 'You're not here to get your ashes hauled, are you?'

'Who cares why I'm here. It's a free country, ain't it?' Jimmie replied. Then wondered why he had just used bad grammar.

Lou Kale made a sucking sound with his teeth, his eyelids fluttering as he watched a fly buzzing on the wall. Then he jiggled his fingers in the air, as though surrendering to a situation beyond his control. 'You give your present to Connie, then you beat feet. This place is off limits for you and so is Connie. That means you find your own girlfriend and you don't try to get a punch on somebody else's tab. We connecting here?'

'No.'

'That's what I thought,' Lou Kale said. 'Connie, get down here!'

When Ida Durbin came down the stairs she was wearing a pair of tight, blue-jean shorts and a blouse that looked made of cheesecloth that outlined the black bra she wore underneath. She had been asleep, and her face was flushed from the stored-up heat in the upper levels of the building and marked with lines from the pillow she had been sleeping upon. Even in the gloom Jimmie could see the injury in her eyes when she realized who her visitor was.

'Let's have a quick exchange of pleasantries, then your friend is gonna be on his way,' Lou Kale said to her.

Jimmie stepped toward her, his arm brushing Lou Kale's shoulder. 'I paid off your loan on the mandolin,' he said.

'Jimmie, you shouldn't be here,' she said.

'I just thought I'd drop the mandolin by, that's all,' he said. He handed it to her, his movements stiff, his voice tangled in his throat. Lou Kale clicked a fingernail on the glass cover of his wristwatch.

'Thank you. You better go now,' she said.

Then Jimmie couldn't hold it in any longer. 'Who is this guy?' he asked, pointing sideways at Lou Kale. 'What are you doing here?'

'Connie, two Panamanian tankers docked this morning. Go finish your nap,' Lou Kale said. 'Everything is solid. Believe me, I like this guy. He's a cute boy, that's what he is.'

She went up the stairs, glancing back once at Jimmie. Lou Kale moved into Jimmie's line of sight. 'You've done your good deed. That's reward enough, right?' he said. *'Right?'*

'Yeah,' Jimmie said. But he didn't move from his position.

'We don't want insincerity here,' Lou Kale said, resting his hand on Jimmie's shoulder, his breath touching Jimmie's skin.

Then Lou Kale walked him to the door, as though Jimmie had no volition of his own, and before Jimmie knew it, he was back outside, the door shutting loudly behind him.

The sun was white and hot in the sky, and the humidity felt like damp wool on his skin. For a moment he could hear no sound, as though he were trapped inside a glass bell. Upstairs, someone turned on a radio, and from the window he heard the adenoidal voice of Kitty Wells singing 'It Wasn't God Who Made Honky-Tonk Angels.'

After Jimmie told me of his visit to Post Office Street, I took him to breakfast and thought our misadventure with Ida Durbin was over. But I was wrong. She called him that afternoon and asked to meet him on the amusement pier.

'Leave her alone,' I told him.

'She paddled through sharks to get us off a sandbar,' he said.

'She's a prostitute. You can't change that. Act like you have a brain,' I said.

Once again, I had spoken without thinking. Our father, known as Big Aldous Robicheaux in the oil patch, had been a good-hearted, illiterate Cajun and notorious barroom brawler whose infidelities had included a prostitute in Abbeville. The prostitute died of Hansen's disease in a federal facility at Carville, Louisiana. She was also Jimmie's mother.

I went to the pier with Jimmie and listened to Ida Durbin's story about her background, a story that neither Jimmie nor I had the experience to deal with or even evaluate in terms of veracity. She told us she had been raised by her grandmother in a sawmill town just south of the Arkansas line, and that she had borrowed twenty-seven hundred dollars from the mortgage holder of their house to pay for the grandmother's cancer treatment in Houston. When Ida couldn't pay back the loan, she was offered a choice of either eviction or going to work in a hot pillow joint.

'Stuff like that doesn't happen, Ida. At least, not anymore,' Jimmie said. His eyes clicked sideways at her. 'Does it?'

She turned one cheek into the light. It was layered with makeup, but we could see the swelling along the jawline, like a chain of tiny dried grapes. 'I talked to Lou Kale about getting out. He said if I worked what they call special trade, that's girls who do everything, I can be even in a month,' she said.

'He put those bruises on your face?' Jimmie said.

'A cop did. He was drunk. It's nothing,' she said.

We were on the end of the pier, and we could see gulls dipping sand shrimp out of the waves. The sun was hot on the boards, the wind blowing, and blood had dried on the railing where someone had chopped up fish bait.

'A cop?' Jimmie said.

'They get free ones sometimes,' she said.

I didn't want to listen to it anymore. I went back to the

motel by myself. Later, I heard Jimmie outside with Ida, then the two of them driving away in our convertible.

Jimmie didn't go back on the job with me the next day and instead hung out with Ida in Galveston. He bought her clothes and paid four dollars apiece for four recordings of her songs in a recording booth on the amusement pier. This was in an era when we were paid one dollar and ten cents an hour for work that, outside of building board roads in swamps, was considered the lowest and dirtiest in the oil field. He also withdrew his one hundred and twelve dollars in savings from the bank, money put away for his college tuition, and gave it to Ida. When I came back off the hitch, I wanted to punch him out.

'What'd she do with it?' I said. He was doing push-ups on the floor in his underwear, his feet propped up on the windowsill. His hair was black and shiny, his wide shoulders as smooth as tallow.

'Gave it to this guy Lou Kale to pay off her debt,' he replied. He dropped his feet from the sill and sat up. From outside I could hear the surf crashing on the beach. 'Quit looking at me like that.'

'Nobody is that stupid,' I said.

'We sent one of her recordings to Sun Records in Memphis. That's where Johnny Cash and Elvis Presley got started. Jerry Lee Lewis, too,' he said.

'Yeah, I heard the Grand Ole Opry has a lot of openings for singing prostitutes.'

'Why don't you show a little respect for other people once in a while?' he said.

Was I my brother's keeper? I decided I was not. I also decided I did not want to be held hostage by what I considered the self-imposed victimhood of others. I let Jimmie take the convertible and I went back to Louisiana until it was time to rejoin the doodlebug crew on the quarter boat. I hoped by the end of the next hitch, Jimmie would be free of his entanglement with Ida Durbin.

It was a hot, windblown day when Jimmie picked me up at the dock. A storm was building, and in the south the sky was the blue-black of gunmetal, the inland waters yellow with churned sand, the waves capping as far as the eye could see. Jimmie had the top down on the convertible, and he grinned from behind his shades when he saw me walking toward him with my duffel bag over my shoulder. A bucket of iced-down Pearl and Jax sat on the backseat, the long-neck bottles sweating in the sunlight.

'You look like a happy man,' I said.

'Ida's getting out of the life. I'm moving her out of that house tonight. We're going to Mexico,' he said. He reached in back and slid a beer out of the ice. He cracked off the cap with a bottle opener that hung from a cord around his neck and handed the bottle to me. 'You don't have anything to say?'

'It's a little more than I can think my way through right now. How do you get somebody out of the life?' I said.

'I went to the cops. This is a free country. People can't make other people work in whorehouses,' he said.

I didn't speak until after he started the engine and began backing out of the parking area, the sun hot on the leather seats, the palm trees clattering in the wind. 'The cops who get free ones are on the side of the good guys now?' I said.

'There *was* one little bump in the road,' he said. 'Remember the hundred and twelve bucks Ida and I gave this guy Lou Kale? He says the guys he works for consider that the interest, so Ida still owes the principal. I don't quite know what to do about that.'

He lifted a beer out of a wire holder on the dashboard and drank it while he steered with one hand, his sunglasses patterned with the reflected images of trees, sky, and asphalt, all of it rushing at him, like a film strip out of control, as he pushed the accelerator to the floor.

That evening Jimmie went off with Ida in the car, supposedly to confront Lou Kale about the one hundred twelve dollars Kale had obviously stolen. I walked down on the amusement pier and ate a burrito for supper. The thunderheads in the south rippled with electricity and I could see the lights of freighters on the horizon and I wondered if Jimmie was actually serious about going to Mexico with Ida Durbin. In three weeks the fall term would be starting at Southwestern Louisiana Institute, in Lafayette, where we were both enrolled. We were three weeks away from normalcy and football games on crisp Saturday afternoons, the booming sounds of marching bands, the innocence of the freshman sock hop in the school gym, the smell of leaves burning and barbecues in the city park across the street from the campus. In my mind's eye I saw my self-deluded half brother sinking in quicksand, while Ida Durbin sat astride his shoulders.

My own mother had long ago disappeared into a world of low-rent bars and lower-rent men. Big Aldous, our father, had died in an oil well blowout when I was eighteen. Jimmie'd had little or no parental authority in his life, and I had obviously proved a poor substitute for one. I threw my burrito in a trash can, went to a beer joint down the beach, and drank until 2:00 a.m. while hailstones the size of mothballs pelted the surf.

I woke before dawn, trembling all over, the distorted voices and faces of the people from the bar more real than the room around me. I couldn't remember how I had gotten back to the motel. Water was leaking through the ceiling, and a garbage can was tumbling end over end past the empty carport. I sat on the edge of my bed, my hands shaking, my throat so dry I couldn't swallow. The window curtains were open, and a network of lightning bloomed over the Gulf, all the way to the top of the sky. Inside the momentary white brilliance that lit the clouds and waves I thought I saw a green-black lake where the naked bodies of the damned were submerged to their chests, their mouths crying out to any who would hear.

I didn't know it at the time, but I had just booked my first passage on the SS *Delirium Tremens*.

I buried my head under a pillow and fell into a sweaty dream. Thunder shook the walls and sheets of rain whipped against the windows. I thought I heard the door open and wind and a sudden infusion of dampness blow into the room. Maybe Jimmie had returned, safe and sound, and all my fears about him had been unjustified, I told myself in my sleep. But when I looked up, the room was quiet, his bed made, the carport empty. I felt myself descending into a vortex of nausea and fear, accompanied by a dilation of blood vessels in the brain that was like a strand of piano wire being slowly tightened around my head with a stick.

When I woke a second time, I could hear no sound except the rain hitting on the roof. The thunder had stopped, the power in the motel was out, and the room was absolutely black. Then a tree of lightning crackled over the Gulf and I saw a man seated in a chair, no more than two feet from me. He wore sideburns and a striped western shirt, with pearl-colored snap buttons. His cheeks were sunken, pooled with shadow, his mouth small, filled with tiny teeth. A nickel-plated automatic with white grips rested on his thigh.

He leaned forward, his eyes examining me, his breath moving across my face. 'What's your name?' he said.

'Dave,' I said. 'Dave Robicheaux.'

'If you ain't Jimmie, you're his twin. Which is it?' he said.

'Tell me who you are,' I said.

He touched the pistol barrel to the center of my forehead. 'I ask the questions, hoss. Lay back down,' he said.

I saw a swelling above his left eye, a cut in his lip, a clot of blood in one nostril. He pulled back the receiver on the pistol and snicked a round into the chamber. 'Put your hands on top of the covers,' he said.

With one hand he felt my knuckles and the tops of my fingers, his eyes fastened on my face. Then he stood up, dropped the magazine from the butt of the automatic, and ejected the round in the chamber. He reached over, picked up the cartridge from the rug, and snugged it in his watch pocket. 'You got a lot of luck, kid. When you get a break, real slack, like you're getting now, don't waste it. You heard it from the butter and egg man,' he said.

Then he was gone. When I looked out the window I saw no sign of him, no automobile, not even footprints in the muddy area around the room's entrance. I lay in bed, a bilious fluid rising from my stomach, my skin crawling with a sense of violation and the stale odor of copulation from the bedcovers.

Unbelievably, I closed my eyes and fell asleep again, almost like entering an alcoholic blackout. When I woke it was midmorning, the sun shining, and I could hear children playing outside. Jimmie was packing an open suitcase on top of his bed. 'Thought you were going to sleep all day,' he said.

'A guy was looking for you. I think it was that pimp from Post Office Street,' I said.

'Lou Kale? I don't think so,' Jimmie replied.

'He had a gun,' I said. 'What do you mean you don't think so?'

'He didn't want to pay back the hundred and twelve bucks he stole. He pulled a shiv on me. So I cleaned his clock. I took the money off him, too,' he said. He dropped his folded underwear in the suitcase and flattened it down, his eyes concentrated on his work. I couldn't believe what he had just said.

'Where's Ida?' I asked.

'Waiting for me at the bus depot. Get dressed, you got to drive me down there. We'll be eating Mexican food in ole Monterrey tonight. Hard to believe, isn't it?' he said. He touched at the tops of his swollen hands, then grinned at me and shrugged his shoulders. 'Quit worrying. Guys like Kale are all bluff.'

But Ida was not at the bus depot, nor, when the cops checked, was she at the brothel on Post Office Street. In fact, she had disappeared as though she had been vacuumed off the face of the earth. We didn't know the name of the town she came from, nor could we even be sure her real name was Ida Durbin. The cops treated our visits to the police station as a nuisance and said Lou Kale had no criminal record, that he denied having a confrontation with Jimmie and denied ever knowing a woman by the name of Ida Durbin. The prostitutes in the house where she had worked said a cleaning girl named Connie had been around there for a while, but that she had gone back home to either Arkansas or Northeast Texas.

The years passed and I tried not to think about Ida Durbin and her fate. As I began my long odyssey through low-bottom bars and drunk tanks and skin joints of every stripe – in the Deep South, the Philippines, and Vietnam – I would sometimes hear a voice on the jukebox that reminded me of Kitty Wells. I wanted to believe the voice was Ida's, that somehow the four-dollar discs she and Jimmie had sent to Sun Records had worked a special magic in her life and opened a career for her in Nashville and that she was out there now, under another name, singing in roadhouses where a sunburst guitar and a sequined western costume were proof enough of one's celebrity.

But I knew better, and when my booze-induced fantasy faded, I saw Ida in the backseat of a car, a man on either side of her, speeding down a dirt road at night, toward a destination where no human being ever wishes to go.

chapter three

I would almost forget about Ida Durbin. But a sin of omission, if indeed that's what it was, can be like the rusty head of a hatchet buried in the heartwood of a tree – it eventually finds the teeth of a whirling saw blade.

Troy Bordelon was a bully when I knew him at Southwestern Louisiana Institute in Lafayette. SLI, as it was called, had been the first integrated college in the South. As far as I knew, there were no incidents when the first black students enrolled, and by and large the students, both white and black, treated one another respectfully. Except for Troy Bordelon. His name was French, but he came from a sawmill town north of Alexandria, an area where the deeds of the White League and the Knights of the White Camellia were burned into Reconstruction history with a hot iron.

Troy kept the tradition alive and well.

A black kid from Abbeville by the name of Simon Labiche was the only person of color in my ROTC unit. Troy did everything in his power to make Simon's life miserable. During drill he stepped on Simon's heels, throwing him off-step, constantly murmuring racial and sexual insults in his ear. When Simon made the drill team and was scheduled to perform at the halftime ceremonies during the homecoming game, Troy brought him a goodwill offering of a cold drink from the refreshment stand. It was loaded with a high-powered laxative that can cause the red scours in cattle.

Simon, dressed in chrome-plated helmet, white scarf, and white leggings, fouled himself in front of twenty thousand people, dropped his M-1 in the mud, and fled the field in shame.

But Troy did not confine his abuse to minorities. He bullied anyone who exposed a chink in his armor, and most often these were people who reminded Troy of himself. Nor did the passage of time bring him the wisdom that would allow him to understand the origins of his sadistic inclinations. He returned to his hometown, where he was related to the sheriff and the president of the parish police jury, and went to work for a finance company, one that was owned by the same family who owned the cotton gin and the lumberyards in town.

His power over poor whites and people of color was enormous. He was loud, imperious, and unflagging in his ridicule of the vulnerable and the weak. For Troy, an act of mercy was an act of identification with his victim.

Oddly, when traveling through New Iberia, he would always call me up for coffee or to share a meal. I suspected I belonged in Troy's mind to a self-manufactured memory about his college days in Lafayette, a time he evidently looked back upon with nostalgia. Or maybe because I was a police officer, he enjoyed being in the company of someone who represented power and authority.

'We had some real fun back then, didn't we?' he'd say, and slap me hard on the arm. 'Dances and all that. Playing jokes on each other in the dorm. Hey, you remember when –'

I'd try to smile and avoid looking at my watch.

Then one fine day in early June, after I had hung it up with the Iberia Parish Sheriff's Department, I got a call from Troy's estranged wife, a schoolteacher named

Zerelda. Years ago, at age thirty-five, she had looked sixty. I couldn't even imagine what she probably looked like today. 'He wants to see you. Can you drive up this afternoon?' she said.

'He doesn't have a telephone?' I said.

'He's at Baptist Hospital. As far as I'm concerned, you can rip out his life-support system. But the poor fuck is scared shitless of dying. So what's a Christian girl to do?' she said.

Evidently Troy's denouement began with the new waitress in the Blue Fish Café – an overweight, big-boned country girl whose mouth was painted bright red, her hair shampooed and blow-dried for her first day on the job. She was eager to please and thought of her new situation as an opportunity to be a cashier or a hostess, a big jump up from her old job at the Wal-Mart. When Troy came in for his breakfast he lit up a cigarette in the non-smoking section, sent his coffee back because it was not hot enough, and told the waitress there were dishwater spots on his silverware. When his food was served, he complained his steak was pink in the middle, his eggs runny, and he had been given whole wheat rather than rye toast.

When the girl spilled his water, he asked if she was an outpatient at the epileptic rehabilitation center. By the end of his meal she was a nervous wreck. While she was bent over his table, clearing his dishes, he told others a loud joke about a big-breasted woman and a farm equipment salesman who sold milking machines. The girl's face burned like a red lightbulb.

Then one of those moments occurred that no one in a small town ever expects. The owner of the restaurant was a hard-packed, rotund Lebanese man who attended the Assembly of God Church and whose taciturn manner seldom drew attention to him. Without saying a word, he picked up a Silex of scalding hot coffee and poured it over the crown of Troy Bordelon's head.

After Troy stopped screaming, he attacked the owner with his fists and the fight cascaded through the dining area into the kitchen. It should have ended there, with two over-the-hill men walking away in shame and embarrassment at their behavior. Instead, when they had stopped fighting and a peacemaker asked both men to apologize, Troy gathered the blood and spittle in his mouth and spat it in the owner's face. The owner responded by plunging a razor-edged butcher knife four times through Troy's chest.

It was dusk when I arrived at the hospital in the little town where Troy had spent most of his life. It was a beautiful evening, the summer light high in the sky, the moon rising over red cotton land and a long bank of green trees on the western horizon. The air smelled of chemical fertilizer, distant rain, night-blooming flowers, and the fecund odor of the ponds on a catfish farm. I didn't want to go into the hospital. I was never good at deathbed visits, nor at funerals, and now, with age, I resented more and more the selfish claims the dead and dying lay on the quick.

Troy was spread out on his bed in the intensive-care unit like a pregnant whale that had been dropped from a high altitude, his blond hair still cut in a 1950s flattop, now stiff with burn ointment. What his wife had referred to as his life-support system was a tangle of translucent tubes, oxygen bottles, IV sacs, a catheter, and electronic monitors that, upon first glance, made me think that perhaps technology might give Troy another season to run.

Then he took a breath and a sucking noise came from inside his chest that I never wanted to hear again.

He had vomited into his oxygen mask, and a nurse was wiping off his face and throat. He wrapped a meaty hand around mine, squeezing with a power and strength I didn't think him capable of.

'Sir, you'll need to lean down to hear your friend,' the nurse said.

I put my ear close to Troy's mouth. His breath rose against my skin like a puff of gas from a sewer grate. ''Member that colored . . . that black kid, the one we played the joke on with the laxative?' he whispered.

'I do,' I said, although the word 'we' had not been part of what happened.

'I feel bad about that. But that's the way it was back then, huh? You reckon he knows I'm sorry?'

'Sure he does,' I replied.

I heard him swallowing, the saliva clicking in his windpipe.

'Years ago, you knew a girl who was a whore,' he said. 'They snatched her up. My uncle was a cop in Galveston. He was one of the guys who snatched her. I saw where they took her. I saw the room she was in.'

I looked down at him. His eyes were wide-set, round, his youthful haircut and porcine face like a grotesque caricature of the decade he never allowed himself to grow out of. 'What was the name of the girl?' I said.

He wet his lips, his hand knotting my shirt. 'I don't know. She burned some people for a lot of money. You and your brother took her out of a cathouse. So they snatched her up.'

I could feel my heart thumping in my chest. 'Your uncle and who?' I asked.

He shook his head. 'Cops and a pimp. She had a mandolin. They busted it up.'

'Did they kill her?'

'I don't know. I saw blood on a chair. I was just a kid. Just like you and Jimmie. What's a kid s'pposed to do? I took off. My uncle's dead now. Nobody probably even remembers that girl now 'cept me.'

He was the saddest-looking human being I think I had ever seen. His eyes were liquid, receded in his face. His body was encased in beer fat that seemed to be squeezing the breath out of his lungs. He let go of my shirt and waited for me to speak, as though my words could exorcise the succubus that had probably fed at his heart all his life.

'That's right, we were all just kids back then, Troy,' I said, and winked at him.

He tried to smile, his skin puckering around his mouth. Without his consent, the nurse fitted the oxygen mask back on his face. Through the window I saw a TV news van in the parking lot, with the call letters and logo of an aggressive Shreveport television station painted on the side. But if the news crew was there to cover some element in the passing of Troy Bordelon, it was of little import to Troy. He looked out the window at the sun's last red ember on the horizon. A flock of crows rose from the limbs of cypress trees in a lake, lifting into the sky like ashes off a dead fire. The look in his eyes made me think of a drowning man whose voice cannot reach a would-be rescuer.

Outside, I walked toward my truck, my head filled with nightmarish images about what may have been Ida Durbin's last moments. How had Troy put it? He had seen 'blood on a chair.'

'Hold on there, Robo,' a voice called out behind me.

Robo?

There were two of them, angular in build, squared away, military in bearing, their uniforms starched and creased, wearing shades, even though it was almost dark, their gold badges and name tags buffed, their shoes spit-shined into mirrors. I had seen them at various times at law enforcement gatherings in Baton Rouge and New Orleans. I didn't remember their names, but I remembered their manner. It was of a kind every career lawman or military officer recognizes. These were men you never place in situations where they have unsupervised authority over others.

I nodded hello but didn't speak.

'On the job?' one of them said. His name tag read *Shockly, J. W.* He tilted his head slightly with his question.

'Not me. I hung it up,' I replied.

'I saw you go into Troy Bordelon's room. You guys were buds?' he said.

'I went to school with him,' I said.

The second deputy was grinning from behind his shades, as though the three of us were in a private club and the inappropriateness of his expression was acceptable. The name engraved on his tag was *Pitts, B. J.* 'Poor bastard was a real pistol, wasn't he? Half the blacks in the parish are probably drunk right now,' he said.

'I wouldn't know,' I said.

'Ole Troy didn't want to unburden his sins?' the second deputy, the one named Pitts, said.

Shockly pulled on his nose to hide his irritation at his friend's revelation of their shared agenda.

'Nice seeing you guys,' I said.

Neither one of them said good-bye as I walked away. When I glanced in my rearview mirror, they were still standing in the parking lot, wondering, I suspect, if they had said too much or too little.

I decided I needed to talk to Troy again, when the two sheriff's deputies were not around. I checked into a motel in the next town, then returned to the hospital at sunrise, but Troy had died during the night.

I was a widower and lived by myself in New Iberia, a city of twenty-five thousand people on Bayou Teche in the southwestern part of the state. For years I had been a detective with the Iberia Parish Sheriff's Department and also the owner of a bait shop and boat rental business outside of town. But after Alafair, my adopted daughter, went away to college and the home my father built in 1935 burned to the ground, I sold the baitshop and dock to an elderly black man named Batist and moved into a shotgun house on East Main, on the banks of the Teche, in a neighborhood where the oak and pecan trees, the azaleas, Confederate roses, and philodendron managed to both hide and accentuate the decayed elegance of a bygone era.

After I returned from my visit to Troy's bedside, I could not get Ida Durbin out of my head. I tried to convince myself that the past was the past, that Ida had involved herself with violent and predatory people and that her fate was neither my doing nor Jimmie's.

But over the years I had seen the file drawer slammed on too many unsolved disappearances. These cases almost always involved people who had no voice and whose families had no power. Sometimes a determined cop would try to keep the investigation alive, revisiting his files and chasing leads on his own time, but ultimately he, too, would make his separate peace and try not to think, as I was now, about voices that can cry out for help in our sleep.

I had no demonstrable evidence that a crime had actually been committed, nothing except the statement of a guilt-driven man who said he had seen blood on a chair decades ago. Even if I wanted to initiate an investigation, where would I start? In a Texas coastal town where most of the players were probably dead?

I had another problem, too. For a recovering alcoholic, introspection and solitude are the perfect combination for a dry drunk, a condition that for me was like putting a nail gun in the center of my forehead and pulling the trigger.

I mowed the grass in the front yard and began raking up layers of blackened leaves on the shady side of the house, burning them in a rusty oil barrel under the oak trees down by the bayou. A speedboat went by with water-skiers in tow, churning a frothy yellow trough down the center of the bayou. On the far bank, in City Park, the camellias were in bloom, kids were playing baseball, and families were fixing lunch in the picnic shelters. But I couldn't shake the gloom that had clung to me like cobwebs since I had listened to Troy Bordelon's deathbed statement.

I went back in the house and read the newspaper. The lead story was not a happy one. Thirty miles from New Iberia, the body of a young black woman, bound at the wrists and ankles, had been found in a cane field, not far from the convent in Grand Coteau. Her car was discovered only two miles away, at a rural cemetery where she had been visiting her brother's grave site, the driver's door ajar, the engine still idling.

In the last six months two women had been abducted in Baton Rouge and their bodies dumped in wetlands areas. The murder of the black woman in Grand Coteau bore similarities to the homicides in Baton Rouge, except this was the first time the killer, if indeed the same perpetrator murdered all three women, had struck in the area we call Acadiana.

A one-paragraph addendum to the wire-service story mentioned that over thirty women in the Baton Rouge area had been murdered by unknown perpetrators in the last decade.

Clete Purcel, my old friend from NOPD, had opened a branch of his P.I. business in New Iberia, and was now dividing his time between here and his office on St. Ann in New Orleans. He claimed he was simply expanding his business parameters, but in truth Clete's shaky legal status and his penchant for creating chaos and mayhem wherever he went made instant mobility an imperative in his day-to-day existence.

How many cops have longer rap sheets than most of the criminals they put in the can? Over the years, some of

Clete's antics have included the following: forcing an entire dispenser of liquid hand soap down a button man's mouth in the men's room of the Greyhound bus depot; leaving a drunk U.S. congressman handcuffed to a fire hydrant on St. Charles Avenue; filling a gangster's convertible with cement; dangling a gang-banger by his ankles off a fire escape five stories above the street; driving an earthmover back and forth through Max Carlucci's palatial home on Lake Pontchartrain; stuffing a billiard ball inside the mouth of a child molester; parking a nine-Mike round in the brainpan of a federal snitch; and, top this, possibly pouring sand in the fuel tank of an airplane, causing the deaths of a Galveston mobster by the name of Sally Dio and a few of his hired gumballs.

More unbelievably, Clete did all these things, and many others, in a blithe, carefree spirit, like a unicorn on purple acid crashing good-naturedly through a clock shop. He was out of sync with the world, filled with self-destructive energies, addicted to every vice, still ridden with dreams from Vietnam, incredibly brave, generous, and decent, the most loyal man I ever knew, and ultimately the most tragic.

What Victor Charles and the NVA couldn't do to him, or the Mob or his enemies inside NOPD, Clete had done to himself with fried food, booze, weed, whites on the half shell, and calamitous affairs with strippers, junkies, and women who seemed to glow with both rut and neurosis. Sometimes I believed his dreams were not about Vietnam but about his father, a milkman in the Garden District who thought parental love and discipline, the latter administrated with a whistling razor strop, were one and the same. But no amount of pain, either inflicted by himself or others, ever stole his grin or robbed him of his spirit. For Clete, life was an ongoing party, and if you wanted to be a participant, you wore your scars like crimson beads at Mardi Gras.

Clete lived on Main, too, farther down the bayou, in a

stucco, 1940s motor court, set back from the street in deep shade. Because it was Sunday, I found him at home, reading in a deck chair, his glasses perched on his nose, his leviathan body glistening with suntan oil. An iced tomato drink with a stick of celery floating in it rested on the gravel by his chair. 'What's the haps, noble mon?' he said.

I told him about my visit to Troy's bedside and how Jimmie and I met Ida Durbin in Galveston on the Fourth of July in 1958. I told him about the beating Jimmie gave the pimp, Lou Kale, and how Ida disappeared as though she had been sucked through a hole in the dimension.

Clete was a good investigator because he was a good listener. While others spoke, his face seldom showed expression. His eyes, which were smoky green, always remained respectful, neutral, occasionally shifting sideways in a reflective way. After I had finished, he ticked a fingernail at a scar that ran diagonally through his left eyebrow and across the bridge of his nose. 'This guy Troy was working with pimps?' he said.

'The uncle was a cop on a pad. Troy was evidently a tagalong,' I said.

'But he believed they killed the girl?'

'He didn't say that,' I replied.

'House girls are full-time cash on the hoof. Their pimps usually don't kill them.'

But Clete knew better. He raised his eyebrows. 'Dave, a thousand things could have happened. Why think the worst? Besides, if there's any blame, it's on your half-crazy brother. Remodeling a pimp's face on behalf of a whore probably isn't the best way to do P.R. for her.'

He laughed, then looked at my expression. 'Okay, mon,' he said. 'If you want to scope it out, I'd start with Bordelon's ties to other people. Run that by me again about the two sheriff's deputies.'

'They braced me in the hospital parking lot.'

'They thought Bordelon gave up somebody?'

'That was my impression.'

'So Troy Bordelon's family is –'

'They do scut work for the Chalons family in St. Mary Parish.'

Clete removed the celery stalk from his drink and took a long swallow from the glass. His hair was sandy, with strands of white in it, cut like a little boy's. When the vodka and tomato juice hit his stomach, the color seemed to bloom in his face. He looked up at me, squinting against the sunlight.

'I have crazy thoughts about going back to 'Nam sometimes, finding the family of a mamasan I killed, apologizing, giving them money, somehow making it right,' he said. He looked emptily out into the sunlight.

'What are you saying?'

'I'd let sleeping dogs lie. But you won't do that. No, sir. No, sir. No, sir. Not ole Streak,' he replied, pressing the bottom of his glass hard into the moist gravel.

Clete was wrong. I disengaged from thoughts about Ida Durbin. During the week, I bass-fished on Bayou Benoit, repaired the roof on the shotgun house I had just taken a mortgage on, and each dawn jogged three miles through the mist-shrouded trees in City Park. In fact, listening to Clete's advice and forgetting Ida was easier than I thought. I even wondered if my ability to give up an obsession was less a virtue than a sign of either age or a newly acquired callousness.

But airliners crash because a twenty-cent lightbulb burns out on the instrument panel; a Civil War campaign is lost because a Confederate courier wraps three cigars in a secret communiqué; and a morally demented man takes a job in a Texas book depository and changes world history.

It was early the next Monday, the rain hitting hard on the tin roof of my house, when the phone rang. I picked up the receiver on the kitchen counter, a cup of coffee in one hand. Between the trees on the back slope of my property, I could see the rain dancing on the bayou, the mist blowing into the cattails. 'Hello?' I said.

'Hey, Robicheaux. What do you say we buy you breakfast?' the voice said.

'Who's this?' I asked, although I already knew the answer.

'J. W. Shockly. Talked to you outside Baptist Hospital last week? Billy Joe and I have to do a favor for the boss. I'd really appreciate your help on this.'

'I'm pretty jammed up, partner.'

'It'll take ten minutes. We're at the public library, a half block down the street. What's to lose?'

I put on a hat and raincoat and walked under the dripping limbs of the live oaks that formed a canopy over East Main. I passed the site of what had once been the residence of the writer and former Confederate soldier George Washington Cable and the grotto dedicated to Christ's mother next to the city library. J. W. Shockly and the other sheriff's deputy from the hospital parking lot, both in civilian clothes, were standing under the shelter at the library entrance, smiles fixed on their faces inside the mist, like brothers-in-arms happy to see an old friend.

'Can we go somewhere?' Shockly said, extending his hand. 'You remember Billy Joe Pitts.'

So I had to shake hands with his partner as well. When I did, he squeezed hard on the ends of my fingers.

'That's quite a grip you've got,' I said.

'Sorry,' he said. 'How about coffee and a beignet down at Victor's?'

I shook my head.

'Here's what it is,' Shockly said. 'The sheriff sent me down here because me and you go back. See, the nurse who was in Troy's hospital room with you is the sheriff's cousin. She says Troy was telling you some bullcrap about a crime involving a prostitute. The sheriff thinks maybe you're working for the defense. That maybe the restaurant owner's family has hired you to prove Troy was a lowlife or procurer or something, that maybe he was propositioning the waitress and the restaurant owner went apeshit. You following me?'

'No, not at all,' I replied.

Shockly's hair was buzz-cut, his pale blue suit spotted with rain. His breath smelled like cigarettes and mints. His gaze seemed to search the mist for the right words to use. 'Nobody wants to see the restaurant owner ride the needle. But he's not going to skate, either. So how about it?'

'How about what?' I said.

'You working for the defense or not?' Billy Joe, his friend, said. He was a shorter man than Shockly, but tougher in appearance, his eye sockets recessed, the skin of his face grainy, his teeth too large for his mouth.

'I already explained my purpose in visiting the hospital. I think we're done here,' I said.

Billy Joe raised his hands and grinned. 'Enough said, then.' He popped me on the arm, hard enough to sting through my raincoat.

When I got back home, I washed my hands and dried them on a dish towel. I fixed a bowl of Grape-Nuts and berries and milk and sat down to eat by the kitchen window. The air blowing through the screen was cool and smelled of flowers and wet trees and fish spawning in the bayou, and in a few minutes I had almost forgotten about Shockly and Pitts and their shabby attempt to convince me their visit to New Iberia was an innocuous one.

But just as I started to wash my dishes I heard footsteps on the gallery. I opened the front door and looked down at Billy Joe Pitts, who was squatted on his haunches, scraping the contents from a pet food can onto a sheet of newspaper for my cat, Snuggs. J. W. Shockly waited at the curb in a black SUV, the exhaust pipe smoking in the rain. 'What do you think you're doing?' I said.

'Had this can in the vehicle and saw your cat. Thought I'd treat him to a meal,' Pitts said, twisting around, his bottom teeth exposed with his grin.

Snuggs had just started to eat, but I scooped him up and cradled him in one arm. He was a white, short-haired, unneutered male, thick-necked, heavy, ropy with muscle, his ears chewed, his head notched with pink scars. He was the best cat I ever owned. 'Snuggs says thanks but he's on a diet. And I say *adiós,* bud.'

I kicked the pet food and newspaper into the flower bed.

'Just trying to do a good deed. But to each his own,' Billy Joe Pitts said, getting to his feet, his face close to mine now, his skin as damp-smelling as mold.

chapter four

It was still raining that afternoon when I drove across the train tracks and parked my pickup behind the courthouse, a short distance from the crumbling, whitewashed crypts in St. Peter's Cemetery. Helen Soileau, my old colleague, had become the parish's first female sheriff. She was either bisexual or a lesbian, I was never sure which, and had the perfect physique for a man. I mention her sexuality not to define her but only to indicate that her life as a law officer was not always an easy one. She started her career as a meter maid at NOPD and became a patrolwoman in Gird Town and the neighborhood surrounding the Desire Project. The notoriety of the latter has no equal in the United States, except perhaps for Cabrini Green in Chicago and neighborhoods in the South Bronx. A white female cop who can enter the Desire at night, by herself, is an extraordinary person. Helen Soileau earned respect from people who do not grant it easily.

After I told her the story about Troy Bordelon's death and the visit to my house by J. W. Shockly and Billy Joe Pitts, she leaned back in her swivel chair and looked at me for a long time. She wore blue slacks and a starched white shirt, with a gold badge hung on the pocket. Her hair was blond and natural but for some reason it had always looked like a wig when she wore it long. So now she had it cut short and tapered on the sides and back, and it gave her an attractive appearance that for the first time in her life caused men to turn and look at her. 'You're asking for your job back? Over these two characters coming to your house?' she said.

'The income wouldn't hurt,' I said.

Helen's eyes had a way of becoming lidless when she asked questions of people. 'Did you ever consider that maybe these two deputies were telling the truth? That they think you're doing P.I. work for the defense in a homicide? That they're just inept and not very bright?'

'How many redneck cops stop by your house to feed your cat?'

She pulled at an earlobe. 'Yeah, that is a little weird,' she said. 'But the real reason you want your shield back is to start looking into this disappearance in Galveston, right?'

'Maybe.'

She tapped the arms of her chair with her palms and made clucking sounds with her tongue. 'Love you, Streak, but the answer is no.'

I cleared my throat and looked out the window. Across the street I could see the mist blowing off the crypts in the cemetery, and the dull red texture of the bricks through the cracked places in the plaster. Someone was honking a horn angrily at the intersection, like an idiot railing at a television set. 'Mind giving me an explanation?' I said.

She leaned forward in her chair. 'Yeah, I do mind, and that's because I'm your friend,' she said.

I didn't try to sort out the meaning in her words. 'Run those two cops for me.'

'Why?'

'They're dirty.'

She clicked her teeth together. 'I forgot what it was like when you were around,' she said.

41

'Would you clarify that?'

'Not in your dreams,' she replied.

The church where I attended Mass was on the outskirts of Jeanerette, down the bayou, in St. Mary Parish. Most of the parishioners were people of color and desperately poor. But it was a fine church to attend, built on a green bend of the bayou by an oak-shaded graveyard, and the people in the church had a simplicity and dignity about them that belied the hardship and struggle that characterized their lives.

That evening I drove down the bayou to attend a meeting of our church-annex committee. The back road to Jeanerette is like a geographical odyssey through Louisiana's history and the disparities that make it less than real and difficult to categorize. The pastureland is emerald green in spring and summer, dotted with cattle and clumps of oak and gum trees, the early sugar cane waving in the richest alluvial soil in America. At sunset, Bayou Teche is high and dark from the spring rains; the air smells of gardenia and magnolia; and antebellum homes glow among the trees with a soft electrical whiteness that makes one wonder if perhaps the Confederacy should not have won the War Between the States after all.

But inside that perfect bucolic moment, there is another reality at work, one that doesn't stand examination in the harsh light of day. The rain ditches along that same road are strewn with bottles, beer cans, and raw garbage. Under the bayou's rain-dented surface lie discarded paint and motor-oil cans, containers of industrial solvents, rubber tires, and construction debris that will never biologically degrade.

Across the drawbridge from two of the most lovely historical homes in Louisiana is a trailer slum that probably has no equivalent outside the Third World. The juxtaposition seems almost contrived, like a set in a Marxist documentary meant to discredit capitalistic societies.

But as I drive this road in the sunset, I try not to dwell upon the problems of the era in which we live. I try to remember the Louisiana of my youth and to convince myself that we can rehabilitate the land and ourselves and regain the past. It's a debate which I seldom win.

It was dark when I came out of the meeting at the church, the wind cool off the Gulf, the clouds in the south veined with lightning that gave off no sound. An elderly black man from the congregation came up to me in the parking lot. 'That guy find you?' he said.

'Which guy?' I asked.

'He was looking at your truck and ax if it was yours. He said he t'ought it was for sale.' The elderly man was named Lemuel Melancon and he had muttonchop sideburns and wore a white shirt and tie.

'It has been, but I took the sign out of the window when I drove here. This was a white or black guy?' I said.

'White. Maybe he'll come back. Pretty good meeting tonight, huh?'

'Yeah, it was. See you Sunday, Lemuel.'

I drove back to New Iberia, past a sugar mill on the far side of the bayou and through cane fields and a rural slum at the city limits, then I crossed the drawbridge onto Old Spanish Trail and entered the long tunnel of oaks that led to my home on East Main. The street behind me was empty, serpentine lines of dead leaves scudding across the asphalt.

I parked the truck under my porte cochere and replaced the for sale placard in the back window. I unlocked the front door of my house, then paused in the gentle sweep of wind across the gallery. Normally, when Snuggs heard my truck, he ran to the front, particularly

43

when he had not been fed. But there was no sign of him. I picked up his pet bowl and went inside, then looked for him in the backyard. Tripod, my three-legged raccoon, was on top of his hutch, staring at me.

'How's it hangin', Tripod? Have you seen Snuggs tonight?' I said.

I patted his head and smoothed down the fur on his back and gave his tail a little tug. He rubbed his muzzle against my forearm.

It was balmy inside the trees, the night alive with wind. A tugboat was passing on the bayou, its wake lit by its running lights. Decayed leaves and pecan husks that were soft with mold crunched under my shoes as I walked back toward the house. Dry thunder pealed slowly across the sky, then I heard Tripod climb down the side of his hutch and jump heavily inside.

'What is it, 'Pod? Thunder got you scared?' I said.

I returned to his hutch and started to lift him up. The tree limbs overhead flickered with lightning, then I heard a sound or felt a presence that should not have been there, a twig snapping under the sole of a shoe, an inhalation of breath, like a man oxygenating his blood in preparation for an expenditure of enormous physical energy.

I set Tripod down and straightened up, just in time to see a man with a nylon stocking over his face swing a two-by-four at the side of my head. I caught part of the blow with my arm, but not well enough. I felt my scalp split and wood splinters bite into my ear and my cheek. I crashed against the hutch, grabbing at the air, just as he hit me again, this time across the neck and shoulders.

I tried to get to my feet, but he kicked me in the ribs with the point of his shoe, then in the armpit, and once right across the mouth. I tumbled backwards, trying to get the hutch between me and the man with the two-by-four. I could hear Tripod's paws skittering on the floor and wire sides of his hutch. I grabbed a handful of dirt and leaves, threw it blindly at my attacker's face, got my pocketknife loose from my pants, and pulled the blade open.

But when I stood erect, I was alone, the yard suddenly gone silent, as though I had stepped outside of time and the world around me had been reconfigured without my consent. Blood was leaking from my hairline and there was a bitter, coppery taste, like wet pennies, in my mouth. Tripod had scampered up into the live oak above his hutch and was peering down at me, his body trembling.

I had no idea where my attacker had gone. I walked off balance toward the house, as though a piece of membrane were torn loose inside my head. In the kitchen I had to sit down to punch in a 911 call on the telephone, then had to spit the blood out of my mouth into a paper towel before I could tell the dispatcher what had happened.

In less than a minute I heard a siren coming hard down East Main. I looked through the kitchen window and saw Snuggs sitting on the outside sill, framed against the philodendron, pawing at the screen to come inside.

The emergency-room physician at Iberia General kept me overnight, and when I woke, the early-morning sun looked like pink smoke inside the oak trees. A nurse's aide brought breakfast to me on a tray, then wheeled me down the corridor for an X ray. When I returned to the room, Helen Soileau was sitting by the window, reading the *Baton Rouge Advocate*. The main story above the fold was about another abduction in Baton Rouge, this time the wife of a state environmental quality official who was serving time in a federal prison. Helen folded the paper and set it on the windowsill. 'Bad night, huh, bwana?' she said.

'Not really,' I said, sitting down on the side of the bed.

'They going to kick you loose?'

'Soon as the doc looks at my X ray.'

'We couldn't find the board your attacker used, so we got nothing we can lift latents off. You think he was the same guy asking about your truck at the church?'

'Maybe.'

'More specifically, you think it was one of those deputies – Shockly or Pitts?'

'Who knows?'

'I ran both of them and got a hit on Pitts. Four years back he was charged with planting coke on some Cambodians. They got pulled over at a traffic stop and their SUV and thirty thousand in cash seized. They'd saved the money to buy a restaurant in Baton Rouge.'

'How'd Pitts get out of it?' I asked.

'Gave evidence against the other cops. Did you say a black man at your church got a look at the guy who was hanging around your truck?'

'He talked to him.'

'I got a mug shot of Pitts for him to look at.'

I nodded and waited for her to go on. But she seemed distracted, as though several things were on her mind at once. She got up from her chair and gazed out the window. The tops of her arms were round and thick, her back stiff. 'Did you read the story in the *Advocate* about another abduction in Baton Rouge?' she asked.

'Yeah, I saw it.'

'I think the perp is using Baton Rouge as his personal hunting reserve. But I don't think he's from there,' she said.

'Why not?'

'I talked with Baton Rouge P.D. The DNA on the girl in Grand Coteau was just matched to DNA on at least five other victims.'

'Five?'

'The locals didn't know they had a serial predator on their hands. They screwed up. It happens. I think the guy has deliberately confined himself to Baton Rouge for years, but he saw the black girl at the cemetery by herself and couldn't resist the opportunity. I think he lives in a small town, maybe in Acadiana, and gets his jollies in Baton Rouge.'

'Why you telling me all this?'

'You still want your shield back?' she asked.

Two days later after the swelling had gone out of my jaw and my mouth no longer bled when I ate, I reported to my old job at the Iberia Parish Sheriff's Department. I was assigned a corner office on the second floor, one that allowed me a view of the cemetery, trees that lined the railway tracks, and the ivy-scaled brick facades of several buildings that, with a little imagination at twilight, provided a glimpse back into nineteenth-century America.

The previous night I had laid out a tie and sports coat, shined my shoes, and pressed a pair of slacks and a soft, long-sleeve blue shirt, pretending I had no anxiety about returning to a job for which I was perhaps too old or, worse, simply unfit to do well. Now, standing in my office by myself, the wire baskets on the desk empty, I felt like a guest who has said good night at a party but comes back later because he has nowhere else to go. But all morning uniformed deputies and plainclothes detectives stopped by and shook hands, and it felt wonderful.

At noon I checked out a cruiser and drove down the bayou to Jeanerette and the community of shacks along the back road where Lemuel Melancon lived. He was sitting in a rocker on his tiny gallery, his body dappled with sunlight that fell through a pecan tree in his front yard. The wind was blowing in the cane behind his house, but his tin roof shimmered with heat.

I showed him front and profile photos of Billy Joe Pitts. Pitts was wearing a starched sports shirt printed with a tropical design, the fabric stretched tight against the expansion of his chest. The booking time on the photo strip was 11:16 p.m., but Pitt's face showed no expression, not even fatigue, like the head of an unrepentant criminal upon a platter. 'Is this the guy who was looking at my truck?' I asked.

Lemuel held the strip close to his face, then handed it back to me. 'Could be. But it was dark. I can't see good no more, me,' he said.

'It's important, Lemuel.'

He took another look and shook his head. 'What'd this guy do?' he asked.

'Helped plant cocaine on some Cambodians so their vehicle and cash could be confiscated.'

'I ain't following you.'

'He's a cop. You see him again, you let me know.'

Lemuel leaned back in his chair and looked out at the road, suddenly disconnected from me and a conversation involving a corrupt white police officer.

'Lemuel?' I said.

'Got to clean my li'l house now. Dust keep blowing out of the yard t'rew the screen, dirtying up my whole house. Just cain't keep it clean, no matter what I do. See you another time, Dave.'

We live in the New South. Legal segregation has slipped into history; the Klan has moved west, into white supremacist compounds, where they feel safe from the people whom they fear; and in Mississippi black state troopers ticket white motorists.

But memories can be long, fear is fear, and race is at the heart of virtually every political issue in the states of the Old Confederacy, particularly in the realignment of the two national political parties. As I drove back to New Iberia, the fields of early sugar cane rippling in the breeze, the buttercups blooming along the rain ditches, I wondered about the memories of violence and injustice that my friend Lemuel Melancon would probably never share with me. But they obviously lived inside him, and I knew that as a white man it was presumptuous of me to ask that he set aside the cautionary instincts that had allowed him to be a survivor.

This was St. Mary Parish, historically a fiefdom where a few individuals controlled mind-boggling amounts of wealth. In the 1970s a group of Catholic Worker nuns tried to organize the sugar cane workers here. Some of the blacks and poor whites who listened to them discovered they had thirty minutes to move their belongings out of their houses.

A journey to the bedside of a dying school chum had led me back to the disappearance years ago of Ida Durbin. Had not two rogue deputies, Shockly and Pitts, tried to turn dials on me, my revisiting of a bad experience in my youth would probably have ended there, at a Baptist hospital, in a backward, piney-woods parish in central Louisiana.

But that parish, its sawmills, corporate cotton and soy bean fields, its catfish farms, along with its politicians and sheriff's department, had always been owned by the Chalons family in St. Mary Parish.

Unconsciously I touched the stitches in my scalp where my attacker had clubbed me with a two-by-four. Was he sent by the Chalonses, over the disappearance or death of a prostitute in 1958? No, that was my old class-conscious paranoia at work, I told myself.

I kept telling myself that all the way back to New Iberia.

That evening, Clete Purcel picked me up at the house and we had dinner at a bar-and-grill that served food on a deck overlooking the bayou. It was dusk, the western sky ribbed with strips of orange cloud, the turn bridge on the bayou open for a barge. Clete had been quiet all evening.

'I think I need to make a home call on this Pitts character,' he said.

'Nope,' I said.

'Nothing dramatic. Maybe drive him out to a quiet spot and give him a chance to get some things off his chest.'

'Clete —'

'Nobody messes with the Bobbsey Twins from Homicide. Every lowlife in New Orleans always understood that, big mon. This dickhead doesn't get slack because he's a cop.'

Some people at the next table stared at us.

'I have no evidence Pitts was the guy,' I said.

'You *know* he was the guy.'

'Maybe.'

'Trust me, I'll get the "maybe" out of the equation. Quit worrying. He'll probably thank me for it,' he said. He took a bite out of his po'boy sandwich. 'These fried oysters are supposed to be aphrodisiacs, did you know that?'

Talking with Clete Purcel about personal restraint or reasonable behavior was like a meteorologist telling an electrical storm it shouldn't come to town. But I couldn't be mad at Clete. He was the first person to whom I always took my problems, and in truth his violence, recklessness, and vigilantism were simply the other side of my own personality. I felt his gaze wander over my face and the stitches I had tried to comb my hair over.

'Will you stop that?' I said.

'What's your brother say about all this?' he said.

'Haven't talked with him about it.'

He looked at me.

'He's got his own problems,' I said.

'Jimmie the Gent is a stand-up guy. Why not treat him like one?' Clete said.

Years ago my brother had taken a bullet for me and

lost an eye. I didn't feel like cluttering up his life with any more grief or the detritus of 1958. I started to tell Clete that when my cell phone rang. The caller number was Helen Soileau's.

'We got a floater out by the St. Martin line,' she said. 'It may be the wife of that DEQ official who's in Seagoville. We've got personal effects, but I don't think we'll get a visual ID.'

'That bad?'

'The guy who did this isn't human.'

'None of them are,' I replied.

'Better see the vic,' she said.

chapter five

The crime scene was only ten minutes from the bar-and-grill on the bayou. But the images there belonged in a medieval painting of a netherworld that should have existed only in the imagination. On a dead-end dirt road lined with garbage was a black pond spiked by gum trees. The sky was tormented by birds, the sun a gush of red on the horizon. The victim lay on her back, her torso half in the water. I felt my stomach constrict when Helen shined her flashlight on the woman's face.

'Get this. The sonofabitch hung her purse in a tree,' she said. 'Money, car keys, driver's license, credit cards, everything was in there.'

'Her husband was with the Department of Environmental Quality?'

'Yeah, he was taking juice from a couple of petrochemical guys. So maybe this isn't the Baton Rouge serial killer.'

The coroner, Koko Hebert, had just arrived. He was a gelatinous, cynical man, a sweaty, foul-smelling chain smoker, given to baggy clothes, tropical shirts, and a trademark Panama hat. I always suspected a Rotarian lay hidden inside his enormous girth and wheezing breath and jaded manner, but, if so, he hid it well. He leaned over with a penlight and stared down at the body. 'Jesus Christ,' he said.

'Got any speculations?' Helen said.

'Yeah, her face looks like a flower pot after a truck ran over it,' he said.

Helen gave me a look. 'Are those ligations around her throat?' she asked.

He made a pained face, as though he were weighing a great decision. 'Could be. But those knots could be the nodules associated with bubonic plague. Been a couple of outbreaks in East Texas. Squirrels and pack rats can carry it sometimes. You didn't touch anything here, did you?' he said. He held Helen's eyes somberly, then his mouth broke at the corners and his breath wheezed like air escaping from a ruptured tire. 'Ligations, shit. The guy who did this had a boner on he couldn't knock down with a baseball bat.'

'The signature on the Baton Rouge serial killings is death by strangulation,' Helen said.

But the coroner ignored her and motioned for two paramedics to bag up the body.

'Did you hear me?' she said.

He stared into space, his eyes askance, a manufactured look of pensiveness on his face. 'Our killer is not into methodology,' he said.

'Say again?' Helen said.

'Our killer is a horny prick who loves beating the shit out of people. He doesn't care how he does it. Are we all better now?' Koko said.

Helen's face blanched. She started to speak, but I placed my hand on her shoulder. Her muscles felt like a bag of rocks. We watched Koko Hebert walk toward an ambulance, its emergency flashers blinking. It was hot and breathless inside the trees, and the air smelled of stagnant water and leaves that had turned black in damp shade.

'Blow him off. He's an unhappy fat man who tries to make other people as miserable as he is,' I said.

She slapped a mosquito on her cheek and looked at the

smear of blood on her hand. The paramedics lifted the body heavily out of the water, their latex-gloved hands sinking deep into the tissue. 'Wrap it up for me, Pops?' Helen said.

'Sure. You okay?' I said.

'I will be after a hot bath and four inches of Jack Daniel's. It's God's compensation for giving me this fucking job,' she said, then grimaced at her own remark.

'Drink two inches of it for me,' I said.

She hit me on the arm with the flat of her fist and walked to her cruiser, her eyes sliding off the face of the coroner.

It was dark by the time the crime scene investigators finished their work. A wind came up and blew the mosquitoes out of the trees, and I could see heat lightning in the clouds over the Gulf and smell distant rain. I thought about four inches of Jack on ice, with a sprig of mint bruised inside the glass. I rubbed my mouth and swallowed dryly. Then I said good night to the other personnel at the scene and got back in my truck.

Just in time to see a television news van rumble down the road and stop squarely in front of me, its headlights burning into my eyes. The first figure out of the van was none other than Valentine Chalons, the one certifiable celebrity in the Chalons family, the same people who owned cotton, sugar cane, oil, and timber interests all over Louisiana and East Texas, including the parish where my former college friend, Troy Bordelon, had lived.

Valentine could have descended from Vikings rather than the chivalric Norman French ancestry his family claimed for themselves. He was tall, athletic-looking, and blue-eyed, with a bladed face and hair that had turned silver on the tips in his late thirties. Unlike the rest of the Chalons family, his views were ostensibly populist or libertarian, although I sensed that inside his populism was the soul of a snob.

He had studied journalism at the University of Missouri, then had worked as a stringer and feature writer for the Associated Press before taking a news anchor position with a television station in New Orleans. But Valentine Chalons's stops on the ladder of success were always temporary, and nobody doubted that he considered ambition a virtue rather than a vice.

Before the 9/11 attacks, he actually interviewed Osama bin Laden high up in the mountains on the Pakistan border. After hiking three days through burning moonscape and razor-edged rocks, Valentine and an interpreter finally trudged up a path to a cave opening, where the man who would help orchestrate the murder of almost three thousand people stood waiting for him, his robes swirling in the wind. According to what had become a folk legend among newsmen, the first words out of Val's mouth were: 'Why don't you build a decent driveway, Jack?'

Now he owned a television station in Lafayette and one in Shreveport and was an editorial contributor on a national cable network. But regardless of his acquisitions, Val remained a hands-on journalist and took great pleasure in covering a story himself as well as immersing himself in the fray.

'You're too late, podna,' I said.

'That's what you think. I got a shot inside the ambulance at the intersection,' he replied. He motioned to his cameramen, who flooded the pond and the trees with light. One of them accidentally snapped the yellow crime scene tape that was wrapped around a pine trunk.

'You guys step back,' I said.

'Sorry,' the offending cameraman said.

But Val didn't miss a beat. He extended his microphone in front of my face. 'Does the victim have a name yet?' he said.

'No,' I replied.

But he slogged on, undeterred, and repeated the question, using the name of the missing DEQ official's wife.

'Cut the bullshit, Val. You want information, talk to the sheriff,' I said.

He lowered the mike. 'How you been?' he said.

'Great.' I slipped my hands into my back pockets and took a step closer to him, maybe because his aggressive manner had given me license I wouldn't have had otherwise. 'Did you know a guy by the name of Troy Bordelon?'

'No, I don't think so. Who is he?'

'A dead guy who worked for your family.'

'A dead guy?'

'He gave me a deathbed statement about the disappearance of a prostitute named Ida Durbin. I think she was killed.' I held my eyes on his.

'I'm listening,' he said.

'A couple of rogue cops paid me a visit. Their names are J. W. Shockly and Billy Joe Pitts. These guys seemed worried about what Troy might have told me. Their names ring a bell?'

'Nope.' He looked idly at one of his cameramen who was filming the pond and the drag marks where the paramedics had pulled the body out of the water.

'And you never heard of Troy Bordelon?' I said.

'I just told you.'

'You're a knowledgeable man, so I thought I'd ask,' I said.

He inserted a piece of gum into his mouth and chewed it, his eyes crinkling at the corners. 'You kill me, Dave. Come out to the plantation. We've got a cook from France now. I want him to fix a dinner especially for you.'

'I'm off butter and cream,' I said.

He laughed to himself and shook his head. 'It was worth every minute of the drive out here. Have a good one.' He patted me on the shoulder and walked away, a self-amused grin on his face.

Let it go, I told myself. But I couldn't take his imperious, fraternity-boy manner. I caught up with him at the passenger window of his van. 'Ida Durbin worked in a hot pillow joint on Post Office Street in Galveston in 1958. Would your old man know anything about those places?' I said.

'You're asking this about my father?' he said.

'Want me to repeat the question?' I said.

He touched at his nose and snapped his gum in his jaws. For a moment I thought he might step outside the vehicle. But he didn't. 'Dave, I'd love to get you your own show. The ratings would go through the roof. Let me make a couple of calls to New York. I'm not putting you on. I could swing it,' he said.

Then the van pulled away, bouncing through the dips in the road, the high beams spearing through the underbrush and trees.

You just blew it, bubba, I said under my breath.

I couldn't find Clete for three days. The owner of the motor court where he lived said Clete had thrown a suitcase in his Cadillac early Friday morning, driven away with a wave of the hand, and had not returned.

But at dawn the following Monday, Clete called the house on his cell phone.

'Where are you?' I said.

'Across the bayou. In City Park. I can see your backyard from here.'

'Why the mystery?'

'My situation is a little warm right now. Anybody been around?'

'What have you done, Clete?'

'It's under control. Haul your butt over here, Streak. Over-and-out.'

I drove down Main and across the drawbridge into the park. The sky was gray, the trees shrouded with mist, the surface of the bayou chained with rain rings. Clete was sitting on a table under a picnic shelter, his restored Cadillac parked back in the trees. But if he was trying to hide his Caddy from notice, he had taken on an impossible task. It was a beautiful automobile, with big fins, Frenched headlights, wire wheels and whitewalls, an immaculate cream-colored top, and a waxed finish that was the shade of a flamingo's wing – all of it the gift of a pornographic actor and drug mule by the name of Gunner Ardoin, who credited Clete with turning his life around.

I sat beside him under the shelter and unscrewed the cap on a thermos of coffee and hot milk I had brought from home.

'You went after Billy Joe Pitts, didn't you?' I said.

'I found out he hangs around the casino in Lake Charles on the weekends. But that's not all he does over there. He's part owner of a motel that operates as a cathouse for high rollers.'

Clete sipped his coffee, the steam rising into his face. He wore a rumpled suit with a white shirt and no tie, and a yellow straw cowboy hat that was bright with dew. The back of his neck was thick and red and pocked with scars below his hairline. I waited for him to go on, but he didn't.

'What happened?' I said.

'He made me at the casino and got me busted. I spent Saturday night in the Calcasieu Parish Jail. I'd still be in there if Nig and Willie hadn't called in some IOUs for me. I was in a cell with a meth freak who tried to talk to his wife in the women's section by yelling into the toilet bowl.'

Wee Willie Bimstine and Nig Rosewater were two New Orleans bondsmen Clete worked for, but I didn't want to hear about them or Clete's night in the can. When Clete's stories digressed, he was usually trying to hide a disaster of some kind inside an incessant stream of minutiae. 'What did you do when you got out, Clete?'

'Hung around town, bought some books at Barnes and Noble, went swimming out at the lake. You ever been to Shell Beach?'

'Clete –'

'Toward evening I made a house call out at Pitts's motel. He was lifting weights in a cottage out back. He was also getting a blow job. The girl was black, maybe sixteen or seventeen years old.' Clete tossed the remainder of his coffee into the grass and stared at the bayou.

'Go on,' I said.

'The girl went into the motel, probably to scrub her teeth with Liquid Drāno. So I ducked into the cottage. I was just going to have a motivational talk with the guy. He was lying on a bench, pressing a bar with maybe a hundred and seventy-five pounds on it. I waited till the bar was down on his chest, then I came up behind him and grabbed it and held it there so he couldn't lift it up again.

'I go, "You busted up my podjo, motherfucker. That means you take the payback or give up the guy who sent you. Want a second to think it over?"

'He goes, "Oh, it's Louisiana Fats again. I thought you were getting your cheeks oiled at the jail."

'I go, "Bad time to be a wiseass, Billy Joe," and roll the bar toward his throat.

'I thought he'd give it up. He was popping with sweat, his face starting to get a little purple. Then he says, "Does Robicheaux make you squat down for your nose lube?"'

Clete blew out his breath. 'What was I supposed to do? The clock was running. The guy almost took your head off with a two-by-four. He made a teenage girl cop his swizzle stick. He's a dirty cop. He should have had his spokes ripped out a long time ago. So I did it.'

'*What?*'

'Maybe hurt him a little when I picked up the bar and dropped it on him.'

Clete looked sideways at me, then back at the bayou again. I could hear the rain ticking on the trees and the camellias that grew along the water's edge. I was afraid to ask the next question. 'Is he –'

'I didn't hang around. Last I saw, he was thrashing around on the floor, holding his throat. Red froth was kind of blowing out of his mouth,' Clete said. He looked at me again, waiting for me to speak, unable to hide the apprehension in his face.

So I slipped back into my old role as Clete's enabler and answered the question that was in his eyes. 'To my knowledge no one has contacted the department. Did you check in with Willie and Nig?' I said.

'Are you kidding? The last thing they want is their hired skip chaser bringing an A and B beef down on their heads.'

He lit a Lucky Strike with an old Zippo and flicked the cap shut. He inhaled on the cigarette, blowing the smoke out through his fingers, then ground it out in the dirt. I could almost see his heart beating against his shirt.

'I'll make some calls. It's probably not as bad as you think,' I said.

St. Augustine said we should never use the truth to injure. Who was I to argue with a patristic saint? Besides, what else can you do when your best friend regularly allows his soul to be shot out of a cannon on your behalf?

I changed the subject and told him about my encounter with Valentine Chalons at the homicide scene Thursday night. At first Clete's eyes remained focused inward on his own thoughts, then I saw his attention begin to shift from his own troubles to mine.

'You say this guy Chalons blew it?' he said.

'He told me he never heard of Troy Bordelon. But his news crew was at the hospital. I'm sure they were covering the knife attack on Troy.'

'That doesn't mean Chalons knew about it,' Clete said.

'He's a good newsman. Nothing slides by him.'

'We're back to this Ida Durbin broad again? And rich people in St. Mary Parish you can't stand. There's a pattern here, big mon,' Clete said.

'Clete, sometimes you can make me wish one of us was stone drunk or down at the methadone clinic,' I said.

'What can I say? You'll never change. If you don't believe me, ask anybody who knows you.'

I wanted to punch him.

I went to the office and buried myself in our newly opened investigation into the death by strangulation and massive head trauma of Fontaine Belloc, the wife of the DEQ officer serving federal time at Seagoville, Texas. She had been raped before she died, and the semen in her body had come back a match with the Baton Rouge serial killer's, pulling us into an investigation that was now drawing national attention and every kind of meddlesome intrusion imaginable.

A famous crime novelist from the East ensconced herself in the middle of the investigation and the attendant publicity; psychics came out of the woodwork; and psychological profilers were interviewed on state television almost daily. The revelation that the murders of over thirty Baton Rouge women had remained unsolved in the last decade left local people stunned and disbelieving. Sporting goods stores quickly ran out of pepper spray and handguns.

Law enforcement agencies in other states began to contact Baton Rouge P.D., looking for ties to their own files of unsolved pattern homicides. The number of serial killings throughout the United States, as well as disappearances that were likely homicides, was a comment about the underside of our society that no humanist would care to dwell upon.

In Wichita, Kansas, a psychopath who called himself BTK, for 'bind, torture, and kill,' had committed crimes against whole families that were so cruel, depraved, and inhuman that police reporters as well as homicide investigators refused to reveal specific details to the public, even in the most euphemistic language.

Baton Rouge P.D. received inquiries from Miami and Fort Lauderdale about a series of silk stocking strangulations back in the 1970s that came to be known as the 'Canal Murders,' which may have been committed by one or several persons.

Years ago, in Texas, a demented man by the name of Henry Lucas confessed to whatever crime police authorities wished to feed him information about. Now some of those same cops who had closed their files at Lucas's expense privately acknowledged over the phone the real killer was probably still out there or, worse, in their midst.

The names of celebrity monsters reentered our vocabulary, perhaps because they put a human face on a level of evil most of us cannot comprehend. Or perhaps, like Dahmer or Gacy or Bundy, they're safely dead and their fate assures us that our legal apparatus will protect us against our present adversaries.

But what troubled me most about this investigation, as well as two other serial killer cases I had been involved with, was the lack of collective knowledge we possess about the perpetrators. They take their secrets to the grave. In their last moments, with nothing to gain, they refuse to tell the victims' families where their loved ones are buried. When a family member makes a special appeal to them, they gaze into space, as though someone is speaking to them in a foreign language.

None I ever interviewed showed anger or resentment. Their speech is remarkably lucid and their syntax shows no evidence of a thought disorder, as in the case of paranoids and schizophrenics. They're polite, not given to profanity, and disturbingly normal in appearance. Invariably they tell you their victims never had a clue as to the fate that was about to befall them.

They look like your next-door neighbor, or a man selling Fuller brushes, or a hardware store employee grinding a spare key for your house. I believe their numbers are greater than we think. I believe the causes that create them are theological in nature rather than societal. I believe they make a conscious choice to erase God's thumbprint from their souls. But that's just one man's opinion. The truth is, nobody knows.

It was raining when I went to lunch. Our drought was broken and Bayou Teche was running high and dark under the drawbridge, and black people were fishing with bamboo poles in the lee of the bridge. Even though it was early summer, the wind was cool and smelled of salt and wet trees. When I got back to the office, I temporarily put away my expanding file on the murder of Fontaine Belloc and kept my promise to Clete, namely, to determine the fate of Billy Joe Pitts after Clete bounced one hundred and seventy-five pounds in iron weights off his sternum.

I knew the police chief in Lake Charles, where Pitts evidently moonlighted as a pimp, but I decided to take the problem straight to its source and called the sheriff's department in the parish north of Alexandria where Pitts lived and worked. The dispatcher said Pitts was off that day.

'Give me his home number, please. This is in reference to a murder investigation,' I said.

'I can't do that,' the dispatcher said.

'Call him and give him my number. I need to hear from him in the next half hour or I'll go through the sheriff,' I said.

Ten minutes later, my extension rang. 'What do you want, Robicheaux?' Pitts said.

'Sounds like you have an obstruction in your throat,' I said.

'I said what do you want.'

Actually his response had already given me the information I needed. Pitts was alive, not in a hospital, and he probably wasn't filing charges against Clete. 'I think Troy Bordelon may have been witness to the murder of a prostitute by the name of Ida Durbin. But I hit a dead end every time I mention her name. So I talked to Val Chalons, you know, the newsman? He told me you might have some helpful information.'

'Me?'

'He mentioned your name specifically,' I lied.

'I see Val Chalons when he fishes up here on my dad's lake. I don't talk police business with him. He doesn't give me tips on the stock market.'

'But you know Val Chalons, right?'

'Listen, I don't know what you're up to, but you tell rhino-butt it's not over between us.'

'Who would rhino-butt be?' I asked.

'Duh,' he replied.

'It's been good talking with you, Billy Joe. Try gargling with some warm salt water. And the next time you come around my house with a weapon in your hand, be advised I'm going to blow your fucking head off,' I said.

Then I made a call to my half brother, Jimmie, in New Orleans, where he owned one restaurant in the Quarter and another uptown, in the Carrollton district. Jimmie had never married, although any number of attractive and interesting women drifted in and out of his life. He was known in the life as 'Jimmie the Gent' and over the years had acquired a kind of benign notoriety as a player in the city's traditional vices – video poker machines, offtrack betting, card clubs, and trafficking in large amounts of illegal Mexican rum and gin. By their nature, all these enterprises took Jimmie into a working relationship with the Giacano family, who had run New Orleans since Governor Huey Long made a present of the state to Frank Costello.

But the patriarch of the Giacanos, a Dumpster load of whaleshit by the name of Didi Gee, paid back Jimmie's trust by putting a contract on me, except the button man mistakenly shot Jimmie and blinded him in one eye.

'This guy Bordelon saw Ida die?' Jimmie said.

'I didn't say that,' I replied.

'Then *what* did you say?'

'He saw blood on a chair. He said they smashed her mandolin. He wasn't sure what happened to her.'

The line was quiet a long time. 'And some redneck cops came after you because they thought you knew too much? Cops who might work for the Chalons family?'

'That about sums it up.'

'I'm coming over there.'

'Not a good idea,' I said.

'You want me to stay at a motel?' he said.

chapter six

After I had hung up I went downstairs and tapped on Helen's door. Her desk was covered with photos of women who were thought to be victims of the Baton Rouge serial killer.

'Val Chalons was covering the story on our DOA Thursday night,' I said. 'I brought up the name of Billy Joe Pitts. He told me he never heard of him.'

Helen was chewing on the corner of her lip, trying to concentrate on what I was saying, her fingers splayed on the photos of the dead women. 'You lost me,' she said.

'I just talked with Pitts. He says Chalons fishes at his father's lake. Chalons was lying.'

Helen closed her eyes and opened them. 'Dave, we've got our hands full here. We're going to get Pitts. We're going to get that other jerk, what's-his-name, Shockly. But right now –'

'Guys like Pitts don't operate without sanction, Helen. Why did Chalons lie?'

'Maybe he isn't interested in the subject. Maybe he couldn't care less about you or Pitts. Maybe everything isn't about you.'

It was quiet in the room. Outside, rain swept across the window. 'The assault against my person is an open investigation. I was bringing you up to date.'

'Good,' she said, her face coloring with embarrassment at her own level of irritation.

I nodded at her desktop. 'I went over those this morning. Pretty grim.'

She stood up from her desk and tightened the tuck of her shirt with her thumbs, her shoulders flexing, her expression recomposing itself. She picked up a glossy plastic folder and handed it to me. 'Here's the Baton Rouge coroner's file. A couple of the women were dead when most of the damage was done to them. Some of them weren't.'

'I'll read it and check with you later.'

'Do that,' she said.

I started out the door.

'Hold on a minute, bwana,' she said. 'I apologize if I'm a little on edge. This is the worst case I've ever seen. How does a guy this sick go undetected for years?'

In my mind's eye I saw an image from years ago of a nineteen-year-old door gunner blowing apart a South Vietnamese wedding party inside a free-fire zone.

'Because he looks like a regular guy, cooking hot dogs on the grill next door,' I said.

After five o'clock, I drove into St. Mary Parish and resumed my own investigation into the fate of Ida Durbin.

To say the Chalons family lived in an antebellum home on Bayou Teche does not go anywhere near an accurate description of the singularity that characterized their home and their way of life. The house was enormous, two and a half stories tall, and had been built in the 1850s inside oak trees that were already mature. Now the trees were centuries old and kept the house in perpetual shade. But rather than restore the home to its original grandeur, as the Chalons's wealth would have allowed them to do, they seemed to treat modernity as an enemy to be kept in abeyance.

According to the legend, the builder had mixed milk and hog's blood in the paint, and it had dried on the cypress and oak planks as hard as iron. I suspected the truth was otherwise. The hardened texture and grayish-green color of the paint was probably due to the smoke from cane stubble fires and the mold and dampness caused by lack of sunlight inside the trees.

Or maybe I just didn't like the romantic legends that seemed to attach themselves to the Chalons family.

Valentine's father was named Raphael. He had become a widower twice and was notorious for his illegitimate children, erotic excursions to the Islands, and his affairs with married women in New Orleans. I wondered sometimes if his home did not mirror his soul. He hired no gardeners and let his grounds run riot. But the result was a rough kind of subtropical Edenic beauty, threaded with snakes and thorned plants that had no names. Even more incongruently, his magnolia trees grew to a huge size, dripping with flowers, his grapefruit trees bursting with golden orbs, without sunlight ever directly touching the leaves.

Formosa termites had eaten through the outbuildings, the old slave quarters, and part of the house's walls and lower veranda, robbing them of any sense of historical severity they might have once contained, as though their edges had been molded by the gentle forces of time and foliage rather than parasitical insects. Raphael had finally relented and allowed chemical treatment of his property, but the accumulative effect of his organized neglect was a tangle of air vines, wild persimmons, palmettos, pecan trees, blooming flowers, and desiccated wood that no film company could replicate.

I stopped my pickup in front of the heavy iron gate that closed off the driveway and prevented tourists from entering the property and photographing it. But before I could get out of the truck, a black man emerged from the shadows and scraped back the gate for me. He was a heavyset, pie-faced man, with big, half-moon eyebrows and a cranium like an inverted pot. What was his name? Andrew? No, Andre. Andre Bergeron. He ran errands and did chores for the Chalons family and used to sell iced-down oysters off the tailgate of a pickup by the drawbridge near Burke Street.

'Thank you,' I said.

'Yes, suh,' he replied. 'You here to see Mr. Val?'

'How'd you know?' I said.

''Cause you a policeman in New Iberia. 'Cause you probably working on a crime and you here to see Mr. Val 'cause he's a TV newsman and he got a lot of information on them kind of t'ings.'

'You got it pretty well figured out,' I said.

'Yes, suh. I do.'

I drove into the grounds, through towering oak trees that creaked with the wind. The rain had stopped and the sky was marbled with purple and gold clouds, and through the trees I could see the sunlight winking on the bayou.

Val opened the front door. He was expansive, jocular, a bourbon and crushed ice in his hand, his sister Honoria seated at the piano in the middle of the living room, a solitary lamp burning behind her. The woodwork was dark, the furniture heavy, the air musky-smelling. 'How you doing, old buddy?' Val said.

'Hope you'll forgive me for not calling first,' I said.

'Oh no, no, no, not a problem. You remember Honoria, don't you?' he said.

Honoria was hard to forget. She was dark-haired and dark-skinned, like her father, with brown eyes and a small red mouth, a mole at one corner. Honoria had received a doctorate from the Sorbonne and had taught music theory for three years at the university in Lafayette. But either her iconoclastic ways or rumors about her libertine behavior caused the university to deny her tenure. Sometimes I would see her in New Iberia's public library, by herself, her glasses perched on the end of her nose, reading until closing time.

'You want a soft drink?' Val asked.

'No, just a word with you,' I replied.

Honoria got up from the piano bench and started toward the kitchen. She wore a spaghetti-strap black dress with purple shoes, and the muscles in her back were deeply tanned and looked as hard as iron when she walked.

'I didn't mean for you to leave,' I said awkwardly.

'I was going to see if there was any iced tea. I thought you might like that in place of a soft drink,' she said. She stared at me, waiting, the sepia-tinted light shining on the tops of her breasts.

'Don't bother,' I said.

She walked away, leaving me with the illogical impression that somehow I had been rude.

'What's up?' Val said.

'You told me you didn't know Billy Joe Pitts. He says you fish on his father's lake. Why would you want to jerk me around, Val?'

'Yeah, I know Old Man Pitts. Maybe I didn't put the names together. Square with me, Dave. What are you trying to prove here?'

'I think Pitts tried to click off my switch. Your family owns the parish he works for. A guy like that doesn't take a dump without somebody's permission.'

'That's a great line. You could be a screenwriter in a blink. I'm serious. I'd like to help you with that. Isn't your daughter studying literature?'

Valentine was slick. He didn't defend or attack. He treated an insult like a compliment and an adversary like a misguided friend. I had acted foolishly in coming to his house. What had I expected? For a man to agree with me when I called him a liar?

'Thanks for your time. I'll let myself out,' I said.

'Don't go away mad. I'm glad you dropped by. Hey, I live in the guesthouse in back. Let's throw a steak on the grill.'

'Another time,' I said.

He placed his arm across my shoulders. He was almost a half head taller than I, even with a slight slouch in his posture. I tried to step away from him, without being rude, but to no avail. He pointed to an ancient parchment sealed in a glass frame on the wall. 'That's our family coat of arms. The parchment is fifteenth century, but the seal goes back a thousand years earlier.'

The coat of arms involved a shield, a gladius or sword a Roman legionnaire would have carried, the cross of the Crusades, and the visored helmet of a medieval knight errant.

'The family name comes from the Battle of Châlons. My ancestors got rid of their own name and substituted the name of a great event,' he said. He removed his arm from my shoulder and gazed benevolently into my face. I couldn't tell if he was feigning humility or actually offering up his family history to inspire awe in others.

'Your ancestors fought against Attila the Hun?' I said.

'We probably didn't do a very good job of it. We had to fight his descendants in that delayed Teutonic migration known as World Wars One and Two.'

I looked at him blankly. He had just lifted a line from F. Scott Fitzgerald's novel *The Great Gatsby* and used it as though it were of his own creation.

'You're not impressed?' he said.

'I had a long day. I'll be seeing you, Val.'

When I shook hands with him, I felt his fingers wrap around my skin and squeeze, his eyes lingering on mine, as though he were trying to read my thoughts. 'I like you, Dave,' he said.

Out in the yard, I unconsciously rubbed my hand on my trousers.

The black man named Andre was picking up litter that had blown into the drive from the highway. He waved at me and I waved back. Then, in the easy sweep of wind through the trees, I heard someone behind me. I turned, expecting to see Valentine Chalons again. But it was his sister, Honoria, her black hair curved under her cheeks, a gold chain and cross askew on her chest.

Her eyes were liquid, almost luminous in the shade, her facial skin smooth, without a wrinkle or crease. She continued to look at me strangely, without speaking.

'Could I help you?' I said.

'Do you remember the night you drove me home from the dance at the country club?' she asked.

'No, I don't remember that.'

'You probably wouldn't. I had to put you to bed rather than the other way around.'

'I used to have blackouts, Honoria. I did a lot of things that are still inside a dark box somewhere. I don't know if I want to revisit them.'

Her eyes went away from mine and came back. 'My father and brother aren't afraid of you. But they are afraid of the nun,' she said.

'The *nun?*'

'The Buddhists believe the dead don't know they're dead. So maybe some people die and go to hell and never know it. It's just another day. Like this one, now. Do you think that's true? That hell is just a place you step into on an ordinary day?'

The wind smelled of humus, lichen, the musky odor of pecan husks broken under the shoe, a sunshower on the fields across the bayou. But any poetry that might have been contained in that moment was lost when I stared into Honoria's face, convinced that human insanity was as close to our fingertips as the act of rubbing fog off a windowpane.

Honoria's eyes remained fixed on mine, expectant, somehow trusting, the redness of her mouth and the mole next to it as inviting as a poisonous flower.

chapter seven

When I got back home later that evening, Jimmie had already arrived from New Orleans and installed himself in the spare bedroom. Jimmie was a funny guy. He had earned the nickname 'Jimmie the Gent' for his manners, intelligence, and sharp dress, but his success in the world was also due to the fact that, like my father and mother, he could do many things well with his hands.

As a Depression-era family we worked from what people used to call 'cain't-see to cain't-see,' which meant from before first light to well after sunset. My father was a natural gas pipeliner and derrick man on drilling rigs out in the Gulf, but he considered industrial work, with regular hours and paychecks, a vacation. Real work was the enterprise you did on your own, with nobody to back you up but your family. We broke corn together, butchered and smoked our own meat, strung 'trot' lines baited with chicken guts through the swamp across the road, milked cows and hoed out the vegetable garden before school, calved in the early spring, trapped muskrat in the winter, sold cracklins and blackberries off the tailgate of a pickup for two bits a quart.

In the summer, Jimmie and I built board roads with our father through tidal marshland where you plodded all day through ooze that was like wet cement. In the spring, we caught crabs and crawfish by the washtub with chunks of skinned nutria, and sold them to restaurants in New Orleans for twice the price we could get in New Iberia or Lafayette.

Before she fixed our breakfast, my mother would return from the barn smelling of manure and horse sweat, a pail of frothy milk in one hand and an armful of brown eggs smeared with chickenshit clutched against her chest. Then she would pull off her shirt, scrub her hands and arms with Lava soap under the pump in the sink, and in her bra fill our bowls with cush-cush and make ham-and-onion sandwiches for our lunches.

Jimmie and I both had paper routes in New Iberia's red-light district. We set pins in the bowling alley and with our mother washed bottles in the Tabasco factory on the bayou. My father hand-built the home we lived in, notching and pegging the oak beams with such seamless craftsmanship that it survived the full brunt of a half dozen hurricanes with no structural damage. My mother ironed clothes in a laundry nine hours a day in hundred-and-ten-degree heat. She scalded and picked chickens for five cents apiece in our backyard, and secretly saved money in a coffee can for two years in order to buy an electric ice grinder and start a snowball concession at the minor league baseball park.

Our parents were illiterate and barely spoke English, but they were among the most brave and resourceful people I ever knew. Neither of them would consciously set about to do wrong. But they destroyed one another just the same – my father with his alcoholism, my mother with her lust and insatiable need for male attention. Then they destroyed their self-respect, their family, and their home. They did all this with the innocence of people who had never been farther away from their Cajun world than their weekend honeymoon trip to New Orleans.

Jimmie's suitcase lay unopened on the bed in the spare

room, but through the kitchen window I saw him in the backyard, wearing shined shoes, pleated dark slacks, a pomegranate-colored tie, and dazzling white dress shirt, his Rolex watchband glinting on his wrist. He had folded his sleeves up on his forearms and was screwing down a new brass hasp on Tripod's cage door. He stepped back and tested the door, then began pouring from a bag of Snuggs's dry food into Tripod's bowl.

'Snuggs might not appreciate your expression of charity at his expense,' I said, walking down the steps into the yard.

'I already checked with him. He said the eats you buy him are third-rate, anyway,' he replied.

I was always amazed at how much we resembled one another, even though we were only half brothers. He didn't have a white patch in his hair, as I did, and his prosthetic eye had a peculiar gleam trapped inside it, but our height, skin coloring, posture, facial structure, even the way we walked, were the same. I sometimes felt a reflection had stepped out of the mirror and would not allow me to be who I thought I was.

'I just got back from talking with Valentine Chalons. I've caught him in at least two lies,' I said.

'Why does he want to lie about Ida Durbin? He wasn't even born in 'fifty-eight.'

'The Chalonses supposedly had business ties to the Giacanos. The Giacanos had part of the hot pillow action in Galveston. Ida was working in one of their joints,' I replied.

'That doesn't make sense. If Ida was killed by a pimp or some cops on a pad, why would the Chalonses care? They wouldn't even know her name.'

'When they lie, they're guilty. Val Chalons is lying,' I said.

'Maybe. Maybe not, Dave. You don't like rich guys. I'm not sure how objective you are.'

I picked up Tripod and set him inside his cage. He felt heavy and solid in my hands, his tail flipping in my face. I started to speak, but this time kept my own counsel.

Jimmie latched Tripod's cage door and poked one finger through the screen to scratch his head. Jimmie's jaws were closely shaved, the small cleft in his chin filled with shadow. 'I keep thinking maybe she got away from whoever abducted her. A few times I thought I heard her voice on a jukebox, singing backup maybe or even doing a solo. I always wanted to believe those demos we sent to Sun Records got her out of the life. Kind of a crazy way to think, huh?'

No different from my thoughts, I started to say. He waited for me to speak. 'What are you thinking?' he asked.

'She's dead. That's why the Chalonses are running scared,' I said.

'No, there's some other explanation,' he replied, wagging one finger back and forth, as though he had the power to change the past.

That night I dreamed of Galveston, Texas, in the year 1958. In the dream I saw the salt-eaten frame houses where girls with piney-woods accents took on all comers for five dollars a pop, while down by the beach snub-nosed hot rods roared past a drive-in restaurant, their exposed V-8 engines chrome-plated and iridescent with an oily sheen, their twin exhausts thundering in a dirty echo off the asphalt. The sky was purple, streaked with fire, the palm trees like scorched tin cutouts against the sun. I woke at four in the morning and could not sleep again, my heart congealed with a sense of mortality that I could not explain.

In the darkness I drove to the cemetery in St. Martin-ville where my third wife, Bootsie, was buried. Bayou Teche was coated with fog, the crypts beaded with moisture as big as marbles. Downstream I could see the steeple of the old French church impaled against the stars, and the massive Evangeline oak under which I first kissed Bootsie Mouton and discovered how the world could become a cathedral in the time it takes for two people to press their mouths against one another.

I sat on a steel bench by Bootsie's tomb, my head in my hands, unable to pray or even to think. I did not want the sun to rise or the starlight to go out of the sky. I wanted to stay inside the darkness, the coolness of the fog, the smell of nightdamp and old brick stained with mold. I wanted to be with my dead wife.

At eight o'clock I sat down at my desk and went to work again on the case of the Baton Rouge serial killer. So far, all of his known victims had been women. Almost all of them had been abducted from their homes or driveways in upscale neighborhoods, often in broad daylight. There were no eyewitnesses. With the exception of the black woman whose body had been found not far from the convent at Grand Coteau, all of the victims had been white and educated.

One woman evidently was taken out of her front yard while she was watering her flowers. One had parked her SUV in the driveway and left a sack of groceries on the kitchen counter and another on the passenger seat of her vehicle before she disappeared. The door to the SUV was open; a solitary jar of gourmet barbecue sauce was broken on the cement.

Another victim must have opened her front door to retrieve her mail, then had spilled a handful of envelopes down the brick steps. Her three-year-old daughter, who was playing in the sunroom, wandered out on the street, looking for her mother, and was stopped from walking into traffic by a passing police officer. A female graduate student jogging along the chain lakes north of the LSU campus rounded a bend, waved at friends eating lunch on a bench, and jogged up a path between a bank of azalea bushes. She was not seen again until her body, dressed only in underwear, was found floating in a pond under a railroad trestle in the Atchafalaya Basin.

Each abduction took place when no male friend or adult family member was at the crime scene. Baton Rouge police and parish sheriff's deputies had interviewed hundreds of people in the neighborhoods where the victims had lived. The interviews had contributed absolutely nothing to the investigation. Obviously an individual who inspired trust was threading himself in and out of residential enclaves where suspicion and exclusion came with the house deed. Could a black man walk up a driveway to a four-hundred-thousand-dollar home, at three in the afternoon, and drag a woman to his vehicle and not be noticed? Could a delivery man, a telephone worker, an inspector from the gas company? Could a police officer? Could a minister wearing a Roman collar?

But no one saw a delivery or official vehicle parked near the crime scene. The black and Hispanic lawn men who worked nearby were questioned and excluded. Every known sex offender in the area was pulled in and run through the ringer. Oddly, the perpetrator had given a free pass to the groups who are usually the targets of misogynistic predators. None of his victims had been a prostitute, runaway, or barroom derelict.

None of the crime scenes showed any sign of struggle or resistance. The broken jar of gourmet barbecue sauce and the spilled mail on a woman's front steps were the only physical indications that in seconds someone's life had turned into a visit to the Abyss.

The serial killer did not have a face or a history that we knew about. His DNA was not in the national database. He had hung Fontaine Belloc's purse in a tree to taunt us and to show his contempt for her and her family.

He sought out victims who were reasonably happy and at peace with the world and left society's rejects alone. His body fluids were left behind as a toxic smear on the rest of us.

I read through the autopsy report on Fontaine Belloc again. The details were not of a kind anyone wishes to remember. But one stuck in my mind and would not go away. I picked up my phone and called the office of Koko Hebert, our parish coroner. 'She swallowed her wedding ring?' I said.

'From its position, I'd say a couple of hours before she died,' he replied.

'He forced her to eat it?'

'Not in my opinion.'

'Spell it out, will you, Koko?'

'Her wrists were bound, probably with plastic cuffs. There were teeth marks on the ring finger. I think she used her teeth to work the ring off her finger and swallow it. What difference does it make?'

'Because if she was that determined to keep this bastard from taking her ring, maybe she figured out a way to leave us a message about his identity,' I said, my blood rising.

'Yeah, that's a possibility, isn't it?' he replied.

I replaced the receiver in the cradle without saying good-bye.

A mockingbird flew into my window glass, flecking it with a pinpoint of white matter. I got up from the desk and looked down onto the lawn. The bird lay still in the shade, one wing at a broken angle.

It was not a good morning. And it was about to get worse.

Just before noon, Honoria Chalons called the office to ask how I was feeling.

'Excuse me?' I said.

'My first husband is buried at the church cemetery in St. Martinville. I saw you there this morning. You didn't look well. Are you all right?' she said.

'Yes, I'm fine.'

'Can you have a drink with me this afternoon?'

'I traded in sour mash for AA. That was after it chewed me up and spit me out.'

'So I'll buy you an iced tea.'

'Another time.'

'You think I'm a mentally ill person?'

'Guys like me don't get to judge other people's stability.'

'The things I said to you about death yesterday? They're all true.'

'I believe you.'

'What I said about the nun is true, too. My father and Val genuinely fear her. They won't even go inside the little church she attends.'

'Which nun are we talking about?'

'Have that drink with me?'

'Give me a number where I can call you after work,' I said.

I went downstairs and caught Helen on her way to lunch. 'You know a nun who's had some run-ins with the Chalons family?' I said.

She thought about it. 'There's one on Old Jeanerette Road. Years ago, she stoked up the sugar cane workers in St. Mary Parish. She runs a group that builds houses for the poor now. Why?'

'I was out to the Chalons house. The nun came up in the conversation.'

Helen sucked in her cheeks, her eyes studying a dead space between us. 'Nothing I say has any influence, does it?' she said.

'Had you rather I not tell you what I'm doing?'

Helen put her hand inside her shirt collar and picked at a mosquito bite on her shoulder, her gaze wandering along the corridor wall, her breath audible in the silence. 'If I remember right, about two years back somebody slashed up her car tires. Check the file. Her name is Molly Boyle. Her middle name is "trouble." She's your kind of gal.'

I went to lunch at Bon Creole and tried not to think about my brief run-in with Helen. When I came out of the restaurant, the sun was like a white flame in the sky, the highway rippling with heat, the air smelling of salt, and water evaporating from backed-up storm ditches. At the office, I pulled a file on the nun and a series of complaints, all involving harassment and vandalism, that she had lodged with the sheriff's department. The deputies' entries in the file were matter-of-fact and made no conclusion about possible perpetrators, other than a mention that several black teenagers in the area had been questioned.

I took a handful of loose mug shots from my desk drawer, dropped them in my shirt pocket, and went to find Sister Molly Boyle.

She had created an administrative center in a restored nineteenth-century farmhouse on the bayou, eleven miles south of town, and lived next door with another nun in a cypress cottage. Ostensibly she worked under the auspices of the diocese in Lafayette, but as I turned into the gravel driveway I had the sense the archenemy of the Chalons family had staked out her own territory.

The entire compound was about three acres in size. The lawn was bright green and freshly mowed, partially shaded by live oaks and pecan trees, the embankment along the Teche planted with elephant ears, caladiums, impatiens, and periwinkles. A large sunny area was devoted to vegetable gardens, beehives, and a huge compost heap piled inside a rectangle of railroad ties. A tractor was parked in a pole shed, and poultry pecked in a bare spot under a spreading oak that grew above the shed and the adjacent barn. A secretary in the office walked with me onto the gallery and said I would probably find Sister Molly in the barn.

She was grinding a machete on an emery wheel, her eyes encased in machinist goggles, the heel of her hand pressed down close to the blade's edge. I waited until she clicked off the toggle switch on the grinder before I spoke. 'I didn't want to startle you, Sister. I'm Dave Robicheaux, from the Iberia Parish Sheriff's Department,' I said.

She pulled her goggles off with one thumb and left a greasy smear by her eyebrow. Her hair was dark red and tied up on her head with a white kerchief, the tails of her denim shirt knotted across her stomach. The heat and trapped moisture inside the barn were stifling. Motes of dust and desiccated manure floated as thick as gnats in the shafts of sunlight through the cracks. But she seemed unbothered by any of it. 'I go by Molly,' she said, and extended her hand.

'It looks like some vandals were trying to give you a bad time a couple of years back. Have any idea who they were?' I said.

'The deputies who came out thought they were kids from the neighborhood,' she replied.

'But you don't?'

'Our dog was poisoned. Our car tires were cut into ribbons. Our secretary was shot in the back with an air rifle. We help impoverished people own their homes. Why would their children want to hurt us?'

I blotted the perspiration out of my eyes on my arm. 'Can we go outside?' I said.

She hung the machete on a nail, the edge of its curved blade like a strip of blue ice. Then she pulled her kerchief loose from her head and shook out her hair. 'How about some lemonade?' she said.

I sat at a spool table on the back porch of her cottage

while she went inside. Through the trees the sunlight looked hard and brittle and unrelenting on the bayou's surface. She came back on the porch with a tray of cookies and two glasses of lemonade, with sprigs of mint in them.

'You tried to unionize the farmworkers hereabouts?' I said.

'For a while. Mechanization took the jobs away, so we turned to other things. We teach people folk crafts and carpentry now.'

'Has the Chalons family ever tried to injure you?'

She gazed at the bayou, her eyes blinking more than they should have. 'They let us know they were around,' she said.

I removed the handful of mug shots from my shirt pocket and placed them on the table. 'Ever see any of these guys?' I asked.

She separated the photos one from the other with her index finger. Then she tapped on the face of a man with grainy skin, recessed eyes, and teeth that were too big for his mouth. 'That's one I won't forget,' she said.

'His name is Billy Joe Pitts. He's a sheriff's deputy.'

'He pulled me over to the side of the highway north of Alexandria. We'd been circulating a union petition among some cannery workers. He made some rather nasty remarks.'

'He threatened you?'

'His remarks were sexual in nature. That night our car was vandalized.'

'Did you ever hear of a woman named Ida Durbin?'

'No, I don't recall that name. Who is she?'

'Someone I believe the Chalons family would like to forget,' I said.

She paused a moment. 'You're not really here about our troubles, are you?'

I felt my face tighten. 'Billy Joe Pitts is part of an

ongoing assault-and-battery investigation. I think he takes his orders from the Chalonses.'

'I see,' she said.

'You've been very helpful.' But I had lost her attention and I believe her trust as well.

She looked at her watch. 'I have to make some deliveries now. We run a folk craft workshop and sell the birdhouses they make. A tough way to raise a dollar, huh?'

Way to go, Robicheaux, I thought.

Just before I drove off the property onto the state road, I saw a group of black people leave the rehabilitated farmhouse that served as Sister Molly's administrative center. They were laughing, clapping one another on the shoulder about a joke of some kind. A dome-headed black man recognized me through the windshield and raised a hand in greeting. It was Andre Bergeron, the handyman who did chores for the Chalons family. I waved out the window in response and headed back to New Iberia.

After work, I fixed supper for Jimmie and me at the house. I was beginning to regret I had told him of Ida Durbin's fate. He blamed himself and kept trying to recall details of their last day together, as though some clue could be extracted from an idle remark she made over forty years ago. He told me he was meeting a musicologist that night at the University of Louisiana in Lafayette.

'I know I've heard Ida's voice on a record. I'm sure of it, Dave,' he said.

I did the dishes and didn't try to contend with Jimmie's obsession. After he was gone, I showered and took a walk downtown in the twilight. From the drawbridge looking south I could see the gardens behind the Shadows, a plantation home built in 1831, and the receding corridor of oak and cypress trees along the banks of the Teche, a tidal stream that had been navigated by Spaniards in bladed helmets, French missionaries, displaced Acadians, pirates, Confederate and Yankee gun crews, and plantation revelers who toasted their own prosperity on paddle wheelers that floated through the night like candlelit wedding cakes.

Jean Lafitte had auctioned off West Indian slaves a few hundred yards from where I stood. As a lesson in terror, Union soldiers under the command of General Nathaniel Banks had raped women, burned crops, and looted the homes of the rich up and down the bayou when they marched through New Iberia in April 1863. People still found minié balls in the heartwood of felled oak trees and pieces of broken china in chicken yards, green depressions carpeted with mushrooms in a woods where soldiers with no names were hurriedly buried.

As the heat went out of the day, the summer light seemed to ascend higher into the sky, so that the bayou itself became a long amber ribbon between the green darkness of the trees, the surface creasing in the wind, somehow disconnected from the present, the alluvial soil along the banks filled with the bones of Indians, Europeans, and Reconstruction-empowered Africans, all of whom had thought their dominion over the land was forever.

But in my reverie about the nature of history and collective vanity I had forgotten a more prosaic detail from my day at the office. Either Jimmie or I had accidentally turned off the message machine on my telephone, and when I returned home the phone was ringing without stop.

'Hello?' I said.

'I wasn't going to call, but principle is principle, I think.'

'Honoria?' I said.

'Yes. Who did you think it was?' she said.

I squeezed my eyes shut. 'I was supposed to call you back after work,' I said.

'To put it more accurately, you asked for my phone number. We were going to have a drink.'

Not exactly, but it wasn't a time to argue. 'I got buried today. I'm terribly sorry,' I said.

She didn't speak, and I could feel my hand tightening on the receiver, my discomfort growing. I had meant to call her back, but not to have a drink. Instead, my whole agenda with Honoria had been about Sister Molly Boyle, whom I had been able to contact on my own. The consequence was I had forgotten about Honoria. The truth was I had tried to use her.

'Where are you?' I said.

'Down the street, at Clementine's.'

'Can I treat you to a dessert?'

'Whatever you like, Dave. It's a strange evening, isn't it? The sky is purple and full of birds. When I think of the color purple, I always think of the passion of Christ or the robe of Agamemnon.'

Don't get mixed up with this one, I thought.

But I was just buying her a dessert, obeying the tenets of basic charity, wasn't I? Why turn a harmless act into self-flagellation? I told myself.

And in that spirit I strolled down to Clementine's and through the door into a bar and supper club where the glad-at-heart gathered and had drinks and étouffée and steaks two inches thick on a candlelit terrace overlooking the Teche, and where, in the cold smell of crushed ice stained with whiskey and bruised cherries, a half century could disappear with the ease of raising a glass to your mouth.

chapter eight

'You can't drink at all?' Honoria said.

'I could but I choose not to,' I replied, and felt instantly stupid at my own rhetoric.

'I thought if you went through the Twelve Steps, you were cured. It must be awful to know that about yourself.'

'To know what?'

'That you're afraid of your own metabolism.'

There was a black shine in both her hair and eyes, and she wore a white cotton dress with eyelets in the bodice that exposed the deep tan in her skin. When she ordered her third vodka collins I made a show of noticing the clock above the bar and told her I should be going. But you didn't get off the hook that easily with Honoria Chalons. She gave the waiter a credit card to pay the check before I could, then asked him to put her drink in a Styrofoam cup. 'Do me a favor?' she said to me.

I waited for her to go on.

'My car won't start. I think it'll have to be towed. Can you give me a lift?' she said.

We walked back down East Main to my house and got in my pickup truck. She tripped once on a pitch in the sidewalk and I felt her body come hard against me. 'I still haven't eaten dinner. Want to stop somewhere?' she said.

'I have work to do,' I said.

'It's a grand evening. I don't want to waste it at home. The House of Chalons is a dark place. Few people know how dark it really is,' she said.

I looked at her profile in the shadowy light of a streetlamp, and wondered if she was being deliberately grandiose. But she was not. Her eyes were fixed on the rooftops of the Victorian and antebellum homes along the street and the birds circling over the chimneys, as though they held the answer to a question she had never resolved.

'Why are you staring at me?' she said.

'I wonder why you live at home.'

'To care for my father. He's quite ill. I don't think he'll live long.'

'I'm sorry to hear that,' I said.

'He'll handle it. He always does. God, I need a bath. Every time I come back to Louisiana, I can't seem to scrub the dirt and humidity out of my skin.'

In the shadows her cheeks were pooled with color, her eyes glazed with an alcoholic shine. She looked up into my face, almost like a little girl, perhaps faintly embarrassed at the visceral nature of her language. 'Take me home?' she said.

We drove down Old Spanish Trail and on through Jeanerette. The moon was low on the horizon, veiled with brown dust from the sugar cane fields, her house lit inside the massive live oaks that surrounded it. I drove through the gate and stopped in front of the porch. My truck windows were down and for a moment I thought I smelled cigar smoke.

The decorum of the era in which Honoria and I were raised would have required me to walk her to the door, or at least offer to do so. But I had already decided Honoria needed to get on with her life, and she didn't need me to help her with it. I was about to say good night, without getting out of the truck, when she placed her hand on my cheek, then tilted her head sideways and pressed her mouth to mine, using her tongue, threading her fingers tightly through the back of my hair.

I could taste vodka and sweet syrup and orange slices and the tartness of crushed cherries in her mouth. I could even taste the coldness of the ice that had been poured from her collins glass into the Styrofoam cup. She took a breath and got up on her knees, then bent down to kiss me again.

'Whoa, kiddo,' I said.

'Kiddo yourself,' she said. She got out of the truck and walked inside, her back stiff, the porch light bright on her white dress.

I turned the truck around and started back toward the gate. Not more than three feet from my window, I saw the red glow of a cigar among a tangle of persimmon trees. I slowed the truck, the tires creaking on the gravel, and looked into the spectral face of Honoria's father, Raphael Chalons.

'My daughter is a vulnerable woman, sir. Be advised I do not abide the man who would take advantage of that fact,' he said.

Good evening to you, too, sir, I thought, and drove on without replying. I also decided that on some occasions good deeds and the obligations of charity should be heaved over the gunnels.

The next morning Jimmie was up before me, fixing breakfast for us, feeding Tripod and Snuggs, whistling a song.

'You must have had a pretty good night,' I said.

'This friend of mine, the professor at UL, he's got this huge collection of country and bluegrass music. Remember we used to always say Ida sang just like Kitty Wells? That's because Kitty Wells sang in B flat. See, my friend has put his whole record library in his computer and he came up with all these recordings that have somebody on them singing like Kitty Wells.'

Jimmie had been cutting toast on the breadboard while he spoke. He turned around, his starched white shirt crinkling, his hair wet and combed, his face shiny with aftershave. 'You know the best part? On a couple of those records somebody's playing a mandolin just the way Ida did,' he said.

I looked away so he could not see my eyes. 'That's good, Jimmie,' I said.

'Yeah, Ida was smart. I always thought she got away from those guys. Why would they want to kill her, anyway? She was just a piney-woods country girl.'

Because they're sonsofbitches and they make examples of piney-woods girls, I thought.

'What?' he said.

'Nothing,' I replied. 'I'd better get to the office.'

'Hey, we're going to find ole Ida. You'll see,' he said.

'You bet,' I said, knowing that Jimmie, like all brave people, would continue to believe in the world, regardless of what it did to him.

A little after nine, Wally, our overweight dispatcher and self-appointed departmental comic, buzzed my phone. 'There's a newsman down here wants to see you. Should I send him up?' he said.

'Which newsman?'

'The one on TV looks like an icicle.'

'Valentine Chalons?'

'That's the one.'

'Why don't you just say so?'

''Cause he looks like an icicle. Or I could call him the TV guy wit' a broom up his ass trying to give me a bad time. By the way, that nun left a note for you.'

I couldn't begin to follow his words. 'Wally –' I began.

'That nun, the one who builds homes for poor people,

she was here to see you. I buzzed your phone but you wasn't at your desk. So she left a note. It's in your mailbox. She went out when the TV guy was coming in. You want to see the TV guy or not?'

Three minutes later Valentine Chalons opened my office door without knocking and closed it behind him, his eyes locked on mine. 'I'll make this simple. My sister is a grown woman and can associate with whomever she pleases. But I'll be damned if you'll use her to get at my father,' he said.

'Sorry to see you interpret things that way, Val,' I said.

'My father is a heart patient. He probably doesn't have long to live. What are you trying to do to him?'

'Your sister had a problem with her car. I gave her a ride home.'

'You're looking me in the face, telling me you have no issue with my father?'

'If I do, it doesn't involve your sister.'

'How about Sister Molly? It's just coincidence I saw her leaving here this morning?'

'I don't know what it is, because I didn't see or talk with her.'

'Our handyman told me he saw you at her office yesterday.'

'Yeah, I did see her yesterday. But that's none of your business.'

'Let me set you straight about that hypocritical bitch. She's a closet Marxist who uses the Church to stir up class hatred in ignorant and gullible people. Except she's not a real nun. She's got some kind of half-ass status that doesn't require her to take vows. So she hides behind the veil and gets to have it both ways.'

'What's she got on you, partner?'

He put his hands on his hips, like a drill instructor, and looked sideways out a window, as though the room was too small for the level of anger he needed to express. Then he snuffed down in his nose and shook it off. 'Give my dad a break, will you?'

'He's a heart patient but he smokes cigars?' I said.

'You're a beaut, Dave,' he said.

Molly Boyle's note was a simple one: *Please call. Thanks – Molly B.* I rang her office number and was told she was mowing the grass and would return my call later. But why wait, I asked myself, and headed down the road in a cruiser toward Jeanerette.

Then I had to ask myself a more serious question: What was so urgent about seeing Molly Boyle? Why not just wait for her call? The answer that started to suggest itself was one I quickly put out of my mind.

When I pulled in to her agency I saw her seated on a tractor, towing a grass-cutter through a field of buttercups, a little black boy in the seat with her. She turned at the end of a long swath, then saw me walking toward her and shut off the engine. She wore a baseball cap and cotton gloves and a sleeveless blouse that was peppered with sweat. The tops of her arms were dusty and sprinkled with sun freckles. She introduced the little black boy as Tee Bleu Bergeron. 'His daddy is our best birdhouse builder,' she said.

'Your father works for the Chalons family?' I said.

'Yes, suh, he work for Mr. Raphael. We live right up the bayou from the big house,' he replied.

The little boy was many generations removed from antebellum days, but he still obeyed the same custom of referring to the main building on a plantation as 'the big house,' just as his antecedents had. Sister Molly asked him to go to her office and wait for her. 'You've been a good helper, Tee Bleu. I'll drive you home in a little bit,' she said.

'Why is he called "Little Blue"?' I asked.

'His daddy says the umbilical cord was wrapped

around his throat when he was born. I think he has some brain damage. But he's a sweet little guy. Why'd you ask?' Sister Molly said.

'I was just curious.' But my answer was not an honest one. The little boy did not look like his father, the black man named Andre Bergeron. He was light-skinned, with high cheekbones, and liquid brown eyes and jet-black straight hair. He looked like Honoria Chalons.

'You asked me yesterday about a woman named Ida —' Sister Molly began.

'Ida Durbin,' I said.

'Yes. Did something happen to her?'

'I think she may have been murdered many years ago.'

'Was she a prostitute?'

'How did you know?' I asked.

'I didn't. But you said the Chalonses would like to forget about her. I think the Chalonses have secrets. I think one of their secrets is their involvement with prostitution. So I should have spoken up when you asked about this Durbin woman.'

'What do you know about the Chalonses and prostitution, Sister?'

'Call me Molly. I grew up in Port Arthur. My father was career army and a policeman. He always said the brothels in Galveston were owned by the Chalons and Giacano families. Raphael Chalons is infamous for his sexual behavior.' She stopped, obviously conflicted with herself and her own motivations. 'I don't feel very comfortable with any of this, Detective Robicheaux. I think I've said too much.'

'Call me Dave.'

The field fell into shadow and the wind came up and wrinkled the bayou and flattened the uncut wildflowers in the field. She removed her cap and blew a wisp of hair out of one eye. Her face looked dilated in the heat. There were beads of field dirt around her neck and a throbbing

94

insect bite on one cheek. She reminded me of a countrywoman of years ago. In a way, she reminded me of my mother.

'I think you've done a lot for poor people in this area, Sister Molly. I think you and your friends are what the Church is all about,' I said, realizing I still could not bring myself to call her by her first name.

Her eyes fastened on mine and her mouth parted slightly. 'Thank you,' she said.

The silent moment that followed was one neither of us had chosen. I looked out at the bayou and the Spanish moss straightening in the trees along the banks. She fitted her cap back on her head and took the keys out of the ignition for no reason, then tried to reinsert them in the slot. They dropped from her fingers into the uncut grass below the tractor.

'I'm all thumbs some days,' she said.

I found the keys for her and placed them in her hand, my fingertips touching the graininess of her skin and the wetness in the cup of her palm. On the way back to New Iberia, I tried to keep an empty place in the center of my mind and not think the thoughts I was thinking.

Question: What can dumb and fearful people always be counted on to do?

Answer: To try to control and manipulate everyone in their environment.

Question: What is the tactic used by these same dumb people as they try to control others?

Answer: They lie.

That night I got a call from a man out of my past, an anachronism from a more primitive time by the name of Robert Cobb, also known as Bad Texas Bob. Years ago in Louisiana, when a convict escaped from a work camp, the state police always assigned the recapture to Bad Texas Bob. Bob's lifetime record was eight for eight, all DOA.

He thrived on gunsmoke and blood splatter, and if he ever experienced remorse for his deeds, I never saw any indication of it.

There used to be an all-night café in New Orleans where cops of all kinds hung out. Pimps, wiseguys, junkies, and jackrollers knew to take their business up the street. One night an out-of-town black man walked in, laid a .38 inside a folded newspaper on the counter, and told the cashier to empty the register. Bad Texas Bob climbed out a side window, waited at the entrance for the stickup man to emerge, and blew his brains all over the glass panels of the revolving door.

Over the phone Bob's voice sounded like wet sand sliding through a drainpipe. 'Hear you're working a cold case on a whore gone missing,' he said.

'Yeah, something like that,' I said.

'Galveston, about 1958 or '59?'

'You have some information for me, Bob?'

'Maybe. Galveston is where I started out. I'm having a couple of drinks in Broussard. Hey, guys like us were the real cops, weren't we?'

No, we weren't, I thought. But I had learned long ago not to argue with those who need to revise the past.

I drove on the old Lafayette highway to the little town of Broussard, crossed the train tracks, and parked in front of a low-roofed bar whose cracked windows were held together with silver tape and framed with Christmas tree lights. The interior was dark, the air refrigerated, the cigarette smoke curling through an exhaust fan in back. Bad Texas Bob was at the bar, hunkered over a shot glass and draft beer, wearing a gray suit, string tie, cowboy boots, and a short-brim Stetson canted on the side of his head.

He wore expensive jewelry, smoked gold-tipped, lavender cigarettes, and tried to affect an aura of contentment and prosperity. But the years had not been kind to Bob. His teeth were as long as a horse's, his face emaciated, the backs of his hands brown with liver spots. Bad Texas Bob was the nightmare that every cop fears he might become.

'You still in the Dr Pepper club?' he said.

'No other place will have me. How you been doing, Bob?'

'I do a little consulting work. I work part-time at the casino in Lake Charles. Billy Joe Pitts says you were interested in a whore by the name of −' He snapped his fingers at the air.

'Ida Durbin,' I said.

He tossed back his whiskey and chased it with the draft beer, then wiped the salt from the beer glass off his mouth. 'Yeah, that was her name. I knew her. What do you want to know?'

His eyes were level with mine − watery, iniquitous, harboring thoughts or memories of a kind you never want to guess at, the skin at the corners as wrinkled as a turtle's.

'What happened to her, Bob?' I said.

'Nothing, as far as I know. People who run cathouses don't kill their whores, if that's what you were thinking.'

He pointed for the bartender to refill his shot glass. He seemed to be disconnected from our conversation now, but when I glanced at the bar mirror I saw his eyes looking back at me. 'She had sandy hair, nice-looking, tall gal? I remember her. Didn't nothing happen to her. I would have knowed about it,' he said.

But Bob's confidence level had slipped and he was talking too fast.

'Her pimp was named Lou Kale. Remember a lowlife by that name?' I said.

'I never worked Vice. I just used to see this little gal around the island, is all.'

But I remembered another story connected to Bob and

some of his colleagues, one I had always hoped was exaggerated or apocryphal, in the same way you hope that stories about pedophilia among the clergy or financial corruption in your own family are untrue.

A notorious Baton Rouge madam by the name of Vicki Rochon used to run a house specializing in oral sex. A fundamentalist Christian group was about to close her down when the local cops offered her a deal: Vicki and her girls could take a vacation in Panama City, then return to town in a couple of months and their business would not be interrupted again. No money was involved. Vicki became an invaluable snitch and personally provided free ones for the cops. As a bonus, her son, who was doing hard time in Angola's Camp J, was transferred to an honor farm. Bad Texas Bob became one of Vicki's most ardent free patrons.

'Thanks for passing on the information, Bob. But if I were you, I'd let your friend Pitts drown in his own shit. He's on a pad for the Chalons family. Did you know that?' I said.

'I was trying to do you a favor, for old times' sake. Screw Pitts.' Bob knocked back his whiskey and drew in on his cigarette, the whites of his eyes threaded with tiny veins.

'Let me buy you a round,' I said.

'I'm covered.'

'See you around, partner,' I said.

'You might think I'm pulling your joint, but I remember a Galveston whore by the name of Ida Whatever. She played a fiddle. No, that wasn't it. She played a mandolin. Played the fire out of it.'

'Say that again?'

But he had nothing to add. Bad Texas Bob had outsmarted me. Like all corrupt people, he had wrapped a piece of truth inside a lie. To try to discern the fact from the lie was to empower the agenda of a classical manipulator, I told myself. I left Bob to his booze in Broussard, wondering if I had just revisited my alcoholic past or seen my future.

chapter nine

The coroner, Koko Hebert, was waiting for me when I got to work Thursday morning. He dropped his great weight down ponderously in a chair and fanned his face with his hat. His skin was flushed, his beachball of a stomach rising up and down as he breathed. A package of cigarettes protruded from his shirt pocket. He was probably the most unhealthy-looking human specimen I had ever seen. 'How's life, Koko?' I said.

'Burning up out there,' he said.

He pulled his tropical shirt off his chest and shook the cloth. I could smell an odor like talcum and stale antiperspirant wafting off his skin. 'The contents of the DOA's purse, you got a list in your file?' he said.

'What about it?'

'Were there car keys in there, house keys on a chain, maybe a penlight on a chain, something like that?' he asked.

'Yeah, car keys,' I said.

'On a chain?'

'No, as I remember, they were on a ring. They're in an evidence locker,' I replied.

He held up a small Ziploc bag. Inside it was a thin piece of brass chain, no more than an inch long, with very tiny links. 'Maybe this fell out of her clothes. I'm not sure.

One of the paramedics found it in the body bag,' he said.

'What are you getting at?'

'You said something about the DOA I couldn't forget. You said a woman who'd swallow her own wedding ring might also figure a way to tell us who killed her. So I wondered about this chain.'

It was obvious humility did not come easily to Koko Hebert, and I was reminded of George Orwell's admonition that people are always better than we think they are. Koko fiddled with his Panama hat, then flipped the Ziploc bag and chain on my desk. 'Did Mack Bertrand get ahold of you yet?' he asked.

Mack was our forensic chemist out at the lab. I told Koko I had not heard from him.

'The DOA's clothes had small traces of grease and rubber on them,' he said.

'She was inside the trunk of a car?' I said.

'That'd be my guess. Give me a call if you need anything else.' He stood up from his chair, the bottom of his stomach like a giant watermelon inside his linen slacks.

'There is one other thing, Koko. Why do you always give Helen a bad time? Why not cut her some slack?' I said.

'She's a dyke trying to do a man's job. Get a life, Robicheaux,' he replied.

Lesson learned? Don't expect too many miracles in one day.

Five minutes later, Helen buzzed my extension. 'I just got a call from Raphael Chalons. Clete Purcel was out at his house. Know anything about that?' she said.

'No,' I replied.

'Then why was he out there?'

'Clete's uncontrollable sometimes. I've already talked to him. He doesn't listen.'

There was silence on the line. I wanted to bite my tongue off. 'Talked to him about what? What's he done, Dave?'

'Made a home call on Billy Joe Pitts.'

'And?'

'I think he might have dropped a set of weights on Pitts's chest.'

'I just don't believe this.'

'That Clete went after Pitts?'

'No, that I'm having this conversation. The next time I rehire you, just put a bullet in my brain. In the meantime, straighten out this shit with Chalons.'

'Why not tell Chalons to kiss your ass? He's not even in our jurisdiction.'

'Bwana go now. Bwana write report and put it on my desk when he get back.'

Clete's P.I. office was on Main, in an old brick building hard by the old jail, the front shaded by a solitary oak tree growing out of the sidewalk. A bell tinkled above the door when I went inside. He was sitting at a metal desk, in the middle of a large room that was bare except for two file cabinets, flipping through the pages of a notebook that he always carried in his shirt pocket. 'Glad you dropped by. I did some more checking on Billy Joe Pitts and that casino over in Lake Charles.' He looked at the expression on my face and raised his eyebrows. '*What?*'

'Helen Soileau says you fired up Raphael Chalons,' I said.

'I don't read it that way.'

'So tell me.'

'Chalons is backing a couple of casinos in western Louisiana. He's got a religious crusader fronting points for him with some dudes in Washington. The issue is licenses for some Indian tribes who can siphon off the Texas trade before it goes to casinos deeper in the state.'

'What's new about that?'

'I got a call this morning from Nig Rosewater about a couple of bail skips. Then Nig says, "What's this about some peckerwood cop trying to put up a kite on you?" Get this – Nig says a cop went to Jericho Johnny Wineburger and offered five grand to have me clipped. Except Jericho Johnny knows better and told the cop to get fucked.'

Jericho Johnny Wineburger was an old-time button man for the Giacano family and was called Jericho because his work product traveled to a dead city and did not return from it.

'You sure it was Pitts?' I said.

'Yeah, because I called up Jericho Johnny and he described Pitts exactly,' Clete said.

'Pitts's beef with you is personal. Why would you put it on Raphael Chalons?'

'You're not hearing anything I say. You were right about Pitts. He works for the Chalonses. The old man is a regular with Pitts's chippies. "Personal" is when guys like Chalons look the other way while the hired help splatter your grits. So I went out to his house and told him that. As well as a couple of other things.'

'Like what other things?'

'That if he kept his stiff red-eye in his pants, he'd probably have a lot fewer problems. By the way, the guy is supposed to have a schlong on him like a fifteen-inch chunk of flex pipe. Stop looking like that. He needed a heart-to-heart. He probably appreciated it.'

Clete tried to make light of his encounter with Raphael Chalons, but he and I had reached an age when cynicism and humor become poor surrogates for the rage we feel when our lives are treated with disregard. I bought him lunch at Victor's Cafeteria, then drove up the bayou to the home of Raphael Chalons.

*

I had always wanted to dismiss him as a vestigial reminder of the old oligarchy – imperious, pragmatic, amoral when necessity demanded it, casual if not cavalier regarding the hardship imposed by his society on the backs of blacks and poor whites. He may have been partially all those things but I also believed he was a far more complex man.

He was a strict traditionalist, even to the point of refusing to air-condition his home. But during the Civil Rights era, when a group of black men entered the clubhouse at the public golf course and were ignored by the waiters, who were also black and feared for their jobs, Chalons sat at their table and told the manager to put their drinks on his tab. After that one seminal incident, black golfers never had trouble at our public links or clubhouse again.

He became the legal guardian of orphaned children and paid for their education. I suspected he would not use profane language or be personally abusive at gunpoint. In his own mind the estate he had inherited was a votive trust, and those who would impose their way upon it risked his wrath. Sometimes I wondered if Raphael Chalons heard the horns blowing along the road to Roncevaux.

The rumors that he did business with the Giacanos were I'm sure true. To what degree was up for debate. In the state of Louisiana, systemic venality is a given. The state's culture, mind-set, religious attitudes, and economics are no different from those of a Caribbean nation. The person who believes he can rise to a position of wealth and power in the state of Louisiana and not do business with the devil probably knows nothing about the devil and even less about Louisiana. Chalons was an enigma, a protean creation bound more to the past than the present, and in some ways a mirror of us all. But the best description I ever heard of Chalons came from his own attorney, who once told me, 'Raphael hates lawyers, keeps all his records in his own head, and is a ruthless sonofabitch. But by God he always keeps his word.'

I parked my cruiser in the spangled shade of a live oak and was told by a yardman that Raphael Chalons was in the back, down by the bayou, walking his dog. I went around the side of the building, past slave quarters that were used to store baled hay and a cistern that had caved into sticks on its brick foundation. Down the slope, in the sunlight, I saw Raphael Chalons throwing a stick for his pet Rottweiler to fetch. As I approached him, he snapped his fingers at the dog and clipped a leash onto its collar, then stepped on the end of the leash with one foot.

He was a tall, ascetic-looking man, with shiny black hair and a scrolled and waxed mustache, like the one worn by the legendary Confederate naval officer Raphael Semmes. His hands had the long, tapered quality of a surgeon's, deeply tanned on the backs, corded with blue veins.

I told him I had been sent by the sheriff to investigate his complaint regarding Clete Purcel. 'Did he bother or threaten you in some way, sir?' I asked.

'You're not patronizing me, are you, Mr. Robicheaux?'

'Sheriff Soileau doesn't want someone from our parish threatening people, if in fact that was the case,' I replied.

I saw the veiled challenge to his veracity register in his eyes. 'If he had threatened me, I would have run him off with a shotgun. Did he offend me? Yes, he did. He made an insinuation an employee of mine put a contract on his life. But I have the feeling you know this man.'

'I do.'

'So there's a personal agenda at work here?'

'No,' I replied, my eyes shifting off his.

'My son thinks you're trying to extract information from my daughter about our family. Is that your purpose, Mr. Robicheaux, besides looking out for your friend's interests?'

His tone had become pointed, slightly heated, and I saw the dog raise its head, a string of slobber hanging from the side of its mouth. The dog was heavily muscled, its hair coarse, the same black, shiny color as Chalons's, with tan markings around its rump and ears. Chalons snapped his fingers and the dog got down flat on the ground and rested its head on its paws.

'There's a hit man in New Orleans by the name of Jericho Johnny Wineburger,' I said. 'His specialty is one in the mouth, one in the forehead, and one in the ear. He once told me, "When I pop 'em, I shut all their motors down. Forget life support. They're cold meat when they bounce off the pavement." That's the guy a cop by the name of Billy Joe Pitts was trying to sic on my friend Clete Purcel.'

I could see the offensive nature of my language and its implication climb into his face. He studied the bayou and a powerboat splitting a long yellow trough down its center. Then he bent over and unsnapped the leash from the dog's collar.

Involuntarily I stepped back and rested my palm on the butt of my holstered .45, my heart beating. But Chalons only patted his dog on its head and said, 'Go to the house, Heidi.'

I watched the dog bound up the grassy slope, then I looked back at Chalons's face. There were long vertical lines in it, the mouth downturned at the corners, as though he had never learned to smile. I took my hand from my weapon, feeling strangely disappointed that he had not forced the moment. I could not begin to guess at the thoughts that went on behind the black light in his eyes.

Then, as though he had read my mind, he said, 'Please leave my family alone, Mr. Robicheaux. We've done you no harm.'

*

I went directly from work to New Orleans, driving the four-lane through Morgan City and Des Allemands. I hit rain on the bridge over the Mississippi River, then a full-blown electrical storm as I turned off Interstate 10 and headed up St. Charles Avenue toward the old Irish Channel.

Jericho Johnny Wineburger owned a saloon on a side street between Magazine and Tchoupitoulas, and claimed to have been out of the life for at least a decade. But he had at least a thirty-year history of killing people, and supposedly, with another button man, had taken out Bugsy Siegel's cousin with a shotgun on a train roaring through West Palm Beach. Clete believed Jericho Johnny had turned down the contract on Clete's life either out of fear of Clete or respect for the fact they both grew up in the Irish Channel.

I doubted either possibility. Jericho Johnny had ice water in his veins and I suspect was capable of killing his victim and eating a sandwich while he did it.

The air was cold and smelled of ozone. The streets were flooded, and thunder was booming over the Gulf when I parked in front of his saloon and ran for the colonnade. The only customers in the saloon were some kids shooting pool in back and a white woman in a house robe who slept with her face on her hands at a table. Jericho Johnny stood behind the bar drying glasses while he watched a professional wrestling match on TV. He looked at me and slid a toothpick into the corner of his mouth. 'This about Purcel?' he asked.

His words came out in an accentuated whisper, as though they were filtered through wet grit. Some said his vocal cords were impaired when he was a child and he accidentally drank rug cleaner. But I think the story was romantic in origin. I think Jericho Johnny came out of a different gene pool than the rest of us.

'I need the name of the cop who wanted you to clip Clete,' I said.

I thought he might give me a bad time, but he didn't. He looked at the backs of his nails. 'Pitts,' he said.

'But you told him to get lost?' I said.

'In so many words, yeah, I did. You still on the wagon?'

'Why?' I asked.

''Cause I'll stand you a beer and a shot if you're not. Otherwise, I'll offer you a cup of coffee. Take the two-by-four out of your ass, Robicheaux.'

His accent could have been mistaken for Flatbush or South Boston. He had worked on the docks when he was a kid, and he had silver hair, short, powerful forearms wrapped with tattoos, and a face that could have been called handsome except for the thinness in his lips. He poured me a demitasse of black coffee and placed it on a small saucer with a cube of sugar and a tiny spoon. He saw me look at the woman who was sleeping with her face on her hands. 'She lives up the street. She's scared of lightning and can't sleep during an electrical storm, so she comes down here,' he said.

'You didn't piece off the work?' I asked.

'I never pieced off a job in my life,' he replied.

'Why'd you tell Nig Rosewater about it?'

'I didn't. This cop, this guy Pitts, he went to two or three people in the business about Purcel. I was just one of them. That's how Nig heard about it. I own a saloon today. I live in a nice house out back. I been out of the life a long time now.'

'You think somebody else took the contract?'

'Maybe.'

'Who?'

'Don't know.'

A phone rang in back and he went to answer it. The rain and lightning had quit, and the street was dark and in the light from the saloon I could see the fronds of a banana tree flapping against a side window. The woman who had been sleeping at the table woke up and looked around, as though unsure of where she was. 'I want to go home,' she said.

'Where do you live?' I asked.

'Down the block, next to the grocery store,' she replied.

'I'll take you there,' I said.

'Do I know you?' she said.

'I'm a friend of Johnny's,' I said.

She was very old, quite feeble, and even with her hand on my arm she had to take small steps as we walked toward the front door.

'Where you going?' Jericho Johnny said from behind the bar.

I explained I was taking the elderly woman home.

His toothpick flexed in the corner of his mouth and his eyes looked at a neutral space between us. 'Come back when you're done,' he said.

A few minutes later I reentered the saloon and finished my coffee. The kids who had been shooting pool bought a bagful of cold long-neck beers to go and went out the door. The wind was blowing through the screen doors, and the inside of the saloon smelled like rain and sawdust.

Jericho Johnny leaned on his arms. 'Here's the deal, Robicheaux. That guy Pitts wasn't trying to put a kite on just Purcel. He wanted a twofer – seventy-five hundred for the whole job.'

'Who was the other hit?' I asked.

'Who you think?' he said.

'Pitts used my name specifically?'

'He said it was a friend of Purcel. An Iberia Parish plainclothes. He said the guy had been an NOPD Homicide roach, but got kicked off the force because he was a drunk. He said if this guy gets smoked, no cops around here are gonna be burning candles. Sound like anybody you know?'

'You willing to wear a wire?'

He laughed to himself and began stacking bottles of Bacardi and Beam and Jack Daniel's on a shelf.

'Why'd you tell me all this, Johnny?' I said.

'That was my mother you drove home. I don't like to owe people. You mixed up with politics?'

'No.'

'I think the juice on this deal is coming from up high. Watch your ass. This city is full of dirtbags. It ain't like the old days,' he said.

The next morning was Friday. As soon as I came into the office I told Helen of my visit to Jericho Johnny's saloon.

A deep line cut across her brow. 'You want to have Wineburger picked up?' she said.

'Waste of time. Plus, I'd lose him as an informant,' I replied.

'He said the juice was coming from up high? Who are you a threat to? I don't think this goes any higher than Billy Joe Pitts.'

'Maybe not,' I said.

'Raphael Chalons is not behind this, Dave, if that's what you're thinking.'

'I'm just reporting what happened.'

'I'm going to call Pitts's boss and tell him what we have.'

'Mistake,' I said.

'My life is full of them,' she replied.

Jimmie had been out of town for a day, without telling me where he had gone. Friday evening his Lincoln pulled into the drive, shotgunned with dried mud. He was beaming when he came through the front door. 'Guess where I've been,' he said.

'Galveston,' I said.

'Galveston, then I got a lead on an old guy over in Beaumont. He used to play backup for Floyd Tillman and

Ernest Tubb. Remember Floyd Tillman, wrote "Slipping Around"?'

'Jim –'

'This old-timer used to play in a lot of beer joints along the Texas coast. He said a girl from one of the hot pillow houses used to sit in with his band. He said she played the mandolin and guitar.'

I tried to look attentive, but I could not get my mind off Jericho Johnny Wineburger. Jimmie held up a 45-rpm record in a water-stained paper jacket. 'The old man gave me this. One side is titled "Ida's Jump." He said this gal always played a song by that name. He always thought this recording must have been her song.'

'Can I see that?' I said.

The group was called the Texas Tumbleweeds. The recording had been made at a small studio in Corpus Christi, the same studio where Harry Choates had made his famous recording of 'Jolie Blon' in 1946.

'It was cut in 1960, two years after she disappeared,' Jimmie said.

'The name Ida Durbin is nowhere on the label, Jim.'

'Does that phonograph in the living room work?'

The people who had sold me my house had left behind an ancient combination radio and high-fidelity console, with a three-speed turntable and a mechanical arm that made use of reversible needles. The top squeaked on a rusted hinge when Jimmie raised it up and fitted the small 45-rpm recording on the spindle.

The groves in the record were filled with static, but I could hear a string band of the kind you associate with country music of the 1940s and '50s – a fiddle, stand-up bass, Dobro, muted drums, an acoustical guitar outfitted with an electronic pickup, and a mandolin. Then a woman and two or three men began singing. They reminded me of Rose and the Maddox Brothers or Wilma Lee and Stony Cooper. Their harmony was beautiful.

'It's her,' Jimmie said.

'How can you be sure?' I said.

'It's her,' he repeated.

I gave up. I told him about my conversation with Jericho Johnny Wineburger. 'Are you hearing me?' I said.

'You're talking about Whiplash Wineburger's brother? He's a meltdown. He was cleaning his gun on the toilet and ricocheted a round into his own head,' he replied.

'I don't want you getting mistaken for me again,' I said.

But he'd already blown me off and moved on. 'My friend at UL can re-create an old record through a digital process that removes all the static and leaves only the music. It's Ida, Dave. We didn't get that poor girl killed. Why don't you be happy about something once in a while?'

'Even if that's Ida's voice, there's no way to determine when the recording was made. It could have been recorded on tape, then put on wax later,' I said.

'Why would the studio sit on a tape for two years? You can think up more bad news than any person I've ever known. Are you going to your AA meetings?' he said.

Maybe he was right, I told myself. Jimmie would for-ever be the Renaissance humanist, bearing his faith and optimism like a white light inside a chalice. Who was I to steal it from him?

chapter ten

The days went by uneventfully. I made two weekend trips to Galveston and talked to retired cops, checked death records in the coroner's office, interviewed a madam who had run a house on Post Office Street, called the state attorney in Austin, and found out absolutely nothing about the fate of Ida Durbin. The studio that had cut the recording of 'Ida's Jump' had gone out of business many years ago, and the musician who had told Jimmie a girl named Ida had sat in with his band during the late 1950s turned out to be a lonely old fellow who became more and more confused and contradictory in his account the more I talked with him.

If Ida Durbin was alive, she had left no paper trail of any kind.

I also began to wonder if Jimmie wasn't right about Jericho Johnny. Jericho Johnny's brother was Whiplash Wineburger, a part-time Mob lawyer and full-time gasbag who, when accused by his wife in divorce court of sleeping with the Puerto Rican maid, exclaimed, 'I'm no snob, Your Honor! Guilty as charged!' At best, Jericho Johnny was a sociopath with blood up to his elbows. Why believe anything he said?

For a few nights I slept with my .45 automatic under my bed and kept my cut-down twelve-gauge Remington behind the couch in the living room. But after a while I no longer looked with caution upon the arrival of a deliveryman or a meter reader from the utility company. The world was a good place, the early dawn announced by birdsong and blue shadows on the lawn and fog puffing off the bayou. Why let fear and suspicion invade the heart and lay claim on your life?

Then on a windswept, burning Friday afternoon, when the sky was yellow with dust, Helen called me into her office. The *Baton Rouge Advocate* was spread open on her desk. 'Looks like Billy Joe Pitts won't be bothering you anymore,' she said.

'Say again?'

She tapped her finger on a back-page article. 'A boating accident. He was drunk in an outboard on his old man's lake. He fell out of the boat and it circled around and hit him in the head. I just got off the phone with the sheriff,' she said. She tilted her weight back in her chair and watched my face. 'What bwana say?'

'You buy it?' I asked.

She picked up a ballpoint pen and twisted it in her fingers, then let it drop on her desk blotter. 'I'd already told the sheriff we believed Pitts may have been involved in a murder-for-hire plot. So I asked him why I had to find out about Pitts's death in the newspaper.'

'And?'

'He said he'd been real busy of late.'

'You talk to the coroner?'

'I have a call in. But it's not going anywhere. That place is corrupt even beyond Louisiana standards,' she replied.

'Maybe it was just an accident, Helen. Guys like Pitts eventually blow out their doors.'

'I'm going to ask NOPD to roust Jericho Johnny.'

'Don't do it,' I said.

She scratched her forearm. 'Okay, boss man,' she said.

*

That evening just at dusk, it rained hard, pounding on the tin roof of my house, the raindrops dancing with a strange yellow light on the bayou. Then suddenly it was quiet outside, the trees dripping, the air cool and smelling of flowers and wet leaves. I wanted to believe that Billy Joe Pitts had died accidentally, that there was no contract on my life, that I was no different from any other police officer or, for that matter, any ordinary person who went about his day with goodwill toward others and tried to do the best he could with the life he had. I did not want to believe that somehow I was a harbinger of violence and death, a man who dwelled in the cities of the dead and who trailed the stench of a necropolis wherever he went.

But I had always subscribed to the belief that there is no mystery to the human personality. People are what they do. My own record was one I did not care to examine. The faces of the men I had killed did not appear in my sleep, but sometimes, on the periphery of my vision, I saw a moving shadow, a figure inside the elephant grass, a tiny man in black pajamas and a conical straw hat, or I heard a voice, the phlegmy death rattle of the man who murdered my second wife, Annie, and whose life I took in turn. Or sometimes I sat on the edge of the bed, in the middle of the night, inside a square of moonlight, wondering if indeed the wind in the trees or the thropping of helicopter blades overhead was nothing more than the auditory manifestation of a world at peace or if in fact hell was a place that some individuals carried inside themselves the rest of their lives.

I did not trust myself alone anymore. Sometimes I thought I, too, was infected with bloodlust. There were moments when I could feel shards of color explode behind my eyes, a balloon of anger surge in my chest without cause. I avoided watching the evening news. I would quickly turn off the radio in my truck when I would hear the voices of what we used to call REMFs, rear echelon motherfuckers, cheering on a war they or their family members would never serve in. There were moments when I had thoughts I would never share with anyone.

I wanted to reclaim my dead wife and lead her back from the underworld, as Orpheus did when he stole Eurydice from Hades.

In the Friday issue of the *Daily Iberian* was a feature story about a picnic and hot dog roast at Sister Molly Boyle's self-help housing agency and a race down Bayou Teche involving hundreds of plastic ducks. According to the article, the children would draw numbers from a barrel that corresponded to numbers painted on the bottom of the ducks. Then at 10:00 a.m. the ducks would be released at the drawbridge on Burke Street, when the tidal current was flowing southward. Eight miles down the Teche the first ten ducks across the finish line would determine which children would win a T-shirt with Donald Duck's face ironed on it.

I convinced myself my attendance Saturday morning at the picnic was innocent in nature. It was a fine day, the sun covered by rain clouds, the wind flecked with salt, the Spanish moss straightening in the oak trees along the bayou, Frisbees sailing through the air. What could be wrong in eating ice cream and grilled frankfurters among people of color for whom a plastic duck race down the bayou was a grand event?

But it wasn't long before I found ways to put myself next to Sister Molly Boyle. I helped her set tables, turn franks on a flame-streaked grill, paint margarine on hot dog buns, and finally to dip ten ducks out of the water with a crab net.

It was all in the spirit of fun, wasn't it?

But regardless of what I was doing, my eye would travel to wherever she was on the grounds. I felt foolish and wondered if I had entered that self-deluded stage in an aging man's life when others have to protect him from knowledge about himself.

She was certainly lovely to look at. She was hard-bodied, her jeans stretched tight on her rump and hips, her shoulders powdered with freckles, her red hair feathered with light when the wind blew it, her eyes interested in whatever was being said to her, without any sign of impatience or hidden thoughts in them that I could see. My brother was a light-bearer. I believed Molly Boyle was probably one, too.

I went into the office to use the restroom. As I was coming out, I saw a little boy wandering in the hallway, about to wet his pants. I took him into the restroom and helped him use the toilet and wash his hands. When I came back out, his mother was standing by the door, fat and angry, her print dress damp against her distended dugs. 'You didn't have no bidness taking him in there,' she said. Then she pointed her finger at the little boy. 'You gonna get it, you.'

I started to speak, then saw Molly Boyle come through the door, the sun bright and hot at her back. 'There was a man in a boat up the bayou. The children say he had a rifle in his boat,' she said.

The angry, fat woman pulled her child down the hall and slammed the door behind her.

'Where's this guy now?' I said to Molly.

She went to a window and looked across the lawn at a line of cypress trees on the bayou. I stood behind her and could smell the heat from the grill in her clothes and a warm odor like flowers and shampoo in her hair. 'He's gone. He was just behind those trees. He had a pair of binoculars. I think he was watching you walk into the building,' she said.

When she turned around, her chin was pointed upwards. She seemed smaller, shorter, her face both beautiful and vulnerable, in a way that made my throat dry and caused my loins to tingle. 'Can you describe what he looked like, Sister?' I said.

'Don't call me that again, will you?' she said.

'I won't.'

'He was white. He had a cap on. But I didn't get a good look at him. Is someone after you?'

'Could be.'

Her eyes moved over my face. 'Are you feeling okay? Our air-conditioning is broken,' she said.

'The heat doesn't bother me,' I said.

'Would you like a glass of water?'

'No. No thanks,' I said. I opened my cell phone and punched in a 911 call.

She stepped away from me, then looked back over her shoulder, waiting for me to follow her down the hall. 'I'm glad you came today. The children really enjoyed meeting you. Spend more time with us,' she said.

I stared at her, puzzled, unsure what I should say next. 'By the way, I helped a little boy go to the restroom. I'm afraid I angered his mother.'

'That's Mrs. Poche. You're lucky she didn't club you with her purse. She was angry the day she was born.'

In the next five minutes cruisers from both Jeanerette and New Iberia arrived on the drawbridges to the north and south of us. But no one saw any sign of a man in a boat with binoculars and a rifle. I talked to a little black boy who had seen the man in the boat through a canebrake.

'He had a rifle. It looked like he had a tin can stuck on the end of the barrel,' the boy said.

A silencer?

But contract killers don't pop you in broad daylight in front of large numbers of witnesses, I told myself.

Tell that to President Kennedy or Jimmy Hoffa, I thought.

Jimmie had gone back to New Orleans and I was alone again. I had never done well with solitude. But I had another enemy, too, one that did not depart with age. I suspect monastic saints tossed in their sleep with it, waking fatigued and throbbing at first light, their fingers knotted in prayer as they tried to extricate themselves from the soft shapes that beckoned to them from their dreams. For that reason alone I always admired them, but my admiration for them did not make my own problem with celibacy any the less, perhaps because I was a drunk as well as one of those for whom the sybaritic life was only a wink of the eye away.

Sometimes I thought I heard Bootsie telling me I should not be alone. Didn't the story in Genesis indicate the same? Was it not a form of pride to set a standard above that of ordinary men?

That evening I went to Clete's cottage at the motor court, where he was waxing his Caddy under a mimosa tree. He was bare-chested and wore a Marine Corps utility cap on the back of his head and a huge pair of electric-blue Everlast boxing trunks that hung to his knees. The shadows of the mimosa branches looked like feathers moving on his skin.

'Where have you been for the last three days?' I said.

'Chasing down a couple of child molesters. They run every time. I don't know why Nig and Willie –'

'Why don't you answer your cell phone?' I said.

'I lost it somewhere. I think maybe a gal rolled me. I can't deal with working for Nig and Willie anymore. It's really affecting my stability. You think I could get on with the department?'

'In Iberia Parish?' I said.

'Something wrong with that?'

'Nothing,' I said, my face empty.

'Can you run it by Helen? Salary is not a factor. Long

as it's detective grade,' he said.

'Sure,' I said.

'I'd really like that,' he said, rubbing a soft rag along a tailfin on his Cadillac, whistling to himself, as though somehow I had reassured him that people such as ourselves were not out of sync with the rest of the world.

Then I told him about the death of Billy Joe Pitts. 'Pitts got hit in the head with his own motorboat?' he said.

'That's what the sheriff says.'

Clete opened a Budweiser and drank from it, his throat working, his eyes flat. 'You figure somebody took him off the board?' he asked.

'Who knows?'

He watched the way I was looking at him. He wiped the beer off his lips with his hand. 'Get yourself a Dr Pepper out of the icebox.'

'I don't want one,' I said.

'What's bugging you?' he said.

'Nothing,' I replied.

He picked up a pint bottle of whiskey from inside the open top of his Caddy. It was wrapped inside a brown paper bag, a shaft of sunlight flashing on the broken seal affixed to the cap. He took a hit from the neck and chased it with beer from his Budweiser can. He lit a cigarette and drank again from the whiskey, then ground the cigarette out in the gravel, his cheeks blooming with color. Unconsciously I wet my bottom lip. His eyes wandered over my face and I saw a great sadness in them.

'I'm a bad example. You stop having the thoughts you're having,' he said.

'I'm not having any thoughts. I worry about you,' I lied.

'Right,' he said.

I headed for my truck.

'I'll put the booze up. I'll drive you to a meeting. Dave, come back here. Jesus, Mary, and Joseph!' he said.

I put on my running shorts and lifted weights in the backyard, did three sets of push-ups, with my feet propped on a picnic bench – thirty reps to each set – and jogged two miles through City Park, then hit it hard back across the drawbridge to home. But I could not rid myself of the restlessness that seemed to invade my metabolism without cause, nor the thoughts and images that kept drifting before my eyes.

There was no question about their nature. They had to do with the smell of perfume, the amber splash that sour mash makes when it's first poured on ice, a woman's face framed softly inside the thickness of her hair, the shine of bar light on the tops of her breasts, perhaps a cherry held between her teeth, her hand curved on the neck of a freshly opened bottle of champagne, bursting with white foam.

I opened a bottle of Talking Rain and drank it empty, then showered, put on my pajama bottoms, and tried to read, my shield, handcuffs, slapjack, and .45 on the nightstand beside me. The last of the summer light had gone out of the sky, and in the yard I could hear the bamboo rattling in the breeze and the first patter of rain on the trees. Sometime just before midnight I fell asleep with my hand over my eyes. I had not locked the front door.

When I woke, the room was black. I went to the bathroom and got back in bed. Outside, dry lightning flickered on the trees. I drifted off to sleep and dreamed I was inside a cave, my arm twisted behind me. That's when I heard the rocking chair moving back and forth in the corner.

I opened my eyes and saw a silhouette seated in the chair. When I tried to sit up, my right wrist came tight against the handcuffs that were clipped around it and the brass bedstead. I reached with my left hand for the nightstand, where my .45 should have been. It was gone, along with my slapjack. The figure in the chair stopped rocking.

'I was watching you sleep,' a woman's voice said.

'Honoria?' I said.

'Your front door was unlocked. That's a dangerous thing to do,' she said.

'What are you doing here?'

'I came in to see you.'

My eyes were still adjusting to the darkness, but I could see her face now, a pale orb wrapped in shadow. 'Where's my piece?' I said.

'Your what?'

'My forty-five, where is it?'

She stood up from the chair and walked to the side of the bed. She wore Mexican-style jeans, gold sandals, hoop earrings, and a white blouse that was fluffy with lace. She sat down beside me, her rump pressing deep into the mattress. 'I hid it,' she said.

I couldn't smell alcohol on her, nor even cigarette smoke, which meant she had probably not been in a bar. 'My handcuff key is in my pants. You need to unhook me, Honoria,' I said.

'Why?'

'Because friends don't do this to one another,' I replied.

She looked into my face and brushed back my hair, then leaned over and kissed me on the mouth. 'You like me, don't you?' she said.

'I'm too old for you.'

'No, you're not.' She placed her hand on my stomach and leaned down again.

'What you're doing is no good for either of us, Honoria,' I said.

She took her hand away and sat very still. I could see her breasts rising and falling against the light from the street.

'I think the devil lives under the bayou. I think the devil

lives in my father, too,' she said.

'I believe you need some help with this stuff. I know a doctor in Lafayette,' I said.

'A therapist?'

'I used to see him after my wife Annie was killed. He helped me a lot,' I said.

She looked at nothing, her small hand by my hip. 'Do you mind if I stay with you a while?'

'No, but I –'

'Just say yes or no.'

'No, I don't mind.'

'I didn't think you would. I always liked you, Dave. You're a misplaced figure from Elizabethan theater, you know. Your tragedy is the fact no one ever explained that to you.'

And with that, she curled up next to me, her face on my shoulder, her arm across my stomach, and went to sleep.

The sun was above the rooftops when I woke. The space beside me was empty and my right wrist was free of the handcuffs that hung from the bedstead. My .45 and slapjack had been replaced on the nightstand, along with the key to my cuffs. From the kitchen I could hear someone clattering pots or pans on the stove.

After I used the bathroom, I pulled on my khakis and went into the kitchen. Honoria was dripping coffee, heating a pan of milk and stirring a pot of oatmeal. Both Snuggs and Tripod were eating out of their pet bowls on the floor. Honoria's hair was brushed and her face made up, but when she glanced in my direction her face had the stark expression of someone who has been caught unawares by a photographer's flash.

'There was no water in the cat's bowl,' she said.

'He drinks out of the toilet,' I said.

'That's disgusting.'

'That's what I've been telling him,' I said.

But she saw no humor in my remark. She served oatmeal in two bowls and placed them on the breakfast table, then began hunting for spoons and coffee cups. I looked at my watch. 'I'm running a little bit late for Mass,' I lied.

'Where's your butter dish?'

'I don't have one. Look, Honoria —'

'The oatmeal is getting cold. I fixed it for you. It would be nice if you ate it.'

'Sure,' I said, and sat down at the table.

She poured coffee, and placed toast, jam, and sugar in front of me, preoccupied, her eyes darting about the room, as though somehow she needed to impose order on it. 'Your cat is climbing in the sink,' she said.

'Snuggs is his own man,' I said.

'You should train your animals,' she said, lifting him off the drainboard and scooting him out the back door. 'Don't you ever rake your leaves? A couple of days' work and this place would look fine.'

'Last night you said the devil lived under the bayou and also inside your father.'

'Where'd you get that?' she said, smiling for the first time that morning.

I studied her eyes. They were dark brown, like warm chocolate, possessed of visions and privy to voices and sounds that I believed only she saw and heard. They were the eyes of someone who would never be changed by therapy, analysis, Twelve-Step programs, religion, or medical treatment.

'Do you know what you did in your sleep last night?' she said.

'Nothing,' I said.

'Have it your way. I don't kiss and tell,' she said.

'This bullshit ends now, kiddo. The Robicheaux Fun House is officially closed. Thanks for fixing breakfast,' I said, and dumped my food into a sack under the sink.

She took a half pint of gin from her purse, poured a three-finger shot into a glass, and drank it at the back door, staring in a desultory fashion at the yard. 'Have you ever spent the spring in Paris? I fell in love there with a boy who was gay. My father hounded him without mercy. He drowned himself in the Seine,' she said.

But I was all out of Purple Hearts and had decided that Honoria was going to leave of her own accord or be picked up by a cruiser. My determination suddenly dissipated when I looked out the front window and saw the Chalonses' handyman, with his son and Sister Molly next to him, turn into my driveway.

'I'm going to talk to some people out front. There's no need for you to leave right now,' I said to Honoria.

'Too late, my love,' she said. She walked out the front door and down the street toward the Shadows, her purse swinging from a shoulder string.

I stood on the gallery, barefoot, unshaved, looking down at Molly Boyle, my face burning.

'I should have called first, I guess, but Tee Bleu says he knows where the boat is,' she said, speaking awkwardly and too fast, trying to hide her embarrassment at my situation.

'Which boat?' I said.

'The one the man with the gun was in. Tee Bleu says it's moored in a canebrake the other side of the drawbridge.'

But I couldn't concentrate on her words. 'There's a misunderstanding about what you just saw here. The lady who just left has some mental problems. I left my door unlocked and she –'

'I know who she is. You don't have to explain.'

'No, hear me out. She hooked me up to my bed with my cuffs. I was trying to get her out of the house when you arrived.'

'Locked you in your own handcuffs?'

'Right. I was asleep.'

'I didn't mean to intrude. I thought you should know about the boat.'

'You didn't intrude. Y'all come inside.'

'No, we'd better run. Thank you. It's a beautiful day, isn't it?'

She tried to smile over her shoulder as she got into her car.

Way to go again, Robicheaux, I thought, my stomach churning. 'Give me ten minutes. I'd really appreciate it,' I said.

I followed Molly and the handyman and his son to the drawbridge south of Molly's agency. The little boy pointed at a boat that had floated into a flooded clump of reeds and bamboo. I waded into the water and dragged the boat's hull up on the mudbank. The boat was old, made of wood, the stern printed with rust where the engine mounts had been removed. There were no tags or registration numbers of any kind on it. 'What makes you think this was the man's boat, Tee Bleu?' I asked.

'It got blue paint on the front end,' he replied.

'Thanks for telling me about this,' I said.

'I seen the gun. I ain't made it up. Seen the man, too. He was old,' he said.

'Y'all gonna dust the boat for fingerprints?' his father said.

'It doesn't work quite like that,' I said.

The father's half-moon eyebrows gave him a happy look, even when he wasn't smiling. He had a habit of turning his whole head as he glanced about himself, like a curious owl on a tree branch. 'I got to make my deliveries. Can y'all run Tee Bleu home for me?' he said.

'Show Dave your birdhouses,' Molly said.

'They ain't that much to look at,' he said.

'No, show him,' she said.

He opened up the trunk of his car, exposing a half dozen or so notched and pegged cypress birdhouses lying on a blanket, each with a wood plug in the roof. 'See, the trick is not to get no foreign smells inside the house. I stain the outside with vegetable oil and that way it don't have no paint smell. I got a plug in the roof and a feeder shelf inside so you can pour the feed t'rew the hole and not get no human smells on it. If you stick this house up in your tree, every kind of bird there is gonna be flying around in your backyard. They're t'irty-five dol'ars, if you want one.'

Thanks, Molly, I thought.

'I already have one. Maybe another time,' I said.

''Cause I got 'em, ready and waiting,' he replied.

Molly Boyle and I dropped Tee Bleu off at the gated entrance to the Chalons property, where he lived in a small house down by the bayou with his father and mother. We watched him walk through the shade and around the side of the main house. I could not get over his resemblance to Honoria Chalons.

'You didn't want to take him down the driveway?' Molly said.

I turned my truck back onto the highway and headed toward Jeanerette and New Iberia. 'I don't want any more contact with the Chalonses except in an official capacity. About this morning –' I said.

'I believe what you told me. You don't have to explain your life to others.'

We recrossed the bayou and entered a tunnel of trees that separated the Teche from a row of antebellum homes that were so perfect in their detail and ambiance they looked like they had been constructed only yesterday. The windows in the truck were down, and Molly Boyle's hair kept blowing in her face.

'Can you have lunch with me?' I said.

She continued to stare straight ahead. I could hear the truck keys jiggling against the dash, a flurry of leaves sucking across the windshield.

'Do you like trouble?' she asked.

'I don't seek it out,' I said.

'I heard you were a Twelve-Step person.'

'I'm in AA, if that's what you mean.'

'Maybe that's what you need to keep doing and not complicate things.'

'I'd sure like to have lunch with you.'

She looked out the window at Alice Plantation, the acres of clipped St. Augustine grass and the flowers growing along the brick base of the building. 'Can we invite another person to join us, an elderly lady who volunteers at the agency?' she asked.

'That'd be fine,' I said.

I could feel her eyes on the side of my face. Up ahead, a black cloud moved across the sun, dropping the countryside into shadow. 'Do you have any idea who the man in the boat might have been?' she said.

'Probably just a guy shooting water moccasins,' I said.

'That seems kind of cavalier,' she said.

'When the pros punch your ticket, they're at your throat before you know it. The guy in the boat was just a guy in a boat,' I said.

'I worked at a mission in Guatemala during the civil war. Men with binoculars and guns didn't use them to hunt snakes,' she replied.

chapter eleven

The phone on my kitchen counter rang early Monday morning. 'Is this Mr. David Robicheaux?' a voice said.

I looked at the caller ID. The number was blocked. 'What can I help you with?' I said.

'That one-eyed brother of yours cain't let the past rest. Looks like you cain't, either. Time to stop messing in other people's berry patch.'

'What are you talking about?' I said.

'I knew this was a mistake.'

Where had I heard the voice? Nowhere and everywhere, I thought. The speech pattern and accent were generic, the kind you hear in carnival people – laconic, faintly peckerwood with hard urban edges, the cynicism and private frame of reference always veiled. 'I know you?' I asked.

'Did you lose your cherry in a cathouse? Bet you did. Bet I can tell you the thoughts you had the night you done it. Fantasies about a big-titty girl with a soft ass an ax handle wide. Except she turned out to be a sack of flab that smelled bad and yawned in your face when you got off her. Tell me I'm wrong.'

'Still haven't figured out what you're selling, partner, so I'd better ring off now. Thanks for your call.'

'Ring off?'

I hung up, then punched in 911 on my cell. Wally, our wheezing dispatcher, answered. 'Call the phone company and open up my home line,' I said.

'You got it, Dave,' he said.

The phone on the counter rang again just as I clicked off the cell. 'Hey, man, I ain't your enemy,' the voice said. 'Let Ida go. She don't –'

The transmission broke up and the connection went dead. Fifteen minutes later, Wally called. 'It was from a cell phone, somewhere down in the Keys. What's going on?' he said.

'Some guy with too much time on his hands having dirty thoughts,' I said.

'Anyt'ing I can get in on?' he replied.

I walked to work that morning and decided not to tell Helen about the caller. She was sick of hearing the name Ida Durbin and also sick of hearing the kind of vague, uncentered information I had been offering her. In this instance, I had asked an anonymous caller if I knew him. He had answered my question with a reference to brothels. It wasn't a complimentary response. Also it made little sense and hardly seemed worth passing on to anyone else.

But in truth the caller had made one slip which I suspected he sorely regretted. He had spoken of Ida in the present tense. I also had a feeling I would hear from him again.

Much is written about contract killers. Much of it is accurate. If they're Mobbed-up, they tend to be ethnic, with tribal loyalties. But in the final analysis their race or nationality is coincidental. A button man is a sociopath first and an Italian, Jew, Latino, or Irishman second.

Jericho Johnny Wineburger was a Jew who graduated from a Catholic high school and did hits for a Neapolitan crime family.

The common denominators among professional

assassins, at least in my experience, are greed, sometimes desperation, and total indifference to the fate of their victims and the pain visited upon their families. They possess neither anger nor curiosity and struggle with no problems of conscience whatsoever.

Years ago, when Clete Purcel and I were at NOPD, we had to fly to New York and interview a man being held in the West Street Jail. He had admitted to murdering over thirty people for one of the major crime families, one based in both Queens and Hallandale, Florida. The only emotion he showed was concern about his own situation. He maintained he had cut a deal that should have allowed him to enter the federal Witness Protection Program but the United States Attorney had betrayed him.

He droned on about governmental treachery and a life sentence without possibility of parole that had just been dropped on his head. I finally reached the point where I had to ask the question that lingers in the mind of every homicide cop who finds himself in a small room with a man whose handiwork he has seen up close, before the odors and the body fluids have been scrubbed out of the environment. 'Did you ever have any regrets about the families of the guys you popped?' I said.

'Who?' he said.

'The families – their parents, their wives and kids.'

'I didn't know them,' he said. He shook his head and thought hard to make sure he was being honest. 'No, I'm certain I didn't know none of them. Why?'

When I didn't reply, he snuffed down in his nose, complained about the coolness of the room, and asked if I could get the screw to bring him a box of Kleenex.

The week passed and I made no progress on the case of Fontaine Belloc, the woman the Baton Rouge serial killer had raped, bludgeoned, strangled, and dumped in a pond inside the Iberia Parish line. Sometimes in my dreams I thought I saw her ruined face speak to me. I had long ago learned the dead have their ways, and I was sure that a lady who was so brave that she would swallow her own wedding ring to keep it from the hands of her killer would find a way to tell me who he was.

But on Friday night I decided to put away my cares and go fishing with Clete for two days out on the salt. At false dawn on Saturday morning, just as the trees were turning gray inside the fog, I hitched my boat to my truck, loaded my tackle and an ice chest in the bed, and was about to pull out of the backyard onto the street when I heard the phone ring inside.

Ignore it, I told myself.

But my daughter, Alafair, was attending the summer session at Reed College in Portland, and no father who loves his daughter ever ignores a call that might be related to her welfare. I cut the engine and went back inside the house.

'Wake you up?' the voice said, one that sounded like that of a man with infected membrane on his vocal cords.

'Jericho?' I said.

'I know it's early, but I let Jigger Babineau sleep it off in the back of my saloon. Then he goes crazy about an hour ago and starts breaking out my windows with pool balls. Remember Jigger? He used to wash money for the Giacanos? So I'm sticking his head in a bucket of ice water when he tells me he saw you coming out of my saloon and you're gonna get clipped by a cop. I say, "Why tell me, Jigger?" He goes, "Because Robicheaux is a prick and so are you."

'So I ask him if the hitter is a guy name of Billy Joe Pitts, since Pitts ain't a player anymore. He says no, that ain't the name, it's a cop on a pad who's also a gash-hound and likes to nail young girls but he don't know the name. In fact, he don't know nothing except that Dave Robicheaux, who he called a self-righteous lush, is about to get his wick snuffed. So I thought I ought to pass it on.'

'Anything about Purcel?' I said.

'You're the hit, my man. You know a dirty cop who'd go so far he'd smoke another cop?'

'Pitts's partner, a dude named J. W. Shockly,' I replied.

'If I was you, I'd start hanging around with a better class of people,' he said.

Clete and I fished for speckled trout and gafftop catfish in Atchafalaya Bay, just south of Point au Fer. The trout were not running, but we loaded the ice chest with big, hard-bodied gafftop and that evening put ashore at a camp built on stilts in the sawgrass that Clete leased by the year. We cleaned and filleted the fish on the dock and deep-fried them in a huge skillet, while the sun went down like a red wafer in the Gulf of Mexico.

That night the wind came up and blew the mosquitoes back into the marsh. Then at sunrise it rained hard for thirty minutes and the air was sweet and cool as we headed south through groundswells that burst on the bow in ropes of green and white foam. Clete had not had any alcohol in two days, and his face looked youthful and handsome inside the boat cabin, where he was tying fresh leaders and feathered spoons onto the rods we were about to set in the outriggers. The mist-covered Louisiana coastline fell away behind us, and we left the westward alluvial flow of the Mississippi and entered the smoky green, rain-dimpled roll of the Gulf, flying fish sailing across our bow like sleek, salmon-colored birds.

I could have stayed on that stretch of water the rest of my life.

But a storm broke in the early afternoon, and we headed back for land, eating fried-oyster po'boys, our skin stiff with salt and sunburn, a good thirty pounds of gutted fish in the ice chest.

The problems of the workweek had completely

disappeared from my mind. We winched the boat up on the trailer and washed it down, then started to clean up the cabin. The rain was hitting hard on the tin roof now, and the gum trees and sawgrass in the marsh were turning gray inside the mist. Without explanation, Clete seemed to be growing agitated, faintly irritable, looking at his watch as though he were late for an appointment.

'Give me the keys and I'll gas up and buy some groceries to replace what we used,' he said.

'We can buy gas on the way out,' I said.

'I know that. But I want to restock my canned goods. That's why I just said I wanted to buy groceries,' he replied.

Clete's duration of abstinence from booze was always short-lived. After a maximum of forty-eight hours, a physiological change would take place in him. He would perspire and constantly clear his throat, as though his mouth had turned to cotton, then light up a cigarette and take a deep hit on it, holding it inside, just as if he were toking on a joint. In a short while he would be back on the dirty boogie, tossing back Beam with the happy abandon of a hog rolling in slop.

But who was I to be the expert on somebody else's alcoholic chemistry? I tossed him the truck keys and watched through the back window as he drove down the road through the sawgrass and sheets of rain, the northern sky forked with lightning.

He should have been gone no longer than a half hour. I finished washing the dishes and making our beds, but still no Clete. I tried his cell phone and got no answer. I lay down on top of one of the bunks and by the light of a Coleman lantern read a fine novel titled *The Black Echo* by Michael Connelly. The wind outside made a humming sound in the sawgrass, and when I glanced through the window I could see whitecaps on the bay, like tiny bird wings, all the way out to the horizon.

Where was Clete?

I fell asleep briefly and had a troubling dream that later I couldn't remember. When I woke I heard my truck coming up the shell road, the boat trailer bouncing through the depressions. I sat on the side of the bunk and rubbed the sleep out on my face, resolving not to be angry or impatient with Cletus. The side window of the cabin had fogged in the rain, and I wiped it clean and looked out at the parking spot by the boat ramp. Clete had somebody with him and they were both drunk.

I opened the door onto the small gallery and watched them gather up two bags of groceries and a case of beer and head through the rain. The man with Clete was dressed western – in tight jeans, cowboy boots, chrome belt buckle the size of a car tag, a snap-button shirt that glittered like tin, and a short-brim Stetson tilted on the side of his head. His teeth were long, his face as lined as a tobacco leaf.

'Hey, Streak, look who I ran into – Bob Cobb. Remember Stomp-ass Bad Texas Bob?' Clete said.

They clomped inside the cabin, shaking off the rain, blowing out their breath, sorting out the beer and snacks on the kitchen table. Bad Texas Bob sat down in a chair, removed his hat, and wiped the water out of his hair onto the floor. 'You guys got any chippies down here?' he said.

'Not a good question, Bob,' Clete said.

'I was pulling Dave's joint,' Bob said. 'How's it danglin', Streak?'

'We're just about to head out,' I said, giving Clete a look.

Bob's face wrinkled with hundreds of little lines when he grinned, but his eyes contained a steady, forced brightness, the kind you see in people who claim to be born again or wish to sell you something. I had not shaken hands with him, although I wasn't sure why not. In fact, I had stepped backward, toward my rucksack, which lay against the wall, the flap open.

'I didn't know you were a fisherman,' I said.

'It beats spending your days at the OTB parlor,' he replied. He bent over and began slipping off his boots. 'Y'all got a towel? I'm soaked to my socks.'

His back was to us as he worked the sock off his right foot with his fingers. I could see the whiteness of his ankle, the hair along the bone, the dark yellow, shell-like thickness of his toenails. But more than anything else I could see the liquid glimmer in the corner of his eye.

'Sorry about this, boys,' he said.

But even before Bad Texas Bob spoke or turned toward us, I was reaching down into the pouch of my rucksack.

'What the hell you doing, Bob?' Clete said, lowering a can of beer he was about to drink from.

Bob had pulled a blue-black .25 auto from a Velcro ankle holster. But Clete kicked the table against him, knocking off his aim, and his first shot went wild and broke out the window behind me.

I pointed my .45 in front of me with both hands, pulling back the hammer to full cock. When I fired, the room roared with sound and a hollow-point round cored through the top of Bob's left shoulder. He should have gone down, but he didn't, perhaps because he was standing up against the wall now, shooting wildly, one palm held up in front of his face, as though it could protect him from the impact of a .45 fired at close range.

I think it was my second or third round that punched through his hand and sheared off three of his fingers and part of his palm, but I cannot be sure. My ears were ringing, my heart pounding with fear, my wrists bucking upwards with the recoil of my weapon. Then I saw Bad Texas Bob's face come apart, jaw and teeth and brain matter dissolving like wax held too close to a flame.

Bob crashed across the table and rolled dead-up in the center of the floor, while Clete stared at him, openmouthed, his beer splattered on his pants leg.

I kicked open the front door and walked outside, my weapon hanging from my hand, the rain driving into my eyes. I could smell ozone and fish spawn and the salty odor of dead animals in the marsh, but I could hear no sound, as though both earth and sky had been struck dumb. Clete was shaking me, lifting my weapon from my hand, saying words that were lost in the wind. The marsh was flat and long and green in the mist, and it made me think of elephant grass in a distant country, denting and swirling under helicopters that were painted with shark's teeth and flown by boys who only last season had played American Legion baseball.

chapter twelve

I was on the desk a week while Internal Affairs investigated the shooting death of Robert Cobb. During that time my colleagues stopped by to shake hands and chat, perhaps about baseball or fishing, or they'd inquire about Alafair and her life in Portland, then they'd go away.

The same was true at Victor's Cafeteria and at the Winn-Dixie store up the street, the golf course where I sometimes bought a bucket of balls and hacked them into trees, and at my church down the bayou in Jeanerette. People went out of their way to show both respect and goodwill toward me. They shook hands and patted me on the shoulder or back, as they would do to a family member of the deceased at a funeral.

But if you have ever been seriously ill or have received life-threatening injuries in a war, you know what I am about to say is true. People may be kind to you, but they also fear you because you remind them of their own mortality. The insularity they seem to create around themselves is not in your imagination. We have an atavistic sense about death, and we can smell it on others as surely as a carrion bird can.

The same applies to those who shed blood on our behalf. We collectively absolve them and, if they wear uniforms, we may even give them medals, because, after all, they took human life while defending us, didn't they? But we do not, under any circumstances, want to know the details of what they did or how they did it; nor do we want to know about the images that will come aborning forever in their dreams.

On a Wednesday in July I was cleared by I.A. But I could not shake a pall of depression that seemed to have descended upon me. There were too many shootings and too many dead people in my jacket. With age I had come to believe that each of us is diminished by the death of another. No one is God and no one should have the power of life or death over his brother. Those who say otherwise may have their point of view, but I just don't share it anymore.

But I also knew enough about depression and Sigmund Freud to understand that insomnia, guilt, and night sweats are forms of impotent rage aimed at the self.

Time to change the target, I thought.

Somebody had contracted Bad Texas Bob Cobb to take me and, if necessary, Clete Purcel off the board. Why should I carry Cain's mark because of what others had wrought? There was no mystery about where all this started. One way or another, the Chalonses were connected with the story of Ida Durbin, and that connection was one they did not want the world to know about.

On the day I.A. cleared me I checked out a cruiser and headed to Lafayette and the television station and offices of Valentine Chalons. I kept it at eighty all the way up the four-lane, my flasher on, my chest and arms pumped with an adrenal-like energy, a martial band playing in my head. In AA it's called a dry drunk. Some just call it terminal assholeitis. The bottom line is it bodes well for no one.

I hung my badge holder on my belt and went past Valentine's secretary into his office, thrusting back the door without knocking. His office was huge, done with white furniture and a lustrous black floor and a full glass wall that looked onto an atrium containing a live oak tree circled by a bed of pink and gray caladiums. Several men and women in business suits were sitting in plastic chairs, listening to Valentine Chalons speak to them from behind his desk. Their faces made me think of ceramic that had been painted with flesh tones.

'I've got a story you can put your investigative reporters on, Val,' I said. 'The guy I dusted, Robert Cobb? He was a disgraced state police officer who killed eight escaped convicts and used to get free blow jobs at Vicki Rochon's cathouse in Baton Rouge. Then he ended up doing security work at a casino your family has money in. Is that just coincidence? What do you think about doing a human interest story on ole Bob?'

'I think you're out of your mind, is what I think,' he replied.

'All your news stories featured my name as the shooter. The stories also mentioned I'd shot several suspects in the past. I think you also worked in the fact I'd been canned by NOPD. Is that standard procedure with you guys?'

'Excuse me,' Val said to his friends. He picked up his telephone and called for security.

'This is about Ida Durbin, Val,' I said. 'Get used to hearing that name. She was a decent country girl who fell into the hands of white slavers. Ida Durbin was her name. Your family had money in Galveston whorehouses. She tried to get out of the life, then something happened to her. Ida Durbin, Val. You recognize the name. I can see it in your eyes. Ida Durbin and I are going to take you and your father down, partner. You're going to see Ida Durbin's name on your bedroom ceiling.'

He rose from his chair and faced me. He wore a pink tie and a pale blue shirt with white cuffs. His hair was styled so that it was long on top and trim on the sides, which accentuated both his height and the leanness of his face. 'Under that veneer of the blue-collar knight errant, you're a vulgarian and a bully, Robicheaux. You're tolerated around New Iberia because you've overcome some serious difficulties in your life, but in truth most people consider you an object of pity.'

Two uniformed security men had entered Val's office and were now standing behind me. 'On the job, fellows,' I said.

'No, not on the job. You have no jurisdiction here,' Val said. 'You either walk out of here like a gentleman or you'll be escorted to the front door. Why not make a reasonable choice and stop degrading yourself?'

'Before I shot Bad Texas Bob, some guy in the Florida Keys called me and tried to warn me off an investigation into Ida Durbin's disappearance. I couldn't figure out who that guy was. But the voice was of a kind that sticks in your memory, like a dirty moment in your life you can never scrub out of your head. I think the guy was a Galveston pimp named Lou Kale. The name Lou Kale clang any bells for you, Val?'

He tried to hold his eyes impassively on mine, but I saw an indentation in his cheek, a twitch, as though an invisible fish hook had pricked his skin and pulled at it. *Got you, you bastard,* I thought.

'Take this man out of here,' he said, lifting his chin.

But this time Val wasn't speaking to his security personnel. Three uniformed street cops had just walked through the door. They were Cajuns like myself, basically decent men who pumped iron at Red Lerille's Gym and had families and worked extra jobs to make ends meet. Their hands rested awkwardly at their sides, their eyes avoiding mine. Val Chalons waited for my removal from his office, as though it were a foregone conclusion. In the silence I was sure I heard my watch ticking. 'Hey, Robicheaux, come have coffee wit' us,' one of the cops said.

'Sounds great,' I said.

'Yeah?' he said.

'I wouldn't have it any other way,' I said.

He and his two colleagues were relaxed and confident as we left the building. A potentially embarrassing moment had come and gone, they had not had to arrest one of their own, and their world had become a comfortable place again. They told me they were glad my 'I.A. beef' had not jammed me up.

"'Cause that was a righteous shoot, huh? That old dude tried to cap you and you smoked his sausage. You done what you had to do, wasn't no choice about it?' one of them said. His eyes searched mine as he waited for my answer.

That evening the sky was full of birds, the oaks deep in shade, and out on the bayou white ducks were wimpling the water among the reeds. I could smell meat fires in City Park and hear kids playing softball. I thought I was through with Valentine Chalons for the day. But I should have known you don't publicly challenge a man whose ego is as tender as an infected gland and simply walk away from it. When the phone rang, I picked it up without glancing at the caller ID. Val began speaking as soon as he heard my voice. 'You scum-sucking cretin, if it wasn't for your age, I'd break your jaw.'

'Really?' I said.

'Honoria told me about your tryst and the handcuffs and a few other sickening details about your behavior. You don't seem to have any boundaries, do you?'

'Run that by me again?'

'You screwed my sister, you sorry sack of shit. She's an impaired person.'

'You listen –'

'You're white trash, Robicheaux, the village fraud constantly presenting himself as suffering victim. You latch on to causes that give your life a legitimacy it doesn't rightfully possess. Now you're trying to drag my family through the mud. People like you should be bars of soap.'

My hand was clenched tightly on the telephone receiver, my temples throbbing with a level of anger I was not ready for. I tried to disconnect from his words and speak in a dispassionate tone, but at the moment my only impulse was to hang up the phone and find Valentine Chalons.

'Ida Durbin and Lou Kale,' I said.

'Good try, asshole,' he said. The line went dead.

The rest of the evening I tried to free myself from my anger. I had already missed the 7:00 p.m. AA meeting at the Episcopalian cottage across from old New Iberia High, and now, left to my own resources, I could not sort through my own thoughts or get Valentine Chalons's words out of my head.

Was there a degree of truth in them? Was that why I was so bothered? The unarguable fact was I had blood on my hands and during most of my adult life I had placed myself in situations that allowed me to do enormous physical injury to others, even taking their lives, without being held legally accountable for my deeds.

It's no accident that both cops and recidivists have mutual understandings about the netherworld they share. The heart-pounding rush, the lack of complexity or societal restraint, the easy access to women who love a gladiator, it all waits for the participant like a glittering avenue in Las Vegas or a free-fire zone inside a green country that has been deemed expendable.

A therapist once told me that the id for some people is a quiet furnace that simply needs a jigger of whiskey as an accelerant. He also told me I was one of those people.

I went to Clete's cottage, but he was not home. Jimmie was back in town, staying in my spare bedroom, now determined to rebuild the house we had been raised in. He had gone to Lake Charles to contract a builder who specialized in salvaged hardwoods from torn-down barns and farmhouses and what in South Louisiana is called recovered cypress – huge trees that were sunk in swamps or rivers over one hundred years ago, restored into beautiful, soft wood that seems to shine with an interior glow.

I think Jimmie believed he could correct the past and refashion it with nails and ancient wood, somehow cleansing it of bad memories and leaving only the events that should have defined our childhood. I would have given anything that evening if he had been home so I could talk with him. But he was not there, and Val Chalons's words still burned in my ears.

I drove to the graveyard in St. Martinville and under the rising moon said a rosary by Bootsie's tomb. Lightning crawled through the clouds overhead, and across the Teche I could hear music coming from a nightclub and see the neon beer signs in second-floor windows where a party was taking place. I sat for a long time beside Bootsie's tomb, then drove back to New Iberia and went to bed after midnight.

By Friday I was wired to the eyes, trying to find professional reasons which would allow me to confront Valentine for his insults. I told myself I was allowing pride to do the work of my enemies, but my best self-analysis was of no help to me. I didn't care if someone called me white trash or not, but that insult, when it is used in the South, is collective in nature, and Val Chalons had aimed his words at my origins, my mother and father, their illiteracy and poverty and hardship, and I wanted to back him into a corner and break him apart – bone, teeth, and joint.

At noon, I drove out to Molly Boyle's office on the

bayou. She was behind her desk, the air-conditioning unit in the window blowing on the side of her face.

'Go to lunch with me,' I said.

'Dave —'

'We'll take someone with us.'

'You're suggesting we're doing something illicit,' she said.

'It's what we did before. Don't shine me on.'

She pressed her fingers against her temples. 'You roll in here like a hurricane, then accuse me of being disingenuous. It's a bit hard to take.'

'So drink a Dr Pepper with me.'

'No!'

I was standing in the middle of the room, drowning in my own ineptitude and heavy-handedness.

She put on a pair of reading glasses, then took them off again. 'Is this about the man you had to shoot?'

I felt my right hand open and close at my side, a drop of sweat form and run from my armpit. 'He wasn't the first,' I said.

'Pardon?'

'I've killed others.'

'Have you talked to somebody about this?'

'What do you think?'

'I can't have lunch with you,' she said.

'Why not?'

She looked straight ahead, out the window, her skin flushed, her eyes filming. Then she propped her forehead on the ends of her fingers so I could not see her face. 'I can't be of any help to you. I wish I could. I'm sorry,' she said. When she looked at me again, there were tiny red threads in the whites of her eyes.

That evening, after work, I went shopping at the Winn-Dixie. I filled the basket with items I didn't need, and told myself that perhaps I should invite friends over, maybe barbecue in the backyard or cook a huge gumbo for the people Jimmie and I had grown up with. I dropped frozen packs of veined shrimp and crawfish in the basket, along with gourmet cheese and a smoked ham, a chocolate cake, a gallon of ice cream, crackers and cans of smoked oysters, ginger ale, diet drinks, big jars of fruit juice, a case of Corona, a fat green bottle of Burgundy, and a quart of Jim Beam and one of Black Jack Daniel's.

I could hear a whirring sound in my ears, like wind blowing in a conch shell, as I stacked my purchases on the conveyor belt at the checkout stand. Then the black teen-age girl working behind the register, whom I had deliberately chosen, went on break, and the assistant manager, a man my age, took her place. 'Fixing to have a party at your house, Dave?' he said.

'Yeah, I thought I might,' I said.

'Good weather for a cookout, huh?' he said, scanning the beer and whiskey and wine on the belt, his face empty of expression.

'It's supposed to rain, but who knows?' I said.

'Could be. Everyt'ing all right with you, Dave?' he said.

'Just great,' I said.

'That's good. That's real good,' he said. For the first time, he looked directly at me, his feigned cheerfulness carefully held in place.

I rolled the basket through the parking lot to my truck and began loading my groceries in back, the sky overhead gray and crackling with dry thunder. Then Molly Boyle passed me in a rusted compact, looked back at me, and made a U-turn, almost running over a man on a bicycle. She stopped abreast of me, her windows down, the front windshield spotted with raindrops. 'I want to talk to you,' she said.

'Go ahead,' I replied.

Her eyes lighted on the packages in the bed of my pickup. 'Not here. I'll follow you to your house,' she said.

'I'm kind of tied up right now,' I said.

'No, you're not,' she said.

I tried to lose her in the traffic and reach my house with enough time to unload the pickup and put everything away before I had to invite her inside. But Molly Boyle was a determined adversary. She stayed right behind my pickup, all the way down Main, past the antebellum and Victorian homes that lined the street, past the city library and the grotto dedicated to Jesus's mother, right into my porte cochere.

The rain was ticking on the trees and my tin roof as I hefted up two bags of groceries and started in the house, leaving the case of Corona and bottles of Black Jack and Beam and Burgundy in the truck.

She did not wait on an invitation. She picked up an armload of booze and followed me into the kitchen and set it down with a clunk on the drainboard, pushing a strand of hair out of her eye. 'You wouldn't want to leave this in the rain, would you?' she said.

'I buy it for guests sometimes,' I said.

She raised a finger at me before the words were hardly out of my mouth. 'Lie to others or lie to God, and you're only human. Do it to yourself and you never wash out the stain,' she said.

'How about taking it out of overdrive?' I said.

'I acted in a cowardly fashion this afternoon,' she said.

'I don't under –'

'You were obviously in need of a friend, or you wouldn't have come to my office. I've been a hypocrite, Dave.'

'No need for a confession here. Everything is copacetic,' I said, my gaze drifting back to the booze on the drainboard.

'I led you on, then I sent you away. Please don't drink. You're a good man. Everyone seems to know that except you.'

The light had gone out of the sky, and I could hear hailstones on the roof and see them bouncing in the backyard. Out on the bayou a willow tree turned white when lightning struck in the park. When I looked back at Molly, her face was close to mine, as though it had floated there, out of dream. I put my mouth to hers, then felt her arms around my neck, her stomach against me. I could feel the smoothness and warmth in her skin and smell a fragrance in her hair, like night-blooming flowers. I squeezed her against me, hard, perhaps harder than I should have, but she had the firm, muscular body of a countrywoman and I realized that Molly Boyle was probably not daunted by anyone or anything.

She walked ahead of me into the bedroom and let down the blinds, a look of determination on her face, as though she had set aside the counsel of others for reasons she would probably never share with anyone. Then she did something I had never seen a woman do in my life – she made the sign of the cross on my person, as though I were incapable of doing it myself, touching my forehead, my breastbone, and each of my shoulders. Then she undressed with her back to me, lay down on the bed, and waited.

The hail clattered on the roof and in the trees, and the attic fan drew the breeze across the sheets and rattled the metal blinds. I heard the phone ring and lightning crash in City Park and someone blowing a car horn in the rain, but I could not think about anything except Molly Boyle's hair spread out like points of fire on the pillow, and the rise and fall of her breasts, and the grace and invitation of her thighs, and the heated whisper of my name, over and over, in my own ear.

chapter thirteen

Clete had not been doing well since the shooting death of Bob Cobb. He blamed himself and his own reckless attitudes for bringing Bad Texas Bob back to the fishing camp, putting both of us in harm's way and ultimately causing me to take on the burden of Bob Cobb's exit from the world.

But Clete was not at fault. Cobb was evil and long ago should have been rejected by the system for the pathological creature he was. I told Clete these things, but they seemed to do him no good. He tried to get out of his melancholy mood by smacking the heavy bag at Red Lerille's Gym in Lafayette, clanking iron, and staying in the steam room until he looked like a boiled crab.

Sometimes I believed an incident in the present acted as a catalyst that took him back to Vietnam. But I never could be sure. Clete seldom spoke of Vietnam, even with me, dismissing his experience there as an aberration not worth resurrecting. I knew better, though. Even when we were patrolmen together, he'd fall into the thousand-yard stare, then snap out of it and tell me he couldn't sleep because his wife was hooking up with an alcoholic Buddhist guru in Boulder, Colorado, and was probably going to dump him for love beads and Rocky Mountain weed.

Clete felt he had let me down. I tried to dissuade him by telling him his own attitude was arrogant, that he wasn't the controller and centerpiece of other people's lives. His reply was, 'Leave the church-basement psychobabble at home, Streak.' Clete had many faults, but a lack of devotion to his friends was not among them.

So on Saturday morning I took my troubles to my best friend at his cottage at the motor court and told him about everything that had happened in the last week – particularly my encounter at the television studio with Val Chalons and my experience with Molly Boyle the previous evening. The rain had stopped in the predawn hours, and the morning was bright and cool, the trees dripping behind the cottage. Clete sat outside in a metal chair, dressed in a strap undershirt and oversized scarlet boxing trunks, shining a bagful of shoes. I thought he would react histrionically to the story I told him, but he kept his attention fixed on the shoes he was softly brushing, his face never changing expression.

When I finished, he set down the shoes and looked at them. 'You got it on with a nun?'

'I wouldn't put it in those terms,' I replied.

His eyes lifted into mine. 'But you were in the sack with a Catholic nun?'

'She never took vows.'

'People don't make those kinds of distinctions, big mon.'

'I was going to get loaded. She knew it. So she got in my way.'

His eyes were unblinking, the scar through one eyebrow and across the top of his nose like a flattened pink worm. 'You want advice?'

'I don't know. What is it?'

'Get a lot of gone between you and this situation.'

'Maybe I don't want to.'

'I'm stunned,' he said. And for the first time that morning he grinned.

He went into the cottage and showered and changed clothes. Out on the Teche a barge heaped with glistening piles of mud dredged from the middle of the bayou was being towed downstream, then a speedboat passed, towing water-skiers who sent waves up into the trees along the bank. Clete came back outside combing his hair, dressed in sharkskin slacks, oxblood loafers with tassels, and a starched sports shirt printed with flowers, the sleeves folded up in one neat turn on each of his huge biceps.

'Let's talk about this guy Lou Kale. You told Chalons it was Kale who called your house and tried to warn you off the Ida Durbin disappearance?'

'More or less.'

'How'd you know it was Kale?'

'The guy who called me talked like a pimp. But I wasn't sure it was Kale until I saw Val Chalons's reaction to the name.'

'And you got the feeling Ida Durbin was alive?'

'Yep.'

'This is the way I see it. Somebody hired Bad Texas Bob to leave both of us dead in my fish camp. That's known as a violation of the Eleventh Commandment, which is, don't screw with the Bobbsey Twins from Homicide. Time to get back on the full-tilt boogie, noble mon. Y'all got a fix on Kale's cell phone?'

'It bounced off a tower down in the Keys.'

'Hmmm,' Clete said. 'One way or another, all this stuff is connected to organized prostitution. Doing anything today?'

Jackson Square, across from the Café du Monde, is a fine place to be on Saturday afternoon, as is the rest of the French Quarter. It's a transitional time of day, caught between the tropical freshness of morning when families are exiting St. Louis Cathedral and sidewalk artists are setting up their easels, and the coming of twilight and the tourists and revelers on Bourbon Street, who in their mind's eye probably see themselves as aloof visitors at the Baths of Caracalla – in control, faintly amused by its pernicious influences.

The truth is that during times of high pedestrian traffic the Quarter is a safe place, its vice illusory, designed to titillate conventioneers from Omaha. The Quarter has always been a cash cow the city is not about to give over to jackrollers, crack dealers, Murphy artists, and indiscreet hookers. But after two in the morning, the glad-at-heart are gone, the nightclub and sidewalk bands have packed up, and the streetlamps seem coated with an iniquitous chemical vapor.

If you're really swacked, and without friends to care for you, you will in all probability have experiences you will not want to take with you into the daylight hours. A black pimp may step out of an alley and catch you by the sleeve, his face split with a lascivious grin, his breath as rife as a garbage can. A cabbie with a hooker in the back of his vehicle may pull to the curb and ask if he can help you find a motel room out on Airline Highway. A gang of kids coming out of Louis Armstrong Park may make you wonder if we all descend from the same tree.

Before leaving New Iberia I tried to reach Molly, but her machine had been turned off. When Clete and I got to New Orleans, I called again and this time she answered. I told her I would probably not be back home until late Sunday afternoon.

'Where are you now?' she said.

'In Jackson Square, trying to get a lead on the man I had to shoot,' I replied.

The line was quiet and I could tell Molly's mind was on something else. 'Do you feel any regret about last night?' she said.

'Are you serious?' I said.

'Sometimes people think differently in the morning than they do at night.'

'Can I see you tomorrow evening?' I said.

'Yes,' she replied. Then she said it again. 'Yes, we'll go somewhere. We'll take a boat ride maybe. We'll do something good together, won't we? I really want to see you, Dave.'

After I closed my cell phone, I sat down on a bench in the square and listened to a street band knock out 'The Yellow Dog Blues' while a juggler tossed wood balls in the air and an old man clutching a black umbrella pedaled a unicycle in a circle. But the real song I heard were Molly Boyle's words through the cell phone, like an urgent whisper in the ear.

During the next five hours Clete and I covered the Quarter, the lower end of Magazine, a strip of water-bed motels on Airline, and a half dozen bars across the river in Algiers. New Orleans' tradition of vice and outlawry goes back almost two hundred years, when the French used southern Louisiana as a dumping ground for both criminals and prostitutes. It doesn't take much imagination to guess at the kind of offspring they bred.

The pirates Jean and Pierre Lafitte and their business partner James Bowie made large sums smuggling slaves from the West Indies through the bayous, in violation of the federal prohibition of 1807, which forbade the importation of slaves into the United States. Brothels and gambling halls thrived, shootings and knifings were commonplace, and stolen goods from the Spanish Main could be found in the best homes along St. John's Bayou. The woman considered the wisest person in old New Orleans was a witch by the name of Marie LeVeau. Outside of Mardi Gras, the most well-attended and festive celebrations in the city were the public hangings, conducted in front of St. Louis Cathedral.

Those hedonistic and pagan traditions are still alive

and well in contemporary New Orleans, modernity's influence upon them cosmetic if non-extant. Crack cocaine hit the city like a hydrogen bomb in the 1980s, decimating black communities and the political viability they had gained during the Civil Rights era. Alcoholism is not a disease here but a venerated family heirloom. The Mafia introduced itself in New Orleans in 1890 by murdering the police commissioner and has been here ever since. Upscale brothels with baroque interiors and carriage houses may have become interesting anachronisms, but the industry of prostitution itself is more widespread, uncontrolled, disease-ridden, and dangerous than it has ever been.

Pimps don't have to seek recruits. Crack addicts, runaways, and desperate single mothers are everywhere, many of them glad to have the protection of a pimp who does not physically abuse them. Clete and I talked to a sixteen-year-old girl from Iowa, street name Holly, who had tracks on her arms, doll-like circles of orange rouge on her cheeks, and a black eye a john gave her after he tried to force her to perform oral sex on him without paying. The pimp, who posted bail for his girls regularly through Nig Rosewater and Wee Willie Bimstine, found the john and used a tire iron to extort three hundred dollars from him, half of which he gave to the girl.

'So you think Claude isn't a bad dude?' I said to her.

She was sipping a Coke through a straw at an outdoor table at McDonald's. Her pimp, whose name was Claude Deshotels, had instructed her to tell us whatever we wanted to know. 'He's got his moments,' she said, looking at the intersection, where two black women in skin-tight white shorts were talking to a man through a car window.

'You know a guy by the name of Bob Cobb? Some people call him Bad Texas Bob,' I said.

'What's he look like?' she asked.

'Old, dresses like a cowboy, long teeth, used to be a cop,' Clete said.

She twisted her lips thoughtfully. She was overweight, powdered, her hair dyed gold, hanging in tresses on her shoulders. She looked like a girl who could have worked at a small-town dollar store or the McDonald's where we were eating. 'Got lines around his mouth like a prune?' she said.

'Sounds like our guy,' I said.

'There was an old guy who told me to call him Bob. He put a gun and a blackjack on the nightstand. He kept a cigarette burning in the ashtray while we did it,' she said.

'How long ago?' I said.

'Two, maybe three weeks,' she said.

'Did he say anything about wanting to clip somebody? Anything about a kite being up on somebody?' I asked.

'Kill them?' she said.

'Yep,' I said.

'I don't get in the car with johns like that.'

'How do you know when not to get in a car?' Clete said.

'I can just tell, that's all. That's why nothing real bad ever happened to me. The dangerous ones look at you in a certain way. You can always tell.'

'The old guy named Bad Texas Bob is dead. He can't hurt you. You sure you don't remember anything else about him?' I said.

'Cops don't talk when they do it. They just want to get off, then pretend they don't know you. Can I have another Big Mac?' she said.

But in our search through New Orleans we had little success in finding the individual who was of most interest to us – Apollonaire Babineau, also known as Jigger Babineau because he had served his apprenticeship in the Mob as a lookout man for a gang of smash-and-grab jewel thieves.

Jigger was actually a coonass from Barataria, who had never shed his accent or his Cajun attachment to both his wife and mother. But perhaps because of his christened name, Jigger suffered delusions of grandeur. He claimed he had helped Jack Murphy rob the richest women in Miami and West Palm Beach of their jewels, and on a dare had picked the coat pocket of Meyer Lansky at Joe's Stone Crab. As miscreants go, he was a fairly innocuous character, an anachronism from an earlier era who believed washing stolen and counterfeit money at racetracks was honorable work suitable for a family man.

Unfortunately for Jigger, he was a degenerate gambler and he lost a pile of money from an armored car robbery in a card game run by the Giacano family. The game got busted, two of the Giacanos went away for the armored car job, even though they were innocent, and Jigger had to go into Witness Protection. Clete and I were the cops who busted the game.

We tried Jigger's cottage off Tchoupitoulas and hunted in the bars where he drank. He had left Witness Protection after Didoni Giacano died of colon cancer, but obviously he had learned we were looking for him and had decided to fly under the radar. We began to believe Jigger had blown the Big Sleazy.

That Saturday night we stayed in Clete's apartment above his office on St. Ann Street, and in the morning went to Jigger's cottage again and to a pool hall where he sometimes shot nine ball. No Jigger. We ended up at a lunch counter in the Carrollton district, empty-handed, discouraged, looking through the window at the St. Charles streetcar warping in the heat. Clete glanced at his watch. 'It's twelve-thirty Sunday,' he said.

'So what?' I said.

'I wasn't thinking. Order some meatball sandwiches to go and meet me on the back end of Audubon Park,' he said.

He was out the door and down the street in his Caddy before I could reply.

A half hour later I was laying out our lunch on a picnic table under a live oak dripping with Spanish moss when I saw the Caddy coming hard up the street, swerving in a shower of leaves at the park's entrance. Clete parked in a shady spot among the trees and walked across the grass toward me, a small ice cooler swinging from his hand, an unlit cigarette bouncing in his mouth. 'You get some pecan pie?' he said.

'Where'd you go?' I said.

'The old Washington Street Cemetery.' He ripped the tab off a beer and drank from it. His face was hot and flushed in the heat, the can cold-looking and beaded with moisture in his big hand.

'So why'd you go to the cemetery?' I said.

'Let's eat first. Wow, what a scorcher. You could fry eggs on the sidewalk.'

I began to regret we'd come to New Orleans. We'd revisited the underside of the city, a world of avarice, use, and deceit, even enlisting the aid of a pimp in order to interview a child prostitute, gaining nothing of value in turn except the cynical knowledge that no vice flourishes without sanction. I wanted to take a shower and burn my clothes. I wanted to be back in New Iberia with Molly Boyle.

Clete finished eating and pinched a paper napkin on his mouth, then studied his convertible, his jaw cocked thoughtfully. Some black teenagers had been parked by Clete's vehicle for a few minutes, their radio blaring, but they had driven away and now the Caddy sat by itself in the warm shade of the oak tree. Clete stuffed our trash in a barrel and hefted up his ice cooler. 'Let's rock,' he said.

He fished his keys out of his slacks, but walked to the rear of the Caddy rather than to the driver's door. He propped one of his two-tone shoes on the bumper and brushed dust off it with his handkerchief. 'You going to behave now?' he said to the car trunk.

Inside, I could hear muffled cries and feet kicking against a hard surface. 'Who's in there?' I said, incredulous.

'Jigger Babineau. I forgot it was Sunday. Jigger always visits his wife's tomb on Sunday. The little bastard tried to stab me with the file on his nail clippers.'

Clete slipped the key in the lock and popped the hatch. The smell of body odor and urine mushroomed out of the trunk. Jigger Babineau sat up, blinking at the light, then tumbled onto the grass, gasping for cool air.

Jigger had facial features like a stick figure. He had sprayed hair remover on his eyebrows, for reasons he had never explained, and now daily re-created his eyebrows with black eye pencil so that he looked perpetually surprised or frightened. He was short, pear-shaped, and wore double-soled shoes and suits with padded shoulders and some said a roll of socks stuffed inside his fly. His hands were white and round and as small as a ten-year-old child's. He was plainly disgusted with his circumstances and the indignity that had been visited upon him. 'I figured if elephant-ass was back in town, you weren't far away,' he said.

'*Comment la vie,* Jigger?' I said.

'He's good. Throw him a beer,' Clete said.

'How'd you hear about a cop wanting to pop me?' I asked.

'Why should I tell you anyt'ing?' he said.

'Because we don't mind riding you around in my car trunk some more,' Clete said.

'Do it, you fat fuck. I couldn't care less. I already pissed myself,' he said.

'Not a good choice of words, Jigger,' Clete said.

'Try these – bite my pole. Also, teach your sister to be a little more tidy. She left her diaphragm under my bed again,' Jigger said.

I cracked a beer and handed it to him. 'You could have taken the bounce on that armored car job, Jigger, but we got you into Witness Protection and let the Giacanos go down for the robbery. They're dead, you're on the street, and you never did time. Tell me, you really think you got a raw deal?'

But Jigger was still noncommittal. I tried again, this time using his birth name. 'You're a family guy, Apollo. Clete and I knew that. That's why you got slack and the Giacanos got back-to-back nickels in Angola,' I said.

He lifted his shirt off his chest and smelled himself. 'You got any salt?' he asked.

'Hang on,' I said.

I went back to the trash barrel by our picnic table and dug a tiny pack of salt from our take-out box. Clete could hardly hide his impatience. Jigger sprinkled his beer can and drank from it, then cut a grateful belch. 'The word was out somebody had a kite up on an Iberia Parish detective. But no pro in New Orleans is gonna hit a cop. So they didn't get no takers.'

'Who's "they"?' I said.

'Like they hand out business cards wit' their names on them?' he said.

'How'd you like the side of your head kicked in?' Clete said.

'That's it, Purcel. Tell your sister she's glommed my magic twanger for the last time,' Jigger said.

I thought Clete was going to hit him, but this time he couldn't help but laugh. Jigger drank again from the can and looked at me. 'I heard the juice was coming down from some people who used to own some cathouses. That's how come the work went to this cop. He was tight with the people running these cathouses.'

'Why did these guys want me out of the way, Jigger?'

'I didn't try to find out. It's amateurs who's messed up this city. I stay away from them,' he said. 'You got another brew in there?'

I squatted down, eye-level with him. 'You're not giving us a lot of help here, partner,' I said.

'Jericho Johnny put you on to me?' he said.

'Your name came up in the conversation,' I replied.

'What's that tell you?'

'Excuse me?'

'The number-one button man in New Orleans giving up a made guy to a cop? The old days are gone, Robicheaux. Live wit' it,' he said.

When I got home Sunday evening, I called Molly Boyle, but she was not home. I went to bed early, then was awakened by the phone ringing inside the sound of rain. It was Dana Magelli, an old friend at NOPD. 'Did you and Clete Purcel question a kid by the name of Holly Blankenship, a runaway from Iowa?' he asked.

'Yesterday?'

'Right. Her pimp says y'all talked to her at a McDonald's.'

'She didn't use that last name,' I said.

'She's not using any name now,' Dana said.

'What?'

'Her body was dumped in a trash pit out by Chalmette in the early a.m. The guy who strangled her used a coat hanger. You working on the Baton Rouge serial killer case?'

'Yeah, but that's not why we were in town,' I said, trying to shake the image of a hapless, overweight girl murdered and thrown away like yesterday's coffee grinds.

'You there?' Dana said.

'I was trying to get a lead on a guy I had to shoot. His name was Bob Cobb.'

'Yeah, I know all about that. Funny the girl ends up dead right after she talks to you. Must be just coincidence, huh? Why would anyone kill a girl because she talked to a cop? Her pimp gave you permission, didn't he?' he said.

chapter fourteen

Early Monday morning I was in Helen's office. 'There was semen in the girl?' she said.

'That's what Dana said,' I replied.

'So let's see what their lab says. In the meantime, there's no connection between her homicide and you being in New Orleans, none at least that we can see. You reading me on this?'

'No,' I said.

'We're buried in open cases. Our backlog looks like the national debt. Don't stir up things with NOPD. If they want your help, they'll call. That translates into mind your own business.'

She stared at me steadily, biting at a hangnail, waiting to see if her words had taken effect.

'The girl got it on with Bad Texas Bob, a guy who contracted to kill me. The girl talks to me, then she's dead. What's the point in saying there's no connection?'

Helen removed a tiny piece of skin from her tongue and dropped it in the wastebasket.

I went home for lunch. My next-door neighbor was Miss Ellen Deschamps. She was eighty-two years old, a graduate of a girls' finishing school in Mississippi, and she lived in the two-story, oak-shaded frame house she had been born in. Miss Ellen had never married, and every afternoon at three served tea on her upstairs veranda for herself and her older sister or friends who were invited by written invitation.

Miss Ellen was devoted to gardening and feeding stray cats. Each spring her flower beds and window boxes were bursting with color; her oaks were surrounded by caladiums that looked individually hand-painted. Cats sat or slept on every stone and wood surface in her yard. But Miss Ellen had another obsession as well. She monitored every aspect of life on East Main and wrote polite notes on expensive stationery to her neighbors when they didn't cut their lawns, take in their empty trash cans in timely fashion, trim their hedges, or paint their houses with colors she considered tasteful.

With Miss Ellen on the job, which was twenty-four hours a day, we didn't have to worry about a Neighborhood Crime Watch program.

When I pulled into the drive, she was weeding a flower bed in the lee of her house. She got to her feet and called out to me: 'Mr. Robicheaux, so glad I saw you. Did you find out who that man was?'

'Pardon?' I said.

She walked through the bamboo that separated our property. She wore cotton gloves, a denim dress with huge pockets for garden tools, and rubber boots patinaed with mud. A half dozen cats, including Snuggs, trailed along behind her. 'The man looking in your windows Friday night. I called the police about him. They didn't tell you?' she said.

'No, they didn't,' I replied.

'Well, he surely didn't have any business in your yard. Besides, it was raining to beat the band. So why would he have been by your window if he wasn't a Peeping Tom?'

'What did this fellow look like, Miss Ellen?'

'I don't really know. He was wearing a raincoat, one with a hood.'

'Was he white?'

'I wouldn't know that, either. Are you going to have your cat fixed?'

'Probably not.'

'You should. His romantic inclinations seem to have no bounds,' she said.

I wondered if there was a second meaning in her statement.

Inside, I called the city police department and talked to the dispatcher. He told me a patrol car had been sent to my address at 11:16 Friday night, but no one had been in the yard, and the responding officer saw no point in waking me up. 'Dave, Miss Ellen said the Peeping Tom was in her yard, yours, and maybe two or t'ree yards on the other side of you,' the dispatcher said. 'We would have had to wake up the whole block. You know how many calls we get from that lady every week?'

I went outside and walked through the side yard by my bedroom windows. The flower bed was planted with hydrangeas and camellias, and the mixture of black dirt, coffee grinds, and compost mixed with horse manure that I used in my gardens was still soggy from Friday night's downpour. Underneath the windowsill were the deeply etched prints of a man's work boots. The blinds were just as they had been Friday night – two inches short of the sill, a perfect viewing slot for a voyeur to have watched Molly Boyle and me in the throes of our passion.

After work I drove down Old Jeanerette Road to Molly's agency and caught her at the end of her workday, carrying a shovel, hoe, and steel rake over her shoulder toward the barn, a machete hanging from her other hand. 'How was New Orleans?' she said.

'The same,' I said, not mentioning the death of the

runaway girl from Iowa. Inside the barn, I watched her put away her tools, first wiping each of them clean, hanging them from nails on the walls. 'Molly, would anyone have reason to follow you around?' I asked.

'Why would anyone want to follow *me* around?'

'The neighbor thought someone might have been in my yard Friday night,' I replied. 'But my neighbor is a little eccentric sometimes.'

Molly smiled, as though the subject were of little consequence, then began sharpening her machete on the emery wheel, orange and blue stars dancing on her jeans. She wiped the blade on an oily rag, then hung the machete on a wood peg.

'You keep your tools sharp,' I said.

'My father taught me that. He had simple admonitions: "Feed your animals before you feed yourself. . . . Take care of your tools and they'll take care of you. . . . Put your shotgun through the fence, then crawl after it." My favorite was "Never trust a white person black people don't like."'

'Come to the house,' I said.

'I can't.'

'I know a motel on the other side of Morgan City. It's on the water, off the highway. Not many people go there. There's a restaurant where we can have dinner.'

I could see the conflict in her face. 'Come on, Molly,' I said, my voice almost plaintive.

We were there in under a half hour. Not only *there*, but in the shower stall, the hot water beating down on our heads, her legs clenched around my thighs, her fingers splayed on my back, her mouth wide with a cry that she fought to suppress but could not.

Then we were on the bed and she came a second time, her stomach and thighs rolling under me, her mouth wet against my cheek. Her hair and skin smelled like the ocean, or the smell a wave full of seaweed gives off when it bursts on hot sand. Then somewhere down below a coral shelf a mermaid winked a blue eye at me and invited me to come and rest inside a pink cave where she lived. The sound went out of the room, and when I opened my eyes the shadows of the overhead wood fan were flicking across Molly's face, like clock hands out of control.

New Iberia has always been an insular place, Shintoistic, protective of its traditions, virtually incestuous in its familial relationships and attitudes toward outsiders. It did not take long for the rumors to start about me and Molly Boyle. One week after our tryst in the motel outside Morgan City, Molly received a call from a priest in the diocesan office. He was an elderly, genteel man who obviously did not enjoy the charge that had been given him. He asked about her health, how she was doing in her work, was there any problem in her life that either he or another clergy member could help her with.

'No, but it's very thoughtful of you to ask,' she replied. 'Everything is wonderful here, Father. Come visit us sometime.'

'Well, I guess that answers that,' he said. Then, probably because of his years and his long experience with human frailty and the harsh judgment the world can visit upon the innocent, his voice changed. 'Take care of yourself, Molly. You're a good girl. Don't load the gun so others can hurt you.'

That same day, Helen tapped on my door. 'How you doin', Streak?' she said.

'Right as rain,' I replied.

She sat on the corner of my desk and fed a stick of gum into her mouth. Her triceps were ridged like rolls of nickels. 'I've gotten three phone calls and several anonymous letters about someone you might be seeing,' she said.

'Who might that be?'

She chewed her gum, her eyes roving over my face. 'I'm your friend, bwana. Don't treat me disrespectfully.'

'A person's private life is his private life,' I said.

'That might flush in San Francisco, but not on Bayou Teche. If you're involved with a Catholic nun, I'd damn well better know about it.'

'The person you're talking about never took vows. In fact, she's been thinking about returning to the role of a lay person. She's a person of enormous conscience.'

My words sounded rehearsed, even to me, as though I had read them off an index card. Helen looked out the window at a freight train wobbling down the tracks between two rows of shacks. 'They're going to put you inside the Iron Maiden,' she said.

'Who's "they"?' I said.

'Take your choice,' she replied.

Three more days went by. People were polite to me on the street and at the supermarket or the filling station, but it was obvious that something in my life had changed. Few stopped to talk, and none joined me at a coffee counter or table in a restaurant. Those who could not escape a social encounter with me held their eyes steadily on mine, fearful I would read the knowledge that was hidden there. Frequently another cop gave me a thumbs-up or hit me on the shoulder, as if I were spiritually ill. I even cornered one of them in the department's men's room and learned quickly that acceptance of sympathy is not without a price.

'I look like the walking wounded?' I said, and tried to grin.

'Thought you needed a boost in morale, Dave, is all I was doing. Didn't mean to get in your face,' he said.

'Can you spell that out?'

'My ex spread rumors I molested my stepdaughter. So I know where you're at right now. I say, screw all them people. You know the troot' about my situation? She come on to me. But don't nobody care about the troot'. So I'm like you, screw 'em.'

Then, just before quitting time, a phone call changed my perspective in ways I could not quite put together. It was from Dana Magelli in New Orleans. 'We got the DNA report back on Holly Blankenship. It's a match,' he said.

'Match with what?' I said.

'The Baton Rouge serial killer. He killed her within twelve hours of the time you and Purcel interviewed her. I don't get it, Dave. This guy hasn't struck in New Orleans, but he shows up in town the same day you do and murders a hooker. That's not the guy's M.O. So far, he's left street people alone. Got any thoughts?'

'No.'

'Gee, I wish I had that kind of latitude. Blow into town, blow out of town, body dumped in a trash pit, sayonara, sonofabitch. Can I get a job over there?'

I wanted to be angry at Dana, but I couldn't. The fact the Baton Rouge serial killer had targeted a teenage prostitute, a girl who bore no similarity to his other victims, indicated either a dramatic change in the nature of his obsession or the possibility he was sending a message.

'Did you hear me?' he said.

'Yeah, I did. I wish I hadn't gotten near that girl,' I replied.

That evening I stood outside my bedroom window, staring at the indentations sculpted into my flower bed. Were these from the workboots of the Baton Rouge serial killer? I called Mack Bertrand, our forensic chemist, at his home. 'Can you make some casts in my flower bed?' I said.

'We're a little backed up, but, yeah, what d'you got, Dave?' he said.

'Maybe just a Peeping Tom.'

'Can you be a little more forthcoming?'

'I interviewed the latest serial killer's victim shortly before she was killed. Maybe the guy knows me.'

Mack was quiet a moment, and I realized how grandiose if not paranoid my statement must have sounded. But Mack was always a gentleman. 'We'll get it done first thing in the morning, podna,' he said.

That night I placed flowers on Bootsie's tomb in St. Martinville. The bayou was black, wrinkled with wind, bladed by moonlight. I sat for a long time on the steel bench in the darkness, saying nothing to Bootsie, not even thinking thoughts she might hear. Then I walked to the old church in the square, pressed a folded five-dollar bill into the poor box, and returned with a votive candle burning inside a small blue vessel. I heard a flapping of wings overhead, but could see no birds in flight. Then I told Bootsie about Molly and me.

I believe the dead have voice and inhabit the earth as surely as we do. I believe they speak in our dreams or inside the sound of rain or even in the static of a telephone call, on the other side of which there is no caller. But Bootsie did not speak to me, and I felt an intolerable sense of guilt about the affair I had embarked upon with Molly Boyle.

I not only felt I had betrayed Bootsie, I could no longer deny I was creating scandal for Molly as well as for my church. My rationalizations of my behavior left me exhausted in the morning and agitated during the day.

'What should I do, Boots?' I said.

But there was no answer. On another occasion when I had visited her grave, I had seen two brown pelicans floating on the bayou, farther inland than I had seen pelicans since my childhood. On that day Bootsie had spoken to me. Her voice and her presence were as real as if she had sat beside me, clasped my hand, and looked directly into my face. She said that one day the pelicans would return to Bayou Teche, that hope was indeed eternal, and the world was still a grand place in which to live.

But the wings I had heard earlier were those of bats and the only sound in the cemetery was music from a jukebox in a neon-scrolled bar across the Teche. An evil man once told me that hell is a place that has no boundaries, a place that you carry with you wherever you go. A puff of wind blew out the candle burning on Bootsie's tomb. I could hear the blood roaring in my ears as I walked across the drawbridge toward the town square. The hammering sound in my ears was almost as loud as the music and the shouts of the revelers as I pushed open the door of the bar and went inside.

chapter fifteen

Friday morning I kept myself buried in the case file of the Baton Rouge serial killer. The street outside was blown with leaves and pieces of newspaper, the clouds swollen with rain. I heard a trash can bounce violently across the asphalt, then freight cars slam together on the train track. I picked up the coffee mug from my desk and drank from it, all my movements precise, like a man seated on the deck of a pitching ship, unsure of what might befall him in the next few seconds. My mouth was dry, and no amount of liquid could lessen the level of dehydration in my body. My right hand trembled as I tried to make notes on the death of Holly Blankenship.

Helen opened my office door without knocking and sat on the corner of my desk, which was the only place she ever sat in my office. 'Looks like you nicked up your face this morning,' she said.

'I think I had a defective blade in my razor,' I said. I placed a breath mint in my mouth and cracked it between my molars, my eyes straight ahead.

'Mack Bertrand says you had him make casts of some footprints under your bedroom window,' she said.

'There may have been a Peeping Tom in the neighborhood.'

I could feel her eyes dissecting my face. 'Would you

explain why Mack should spend his time on a Peeping Tom?'

'The Blankenship kid was the eighth known victim of the Baton Rouge killer. She died after I interviewed her. Maybe I know the serial killer. Maybe he was following me.'

'I think we're leaving something out of the story, here. Was somebody with you the night the Peeping Tom was at your window?'

'I'm just not going to answer a question like that,' I said.

'Right,' she said. She snuffed down in her nose. 'You don't look too good.'

'I've got a touch of stomach flu or something,' I replied.

She placed her hand on top of mine and pressed it against the desk blotter. 'I love you, Pops. Don't make me hurt you,' she said.

At lunchtime I ate a bowl of gumbo at Victor's, then threw up in the bathroom. By midafternoon I was sweating, my teeth rattling, the sky outside black and bursting with trees of electricity. I ate six aspirin and washed them down with ice water from the cooler but got no relief. I finally forced myself to call my old AA sponsor, an ex-convict and former barroom owner by the name of Tee Neg. 'I had a slip,' I said.

'You ain't talking about a dry drunk, you? You actually done it?' he said.

'Last night, in St. Martinville. I was in the cemetery. I don't remember getting home.'

'I ain't interested in blow-by-blow. Where you at now?'

'I'm coming apart.'

'I ain't axed you that.'

'At the sheriff's department.'

'Good. You keep your ass there, you. I'm heading into town.'

'No, that's not necessary. Tee Neg, did you hear me?'

But he had already hung up. I swallowed, already envisioning his arrival and the hours if not days of abstinence before my metabolism would have any semblance of normalcy.

Some people say you pick up the dirty boogie where you left it off. Others say you pick it up where you would have been had you never gotten off it. I signed out of the office before Tee Neg arrived and drove through a blinding rainstorm to a bar in the Atchafalaya Basin, where people still spoke French, did not travel farther than two parishes from the place of their birth, and believed, in their incurable innocence, that the smokey, green-canopied swamplands of South Louisiana would always be there for them.

I do not remember Saturday at all. At least twenty-four hours of my life had disappeared, just like a large decayed tooth excised from the gums. Later, the odometer on my truck would show I had driven sixty-three miles I could not account for. When I woke Sunday morning, I was in a cabin that was dry and snug, cool from a breeze that inched along the floor. Through the window was a vast, stump-filled lake dimpled by rain. The sky was gray, and when the wind blew the cypress trees on the far side of the lake, the canopy turned a bright green against the somberness of the day, as though the trees drew their color from the wind.

Inside my head I could hear the original 1946 recording of Harry Choates's 'Jolie Blon,' the song that will always remain for me the most haunting, unforgettable lament ever recorded. Had I dreamed the song? Had I been with someone who had played it over and over again? I had no idea.

I sat for a long time on the side of the bunk bed in the cabin. The flop hat I wore on fishing trips and my raincoat lay on a chair. My skin had no sensation, as though it had been refrigerated or dry-frozen; my hands were stiff and as thick-feeling as cardboard. I didn't have the shakes or sweats, nor were there nightmarish images painted on the backs of my eyelids. Instead, I felt nothing – no hunger, thirst, or erotic need, neither guilt nor remorse, as though I had simply ceased to exist.

My holstered .45 rested on a table, next to a bottle of Scotch, a paper plate containing the remains of a fried-shrimp dinner, a scattered deck of playing cards, and three empty glasses. The .45 was mine; the rest I had no memory of.

I stood up from the bed, then felt my knees cave and the blood drain from my head. I lay back down, my head buried in a pillow that smelled of unwashed hair, my jaws like emery paper.

I slept until early afternoon, and woke trembling and sick, willing to cut off my fingers one at a time with tin snips for the Scotch I had seen earlier.

Except it was gone.

A Creole woman, with one eye that looked like a milky-blue marble pushed deep into the side of her face, sat on a chair by the door, her feet in flip-flops, her wash-faded print dress puffing from a floor fan under her. 'Where you going?' she said.

'To the restroom,' I replied.

'There ain't no restroom. The privy's in back. Don't go up to the bar, Mr. Dave.'

'How do you know me?'

'I belong to your church in Jeanerette. I see you at Mass every Sunday,' she replied. Her face was lopsided, perhaps misshaped at birth. Her good eye held on me just a moment, then looked away.

'Why are you here? Why are you watching me?' I said.

'You had bad men in here. Poachers and men carrying knives. What you doin' to yourself, a Christian man, you?'

I used the outbuilding in back. My truck was parked in a clump of gum trees, the paint and body unmarked by an accident. My credit cards and most of my money were still in my wallet. On the lakefront was a bar nailed together from unpainted scrap wood and corrugated tin. I could hear music inside and through a window see men drinking long-necked beers. The wind shifted, and I could smell the fish in the lake, barbecue grease dripping into an outdoor fire, ozone from another storm building out on the Gulf.

Perhaps it was a happy day after all. Maybe nothing truly bad had happened because of my brief fling with the dirty boogie. Maybe all I needed was a couple of beers to straighten out the kinks, medicate the snakes a bit, whisk the spiders back into a dusty corner. What was wrong with that? I was not sure where I was, but the woods were hung with air vines, the oaks and swamp maples and persimmon trees widely spaced, the coulees layered with yellow and black leaves. It was Louisiana before someone decided to insert it in the grinder.

'Oh, there you are,' I heard Molly Boyle say behind me. She and the Chalons family handyman, Andre Bergeron, walked down a leafy knoll on the edge of the lake. 'We were watching the alligators in the shallows. How about something to eat?' she said.

She drove with me in the truck back toward New Iberia. Her friend, the black man, followed. At Jeanerette, I saw his car turn off the highway. I had hardly spoken since leaving the fish camp deep in the Atchafalaya Basin. Each time we passed a bar I felt as though a life preserver were being pulled from my grasp. 'How'd you know where I was?' I asked.

'The lady who was watching you called me. Her husband owns the bar,' she replied.

'Why was the Chalonses' handyman with you?' I said.

'Andre helps me in any way he can. He's always been

protective of us,' she replied. 'Don't be angry, Dave.'

'I'm not. I just got jammed up,' I said irrationally, my hands tightening on the steering wheel, my breath a noxious fog.

Molly was silent. When I looked over at her, she was staring out the side window. 'I'll go to a meeting with you,' she said.

'I'd better drop you by your house,' I said.

'That's not going to happen, trooper. If you try to pick up a drink today, I'm going to break your arm.'

I looked at her again, in a more cautious way.

We drove down East Main toward my house, the nineteenth-century homes and manicured lawns and wet trees rushing past me, all of it curiously unchanged, a study in Sunday-afternoon normalcy and permanence to which I had returned like an impaired outsider. I pulled the truck deep into the driveway, past the porte cochere, so that it was almost hidden from the street by the trees and bamboo. I cut the engine and opened the driver's door. When I did, a shiny compact disk fell to the ground. Just next to the edge was a tiny reddish-brown smear that looked like blood.

'What's that?' Molly said.

'I don't know,' I said. 'I don't know what it is.' Vainly, I tried to explain to myself where the CD had come from or who could have placed it in my truck. I touched the crusted smear on the surface and was sure I was touching blood. I slipped the CD in my pants pocket and unlocked the back door, my hands shaking.

Even if Molly had not been with me, my home offered no succor for the drunk teetering on the edge of delirium tremens. I had returned all the booze I'd purchased at Winn-Dixie. There was not even a bottle of vanilla extract in a cabinet. But at least my brother was not home and did not have to see me in the condition I was in.

The only other consolation I had was the fact my bender

had not hurt my animals. When I bought my house I had created a small swinging door in the back entrance so Tripod and Snuggs, in case of emergencies, could get to a bag of dry food on the floor. But I couldn't take credit for having thought about them. A drunk on a drunk thinks about nothing except staying drunk.

I got in the shower, turned on the water as hot as I could stand it, and stayed there until the tank was almost empty. Then I dressed in fresh clothes and shaved while my hand trembled on the razor. I could hear Molly clanking pans in the kitchen.

I went into the living room and loaded the CD into my stereo. There was no seal or logo on it, and I suspected it contained nothing more than an Internet download of music someone had not bothered to pay for. But who had left it in my truck? The poachers the Creole woman had mentioned?

I pushed the 'play' button on the stereo and the long-dead voice of Harry Choates, singing his signature song, 'Jolie Blon,' filled the room. That's why I had heard those words over and over in my head when I had woken up that morning, I told myself. Perhaps someone with a cut on his hand had given me Choates's song and I had probably played it repeatedly in my truck's stereo. A blackout didn't necessarily mean I had committed monstrous acts. I had to control my imagination. Yes, that was it. It was all a matter of personal control.

Then a second song began to play, one titled 'Two Bottles of Wine,' which had been written by Delbert Mc-Clinton for Emmylou Harris in the late 1970s. But the singer was not Emmylou. The band was raucous, the recording probably done in a bar or at a party, and the voice on it was the same voice as on the old 45-rpm recording Jimmie believed to have been cut by Ida Durbin.

'Everything in there okay, Dave?' Molly called from the kitchen.

chapter sixteen

Monday morning the Garden of Gethsemane was the 7:35 traffic backup at the railroad crossing. It also included a horn blowing like a shard of glass in the ear, the hot smell of tar and diesel fumes, undigested food that lay greasy and cold in the stomach, waiting to fountain out of my throat. Then, to demonstrate I was in control of things and not bothered by the metabolic disaster inside my body, I blew my horn at a passing streak of freight cars.

I had attended an AA meeting the previous night, determined to leave my weekend bender behind, and this morning I had dressed in pressed slacks, shined shoes, a striped tie, and a white shirt that crinkled with light. But as I walked into the office I knew my affectation of freshness and confidence was the cheap ruse of a willful man who had thrown away years of sobriety, betrayed his friends in AA, and perhaps mortgaged a long series of tomorrows.

By midmorning I could feel a tension band begin to tighten on the right side of my head. I constantly touched at my scalp, as though I were wearing a hat that had begun to shrink. I chewed gum, washed my face with cold water in the lavatory, and tried not to think about where I might go when the clock finally struck noon. But that problem was about to be taken away from me.

The chief of police in Jeanerette was Doogie Dugas. He was not a bad fellow, simply a showboat and political sycophant. But like most sycophants he was inept and lived in fear of people who had power. I was walking past Helen's open door when I saw her talking on the telephone, snapping her fingers at me. 'Hang on, Chief, Dave Robicheaux just walked in,' she said. 'I'm going to put you on the speakerphone. Dave's the lead detective in our own investigation.'

'– get the impression Mr. Val isn't a big fan of Dave Robicheaux,' Doogie's voice said.

'Uh, you're on the speakerphone now, Chief,' Helen said.

There was a pause. 'You got any evidence this guy is local?' Doogie said.

'Which guy?' I said.

'The Baton Rouge serial killer,' he said.

'No, we don't have any evidence to that effect. What's going on?' I said.

'What's going on is it looks like a butcher shop in there. The sheriff and me got road stops set up on the parish line, but I'm gonna need some lab hep here,' he replied.

'Sir, I have no idea what you're talking about,' I said.

'Honoria Chalons, somebody cut all over her. I never seen anyt'ing like this. Y'all coming over here or not?' he said.

Helen and I and our forensic chemist, Mack Bertrand, drove to the Chalons home on the far side of Jeanerette. The homicide had taken place in the guesthouse sometime during the weekend, when Val and his father were in New Orleans on business. Val claimed he had returned shortly after nine on Monday morning and had found the body.

Crime scene tape had already been strung through the trees, sealing off the immediate area around the guesthouse, which was located by a swimming pool that had long ago been abandoned to mold and the scales of dead vines. Crime scene technicians from three parishes were already inside the guesthouse, photographing the body, the walls, the furniture, the tile floors, the glass in the windows, even the ceiling.

Honoria was nude, her body reclining on a white sofa, the incision in her throat so deep she was almost decapitated. But the wounds in the rest of her body had bled so profusely it was obvious that the mortal blow was not the first one the killer had struck.

'Good Lord,' I heard Mack say softly beside me.

The guesthouse was actually the residence of Val Chalons, and so far no one had offered an explanation for Honoria's presence there. The initial assault seemed to have occurred just as she was about to enter the shower. One strip of blood angled down the wall mirror and there was a smear against the doorjamb, as though she had bumped against it on her way to the living room. A second attack must have taken place in front of a huge television screen and stereo center, causing her to lose large amounts of blood that probably drained over the tops of her feet.

The oddity that no one could explain was the pattern of the footprints. They were evenly spaced, firmly patterned in the rug, as though she had still been in control of her movements and was unhurried about her destination. Mack believed she had sat down with deliberation on the couch, and had lain back with her head on a cushion, perhaps even lifting her chin in anticipation of the blow across the throat.

The front door had been unlocked. There was no sign of a weapon on the premises.

I looked at the white furniture, the black marble in the

wet bar, the gleaming stainless-steel perfection of the kitchen area, the stereo player that was still turned on, its dials glowing with a soft green luminescence, and I felt I had been there before. But perhaps I was just remembering the interior of Val Chalons's office at the television station in Lafayette, which was similar in decor, I told myself.

Koko Hebert, our coroner, had gone outside, under a tree beyond the crime scene tape, to smoke a cigarette. His clothes smelled like an ashtray. His lungs made sounds as if he had just labored up a mountainside.

'Was she raped?' I said.

'No marks around the vagina or thighs that I can see,' he replied.

'Any sign of semen?'

'Traces in the pubic hair. St. Mary's forensic pathologist will call me after he gets inside her.'

'Mack says her blood trail doesn't make any sense. The assailant attacked her at least three times, but she made no attempt to run away. There were no defensive wounds, either.'

'Maybe she dug it.'

'You enjoy pissing people off, Koko?'

'Yeah, when they still got booze on their breath and they're blowing it in my face while they're asking stupid questions,' he replied.

A crime scene team from state police headquarters in Baton Rouge had just landed in a helicopter across the bayou, and a St. Mary Parish sheriff's cruiser was bringing them across the drawbridge to the Chalonses' house. The crime scene area had been soggy from the weekend rains, and now the St. Augustine grass had been trod into green mulch. Plainclothes detectives, cops in uniform, and crime scene investigators came and went with the freedom of people for whom the gates of an amusement park had suddenly been opened. I wondered how Raphael Chalons would deal with the intrusion of the twenty-first century into his cloistered domain.

A brief shower rolled across the sugar cane fields and pattered on the trees, then a few minutes later the sun came out and the trees were green and dripping like crystal against a brilliant blue sky. But still I had seen no sign of Valentine Chalons.

It had not been easy looking at Honoria. She had been a bizarre person, but probably no more so than any true artist is. In fact, I believe her pulp fiction sexual behavior and feigned iconoclastic attitudes hid a fragility and childlike emotional need that ultimately was harmful to no one but herself. She had also died with dignity under the worst of circumstances and proved she was capable of extraordinary courage.

Then I saw Val coming through the trees. I started to offer condolences but did not get the chance. His shoulder grazed across mine, as though I were not there, as he charged inside the guesthouse. 'You left her uncovered?' he shouted. 'The next one of you who points a camera at her is going to have it stuffed down his mouth!'

Mack Bertrand tried to explain that a sheet had been placed over Honoria's body but it had been removed upon the arrival of the investigative team from Baton Rouge.

'You're finished taking pictures, fellow. You want me to say it again?' Val said.

The entire crime scene became quiet. Not one person offered a rejoinder, less out of respect or embarrassment than collective acceptance that the Chalons family operated in rarefied air. Then, after a long beat, a Baton Rouge detective said, 'We got all we need, Mr. Chalons. We're sorry about your loss.'

But Val was not finished. He emerged from the guesthouse and pointed a finger at me. 'You degenerate piece of shit! You dare come into my home?'

'Dial it down, Mr. Val,' Helen said.

'He screwed my sister, for God's sakes, a girl who was ten years old inside,' he said.

'If you have a charge to make about one of our personnel, you need to come into the office,' Helen said.

'Maybe I'll just do this instead,' he said. He advanced three steps in less time than I could blink and swung his fist into my face.

The blow knocked me across a garden sprinkler and against a glider that was suspended from a thick oak limb. My nose felt as though hundreds of needles had been shoved up it and into my brain. I grabbed a rope on the glider and sat down, my eyes watering uncontrollably.

'Get a towel,' I heard Helen said.

I saw two St. Mary sheriff's deputies holding Val Chalons by his arms, his wrists cuffed behind him. Someone pushed a clutch of ice cubes wrapped in paper towels into my hands. I held the coldness against my face until my skin began to numb. When I looked at the ice it was speckled with blood. The yard, the trees, the flowers, and Honoria's body inside the open guesthouse door kept warping in the sunlight.

'You call it, bwana,' Helen said.

Val glared at me, his cheeks splotched with color, his hair hanging in his eyes, the rims of his nostrils white, as though he were breathing subzero air.

'Cut him loose,' I said.

'A little time in an isolation cell might take some of that prissiness out of him,' Helen said.

'Val Chalons is a coward and a liar and has guilt painted all over him. Let him go,' I said, loud enough for everyone in the yard to hear.

In the background I saw a uniformed deputy climb down a ladder with a security camera that had been mounted high in the fork of an oak tree.

I went home, changed shirts, and returned to the office. Helen was waiting for me, as I knew she would be, her hands stuck in her back pockets, a quizzical look in her eye, one tooth chewing on the corner of her lip. 'You pumped Honoria Chalons?' she said.

'Why don't you be more direct?' I said.

We were standing in front of her office door, and people were passing in the corridor. 'Answer the question,' she said.

'Val Chalons believes what he needs to believe. End of discussion,' I said.

'Step inside,' she said.

She closed the door behind us. Through the window I could see the cemetery and a black kid trying to fly a red kite among the crypts. I wanted to be outside in the wind with him, away from all the sordid details that my life had taken on in only a few days. 'Why would Val Chalons make up a story like that?' Helen asked.

'I believe there's a form of evil at work inside the Chalons home that we can't even guess at. Honoria tried to tell me about it. Now she's dead.'

'You don't think the Baton Rouge serial guy is involved in this?'

'Honoria's death is connected to the Chalons family and the Chalons family only. Don't let them put it off on somebody else, Helen.'

'That doesn't sound like an entirely objective statement. At the crime scene you seemed a little nervous about something. Have you been inside that guesthouse before?'

'No,' I said, and felt my heart jump, just as though it had been touched with an electrical wire.

'Okay, bwana,' she said, her manner relaxing now. 'By the way, I was proud of you out there.'

I left her office and washed my face in the men's room.

When I looked at my reflection, I felt as though I were looking at the disembodied head of a Judas, that it was I who was the liar, not Val Chalons. But I had no idea why I felt that way.

chapter seventeen

That evening, at dusk, Clete Purcel and I sat in canvas chairs on the edge of Henderson Swamp, pole-fishing with corks and cut-bait like a pair of over-the-hill duffers who cared less about catching fish than just being close by a cypress-dotted swamp while the sun turned into a red ember on the horizon.

I told him of the bender I had gone on and the discovery that morning of Honoria Chalons's body. I also told him of the compact disk I had found in my truck and the fact I had no memory at all of what I had done from Friday night to Sunday morning.

I thought he would take me to task, but sometimes I didn't give Clete enough credit and would forget that he was the man who once carried me down a fire escape with two .22 rounds cored in his back.

'This Ida Durbin broad's voice was on the CD and she was singing a song that wasn't written until years after she disappeared?' He had taken off his Hawaiian shirt and sprayed himself with mosquito repellent, and in the shadows the skin across his massive chest looked as gray as elephant hide.

'You got it,' I said.

'But that's not what's bothering you, is it?'

'At the crime scene, I felt I'd been there before. I knew

where everything was in Chalons's guesthouse.'

'It's called déjà vu. Look at me, Streak. You were drunk all weekend. You clean those kinds of thoughts out of your head.'

'There's blood on the CD. Chalons's stereo was turned on but the CD slot was empty.'

'You're incapable of hurting a woman. Somebody is setting you up. Don't buy into it.'

'Nobody set me up, Clete. I got drunk and had a blackout. I could have done anything.'

'Shut up and give me time to think. This punk Chalons actually hit you in the face?'

That night, just before going to bed, I received a call from Jimmie. He was on his cell phone, and in the background I could hear the sounds of wind blowing and waves bursting against a hard surface. 'Where are you?' I said.

'At the southern tip of the island in Key West. That dude Lou Kale is down here,' he said.

'How do you know?'

'A couple of girls I used to know work the yacht trade here. They say Kale and his wife run an escort service out of Miami. Or at least a guy who sounds a lot like Kale.'

'What about Ida?'

'Hit a dead end. I got to be back in New Orleans tomorrow. I'll see you later in the week. Anything happening there?'

I had to wet my lips before I spoke. 'I had a slip. But I'm all right now.' I cleared my throat and waited for his response, my fingers opening and closing on the receiver.

'You get in any trouble?' he asked.

'I can't remember what I did or where I was. Honoria Chalons is dead. I think maybe I was there when she died. I can't remember and I don't know how to get inside my own head.'

In the silence I could hear the waves smacking against a beach, then receding with a sucking sound, like the underpinnings of the earth itself sliding down the continental shelf.

The first person I saw in my office Tuesday morning was Koko Hebert. He may have showered since the previous day, but I couldn't tell it. Twenty seconds after he closed the door behind him, the entirety of the room smelled like testosterone and beer sweat.

He sat on a chair with the posture of a man sitting on a toilet. 'The post indicates the Chalons girl wasn't raped, although she did have sexual intercourse with someone in the twenty-four-hour period before she died,' he said. 'She also had enough cocaine in her to anesthetize the city of New York.'

'Anything that could connect her homicide to the Baton Rouge guy?'

'I would have already told you that, wouldn't I?' he said.

'I guess so, Koko,' I replied. I tried to be patient and remember that the autopsy had been performed by the forensic pathologist in St. Mary Parish, and that Koko was probably doing the best he could.

'There was an incision at the top of her forehead, just inside the hairline. It was done postmortem, in the shape of a cross,' he said.

His eyes were fixed on mine, his nostrils swelling as he breathed.

'The Chalons family coat of arms?' I said.

'You're the detective. I just run the meat lockers.'

Don't say anything more, I told myself. 'I'll probably regret this, but did I ever do anything to offend you?' I said.

'Let me work up a list and I'll get back to you.'

'Thanks for coming by,' I said.

I turned my attention back to the paperwork on my desk. I thought he would be gone by the time I looked up again. Instead, he stood in the center of the room, breathing loudly, emanating an odor that was close to eye-watering. 'My son by my first marriage was a private first class in the United States Marine Corps. He was killed two months ago outside Baghdad. What was left of his Humvee wouldn't make a bucket of bolts. He was nineteen fucking years old.'

He stared into space, as though he were trying to puzzle out the implication of his own words.

At 10:00 a.m., Helen and I and the Jeanerette chief of police and two St. Mary Parish detectives watched the videotape from the surveillance camera that had been mounted on an oak tree in the Chalonses' backyard. The frames from Saturday night showed Honoria Chalons going to and coming from the guesthouse several times. The footage was grainy, the images and sense of movement elliptic, lit intermittently by the electricity in the clouds, the lens sometimes obscured by rain and blowing leaves. At 9:04 p.m. a man wearing an abbreviated rain slicker with a hood entered the guesthouse. What occurred next would remain a matter of conjecture.

The camera had been positioned so that its lens covered most of the yard but only part of the house. Shadows seemed to break across the house's windows, indicating activity inside but little else. At 9:09 the figure in the raincoat left by the French doors and disappeared from the film. There was a momentary glint of light on metal inside the figure's open raincoat, but the reflection could have been from a belt buckle.

Then, at 11:05 p.m., a second figure crossed the yard, tapped on the door, and entered the house. The figure wore a dark hat with a brim wilted by rainwater, and a coat with a hood that hung loosely down the back. At

11:13 the figure left. It was impossible to tell the gender of either visitor. Neither had looked up at the camera. The hand of the second visitor, who had tapped on the door, appeared to be white.

Doogie Dugas, the Jeanerette chief of police, clicked on the overhead light. He was a middle-aged, close-cropped, gray-haired man who affected the dress and manner of a western lawman. The fact that he was wise enough to avoid speaking in front of microphones had allowed him a long administrative career in small-town law enforcement. But now his taciturnity was of no service to him and it was obvious he was having trouble dealing with the magnitude of the case that had been dropped into his lap. It was also obvious he had not talked to his own forensic pathologist.

'Koko Hebert told you the killer cut a cross in Miss Honoria's head?' he said.

'Right,' Helen said.

''Cause maybe the killer don't like the Chalonses and he put the cross on Miss Honoria 'cause the cross is on Mr. Raphael's family seal?' he said.

'Right,' Helen said.

Doogie pursed his mouth and closed and opened his eyes, like a man for whom the world was simply too much. 'Cooh,' he said, using the favorite Cajun expression for surprise or awe. 'Know how many people that might be?'

Then he winced at his own show of candor about the people whom he loyally served.

But I didn't care about the problems Doogie Dugas might be experiencing. I could not get out of my mind the type of raincoat worn by both visitors to Val Chalons's guesthouse, nor the wilted flop hat the second figure had worn. They were exactly of the kind stuffed behind the front seat of my truck.

*

I went to an AA meeting at noon and another after work. But by sunset I was back into my problems regarding Molly Boyle. For the first time in my life I felt the abiding sense of shame and hypocrisy that I suspect accompanies the ethos of the occasional adulterer. But desire and need, coupled with genuine love of another, are not easily argued out of the room by morality.

If I genuinely loved Molly Boyle, why had I taken her to an off-road motel that almost advertised itself as the perfect situation for a sweaty tryst? If you loved a woman, you didn't make her a partner in what others would inevitably deem a seedy and scandalous affair, I told myself. Most women have a level of trust in the men whom they love that men seldom earn or deserve. As a rule, we do not appreciate that level of trust until it's destroyed. In my case, the fact that I had put Molly's career and reputation at risk indicated that desire and need had not only trumped morality but also concern for the woman I said I loved.

I kept those lofty thoughts in my mind for about fifteen minutes, then picked up the phone and called her. I talked about the meetings I had attended that day, about the fine weather we were having, about the fact my system seemed to be free of booze. But it was quickly apparent that neither of us was entirely focused on what I was saying. 'Do you want me to come over?' she said.

'Yes,' I said, my voice weak.

'If you don't feel comfortable with that, we can go to the motel in Morgan City,' she said.

'No,' I said.

'Are you sure?'

What I was doing was no good. It was foolish to try and convince myself that it was. 'I'll see you tomorrow,' I said.

'I'm leaving the Order, Dave. I've already talked with the bishop. My leaving doesn't have anything to do with us. It's been coming a long time. Stay there. I'll be over shortly.'

She hung up before I could reply. But I was out front, in the yard, when she arrived a half hour later, happy in a way that perhaps I shouldn't have been. She looked beautiful stepping out of her car, too, in straw sandals and pleated khakis and a blouse stitched with cacti and flowers, a big hand-tooled leather purse slung over her shoulder.

'Hi, big stuff,' she said.

'Hi, yourself,' I replied.

I fixed coffee and hot milk and slices of pound cake for us, and served it on a tray in the living room. We sat on the couch and watched part of a movie on television, while the streetlights came on outside and kids sailed by on bicycles. I touched the back of her neck and clasped her hand, and we sat there like married people do, with no sense of urgency about the passage of time.

She told me about her missionary years in Nicaragua and Guatemala. But without being told I already knew the nature of her experience there, in the same way you intuitively know when people have seen organized murder on a large scale, or have stood with hundreds of others inside a barbed-wire compound or languished in a cell run by individuals who are probably not made from the same glue as the rest of us. Their eyes contain memories they seldom share; they seem to exemplify Herodotus' depiction of man's greatest burden, namely, that foreknowledge of human folly never saves us from its consequences.

But why brood upon the bloody work of neocolonial empires on a summer night on a leaf-blown street that belongs back in the year 1945? Why not fall in love with the world all over again and not contend so vigorously with it? Outside, the night was unseasonably cool, scented with shade-blooming flowers, the giant live oaks along the sidewalks lit by streetlamps, Spanish moss lifting in the breeze. Molly Boyle and I made love in the bedroom, in the slow and unhurried fashion of people who are secure in the knowledge the two of them, together, have legitimate claim on the next day, and that mortality and the demands of the world are no longer of great importance. What better moment could human beings create for themselves? Let the world, at least for tonight, find its own answers for a change, I told myself.

I never asked Molly about other men or other lives she might have led. But her attitudes and manner reminded me of other nuns I had known over the years, particularly those who had gone to jail for their political beliefs or been exposed to the risk of martyrdom in Central America. They seem to have no fear, or least none that I could see. As a consequence, they didn't argue or defend, and the church to which they belonged was one they carried silently inside themselves.

Molly Boyle might have been educated, but she was a blue-collar girl at heart, her body thick from work, her breasts full, her nipples as big as half dollars, the honesty and love in her face as she looked down at me untouched by any mark of vanity or self-interest. When she came, her face softened and her eyes seemed to look inward, as though she were experiencing a tender thought that was almost unbearable; then her body grew tense, her mouth opening, and she came a second time, her arms propped stiffly on each side of me, her skin moist and ruddy, her womb scalding.

I put her nipples in my mouth and kissed the two red moles on her stomach, just below her navel. Her head lay on the pillow, the points of her hair damp with perspiration, her breath loud in the silence. She ran her hand through my hair and cupped it on the back of my neck.

'Was it Ernest Hemingway who wrote about feeling the earth move?' she said.

'That was the guy,' I replied.

'Boy, he had it right,' she said.

Our faces were turned one to the other on the pillow. I could hear the wind in the trees, Tripod running on his chain, a boat blowing its horn as it approached the drawbridge on Burke Street. Then I heard other sounds – car doors slamming, feet running through the yard, someone shouting unintelligibly behind the house.

Molly raised up on one elbow, her eyes fastened on mine. 'What's that?' she said.

A shadow went past the window, then another one. 'Cops,' I replied.

I got up from the bed and put on my khakis. A fist hammered on the front door. When I jerked it open, I looked into the slightly distended oval face of Doogie Dugas, who stood on the gallery, with two uniformed Jeanerette cops behind him. The yard was full of television cameras and lights.

'I got a search warrant for the premises,' Doogie said.

'You don't have any jurisdiction here. Get off my property,' I said.

'It's signed by an Iberia judge. Step aside,' Doogie said, as though performing on a stage set.

'Have you gone crazy?' I said.

'Your fingerprints was all over the crime scene, Dave. I ain't got no control over this,' he said, almost in a whisper.

Two television cameramen followed him in, their battery-powered lights flooding the inside of my home, their lenses focusing now on Molly Boyle, who stood speechless, half-undressed, in the bedroom doorway.

Then I saw Val Chalons walk into the apron of light surrounding the gallery, his face suffused with good cheer. 'This is just for openers, rumdum,' he said.

chapter eighteen

While Doogie Dugas and his minions tore my house apart, I was transported to jail in St. Mary Parish. It was extralegal, almost a kidnapping, but legality can be a matter of definition, particularly when some of the players own vast amounts of money. Actually, few of the events that night were aimed at solving the murder of Honoria Chalons. I believed the agenda was to dismember my life.

Television programming in Acadiana was interrupted to show live coverage of my house being searched. I was shown being spread-eagled against a cruiser, shaken down, and hooked up. Molly was captured on camera leaving the house, her clothes and hair in disarray, refusing to answer questions asked by reporters who identified her as a Catholic nun. A plainclothes state police officer was interviewed on site about the possible connection between the death of Honoria Chalons and the homicides committed by the Baton Rouge serial killer.

The sweep of the tarbrush didn't end there, either. The cameras were waiting when I was taken into the parish prison at Franklin. A television newsman, holding a microphone in my face, said, 'Is it true you're being called a person of interest in the death by strangulation of a New Orleans prostitute by the name of Holly Blankenship?'

Another asked, 'Can you comment on the fact that under questionable circumstances you have shot and killed at least five people while serving as a police officer?'

The aim of the reporters, none of whom I knew, was obviously to slander. They were good at it, too. Their questions were predicated on distortions or flawed syllogisms that were presented as given facts. To try to defend oneself in those circumstances is to legitimize the question. To remain silent seems an admission of guilt. I was beginning to understand how character assassination can be a telecommunications art form. 'Can you explain why a Catholic nun was in your home at the time of your arrest?' the first reporter asked.

'I'm under arrest because I shoved a Jeanerette detective who was wrecking my house,' I said.

But my attempt at evasion was that of an amateur. 'Was the nun Sister Molly Boyle?' the reporter said, working Molly's name into the story for the second time.

I pushed by him, my wrists cuffed behind me, my un-shaved jaws like coal smut inside the blinding glare of strobe lights.

A jail is not a geographical place. A jail is a condition. It rings with the sounds of steel clanging against steel, people yelling down stone corridors, toilets flushing, a screw losing it after an inmate throws feces through the bars into his face. Sometimes a gigantic biker arrives wrapped in leg and waist chains, wiped out on meth, his body crawling with stink, his beard and hair as wild as a lion's mane. The elevator stalls between floors. Later, the cops say he went apeshit. The walls shake, and when the elevator doors open, the biker is curled on the floor, bleeding from the mouth and ears, his eyes rolled up in his head from the voltage injected into him by a stun gun.

The external world and the inside of a can – state, federal, city, county, or parish – do not have connection points based on reason, humanity, psychiatry, or penology. Jails represent human and societal failure at its worst, nothing more, nothing less. Jails are a short-stop way of separating aberrant and undesirable people from the rest of us and rendering them as invisible as possible. Anyone who believes otherwise has never been there. The people who believe jails rehabilitate usually need jobs.

In any slammer, powerlessness is the norm. You defecate in full view of others; you eat when you're fed. If you're truly unlucky, or young and very frightened and physically weak, you will be the daily punch of sexual predators, a bar of soap passed around in the shower, an item gambled away in a card game or rented out for a deck of smokes.

But as I lay on a steel bunk suspended from chains screwed into the wall, I really didn't care about any of these things. My nemesis was not jail, the unraveling of my career, or even the machinations of Val Chalons. It was me. I remembered a line written by Billy Joe Shaver: 'The first time the devil made me do it/ The second time I done it on my own.' I had stoked my resentments, fed my sense of loss over Bootsie, and turned my depression into a wardrobe of sackcloth and ashes in order to get drunk again.

I felt like a man who had set fire to his own home in order to warm up an unappetizing dinner.

Then I had a peculiar experience, not unlike one of many years ago when I heard a metallic sound, a brief *klatch*, on a night trail in a tropical country that no one talks about anymore. There was a moment's silence, the kind you automatically know is a prelude to your entrance into eternity, just before a waist-high explosion cut a black PFC nicknamed 'Doo-Doo Dogshit' in half and laced my side and thigh with shrapnel that looked like twisted steel fingers.

A white light filled the inside of my head. I felt myself float up toward the canopy, then crash to the earth. Later,

I would swear I saw Doo-Doo walking through the jungle, unharmed, strings of smoke rising from his clothes. He turned, gave me the peace sign in farewell, and said, *Got to dee-dee, Loot. Big Boss Man upstairs need me to hep out. Hey, don't you worry none. Chuck going back alive in '65.*

My men could have left me there. I'd screwed up and taken them down a night trail that was strung with bouncing betties and trip-wired 105 duds. But that was not their way. They came from barrios and southern shitholes and black northern slums and were the bravest and finest kids I ever knew. While I lay on a poncho liner and a mountain boy from North Georgia rigged up a litter with web gear, I could hear the rounds from an offshore battery arcing with a whooshing sound out of their trajectory, exploding in the jungle, shaking the earth under me. I was laced with morphine and blood-expander and knew I was going to die unless I got to battalion aid. I heard someone calling for the dust-off, then a voice whispering, 'They can't get the slick in. He's fucked, man. Oh Jesus Christ, they're coming through the grass.'

But they carried me all night, with no sleep, their arms straining against one hundred eighty pounds of dead weight, while they humped their own weapons and packs and radios and sweltered inside their flak vests, their exposed skin a feast for the mosquitoes that boiled out of the elephant grass.

That's when I felt my long-held fear of death finally use itself up and lift from my soul the way ash floats off a dead fire. I closed my eyes in surrender to my fate and placed my trust in the tender mercies of those who bore me toward an uncertain destination, perhaps one that would be lit by flame and filled with explosions that sounded like ships' boilers blowing apart.

But I was not a player any longer. The dice had rolled out of the cup, and if the numerical sum on them was snake-eyes or boxcars, the matter was out of my control, and that simple conclusion about my lifespan on earth set me free.

I fell asleep in the jail cell, even though a drunk snored loudly on the floor and a deranged man in sweatpants and a woman's blouse kept shouting accusations through the bars at a city cop he claimed had stolen his airline tickets to Paris.

When the sun came up, I realized I'd just had the first restful sleep since I had gotten drunk. With my cell partners I ate a breakfast of scrambled eggs, tiny sausages, toast, jelly, and coffee. Then I heard Helen Soileau's voice in a foyer and a moment later a screw unlocked my cell door and walked me to the front of the jail.

'Saw you on early-morning TV,' Helen said as she drove us back to New Iberia.

'Val Chalons doesn't take prisoners,' I said.

'What were your latents doing at the crime scene, Dave?'

The sky was still pink with sunrise, the air sweet with the smell of flowers and rain, the cane waving in the fields. I started to lie, to say that perhaps indeed I had been at Val's guesthouse on another occasion, even though earlier I had already denied that possibility to her. But I couldn't do it. 'I'm not sure how they got there. I got back on the juice. I was drunk all weekend,' I said.

She took a call on her radio, her expression frozen in place. Then she hung her microphone back on the dash. 'What was that last part?'

'I've got two days' sobriety now,' I said.

'Two days?'

I waited for her to go on. But she didn't. In the silence I could hear the tires of the cruiser on the asphalt. 'I think maybe I went to Val Chalons's guesthouse in a blackout. I think I took a CD from his stereo, one with Ida Durbin's voice on it,' I said.

'Ida Durbin again?'

'The CD is at the house. I think there's a blood smear on it, maybe from my own hand.'

She rubbed at one temple with the ends of her fingers, as though an intolerable migraine had begun to eat its way through her head. 'Maybe it's time for you not to say any more without a lawyer.'

'I didn't kill Honoria.'

'You don't know what you did, so don't give me your doodah. Dave, you make me so mad I want to stop the car and beat the shit out of you. God*damn* it!'

'I'm sorry,' I said.

She swerved the cruiser to the shoulder and got out under a spreading oak tree. She walked up and down by my window, her fists on her hips, the corner of her mouth bitten white. For a moment I thought she was truly going to lose it. She stood still for a long time, her back to me, then got back in the vehicle.

'Helen –'

'Shut up,' she said.

She did not speak again until she turned into my drive. 'Be in my office in one hour, looking sharp, your head out of your ass for a change,' she said.

Doogie Dugas and his posse comitatus had tossed my house from one end to the other. They had even pulled all my lawn tools out of my shed and left them scattered in the yard. The doors to my truck were ajar, the lock on the steel toolbox I had welded to the bed sheared in half by bolt cutters. The driver's seat was still pushed against the steering wheel, the floor area behind it empty of the flop hat and hooded raincoat I had worn during my blackout Saturday.

The irony of Dugas's search was that he had probably tainted any evidence he had seized by using an improperly acquired warrant. The greater irony was the fact that he and his friends had evidently ignored an item they should have picked up.

It was a sheet of yellow legal pad paper, now rain-damaged, speckled with mud, blown into the canebrake that separated my yard from Miss Ellen's. I would have probably paid little attention to it as well, but every day I picked up litter that either blew or was thrown into my yard. It was dated Saturday, 9:15 p.m. and read:

Dear Dave,

Why don't you stay home? Who's taking care of your cat and raccoon? Anyone who neglects or who is cruel to a defenseless creature deserves to be tortured.

I have to tell someone about the secrets nobody in our family will deal with. My father won't admit the harm our silence has caused. Maybe our souls are damned. My prayer today is that hell is oblivion and not a place of torment.

You must call me. I can tell you about Ida Durbin.

Love,

H.

Was she insane? Twisted on coke and booze? Or perhaps touched with an insight into evil that would make most of us shudder? Whatever the answer, she had taken her secrets to the grave.

After I shaved and showered and changed clothes, I placed Honoria's note in one Ziploc bag and put the CD with the blood smear on the surface in another, and drove to the department. Helen was waiting for me, her mood still rumpled. 'What's that?' she said, indicating Honoria's note.

I placed it on her desk. She was standing up, her palms propped on her desk blotter as she read Honoria's words, her chest rising and falling. The door was closed now, the blinds open, and people passing in the corridor made a point of not glancing inside. The room seemed to grow warmer, the sunlight through the window more intense.

'This was in your yard?' Helen said.

'Right.'

'This is your parachute on a murder beef?'

'I don't know what it is. My guess is Honoria was an incest victim.'

'Where in the name of God do you get these ideas?'

'Koko Hebert says Honoria had intercourse in the twenty-four-hour period before she died. She was about to shower in the guesthouse, where Val Chalons lives, not in the main house, where she lived. She had every behavioral characteristic of someone who has been the long-term victim of a sexual predator.'

'Dave, AFIS came back with only one match that didn't belong in that guesthouse – yours.'

'Except I had no motive to murder her. There was DNA in her genital area. I'll bet the lab will show it was left there by a relative. My guess is it belongs either to the father or the brother.'

But I had already lost her attention. 'I must have had two dozen calls this morning,' she said. 'They want you skinned, salted, and hung in a gibbet.'

'Am I suspended?'

'Suspension might be the least of it.'

'What do you want me to do, Helen?'

'Lose the nun.'

'Can't do it.'

'Then please go somewhere else for a while.'

And that's what I did. As far as the water cooler, my face burning as though I had been slapped. Then I went back into her office, the door hanging open behind me.

'You want my shield, just say it.'

'You're always psychoanalyzing other people. Why don't you look inside your own head for a change?'

'What's that supposed to mean?'

'Bootsie died on you and it made you madder than hell.

Your daughter is gone and every day you wake up, you're scared you'll drink again. So you figured out a way to climb on a cross, a place where it's safe and people can't do anything else to you. I don't think you're going to like it up there, bwana.'

The week was not going well. Worse, Clete had called early the previous morning and, without thinking, I told him Jimmie had gotten a lead on Lou Kale and that Kale might be running an escort service out of Miami. *That* was a mistake.

chapter nineteen

By Tuesday afternoon Clete was standing at the registration desk in the lobby of an old ten-story stucco hotel on the beach in Hollywood, Florida, decked out in shades, his pale blue porkpie hat, a tropical shirt printed with bare-breasted hula girls, white polyester Bermuda shorts, and blue tennis shoes threaded with brand-new white laces. He carried a set of golf clubs on one shoulder, a flight bag on the other, registered as C. T. Perkins from Gulfport, Mississippi, and paid cash for his room.

The walls of the hotel were spiderwebbed with cracks, the patio in the center of the building spiked with weeds, the potted jacaranda dying from lack of water. But the view of the ocean from his open window on the top floor was magnificent, the overhead fan adequate to cool the room, the salt air wonderful. Clete propped his feet on the windowsill and punched in the telephone number of the Sea Breeze Escort Service. Down below, the tide was sliding high up on the sand and children were running into the waves, leaping in the froth that sucked back over their tanned bodies. On the third ring Clete found himself talking to a man who called himself Lou Coyne.

'You got the referral where?' Coyne said.

'Stevie Giacano, in New Orleans,' Clete replied.

'Oh yeah, Stevie Gee. In the Teamsters, right? How's ole Stevie doin'?'

'Not too good. He's dead. But he always said your service was tops.'

'We like to think so. So you're hosting a convention, that's what you're saying?'

'I'm about three blocks away from your office. What if I come on down there and maybe we work out a group rate? You give finder fees? I'll take mine in trade.'

'Tell you what, I'll meet you in a half hour at that little outdoor joint by your hotel, the one looks like a straw hut.'

'How will I know you?'

'You won't,' the man who called himself Lou Coyne said, and hung up.

Clete read the newspaper in the lobby, then strolled down the boardwalk to a frozen daiquiri stand, one with a thatched roof, set among a grove of coconut palms. A red-headed woman with a Hawaiian skirt hooked over her bikini sat on the stool next to him and ordered a daiquiri. She looked around at the beach, then said, 'Hi.'

'Hello,' Clete replied.

'Beautiful day,' she said.

'They don't get any better.'

'On vacation?' she said.

'I wish. With me it's all business,' Clete said. He paid for her drink, pushing the five-dollar bill across the counter to the bartender with the heel of his hand, not asking the woman if it was all right. 'C. T. Perkins is the name. I'm staying at the hotel, down the boardwalk there.'

Her eyes were green and there was a smear of lipstick on her teeth. Her breath smelled heavily of cigarettes, and she had a habit of repetitively touching the pads of each of her fingers with her thumb on her left hand while she sipped from her drink.

'I bet you're in the construction business,' she said.

'How'd you know?'

'You've been out in the sun a lot. You have big arms. There're calluses on your hands. But you're probably a supervisor or engineer.'

'I used to be a general contractor. Now I put shopping mall deals together. Whatever blows up their skirt, that's what I do.'

'You up for anything this afternoon?'

'Could be. You got a cell?' he said.

She took a gold retractable pen from a canvas tote and wrote a number on a napkin. 'Thanks for the drink. Keep that number under your hat, will you?' she said.

'They couldn't get it from me at gunpoint,' he replied.

Clete watched her walk away, her face turned in a regal fashion toward the ocean, her hooked skirt molded tightly across her rump. She passed close to a man who wore linen slacks and a purple shirt with white suspenders, and who combed his hair as he walked toward the daiquiri stand. The two of them seemed to exchange glances, then the man sat at a table among the coconut palms, grinned, and pointed a finger at Clete. 'Come talk to me, big man,' he said.

Clete carried his daiquiri to the table and sat down. Lou Coyne's hair was the color of gunmetal, greased, long on the neck. His facial skin had an unnatural shine and hardness to it, as though his youth had been surgically restored at the cost of the softening influences purchased by age.

'If you knew Stevie Gee, you must know his old sidekick, Benny Frizola. Some people call him Benny Freeze,' the man named Lou Coyne said.

'Never heard of him,' Clete replied.

Lou Coyne grinned again. 'So if I understand you, you're organizing a convention here – builders, Teamsters, subcontractors, those kinds of guys – and you need some escorts to show them the city?'

'Not exactly a convention, just a little P.R., get everybody lubricated and in a free-spending mood. Maybe around Thanksgiving. We'll be in town for five days,' Clete said.

Lou Coyne's cheeks were sunken, as though he were sucking the spittle out of his mouth. His ears were small, the way a club fighter's get when he's been too long in the ring. 'So, up front, you know an escort service offers nothing besides sightseeing, companionship, a walk on the beach if you want it, these are nice girls we're talking about here, we're clear on all this?'

'I respect what you got to do, but I don't have time for people's bullshit,' Clete said.

'What'd you say?'

'I can put together a package in Vegas for the same prices I get here. Except some of the guys like to go deep-sea fishing. Besides, the seafood is better here. What can you do for me, Lou?'

Lou Coyne pulled on his nose. 'Slip on a swimsuit. Let's take a dip,' he said.

Clete went back to his hotel and changed into his Everlast boxing trunks and rejoined Lou Coyne on the beach.

'You going to swim in your clothes?' Clete asked.

Coyne began walking toward the surf, dropping his suspenders, pulling off his shirt as he went. 'I ain't got a problem with the human body. Other people do, it's on them,' he replied.

He removed a weighted-down copy of the *Miami Herald* from someone's beach blanket and laid his shirt, shoes, socks, and finally his folded slacks on top of it. He stood raw and white in the sunlight, wearing only a black silk thong that was little more than a sling for his phallus. While other bathers gaped, he flexed his back and rolled his shoulders. 'Let's hit the waves, big man,' he said.

They crashed through the breakers until they were chest-deep in the water, in a flat space between the swells, the beach behind them biscuit-colored and lined with palm trees and hotels that had fallen into decay.

'You thought I was a cop?' Clete said.

'Me? I love cops. I got all the original episodes of *Miami Vice*.'

'Need your prices, Lou.'

Lou Coyne pursed his mouth and thought. 'I can give you ten, no, fifteen percent discount on the item. In terms of girls, I got the whole rainbow. The client acts like a gentleman or the service is discontinued. Before the discount, the various prices are as follows –'

Clete waited until Coyne finished, then said, 'Sounds okay. You remind me of a guy I used to know.'

'Yeah?' Coyne said.

'But his name was Kale. It was back when I was subcontracting on the Texas coast. The guy's name was Lou Kale.'

'No kidding? You never know, huh?'

'Know what?' Clete said.

'Who you're talking to these days. Hey, one other thing? We don't take coupons from *Screw* magazine.'

Clete stared at him blankly.

'That was a joke,' the man who called himself Lou Coyne said.

Clete called me that night from his hotel room and told me of what he had done.

'Get out of there. He's made you,' I said.

'No, the phony name I gave him will check out on the Internet. He bought it. But tell you the truth, I'm not sure he's our guy.'

'Why not?'

'The broad he sent ahead of him to scope me out came by the hotel and asked me to dinner. If they were jobbing

207

me, she would have gone straight for my Johnson.'

'They made you, Cletus.'

'You never worked Vice. These people are not that complicated. Dave, you and I got inside the Mob and they were never on to us. Coyne or whatever bought it. I think this broad Babette is just a working girl.'

'*Babette?*'

'Kind of cute, don't you think?'

How do you tell your best friend that his old enemy, a weakness for female validation, has just deep-sixed his brains?

'Call me on your cell in three hours,' I said.

'Everything is solid. I'm going to exclude Lou Coyne as our Galveston pimp or find Ida Durbin. Now, pull your dork out of the wall socket.'

But I did not hear from Clete again that evening and he did not respond to my calls.

She gazed out at the ocean, her chin tilted up in the breeze, and said she was originally from Hawaii, that she had been a bookkeeper before coming to Miami to work as a hostess at a supper club. But after her ex had blown town on a bigamy charge and stopped her alimony payments, she had drifted into the life. She said Babette was her real name, and that it had been the name of her grandmother, who had been born in Tahiti. Her knees touched Clete's under the table as she said these things, on a fishing pier that was framed darkly against the ocean and the wan summer light that still hung in the sky, even though it was after 9:00 p.m.

She had paid for the hamburgers and beer herself, and had made no commercial proposition to him of any kind. Her hair was mahogany-colored, bleached on the tips by the sun, and hung loosely on her bare shoulders. She lit a cigarette with a tiny gold lighter, crossed her legs, and smoked with her spine hunched, her posture like a question mark, as though she were cold.

'Want to get out of the wind?' Clete said.

'No, I like it here. I come here often to be by myself. I write poetry sometimes.'

'You do?'

'It's not very good. But I'm gonna take a creative writing class at Miami-Dade Community College this fall. I showed my poems to a professor there. He said I had talent but I needed to study.'

'I bet your poems are good,' Clete said.

The sun had sunk beyond the Everglades, and the ocean was dark and flecked with whitecaps. At the end of the pier some Cuban kids had hooked a hammerhead shark and were fighting to hoist it clear of the water and over the guardrail. The woman smoked her cigarette and watched them, the thumb on her left hand repeatedly tapping the tips of her fingers. One of the kids drove a knife into the shark's head, impaling it on a plank. 'Yuk,' Babette said.

'I got to ask you something,' Clete said.

'Go ahead,' she replied, screwing her cigarette out inside a bottle cap.

'You work for Lou Coyne?'

'Yes, I do,' she said, smiling in a self-deprecating way.

'You were checking me out at the daiquiri stand?' he said.

'It comes with my paycheck.'

'I'm not knocking it.'

'I know you're not,' she said.

'I just thought Coyne might be a guy I knew a long time ago, a Galveston guy by the name of Lou Kale.'

'He's always used the name "Coyne" since I've worked for him. He's a pretty good guy, actually. He's just got to be careful.'

'Dude I knew was hooked up with a gal by the name of Ida Durbin.'

209

'You got me. Ask Lou. You like the hamburgers?'

'They're swell.'

'You seem like a sweet guy. Look, I've got to check on my cousin's house. I'm taking care of her parakeet while she's out of town. You want to come?'

They drove in her compact down I-95 and took an exit into a neighborhood of cinder-block apartment buildings and one-story wood-frame homes that looked like they had been built during the Depression years. Babette entered a dark street and turned into the driveway of a paintless house. The front porch was lit and the screens on it were stained with rust, the yard filled with waving shadows from clusters of untrimmed banana trees.

'Your cousin lives in Little Havana?' Clete said.

'She's not Hispanic, if that's what you mean,' Babette replied.

'No, that's not what I meant,' he said.

'Before we go in, I need to tell you something. The cell number I gave you, it wasn't mine. It belongs to a dial-in prayer service.'

'Really?'

'See, Lou took a bunch of us to Lake Charles, to the hotel and casino on the lake there. We met this famous evangelical leader. It was like a spiritual experience for me. I think for the first time in a long while I can stop living the way I do. But I don't have enough money to quit yet and plus I got a little drug problem.'

'That's why they have Twelve-Step programs,' Clete said.

She had cut the engine and now she opened the door partway, lighting the interior of the compact. 'I just wanted you to know how it is with me and why I gave you the prayer number,' she said. 'I'm just trying to be honest.'

Clete did not try to follow her reasoning. He waited for her to ask him for money. But she didn't. 'I need to use the bathroom. Then I'll clean the birdcage and we can go,' she said.

The inside of the house was clean and squared away, the furniture bright, the rooms air-conditioned by two window units. Through a bedroom door he could see a water bed and a lava lamp on the nightstand. Babette went into the bathroom, then Clete heard the toilet flush and the faucet running before she came back out.

'Why do you have that funny look on your face?' she said.

'Sorry.'

'You think this is a fuck pad?'

'Hey –' he said.

'If that's what you think, say so.'

'Not me,' he said, and tried to smile.

'I've got a pitcher of rum punch in the fridge. You want some?' she said.

'I'm good,' Clete said.

'I can't find my aspirin. My head is coming off. Somebody is always hiding my aspirin,' she said, opening and slamming cabinets all over the kitchen.

'I thought this was your cousin's place.'

'It is. I just visit here sometimes.'

Clete decided he would have a drink after all. Babette broke apart a tray of ice, dropped cubes in two tall glasses that had been standing straight up in the dry rack, and filled them with rum punch from the pitcher. She took a long drink and the color bloomed in her face. 'Oh, that's a lot better,' she said.

'You got a pretty heavy jones?' Clete said.

'I got into smoking China white because I didn't want to infect. But I ended up using needles anyway. I've got it down to two balloons a day. They say if you can get it down to one, it's mostly manageable.'

Clete drank from the punch, crunching ice between his molars, and tried to look attentive. He put a cigarette in his mouth and asked to borrow her cigarette lighter.

'I didn't think you smoked,' she said.

'Just once in a while.' He opened and closed his mouth to clear a popping sound from his ears. 'You never heard of a hooker name of Ida Durbin?'

'I already told you. You think I'm lying?'

'No, I just feel kind of weird,' he replied.

He reached out to take the lighter from her hand, but the gold surface seemed to turn soft and sink in the middle, like a lump of butter inside the warmth of a stove. His fingers went past her hand and knocked over a salt shaker, as though his motors had been snipped in half at the back of his brain. His mouth and throat became instantly dry; the overhead lighting caused his eyes to well with tears.

'What's happening?' he said.

She stared at him mutely, her expression caught between fear and guilt. 'I have a little girl. I've got to get clean. Just don't lie to them. It makes them really mad,' she said.

'Come here,' he said, catching a piece of fabric with one hand.

But she pulled her canvas tote from him, looked back once, and rushed out the back door into the darkness.

Clete felt himself slip from the chair and crash on the linoleum, his drink glass shattering inches from his face.

Both the men who came through the front door carried lengths of chain and looked Hispanic. One wore a formfitting strap undershirt and had shaved armpits and the tapered lats and flat chest of a boxer. The other man was much bigger, his skin slick with black hair. The fingers of his right hand were inserted in the holes of a pair of brass knuckles.

A third man entered the house. He wore white slacks belted high up on his waist and a western shirt sewn with chains of purple and red flowers. 'We tossed your room and found your P.I. buzzer. Sorry to do this to you, big man, but it's out of my control,' Lou Coyne said.

'Yeah, you came here to get fucked, and that's what you got, spermo – fucked,' the man in the formfitting undershirt said. Both he and the other Hispanic man laughed.

Lou Coyne squatted down eye-level with Clete. 'You working for Robicheaux? You working for some political people? These guys here are serious. Don't underestimate their potential,' he said.

Clete tried to rise to his feet, then collapsed again, pieces of broken glass knifing into his back.

'This ain't my way, big man. *Please* don't do this to either one of us,' Coyne said.

But the words Clete heard were muffled, distorted, like someone shouting inside the downdraft of a helicopter. In his mind's eye he saw a hooch burning brightly on the edge of a flooded rice field. Boxes of AK-47 rounds were exploding inside the heat, and in the distance, against a storm-sealed sky, he could see a Zippo-track with a Confederate battle flag tied to the radio antenna grinding over a dike that flanged the rice field, automatic weapons fire dancing across the water's surface.

Clete got on his hands and knees and began crawling.

That's when a chain whipped out of the air and raked across his neck and the side of his face. Then the man with animal hair on his skin straddled him and drove the pair of brass knuckles deep into his back and a second time into his neck.

What had they given him? Clete guessed it was chloral hydrate. Or maybe acid. Or maybe both. The room had melted, the colors in the walls and floor dissolving and running together. One of the men was now wrapping a chain around his forehead, tightening the links into his scalp. Clete drove his elbow into the man's scrotum and heard him scream and the chain rattle to the floor.

Clete crashed into a laundry room off the kitchen, knocking over an ironing board and a plastic basket filled with dried clothes. On his knees, he slammed the door behind him and shot the bolt. A cast-iron pipe, an old drain of some kind, extended four feet high up on one wall. He gripped it at the top, wrenched it back and forth until it broke loose from a rusted connection, then ripped it out of the floor.

The pipe was heavy and thick in his palms. The floor seemed to be pitching under his feet, the roar of helicopter blades still thundering in his head. Or was that one of his attackers throwing his weight into the bolted door? The sounds in his head were so loud he couldn't tell where they originated, but the door was shaking hard, vibrating through the walls and floor. Then the bolt splintered loose from the jamb and the door flew open in Clete's face. Clete looked into the close-set pig-eyes of the man with brass knuckles, and drove the pipe into his mouth, breaking his lips against his teeth.

The man held his hands to the lower portion of his face, his brass knuckles shiny with the blood and saliva that drained through his fingers. Clete lifted the pipe like a baseball bat and swung it into the other Hispanic man's jaw, then across his back and rib cage. Both Hispanic men tried to shield their heads with their forearms and escape the blows raining down on them, but Clete followed them into the backyard, hitting them again and again, the pipe ringing in his palms.

'They're done! Jesus Christ! *We're* done!' Lou Coyne said. 'You're gonna kill them guys! Hey, are you hearing me?'

Clete stumbled out of the backyard, dropping the pipe on the front sidewalk. The air smelled of smoke, perhaps from outdoor barbecue pits, and mist was blowing off an elevated highway in the distance. He staggered down the street toward a clapboard bar that glowed with the hazy iridescence of a pistol flare burning inside fog. Again, he thought he heard the downdraft of helicopter blades and the labored breath of people running, clutching at his arms, speaking words to him that made no sense.

Totally stoned, zoned, and shit-blown up the Mekong. I'm not going to make it, he thought.

Then, while a Miami P.D. helicopter with a searchlight roared by overhead, the loving hands of women who made him think of black angels guided him into the backseat of a car. Their lips were arterial-red, their perfume like that of an enclosed garden inside the car, their hands cool and gentle as they wiped his face and hair and the cuts in his scalp.

'What's the haps, ladies?' Clete said, and passed out.

chapter twenty

Clete arrived back in New Iberia the following evening on the Sunset Limited, ensconced in a Pullman bedroom with his flight bag and golf clubs, although he had little memory of being put aboard the train.

'These were black hookers?' I asked as I drove him to his cottage at the motor court.

'Except the woman driving. She was white. A beanpole with a corn bread accent, but definitely in charge,' he replied. 'She got on the cell phone and gave hell to this guy Lou Whatever.'

'The pimp asked you if you were hooked up politically?'

'Yeah, that brings up another subject. Remember I told you Raphael Chalons had this televangelical character fronting points for his casino interests and you blew me off?'

'Vaguely.'

'The dial-a-prayer number Babette gave me belongs to a TV huckster named Colin Alridge. He's the same guy who's working for Chalons. Babette said she and Lou Whatever and some other whores visited the casino in Lake Charles and met him. He looks like a college kid out of the 1940s. I think Babette creamed her pants when she shook his hand.'

'Why should people be beating you up with chains because of Raphael Chalons's connection to a lobbyist?'

'I don't know,' he replied. He was quiet a long time, lost in thought, his back and neck marbled with bruises. 'There's one other thing I didn't tell you.'

I looked at him.

'The white woman, the beanpole with corn fritters in her mouth? Before she and the black girls poured me into the Pullman, I'm pretty sure she said, "Tell Dave and Jimmie Robicheaux I said hello." What do you think of that, noble mon?'

Was the white woman Ida Durbin? There was no way to know. When Clete told me of his experience in Miami, he was still half-swacked on the drugs that the prostitute named Babette had probably dropped in his glass before she poured the rum punch into it.

I also wondered if the story about Raphael Chalons's connection with an evangelical political huckster had any relevance. If a political operative wired into the White House was on his payroll, Chalons's breeding would probably restrain him from revealing that fact at a formal dinner, but he would not care if someone else did. He was jaded, corrupt, sexually profligate, politically pragmatic, but not a hypocrite, a gentleman in the same way the Prince of Darkness is.

Friday morning Jimmie got back to town from New Orleans and I met him for lunch at Victor's Cafeteria.

'The white woman who saved Clete's butt said to tell you and me hello?' he said.

'That's what he says. But he was still half-loaded when he got off the train.'

'She was a beanpole with a peckerwood accent?'

'Something like that.' I was beginning to regret I had brought up the possibility that Ida Durbin was indeed

217

alive and in Miami and hooked up with Lou Kale. 'Jim, if this woman is Ida, she's better forgotten. Let the past slide.'

'*That* from you? I've had her death on my conscience since 1958.' He had stopped eating. His eyes glistened, and he coughed slightly into his napkin to hide his emotion.

'I've got a couple of calls in to Miami P.D. to check out the house where Clete got knocked around. Give me some time before you do something rash,' I said.

'I need to go back over there,' Jimmie said, picking up the check, his lunch unfinished.

The technical processes involving DNA identification are complicated and time-consuming. There is often a long waiting list at both federal and state laboratories, particularly in an era when large numbers of homicide and rape cases are appealed based on evidence that was gathered and stored years ago, before DNA identification was possible. But Mack Bertrand at our crime lab had pushed through the work on Honoria Chalons in less than four days. He called me at the office just before five on Friday.

'No match with the Baton Rouge serial killer, no match with anything in the national database,' he said.

'I never thought the Baton Rouge guy did this,' I said.

'What *did* you think?'

'Did the semen come from a relative?'

'No.'

'You're sure?'

'What kind of question is that?'

'It speaks for itself,' I replied.

'If you're talking about incest, this lab has no evidence of that.' He paused a moment. 'Dave, can I offer some advice?'

'What?'

'I'm not a fan of either Raphael or Valentine Chalons. But I think you're barking at the moon on this one.'

'Thanks for your time.'

'My wife and I are taking the kids to the Little League game tonight. Care to join us?'

'Tied up. But you're the best, Mack,' I said.

I had learned long ago you can have all the friends you want when you're in tall cotton. But your real friends are the ones you meet during hard times, when you've blown out your doors and every sunrise comes to you like a testimony to personal failure. Mack Bertrand was a real friend.

It was Friday night and Molly was at a meeting of Pax Christi at Grand Coteau. I had deliberately stayed away from her since Doogie Dugas had arrested me on camera at my home and Val Chalons had used footage on his various news channels of Molly standing half-undressed in the bedroom doorway. She herself was undaunted by the experience and I suspect had long ago become inured to the wickedness that the socially respectable were capable of. But I did not want to see her hurt more than she already had been, and at the same time I wanted to see her terribly.

At sunset I took a long walk down Main, through the business district and out to the west side, where there is a neatly mowed green lot that is the only reminder of a smithy and wagonworks that was there when I was a child during World War II.

The wagonworks was a very old structure even then, its red paint cracked and faded by the elements, the wood planks shrunken and warped by the heat in the forge. The owner was Mr. Antoine, a small, wizened man who spoke beautiful French but little English. At that time in New Iberia there were black people still alive who remembered the Emancipation, what they came to call 'Juneteenth,' and there were white people who had seen General Banks's Federal soldiers, twenty thousand of them, march through town in pursuit of the chivalric Confederate general, Alfred Mouton. But our only surviving Confederate veteran was Mr. Antoine.

He loved to regale us with tales of what he always referred to as 'La Guerre.' He had served in Jackson's Shenandoah Campaign and had been with Jubal Early when Early had thrown twenty-five thousand men against the Union line just before Lee's surrender at Appomattox. Mr. Antoine's regiment was caught in a cornfield and blown into piles of gray and butternut rags by canister and grapeshot. But the point of Mr. Antoine's tale about the last days of the war was not the carnage, or the crows that pecked out the eyes of southern dead, or the snuffing sounds of feral hogs that would come at dusk. Instead, Mr. Antoine's story was about a fourteen-year-old drummer boy from Alabama who found his regimental colors in the dust, tied them to a musket barrel, and mounted a terrified stray horse.

The Union soldiers two hundred yards up the slope could not believe what they saw next – a boy without shoes, clamped on the spine of a horse like a clothespin, charging across his own dead toward a line of pointed weapons that could have reduced him and his animal to a bloody mist.

But no soldier fired a shot. When the boy's horse leaped across their wall, they pulled him from the saddle and pinned him to the dirt, all the while laughing, one of them saying, 'You ain't got to fight no more, son. You're on the Lord's side now.'

Mr. Antoine still carried a pistol ball in his forearm and would let us children run our fingers over the hard lump it made under his skin. Once, in a dark mood, he decried the war and described the bloody shuddering and gurgling sounds of a young Union soldier who had died on Mr. Antoine's bayonet. But the story he obviously took most pleasure in retelling was that of the Alabama drummer boy. Now, after many years, I think I understand why.

Mr. Antoine did not let the evil of the world overcome him, just as the Union soldiers behind the limestone wall did not let the war rob them of their humanity; just as military defeat and fear of death could not undo the drummer boy who placed honor and loyalty to the dead above concern for his own life.

As I stood on the sidewalk, looking at a green lot bordered in back by live oaks and Bayou Teche, I could almost see Mr. Antoine's forge puff alight in the shadows and hear his burst of laughter at the completion of his story about the Alabama drummer boy. I wanted to tell him that flags were emblematic of much more than national boundaries. But I suspected Mr. Antoine had learned that lesson a long time ago.

The funeral Mass for Honoria Chalons was held Saturday morning in Jeanerette. I attended it, although I took a pew at the back of the church and made no attempt to offer condolences or to accompany the funeral procession to the cemetery. That afternoon I was at Wal-Mart and had one of those experiences that make me wonder if our commonality lies less in our humanity than the simple gravitational pull of the earth and a grave that is already dug and numbered.

The sweeping breadth of the store's interior was crowded with people for whom a Wal-Mart is a gift from God. In my hometown, most of these are poor and uneducated, and assume that the low-paying jobs that define their lives are commonplace throughout the country. The fact that the goods they buy are often shoddily made, the clothes sewn in Third World sweatshops by people not unlike themselves, is an abstraction that seems to have no application to the low price on the item.

By late Saturday afternoon every trash can in front of the store is overflowing on the sidewalk. The parking lot is littered with dumped ashtrays, fast-food containers, chicken bones, half-eaten fruit, soft drink and beer cans, and disposable diapers that have been flattened into the asphalt by car tires. It's the place where the poor go, or those who don't want to drive twenty miles to Lafayette. It's not where I expected to see Raphael Chalons on the day of his daughter's burial.

But he was three places in front of me at the cash register, dressed in a dark suit and a tie and starched white shirt, even though the temperature had been in the nineties all day. His hair was as sleek and black as a seal's pelt, his face that of a stricken man.

In one hand he held a jar of peanut brittle while he stared out the front window. In his tailored suit and shined shoes, he looked like a visitor from an alien world.

'You got to put it on the counter, suh,' the cashier said. She was a short, overweight Cajun woman, with a round face and thick glasses and hair pulled back tightly on her head.

'Pardon?' he said.

'You got to put the peanut brittle down so's I can scan it,' she said.

'Yes, I see,' he replied.

'Wit' the tax, that's fo' dol'ars and t'ree cents,' she said.

'It's what?'

She repeated the amount. But he didn't take his wallet from his pocket. She tried to smile. Her eyes seemed unnaturally large behind the magnification of her glasses and it was obvious she knew something was wrong and that she could not correct it. The two people waiting in line immediately behind Raphael Chalons took their purchases to another counter.

'Suh, you want to pay me? It's fo' dol'ars and t'ree cents,' the cashier said.

'Oh yes, excuse me. I'm sure I have my wallet here somewhere. How much did you say?'

I pushed a five-dollar bill across the counter to the cashier. She took it without speaking, returned my change, and dropped Raphael Chalons's jar of peanut brittle in a plastic sack. I picked it up and handed it to him. He walked a short distance away, then stopped in the concourse and removed the jar from the sack and read the label on it, oblivious to the shoppers who had to walk around him.

'Can I offer you a ride to your automobile, Mr. Chalons?' I said.

'No, I'm quite all right. But thank you for your courtesy,' he replied, looking at me as though my face were not quite in focus.

'May I speak with you outside?' I asked.

He walked ahead of me, the jar of peanut brittle clasped in his hand, the sack with the receipt inside it blowing away in the draft through the sliding doors. The woman who checked purchases at the entrance held up her hand to stop him. I knew her and placed my palm on Mr. Raphael's shoulder and gestured at her in a reassuring way.

He entered the crosswalk and was almost hit by an SUV.

'Let me arrange to have someone drive you home,' I said.

He stared at the label on the jar and either did not hear me or chose to ignore the content of my words. 'The store didn't have the kind she liked,' he said.

'Sir?'

'Honoria loved peanut brittle and pralines. I was going to bring her back some from New Orleans, but I forgot. It was such a small gift. But I forgot to buy it.'

'Mr. Chalons, I know your family bears me enmity, but I want to offer my sympathies. I also want you to understand that I never had a romantic liaison with your daughter and that I always respected her. Both my mother and my second wife, Annie, died at the hands of violent men, and for that reason I think I can understand the nature of your loss. I thought your daughter was a good person. It was an honor to have been her friend.'

He looked at the parking lot, the heat shimmering on the rows of vehicles, an American flag popping on an iron pole.

'That's very kind of you,' he said. 'But you're a police officer, and you were in our guesthouse for reasons of a romantic nature or to make use of my daughter in a legal investigation. Whichever it was, sir, it belies your statement now.'

I should have walked away. But there are certain moments in our lives that even the saints would probably not abide, and I suspect being impugned as a liar is one of them. 'I think your son is at the heart of a great iniquity,' I said.

'My son?' he said, one eye narrowing with confusion. 'Which son are you talking about? What are you saying to me? My son is —'

He pinched his temples and broke off in midsentence, as though both his words and thoughts had been stolen from him. A gust of hot wind blew a fast-food container tumbling past the cuffs of his trousers, splattering the fabric and the tops of his shoes.

Later, I went to Molly's cottage on the bayou. There was probably every reason not to go there, but I had tired of wearing the scarlet letter and seeing others try to sew it upon Molly's blouse as well. The truth was Molly had no official or theological status as a nun and in the eyes of the Church was a member of the laity. Let Val Chalons and those who served him do as they wished. I'd take my chances with the Man on High, I told myself.

My father, Big Aldous, spoke a form of English that was hardly a language. Once, when explaining to a neighbor the disappearance of the neighbor's troublesome hog, he said, 'I ain't meaned to hurt your pig, no, but I guess I probably did when my tractor wheel accidentally run over its head and broke its neck, and I had to eat it, me.'

But when he spoke French he could translate his ideas in ways that were quite elevated. On the question of God's nature, he used to say, 'There are only two things you have to remember about Him: He has a sense of humor, and because He's a gentleman He always keeps His word.'

And that's what I told Molly Boyle on the back porch of her cottage, on a late Saturday afternoon in New Iberia, Louisiana, in the summer of the year 2004.

'Why are you telling me this?' she said.

'Because I say screw Val Chalons and his television stations. I also say screw anyone who cares to condemn us.'

'You came over here to tell me that?'

'No.'

'Then *what?*'

The sun went behind a rain cloud, burning a purple hole through its center. The cypress and willow trees along the bayou swelled with wind. 'I say why do things halfway?'

'Will you please take the mashed potatoes out of your mouth?' she said.

'How about we get married tonight?'

'Married? Tonight?'

'Unless you're doing something else.'

She started to remove a strand of hair from her eye, then forgot what she was doing. She fixed her eyes on mine, her face perfectly still, her mouth slightly parted. 'Get married where?' she asked.

'In Baton Rouge. I have a priest friend who's a little unorthodox. I told him we wanted to take our vows.'

'Without asking me?'

'That's why I'm doing it now.'

She was wearing jeans without a belt, a Ragin' Cajun T-shirt, and moccasins on her feet. She made a clicking sound with her mouth, and I had no idea what it might mean. Then she stepped on top of my shoes and put her arms around my neck and pressed her head against my chest. 'Oh, Dave,' she said. Then, as though language were inadequate or she were speaking to an obtuse person, she said it again, 'Oh, Dave.'

And that's the way we did it – in a small church located among pine trees, twelve miles east of the LSU campus, while lights danced in the clouds and the air turned to ozone and pine needles showered down on the church roof.

chapter twenty-one

We slept late the next morning, then had breakfast in the backyard on the old redwood table from my house that had burned. I had forgotten how fine it was to eat breakfast on a lovely morning, under oak trees on a tidal stream, with a woman you loved. And I also had forgotten how good it was to be free of booze again and on the square with my AA program, the world, and my Higher Power.

At first Tripod had been unsure about Molly, until she gave him a bowl of smoked salmon. Then she couldn't get rid of him. While she tried to eat, he climbed in her lap, sticking his head up between her food and mouth, turning in circles, his tail hitting her in the face. I started to put him in his hutch.

'He'll settle down in a minute,' Molly said.

'Tripod has a little problem with incontinence.'

'That's different,' she said.

But before I could gather him out of her lap, his head lifted up suddenly and his nose sniffed at the wind blowing from the front of the house. He scampered up a live oak and peered back down at us from a leafy bough. I heard the doorbell ring.

'Be right back,' I said to Molly.

Raphael Chalons was at my front door, dressed in

slacks and a sports coat out of the 1940s, a Panama hat hooked on one finger, his shoulders and back as straight as a soldier's. 'You were very thoughtful in paying for my purchase yesterday at the Wal-Mart store. But I forgot to reimburse you,' he said. He held up a five-dollar bill that was folded stiffly between two fingers.

I opened the screen and took the money from his hand. I had hoped his mission was a single-purpose one. But he remained on the gallery, gazing at the trees in the yard and the squirrels that darted across the grass. 'Can I invite you in?' I said.

'Thank you,' he said, and stepped inside, his eyes examining the interior of my home. 'I want to hire you to find the man who murdered my daughter, Mr. Robicheaux.'

'I'm a sheriff's detective, Mr. Chalons, not a private investigator.'

'A man is what he does. Titles are a distraction created to deceive obtuse people. I want the monster who killed my daughter either in jail or dead.'

'My fingerprints were at the crime scene. In some people's eyes I should be a suspect.'

'Those might be my son's perceptions, but they're not mine. Valentine is sometimes not a good judge of character. You may have a penchant for alcohol, Mr. Robicheaux, but you're not a murderer. That's an absurdity. I know it and so do you.'

'I'm complimented by your offer, but it's not an appropriate one.'

'I think a degenerate or psychotic person wandered in from the highway and did this terrible thing to my daughter. But I can't seem to convince anyone else of that. Some speculate it's the Baton Rouge serial killer.'

'The Baton Rouge guy abducts his victims and rapes them before killing them. Bondage is part of his M.O., as well as baiting the authorities. The guy who killed Honoria is somebody else.'

He pulled at an earlobe. 'I have to find out who. If nothing else, I have to exclude people who might have had opportunity or motivation,' he said, glancing sideways at me. 'I can't live in ignorance about the circumstances of her death. I just cannot do that. No father can.'

There was no point in continuing the conversation. For a lifetime his money had bought him access and control, and now it was of no value to him.

'As you suggest, it may have been a random killing, Mr. Chalons. Deranged and faceless men wander the country. Sometimes they commit horrible crimes over a period of decades and are not caught.' I made no reference to the fact a cross had been incised inside Honoria's hairline.

'So you do think that could be the case with my daughter?'

I saw what seemed a hopeful glimmer in his eye, as though I had presented him with good news. Or maybe I was reading him wrong. 'I have no idea, sir,' I replied.

He unhooked his hat from his finger and straightened the brim, then glanced through the back window into the yard. 'Ah, the outlaw nun who's purchased you an inordinate amount of negative attention,' he said.

'The outlaw nun is now my wife.'

'Is that meant as a joke?'

'That's Molly Robicheaux out there, Mr. Chalons — not a nun, not an outlaw, but my wife.'

'Well, she's a disciple of liberation theology and has been at odds with our government's policies in Central America, but no matter. *Chacun à son goût*, huh?'

He let himself out without saying good-bye, then paused on the gallery and fitted on his Panama hat. I followed him outside. 'Run that statement by me again?'

'Your wife is a traitor, Mr. Robicheaux. Perhaps she's done many good deeds for the Negroes in our area, but she is nonetheless a traitor. If you choose to marry her, that's your business. I'm an old man and many of my attitudes are probably overly traditional.'

I stepped close to him. 'I don't wish to offend you, Mr. Chalons –' I began, a phosphorous match flaming alight somewhere in the center of my head.

'But what?'

I sucked in my cheeks and widened my eyes and looked out at the tranquility of the day. 'Nothing, sir. My wife and I both wish you the very best and extend our sympathies and hope that all good things come to you and your family.'

Then I rejoined Molly in the backyard and did not mention my exchange with Raphael Chalons. Tripod climbed down from his perch in the live oak, and Snuggs appeared out of the bamboo, his tail pointed straight up, as stiff as a broomstick. The four of us commenced to share breakfast at the redwood table.

When the world presents itself in the form of a green-gold playground, blessed with water and flowers and wind and centuries-old oak trees, and when you're allowed to share all these things on a fine Sunday morning with people and animals you love, why take on the burden of the spiritually afflicted?

That afternoon I jogged through City Park and saw Clete sailing a Frisbee with a bunch of black kids by the baseball diamond. He was bare-chested, wearing only a pair of swim trunks and his porkpie hat, his skin running with sweat.

'Married?' he said.

'Right. Last night. Got something smart to say?' I said.

'Know somebody a few weeks, start a shitstorm all over town, then hit the altar with about three hours' planning . . . Seems normal to me,' he said.

I told him about Raphael Chalons's offer to put me on his payroll.

'That's what rich guys do. I don't see the big deal there,' he said.

'No, I think he wants to prove to himself that someone close to him didn't kill his daughter.'

Clete sailed the Frisbee to a black kid, then sat on a bench in the shade and drank from a glass of iced tea. He wiped his hair and chest with a towel. There were strawberry bruises ringed around his brow and scabs in his scalp where his tormentors in Miami had wrapped a chain around his head. 'So you told the old man to fuck himself?' he said.

'Not in those words.'

'You should have. We need to take it to them.'

'In what way?' I said.

'Same rules as when we were at NOPD – bust 'em or dust 'em.'

'That's why we're not at NOPD any longer.'

'It's not over between me and this Lou Kale dude, either. By the way, where's Jimmie?'

'I think he may have gone to find Ida Durbin.'

'Think?'

'I don't have his umbilical cord stapled to the corner of my desk. You're the one who brought back the story about Ida saving your ass. Now, give it a rest.'

'Married life must really be agreeing with you.'

'Clete, you can absolutely drive people crazy. I mean it. You need your own Zip code and time zone. Every time I have a conversation with you, I feel like I have blood coming out of my ears.'

'What'd I say?' he replied, genuinely perplexed.

The only sound was the creak of the trees and the kids playing by the ball diamond. 'Molly wants you to come over for dinner this evening. We called earlier but you weren't home,' I said.

'Why didn't you try my cell?'

'I don't remember.'

'Better check with your wife again.'

You didn't put the slide on Clete Purcel. But at 6:00 p.m.

he was at the house anyway, resplendent in a new blue suit, his face glowing with aftershave. He clutched a dozen red roses in each meaty paw, a wedding gift wrapped in ribbon and satin paper clamped under one arm. It contained a sterling silver jewelry box that probably cost him several hundred dollars. 'I'm really happy for Dave,' I heard him say to Molly when I was in another room. 'He's got polka dot giraffes running around in his head, but he's the best guy I've ever known.'

On Monday morning I undertook a task that no drunk willingly embarks upon. I tried to find out what I had done during a blackout, where I had gone, and the identity of the people who had seen me commit acts that were so embarrassing, depraved, or even monstrous that my conscious mind would not allow me to remember them.

I checked out a cruiser and returned to the camp in the Atchafalaya Basin where I had awakened on a Sunday morning, hovering on the edges of psychosis, praying the sky might rain Jack Daniel's at any moment and let my drunkard's game go into extra innings.

I found the Creole woman who had watched over me that morning and who had told me I had been in the company of poachers and men who carried knives. Her name was Clarise Lantier, and she was picking up trash behind the lakefront bar her husband operated, stuffing it heavily into a gunnysack. She wore trousers and men's work shoes, and when she stooped over and stared at me sideways, her recessed, milky-blue eye and misshapen face were like those of a female Quasimodo.

'Who were these poachers and men with knives, Miss Clarise?' I asked.

'They live yonder, 'cross the lake. Don't ax me their names, either, 'cause they don't give them. Maybe they from up nort'.'

'How do you know?'

'They talk different from us.'

'You're not telling me a whole lot.'

'They dangerous men, Mr. Dave. That's enough to know, ain't it?' she said.

But she gave me directions to their camp, anyway. I drove on a dirt track around the northern rim of the lake, through stands of swamp maples and persimmon and gum trees. The interior of the woods was dark with shade, the grass a pale green, the canopy rippling in the wind. On the east shore I saw a shack built on stilts by the water's edge, an outboard and a pirogue tied under it. A pickup with crab traps in back and a Tennessee plate was parked up on the high ground, a bullet hole in the rear window.

There are not many places left in the United States where people can get off the computer, stop filing tax returns, and in effect become invisible. The rain forests in the Cascades and parts of West Montana come to mind, and perhaps the 'Glades still offer hope to those who wish to resign from modern times. The other place is the Atchafalaya Basin.

I got out of the cruiser and stood behind the opened door, my right hand on the butt of my .45. 'It's Dave Robicheaux, Iberia Parish Sheriff's Department. I need somebody to come down here and talk to me,' I called up at the shack.

A dark-haired man with a ragged beard appeared in the back doorway, just above the wood steps that led down to dry ground. 'Holy shit, you're a cop?' he said.

'Keep your hands where I can see them, please,' I said. 'Who else is in the camp?'

'Nobody. They went to run the trot line.'

'Come down here, please,' I said.

His body was so thin it looked skeletal. His jeans and T-shirt were filthy, his neck beaded with dirt rings. He

233

walked slowly down the steps, as though his connective tissue barely held his bones together. It was impossible to tell his age or estimate his potential. He seemed ageless, without cultural reference, painted on the air. He had teeth on one side of his mouth and none on the other. There was a black glaze in his eyes, a long, tapered skinning knife in a scabbard on his belt. His odor was like scrapings from an animal hide that have burned in a fire.

'I sure didn't make you for no lawman,' he said.

'What's your name, podna?'

'Same name it was when we met you 'cross the lake at the bar – Vassar Twitty.'

'I'm not here to bother you guys about game regulations, Vassar. I don't care what kind of history you might have in other places, either. But I've got a personal problem I think you might be able to help me with. I went on a bender and don't know what I did.'

It felt easier saying it than I had thought. He sat down on a step, his knees splayed, and looked about the ground with an idiotic grin on his face.

'Want to let me in on the joke?' I asked.

'You was pretty pissed off. We kept telling you to just have another drink and come coon hunting with us. But you was set on getting even with some guy.'

'Which guy?' I said.

'Some TV newsman you said was jamming you up. We tried to get your keys away from you, but there wasn't nothing for it.'

'For what?' I said, swallowing.

'When a man wants to rip somebody from his liver to his lights, you leave him alone. We left you alone. I reckon nothing bad happened or you wouldn't be driving a cruiser. Right? Boy, you was sure stewed,' he said.

The wind gusted off the lake. It must have been ninety in the shade, but my face felt as cold and bright as if I had bathed it in ice water.

I wasn't in a good state of mind when I got back to the department. Could I have gone to Valentine Chalons's guesthouse and in a bloodlust attacked his sister? How do you reach memories that are locked inside a black box?

I had another problem, too, one I had kept pushing to the edges of my consciousness. I went into Helen's office and closed the door behind me. 'You don't look too hot,' she said.

'I found a guy in the Basin I was drinking with the night Honoria Chalons was murdered. He said I talked about ripping up Val Chalons. He said he and his friends tried to stop me but I took off in my truck.'

'I think we know all that, don't we?'

'You've been protecting me, Helen.'

'No,' she said.

'I gave you that CD with a blood smear on it. You didn't turn it over to Doogie Dugas.'

'Because it didn't come from the crime scene. Because Doogie is an incompetent idiot.'

'I know that's Honoria's blood on it.'

'No, you don't. Listen, Dave, Val Chalons has done everything in his power to put your head on a stick. But luminol doesn't lie. There were no blood traces in your truck, your clothes, or in your house. Now stop building a case against yourself.'

'Raphael Chalons came to my house yesterday and tried to put me on his payroll,' I said.

'That's interesting,' she said, looking at the tops of her nails.

'One other item. Molly Boyle and I got married Saturday night.'

Her elbow was propped on her desk. She rested her chin on her knuckles, her face softening. She seemed to think a long time before she spoke. 'You did it.'

'Did what?'

'Figured out a way to marry your own church. No, don't say anything. Just quietly disappear. Bwana say "bye" now.'

Jimmie's resourcefulness rarely let him down. His friendship with police officers, private investigators, and people in the life extended from Key Biscayne, Florida, to Brownsville, Texas, which was the long, sickle-shaped rim of America's sexual playground long before the invention of Vegas or Atlantic City. Three hours after his flight had arrived in Miami, he obtained the home address of the man who now called himself Lou Coyne. He also obtained the name of his wife, a woman who called herself Connie Coyne and who lived three houses down from her husband on a canal in Miami Beach.

Jimmie stayed that night in a hotel that fronted the ocean. In the morning, he dressed in a linen suit and lavender silk shirt, had his shoes shined in the hotel lobby, then took a cab to a two-story white stucco house, one with a faded red tile roof, scrolled iron balconies, heavy, brass-ringed oak doors, and gated walls that towered over the grounds. Each house on the street was similar in ambiance, a fortress unto itself, the name of its security service prominently displayed. But even though it was Saturday, there were no people on this dead-end street, no sounds of children playing on a ficus-shaded lawn.

A Hispanic gardener came to the gate after Jimmie pushed the buzzer. The St. Augustine grass was closely clipped and thick, the bluish-green of a Caribbean lagoon. The flower beds bloomed with every tropical plant imaginable, and royal palms touched the eaves of the second story. Off to one side of the yard Jimmie could see a lime-colored swimming pool coated with leaves, the cracked dome of a 1950s underground atomic-bomb shelter protruding from the sod, like the top of a giant toadstool, and a boat dock that offered a sweeping view of the ocean.

'Is Ms. Coyne at home?' Jimmie asked.

'*Sí,*' the gardener replied.

'Would you tell her Jimmie Robicheaux would like to speak to her?'

'*Sí,*' the gardener replied, staring into Jimmie's face.

'Would you go get her, please?'

'*Sí,*' the gardener replied, obviously not comprehending a word.

'*¿Quién es?*' a woman said from inside the fronds of a giant philodendron, where she was pulling weeds on her knees and dropping them in a bucket.

'My name is Jimmie Robicheaux, Ms. Coyne. I'm looking for an old friend and thought you might be able to help me,' Jimmie said.

The woman stood up, brushing grains of dirt off a pair of cotton work gloves. She was slender, her hair a silvery-red. She wore a straw hat on the back of her head and a halter and Capri pants, and her shoulders were sprinkled with freckles. She walked to the gate, her eyes examining Jimmie's face.

'How can I help you, Mr. Robicheaux?' she said.

But the formality of her speech couldn't hide her regional inflection, nor disguise the fact she had correctly pronounced Jimmie's last name, after hearing it only once, which most people outside Louisiana are not able to do easily.

'Ida Durbin is the name of the lady I need to find,' he said.

She looked at her watch and rubbed the glass with her thumb, more as an idle distraction from her own thoughts than as an effort to know the time.

'How's your friend, the private investigator?' she said.

'Clete Purcel? He's doing all right. I think he'd like to have a talk with your husband, though.'

She stepped near the gate and closed her hand around one of the twisted iron spikes inside the grillework. 'And yourself? You been doin' okay, Jimmie?'

'Life's a breeze. How's it with you, Ida?'

She reached into the bugle vine growing on the wall and pushed a button, buzzing the gate open. 'Come on in, sailor, and let me tell you a story of hearts and flowers,' she said.

chapter twenty-two

On the morning they had planned to leave Galveston and start a new life in Mexico, Ida had asked Jimmie to drop her off at the bus depot so she could buy a few items downtown for the trip while he returned our Ford convertible to me and packed his clothes at the motel. She stored her suitcase in a coin locker, bought a pair of shoes and a kerchief and a small box of hard candy up the street, drank a lime Coke at a soda fountain, then retrieved her suitcase from the locker and took a seat in the whites-only section of the waiting room. The bus to Monterrey was due in twenty minutes.

Then she looked through the window and saw Lou Kale's '56 Bel Air pull to the curb, followed by an unmarked police car in which sat two plainclothes cops whom she recognized as regular visitors to the house on Post Office Street. Their names were Robert Cobb and Dale Bordelon. Both were rawboned men with cavernous eyes and square, callus-edged hands and mouths that did not smile, their hair mowed so closely into their scalps the ridges in their skulls glistened through the bristles. They followed Lou Kale into the waiting room, then approached Ida while Kale fished for change in front of a cigarette machine. Lou's lip was puffed, one eyebrow distorted by a knot, one nostril darker than the other from the beating Jimmie had given him.

'Take a walk outside with us, Missy,' Cobb said, looking down at her from a great height.

'I'm waiting on my bus,' she replied.

Cobb reached down and cupped her by the elbow. She felt herself rising to her feet, even though she had not been told she was under arrest or that she had violated any law. Her eyes swept the waiting room. The Negroes sitting in the section marked colored preoccupied themselves with their children or twisting about in their seats to watch the traffic on the street. The two clerks behind the ticket counter had suddenly discovered concerns of great import on printed fare and schedule sheets that moments earlier had seemed of little significance to them.

In her mind's eye she saw herself inside a single frame of a filmstrip that had suddenly frozen inside the projector. The sound was gone and all the figures were stationary, robbed of motion and breath, the selfishness of their ulterior motives in the script as stark as the grain in the film. Every figure in the frame, including herself, was complicit in a deed that the larger society would say could not occur. In this case, the deed was the abduction of an innocent person by law enforcement personnel in the middle of an American city, in full view of people who hid their eyes.

But the onus was on her, not them. She was a whore. She existed beyond the invisible boundaries of respectability and was not entitled to histrionic displays. To resist her abductors, who were also her users, was to make herself visible and to call into question the legitimacy of an entire system. As she rose from the bench, she could smell the detectives' armpits through their clothes.

She walked between the two men to their car, without either of them touching her person again. In the filmstrip that recommenced in her mind's eye, she saw herself as a gray, nondescript creature in the back of the car, disconnected from the rest of the world, the air tinged with the hot musty odor of the fabric in the seats. The detective named Cobb set her suitcase by her side and said, 'It's gonna be all right, kid.' For reassurance he grinned, his lips stretching back over teeth that were as long as a horse's.

As the car pulled away from the curb, with Lou Kale's Bel Air following close behind, she looked down the street and saw a canary-yellow convertible at the traffic light, with me behind the steering wheel and Jimmie in the passenger seat. Jimmie was tapping his hands on the dashboard to music she could not hear.

They drove her to a farmhouse, down in the Texas wetlands east of Beaumont. It was raining when they arrived, and through the bedroom window she could see acres of sawgrass and a flooded woods and, out in a bay, the gray outlines of mothballed U.S. Navy warships. The room was bare, except for a chipped chest of drawers and a bed that puffed with dust when she sat upon it. The sky was black now, and when lightning flared in the clouds she saw a solitary blue heron lift from the sawgrass and glide on extended wings toward the protection of the woods.

The man named Cobb was the first to take her. She kept her eyes shut and rested her hands lightly on the tips of his shoulders while he labored on top of her, his breath washing over her face. Inside her mind she watched the heron's flight across the points of the sawgrass, its wings flapping, its grace undisturbed by the storm raging in the sky.

The second detective, Dale Bordelon, tried to give her whiskey, then he brought her food that she wouldn't eat. When he placed his hand on her, a tremor went through her body. 'Something you don't like about me?' he said.

'I'm sore,' she replied.

'Whores don't get sore.'

'I need to use the bathroom.'

When she came back into the bedroom, he was already in his underwear and socks, smoking a cigarette on the side of the bed, tipping the ashes into the neck of an empty beer bottle. 'Time's a-wasting, girl. Get them clothes off. I mean all off, too,' he said.

'Where's Lou?' she asked.

'What d'you care about him? We're the best friends you got.'

'I told you, Bob Cobb hurt me. I cain't do it anymore today.'

He looked meanly into space, exhaling cigarette smoke from his nostrils. He hadn't shaved that morning and his jaws were like dirty sandpaper. 'To heck with it,' he said. Then he dressed and went out of the room, slamming the door behind him.

She curled up in a ball on the bed. When she awoke the sky was still dark, the clouds quaking with thunder, rain ticking in pools below the eaves. Lou Kale was sitting in a wood chair by the bed, leaning forward, his face gathered with a strange look of concern. A candle burned in a bottle on a nightstand someone had brought into the room. 'Gonna give you a little bump, Connie. It'll hep you ride over the hard spots for a while,' he said.

'My name is Ida. I left Post Office Street, Lou.'

'Like it or not, we're in the life, hon. Folks like us ain't got yesterdays. Forget that Robicheaux kid.'

He held a bent spoon over the candle. Inside the curl of flame around the spoon she could see a yellowish-brown liquid boiling, like the broth that rises to the top of chicken soup. The syringe was fashioned from an eyedropper; the tourniquet was a necktie.

'I don't want it,' she said.

'We got to do what those Vice roaches say. We're little people, Connie . . . excuse me . . . Ida.'

'I don't want no dope, Lou.'

'Those guys will be gone by tomorrow night. Just go with it. Don't do anything else to get us in trouble. Now give me your arm.'

Her elbow jerked slightly when the needle punched into an artery. For a brief moment the room was still, the lightning frozen inside the clouds, then she saw the headlight on a train engine wobbling in front of her eyes and felt a warm rush through her body that was like a long-delayed orgasm.

Her head lolled on the pillow, her mouth open. Even though her eyes were closed, she could see Lou Kale through the lids, which somehow had become translucent, as thin as Japanese paper. She had never felt this warm inside her skin before, this content and serene. Lou put away his works and stroked her forehead.

'I'll come by later and give you another one,' he said.

'Get in bed with me.'

'That's the dope talking, Ida.'

'No, I want you.'

'I guess it goes with the job,' he said.

He propped the chair under the doorknob and made love to her, at first mechanically, then he found himself caught up in it, looking at her eyes and mouth and the sandy red color of her hair in a new way. When he got off her, he was self-conscious about his nakedness, confused about what he had just done or why he felt affected by it.

'Be nice to that cop,' he said, dressing with his back to her. 'I'm jammed up on this deal, too.'

'Don't leave, Lou. I'm afraid of them.'

'It wasn't really me you wanted, was it? You got me mixed up with that warm feeling the dope gave you.'

'I always said you weren't a bad guy, Lou. You never

made the girls do anything they didn't want to. You never hit nobody, either. Remember when you told me I could sing as good as Texas Ruby?'

He pulled on his trousers and walked back and forth in front of the window, pushing at his temple with the heel of his hand. 'I ain't suppose to be having these kind of thoughts. I'm breaking a big rule here,' he said.

'You already said it – "We're little people." We have to be smarter than they are.'

'Cobb can have me on Sugarland Farm in twenty-four hours. Why didn't you stay up in Snerdville where you belong? You're a king-size migraine, Ida,' he said.

'Is that what you really think of me?'

'I don't know what I think. You messed with my head.'

He lay down beside her. She curled against him, placing her face against his chest. A moment passed and she felt the tension go out of his body. He exhaled loudly and slipped his arms around her back and tucked her head under his cheek.

'I'll get us out of this,' he said.

'I know you will, Lou.'

'But you got to promise me something.'

She spread her fingers over his heart and waited.

'There ain't no turning back. They'll pour gasoline on you and set you afire. I seen them do it. Say "promise," Ida. Say it now,' he said.

Before Lou left that night, Ida heard him lie to the detectives and tell them he had injected her a second time. He also told them she'd had a seizure from the heroin and that she should not be bothered again, at least until the next day. During the night she heard the voices of several men who were playing cards and drinking. Once, somebody opened the bedroom door, blading her face with a band of white light. The figure stared at her, motionless, in silhouette, his upper body and head like a buffalo's. Then someone called him back to the poker game and he shut the door.

In the morning she waited until the men were finished with the bathroom, then took fresh clothes from her suitcase and cleaned a gray film out of the tub with a wad of toilet paper. The men had used up the hot tank, so she bathed in cold water and washed her hair with a cake of harsh soap.

She fixed breakfast for herself in a tiny kitchen, her hair wrapped in a towel, while outside the cop named Bordelon and a teenage boy played pitch-and-catch with a baseball. In the distance she could see carrion birds turning in circles over a flooded woods and a powerboat splitting a bay in half. The breeze was up and a salty, gray odor from the sawgrass struck her face and made her shut the window, even though the house was already warm.

Her mandolin was in her suitcase, wrapped inside a soft flannel shirt from which she had removed all the buttons so they could not scratch the mandolin's finish. She sat on the edge of the bed and tuned the strings, using a plectrum and a small pitch pipe, then sang Kitty Wells's 'It Wasn't God Who Made Honky-Tonk Angels' in B flat.

The maudlin lyrics and the melody that was borrowed from a hymn titled 'The Great Speckled Bird' gave an emotional focus to her life that she intuitively knew was illegitimate but somehow indispensable. The lost lover was Jimmie Robicheaux. Beer joints and back-street bars became blue-collar purgatories where angels with impaired wings could float above a fire that purged but did not consume. The incremental dismemberment of their lives with alcohol, drugs, and lust was a form of penance that ultimately made them acceptable in the eyes of God.

'You play that pretty good,' Dale Bordelon said from the doorway. He was sweaty and hot from throwing the baseball in the yard, and she could smell an odor on him like sour milk and hay when it's wet. 'That's my nephew out yonder. We're going fishing directly.'

She looked out the window at the boy, as though the detective's words held meaning for both of them.

'He's going to town to get us some bait and such. That leaves just you and me,' he said.

Her left hand formed a cord on the mandolin's neck, but she didn't move the plectrum across the strings.

'Want me to bring you a cup of coffee or tea?' he asked.

'No, thank you,' she replied.

'You're a prissy thing.'

His words were spoken in such a way that they could have contained either an insult or a compliment. But she let no reaction to them register in her face.

'When's Lou coming back?' she asked.

'How the hell should I know?' he replied.

Later, she heard a starter grind on a car, then saw the teenage boy drive past the window onto the county road. Dale Bordelon opened the bedroom door without knocking and leaned inside, his hand fitted like a starfish on the glass knob. 'Want me to fix some sandwiches?' he said.

'I'm not hungry.'

'Bob Cobb says he didn't hurt you. Says you liked it just fine,' he said.

She scratched her neck and stared idly at a horsefly sitting on the windowsill. She could hear the detective breathing heavily in the silence. He stepped into the room and shut the door behind him, then walked within two feet of her, his belt buckle almost eye-level with her. He lifted a strand of hair off her head and rubbed it between his fingers. She could see whorls of dirt in the ball of his thumb.

'I kept a man from going in your room last night,' he said.

'Thank you.'

'You talk like a goddamn phonograph,' he said.

His knuckles were as big as quarters, his odor like a damp locker room. The gold-embossed outline of the state of Texas glittered on his silver belt buckle, inches from her eyes. He clamped his hand over the top of her head. Where was Lou?

'I didn't mean to hurt your feelings,' she said.

'I 'preciate it. But a verbal apology is kind of like getting served ice cream in hell. It don't really address the problem.'

'I got my period this morning.'

But he didn't even acknowledge her deceit. 'I sent the boy on an errand in Orange. He's gonna bring us back some fried-chicken dinners and blackberry cobbler. You'll like them dinners, believe me. But no more excuses. One way or another, you're gonna take care of ole Dale.'

The nakedness of his desire made his face feral. He put a breath mint in his mouth and cracked it between his molars, chewing hard, as though he could relieve himself of the passion that made him rotate his neck against his collar. 'Don't just sit there, woman. You know what you got to do,' he said.

'I got my period at three o'clock this morning,' she said, ignoring the implication of his last words.

That's when he ripped her out of the chair and hit her with the flat of his hand across the face, breaking her upper lip, streaking blood from her nose on the wall. Then he smashed her mandolin on the chair and threw it to the floor, grinding the delicate wood of the sound chamber into splinters with his heel, snapping the tuning pegs from the head like broken teeth.

Lou Kale returned to the farmhouse that afternoon and put ice on her face and brought her strawberry ice cream from the kitchen. He swept the broken pieces of her mandolin and the tangle of strings into a dustpan, sliding them into a garbage sack. Outside, the men were popping skeet with a shotgun, the clay disks exploding into puffs of orange smoke above the sawgrass.

'I'll buy you a new one. Or a guitar. You're always talking about a Martin guitar,' he said.

'Why'd you leave me alone, Lou?'

He sat next to her on the bed and spoke to her with his hands clenched between his knees, his voice lowered. His hair was shiny and black, combed in a wet curl on the back of his neck. His profile looked like a sheep's. 'I heard some talk, Ida. They know you're smart. You've seen important people at the house and you know their names and who they are. They think you'll run off again. They think you're gonna cause a shitload of trouble. They make examples, Ida. Sometimes it's out there in the Gulf with the crabs.'

'Just give me some money and get me to a train station or airport,' she said.

'You're not hearing me. It takes guts to be a whore or a pimp. I'm proud of what I am. We were born on the hard road, Ida. Them cops out there couldn't hack it. I'm not gonna let them push us around. I got us a way out.'

'How?' she said.

'I called this big plantation man over in Louisiana. I used to chop bait on his old man's boat when I was a kid. He's got money with the Giacanos, but he's not like the Giacanos. His name is Raphael Chalons. He's a classy guy and those Vice roaches know it. One thing, though?'

'What?'

'The Giacanos got long memories. As long as we stay under Mr. Raphael's protection, we're gonna be okay. But you owe money and so do I. In the life, that's the dog collar around your neck. It don't go away easy.'

'You?' she said.

'I owe every sports book in Houston and New Orleans.

People like us all got some kind of jones. That how come we're pimps and whores. Who wants to be normal, anyway? It's a drag.'

He thought he had both reassured her and lightened her mood.

'Lou?'

'*What?*'

'You're not gonna try to hurt Jimmie Robicheaux, are you?'

He stood up from the bed, screwing his fingers into his temples, a squealing sound leaking from his teeth.

During the next hour, Lou paced the floor, hyperventilating, drinking ice water, blowing out his breath as though he had pulled a freight car up a grade.

'Stop climbing the walls,' she said.

'If this don't work, bucketloads of shit are going through the fan.'

'Maybe we end here. Maybe our names are written in water and one day the water just dries up,' she said.

'Don't say stuff like that. We're not living inside a country-and-western song.'

'Come on, sit down,' she said. She took him by the arm and guided him to the wood chair by the window. His arm was as hard as a log in her hands. He was chewing gum rapidly in one jaw, snapping it loudly, his throat cording with blue veins.

'I got a confession to make. I was gonna let them hang you out to dry,' he said.

'But you didn't.'

She pushed her fingers deep into his shoulders. His eyes closed briefly, then he surged to his feet, like a man who believed the Furies awaited him in his sleep.

'What are you doing?' she said.

'Coming apart. I ain't up to this.' He jammed a chair under the doorknob and shot himself up with enough heroin to blow the heart out of a draft horse, his mouth rictal when the rush took him.

That afternoon Ida heard the strangest conversation she had ever heard in her life, one that would always remain with her as a testimony to the efficacy of fear.

Another rainfront had swept across the wetlands, smudging out the woods and the fleet of mothballed ships rusting in the bay. She heard the engine of a powerful car coming up the road, then a black Cadillac driven by a Negro chauffeur turned into the yard, the hood steaming in the rain. A tall man got out of the back and walked quickly under an umbrella into the house, lifting his shined shoes out of the puddles like a stork. It was obvious the men drinking beer in the living room had not been expecting him. The rhythm of their conversation faltered, the loud laughter fading, then trailing into total silence. Through a space in the door, she saw them all rise as one from their chairs while the tall man folded his umbrella and hung the crook on a hat rack.

The tall man's cheeks were lean, his hair freshly clipped and as black as India ink, the press in his suit impeccable. He removed a slip of paper from his shirt pocket and read silently from it, then replaced it in his pocket. Lou Kale watched from the kitchen door, the China white he'd shot up singing in his blood, his face incapable of forming a definable expression. Oddly, Lou was the only person in the room the tall man acknowledged.

Then he said, 'I understand there's a woman here by the name of Ida Durbin.'

'Yes, sir, she's back yonder,' the voice of Bob Cobb said.

'Why are you keeping her here?' the tall man said.

'She's just visiting, helping clean and such, Mr. Chalons,' Cobb said.

'That's not my understanding,' Raphael Chalons replied.

'I was gonna fix her lunch, but she didn't want –' Dale Bordelon began.

'Would you ask her to come out here, please?' Chalons said.

Ida heard a chair creak, then footsteps approaching the bedroom. She stepped back from the door just as Bordelon opened it. A smile was carved on his face, like a crooked gash in a muskmelon. 'Mr. Chalons wants to know if everything is okay,' he said. 'We was telling him you can leave anytime you want.'

He tried to hold her with his eyes and to force her to make his words hers. But she walked past him into the living room as though he were not there. The men who only moments earlier had been relaxed and confident about their place in the world were still standing, afraid to sit down without permission.

'You're Miss Ida?' Chalons asked.

'My name is Ida Durbin, yes, sir. It's nice to meet you,' she replied.

'What happened to your face?' he asked.

She knew the most injurious response she could make would be none at all. She lowered her eyes and folded her arms on her chest. Inside the boom of thunder and the slap of rain against the window, she became a replica of the medieval martyr, abused and bound and waiting for the bundled twigs to be set ablaze at her feet.

'Do any of you gentlemen care to tell me what happened here?' Chalons said.

'Somebody got carried away. There's no good hat to put on it,' Bob Cobb said.

'I won't abide this.'

'Sir?' Bob Cobb said.

'I won't have a young woman held in captivity or beaten on my property,' Chalons said, his eyes lighting in a way that made Bob Cobb blink. He mentioned the name of an infamous Cosa Nostra figure in New Orleans, a man who was literally given the state of Louisiana by Frank Costello and United States Senator Huey P. Long. 'This woman and Lou Kale are going to leave with me today. You gentlemen can use the house through tonight. But by ten in the morning you'll be gone. I have no hard feelings against any of you. But you will not have use of this property again. Thank you for your courtesy in listening to me.'

An hour later, Lou Kale and Ida Durbin were aboard Raphael Chalons's cabin cruiser, headed southeast through a squall toward the Florida coast, the waves bursting into ropes of foam on the bow. The cabin in which she slept that night vibrated with the reassuring throb of the engines, and when she woke in the early hours, unsure of where she was, she looked through a porthole and saw the sleek, steel-skin bodies of porpoises sliding through the water next to the boat. Their steadiness of purpose, the hardness of their bodies inside the waves, the fact they were on the same course as she, filled her with a sense of harmony and confidence and power.

Lou Kale slept in the bunk across from her. His sheet had fallen down over his hip, and his exposed arm and naked back and boylike face gave him an aura of vulnerability that she had never associated with the Lou Kale she had known on Post Office Street. She rose from her bunk and lifted the sheet carefully so as not to wake him and replaced it on his back, then looked again at the immensity and mystery of the night.

The Gulf was green and black, domed by a sky bursting with stars, so cold in their configurations they seemed to smoke like dry ice. She saw coconuts tumbling out of a wave, and an enormous sea turtle, its shell encrusted with barnacles, bobbing in a swell. A waterspout, its belly swollen with light, wobbled on the southern horizon, sucking thousands of gallons and hundreds of fish out of the waves into the clouds. She opened the porthole glass and felt the salt on her tongue, like the taste of iodine, and she knew she would not sleep again that night. She longed for the sunrise, to be up on deck, to eat breakfast in a breeze that contained the green heaviness of the ocean and the hint of islands banked with coconut palms. She longed to be a young girl and to fall in love with the world again.

Jimmie Robicheaux had already disappeared from her mind. What a trick life had played on her, she thought. Jimmie was gone and ironically her future was now wed to Lou Kale, the man she had tried to flee and who in turn had probably saved her from a terrible fate.

But when the boat docked in Key West, Lou hung around only long enough to refuel the gas tanks and re-stock the larder in the galley.

'Where you headed?' she asked.

All morning he had been morose, vaguely resentful, his eyes evasive, his speech unusually laconic. 'Up to Lauder-dale on the Greyhound,' he said, a duffel bag packed with his clothes balanced on his shoulder.

'What about me?' she said.

'I got to get things set up. I'll see you when you get back.'

'Back from where?'

'You're going fishing in the Dry Tortugas with Mr. Chalons.'

'Lou, I didn't take care of myself at the farmhouse. I had all that dope in me.'

'You're all right. You've always been all right,' he said. 'Everything is extremely solid. I never lied to you, right? Keep saying, "Everything is righteously solid." Just don't let no problems get in your head. It's all a matter of attitude.'

'Get what things set up?'

But he walked up the dock and did not reply, staring

wide-eyed at the gulls that glided over the dock, his back
knotted under his see-through shirt with the weight of the
duffel.

chapter twenty-three

Jimmie told me all this late Tuesday afternoon, at my house, just after arriving back in New Iberia. Outside, the sunlight was gold inside the trees, more like autumn than late summer, and there was a tannic smell in the air that I only associated with fall and the coming of winter. I could hear Molly nailing up a birdhouse that had been blown out of live oak, like a reassuring presence who told me I still had another season to run.

'So Ida and Lou Kale have been in the prostitution business ever since?' I said.

'More or less,' he replied. 'You actually married a nun?'

'Stick to the subject. Both of us have felt guilty all these years about a woman who didn't have the courtesy to drop a postcard indicating she was alive. Do you feel like you've been had, maybe just a little bit?'

'What do you guys say at meetings? Live and let live?' he said.

'She was Raphael Chalons's punch?'

'More than that,' he said. We were in the guest bedroom, where he was packing his clothes in a suitcase, preparing to move to an apartment he planned to use while he supervised the reconstruction of our destroyed home south of town. 'She had a kid. Almost nine months to the day after Chalons rescued her at that farmhouse.'

'What happened to the kid?'

'Guess?'

I stared at his back as he bent over his suitcase, arranging his shirts and balled-up socks. 'Valentine Chalons?' I said.

'That's the way I'd read it.' He straightened up, his long-sleeve white shirt still fresh and clean, even after a long drive from New Orleans through heavy traffic.

'And Raphael Chalons raised him? And that's what all this bullshit has been about – the Chalons family doesn't want anyone to know Val's mother was a prostitute?'

'You don't buy it?' Jimmie said.

'No.'

'Why not?' he asked.

'The old man doesn't care what anybody thinks of him.'

'Maybe Val does.'

'It's something else.'

'Why not ask Ida?' he said.

'I don't plan on seeing Ida.'

'You might see her whether you want to or not. She's in New Orleans. I put her up at a friend's house on the lake.'

'Don't you ever tire of grief?' I said.

'She wants to see her son. Whores have souls, too,' he replied.

'What was the cost of a postage stamp in 1958?' I said.

He straightened up from packing his suitcase and looked at me, a ray of sunlight falling across his prosthetic eye, which remained fixed and staring in the socket, like the eye of a stranger. 'Thanks for the use of the room,' he said.

That night the temperature dropped suddenly and chains of dry lightning pulsed inside the clouds, flooding our yard with a white brilliance that turned the tree trunks the pale color of old bone. On the edges of sleep I kept waiting to hear the small pet door in the back entrance swing on its hinges, signaling that Snuggs and Tripod had sought shelter from the impending storm. I got up and pushed open the back door and immediately felt the weight of a tree branch that had fallen on the steps. I cleared it away and went out into the yard in my skivvies, the canopy flickering whitely above my head. Both Snuggs and Tripod were inside the hutch, which I left open at night so Tripod could come and go as he wished.

'Let's go, fellows,' I said, and hefted up one in each arm. They both lay back against the crook of my arms, content, enjoying the ride, their feet in the air, heavy and compact as cannon balls.

Then at the corner of my vision I saw a shadow move behind a row of camellia bushes in my side yard. I started to turn my head but instead looked straight ahead and went inside the house. I removed my .45 from the dresser drawer and, still in my skivvies, went out the front door and circled around the side of the house.

Lightning rolled silently through the clouds overhead, flaring suddenly in a yellow ball, as though igniting a trapped pocket of white gas inside each individual cloud. 'Come out,' I called to the darkness.

The wind gusted off the bayou and all the shadows in the yard thrashed against one another except one. A figure stood at the rear of my property, his silhouette framed against the bands of light on the bayou's surface.

'I can drop you from here,' I said.

The figure hesitated, measuring his chances, a sheaf of compacted leaves cracking under his weight. Then a tremendous explosion of thunder shook the trees, the electricity died in the clouds, and the figure's silhouette disappeared inside the shadows.

A voyeur? A disoriented reveler from one of the bars downtown? An imaginary visitor from a sea of elephant grass in a forgotten war? It was possible. I searched along the bank of the bayou and saw no footprints, although someone had recently broken down a banana tree on the edge of my neighbor's property.

I called in a 911 and lay back down. Molly had slept through it all. Those who live with insomnia and who consider sleep both an enemy and a gift will understand the following. Some of us cannot comprehend how anyone except the very good or those who have no conscience at all can sleep from dark to dawn without dreaming or waking. We hear William Blake's tiger padding softly through a green jungle, his stripes glowing, his whiskers spotted with gore. Psychoanalysis does no good. Neither does a health regimen that induces physical exhaustion. The only solution that is guaranteed is the one provided by our old friend Morpheus, who requires our souls in the bargain.

Audie Murphy, the most decorated United States soldier of World War II, slept with a .45 under his pillow for twenty years. Ernest Hemingway slept with a night-light on all of his adult life.

But I sleep with Molly Robicheaux, I told myself. I sleep inside her goodness, the smell of her hair, the flush of her skin when I touch her rump and kiss the baby fat on her sides. I sleep inside a flowerlike odor that she leaves on the pillow. Let the devil have prowling tigers and the shadows in the yard.

The next day I assembled all the investigative material I could on the case of the Baton Rouge serial killer. I still believed the murder of Honoria Chalons was not related. But I had also believed Honoria was an incest victim, and that perhaps her brother was the predator, since she had died in his quarters. There was no doubt this was what I wanted to believe because I had come to personally despise Val Chalons and the self-righteous sneering arrogance that he represented. Unfortunately for me, the

DNA evidence taken off Honoria's body pointed away from Val Chalons as a current sexual partner and possible suspect in his sister's death.

Koko Hebert had said a small cross had been incised postmortem inside Honoria's hairline, forcing us to conclude the killer had not acted randomly and that he bore the Chalons family an enormous animus.

But the Chalons's coat of arms hung in Val's quarters as well as in the main house. In the past, the Baton Rouge serial killer had already demonstrated his proclivity and skill at making others besides his immediate victim suffer as long as possible. He made sure the rest of us knew he had sexually degraded the victim before killing her. He left the instruments of bondage and torture with the body. He mutilated the features after death. He hung a purse in a tree to ensure we would find his handiwork while it was still fresh. Why not mock the Chalons family by lifting the Cross of Jesus from their family seal, then leaving it as an insult to be discovered hours later by the probing fingers of a parish coroner?

But I still couldn't figure out Val Chalons. Had he hired Bad Texas Bob Cobb through intermediaries to cancel my ticket and Clete's as well, just to hide the fact he was illegitimate? It didn't seem plausible.

Over the years I had known many people of his background. They revised the past on a daily basis and lived vicariously through their dead ancestors. Inside termite-eaten historical homes, they stayed drunk and talked endlessly of a grander time and thought of themselves as characters in a Greek tragedy. In their own minds, they were not dissolute or effete but simply bacchanal eccentrics living in an intolerable century. They absolved themselves of their own sins, believing them to be the price one paid for the gift of gentility. Robert Lee had long ago proved that penury and failure could be borne with the dignity of a battle-stained flag. They were not bad people and meant no harm to anyone, not unless you counted the loss they imposed upon themselves.

But my objectivity was gone and I couldn't sort any of these things out. My anger toward Val Chalons had helped me get drunk once and I was sure my next slip would probably be my last. Maybe it was time to take it to Val on a different level, one that he would not be expecting.

I went to his home after work and was told by the handyman that Valentine was having dinner with friends at Clementine's in New Iberia. I drove back to town and parked by the bayou and entered the supper club through the terrace. Clementine's was once a saloon and pool hall called Provost's, a workingman's place with a sports wire and green sawdust and scrolls of ticker tape on the floor. On Thursday nights the owner covered the pool tables with dropcloths and served free sausage and robin gumbo. Those things are gone, but the cavernous rooms, the stamped tin ceilings, and the hand-carved mahogany bar remain. In the shadowy light I could almost see the ghost of my father, Big Aldous, knocking back two inches of Jack at the bar, bellowing at his own jokes, his pinstripe strap overalls still spotted with drilling mud.

I ordered coffee at the end of the bar, where I could see through a wide door into the dining room. Val was with a group of well-dressed people, his back to me. He was the only man at the table without a jacket. His hair had just been barbered, the sides clipped close to the head, which accented the severity of his angular features. He wore a starched white shirt, but without a tie and with the collar unbuttoned, as though he were demonstrating a deliberate disregard for the decorum of the evening. The austerity in his expression and posture made me think of a photograph I had once seen of the Confederate guerrilla leader, William Clarke Quantrill.

In fact, I think he was assuming a persona I had seen him play before. He had been a guest narrator on a Louisiana Public Television broadcast regarding the activities of the White League and the Knights of the White Camellia during Reconstruction. He had spoken of his ancestors' participation in the White League with veiled pride, even dismissing their moral culpability for the execution of fifty black soldiers in what came to be known as the Colfax Massacre. 'It was a violent era. My great-grandfather did what he had to. It's facile to impose our standards on the past,' Val had explained.

Now, in the glow of candlelight at his table, he was holding forth about contemporary wars, his rhetoric threaded with moral certitude, although he himself had never heard a shot fired in anger.

I had resolved earlier to approach Val Chalons with a new and objective attitude. But my thought processes were deteriorating rapidly. I saw him excuse himself from the table and walk through the back hall toward the restrooms, which were housed on the terrace.

Don't confront him here, not in this state of mind, I told myself.

But if not here, where? Val Chalons wouldn't change and I wouldn't, either. Just stick to principles and keep personalities out of it, I thought. The fate of the world didn't hang on what I might say to a member of the Chalons family.

As chance would have it, Clete Purcel came through the front door, just as I got up from the bar stool. 'Where you going?' he asked.

'To the head,' I replied.

'Did I just see Val Chalons?'

'Maybe,' I said.

'Why waste your time bird-dogging a bucket of shit?'

'I dropped in for a cup of coffee and a piece of pie.'

'Yeah, I used to go on skivvy runs in Cherry Alley to play the piano. Let me handle this, Streak.'

'There's no problem here. Stay out of it,' I replied.

I followed Chalons out onto the terrace, into a fragrance of flowers and bourbon and grilled steaks and the fecund summertime odor of the Teche. He was at the urinal when I entered the restroom.

'Unless you're in here to hang out your dick, I suggest you leave,' he said.

'You seem to have many personalities, Val,' I said.

'Don't think your current environment protects you, Robicheaux. I'm going to boil you in your own grease.'

He continued to urinate, his chin tilted slightly upward, his fingers cupped under his phallus.

'I think there's reason to believe your sister may have been murdered by the Baton Rouge serial killer,' I said. 'I had dismissed that possibility because I was carrying a personal resentment against you. I was wrong in doing that, both as a police officer and as an AA member.'

He laughed to himself and shook off his phallus. 'God, I love you people,' he said.

'Which people is that, Val?'

'Guys who constantly confess their guilt in public with doleful faces. Why is it I always feel you're up to something?' He brushed past me and began washing his hands in the basin.

'It's called "transfer." The person assumes other people think in the same duplicitous fashion as himself,' I said.

'You still don't get it, do you?' he said, drying his hands on a paper towel.

'Get what?'

'You're our local Attila. A little campfire smoke and animal grease in your hair and you'd be perfect. You're shit, Robicheaux. So is your wife. She's a poseur and a cunt. You just haven't figured it out yet.'

He was standing within arm's reach of me now. He balled up the paper towel and dropped it in the waste can. I started to speak, but instead stepped back from him and looked into empty space, my thumbs hooked into the sides of my belt. The heavy metal door slammed behind him.

Don't take the bait, I told myself.

But there are instances when that old-time rock 'n' roll is the only music on the jukebox.

I followed Val Chalons through the bar area into the dining room. He had taken his chair and was spreading his napkin on his lap. His friends looked up at me, expecting to be introduced.

'We finally got to the bottom of Ida Durbin's disappearance, Val,' I said. 'Your father rescued her from a whorehouse he had money in. So out of either obligation or reasons of opportunity, Ida became his regular punch. Then you came along about nine months later. If you'd like to check out the story, your mother is staying with a friend of my brother on Lake Pontchartrain. Your mother is married to her former pimp, Lou Kale. They run an escort service together in Miami.'

He rose from his chair and threw his martini in my face. I hit him high up on the cheekbone, so hard that his opposite eye bulged from the socket. He crashed through empty chairs into the wall, then caught me with a sliding blow on the forehead and one on the ear that I could feel burn right through the cartilage into the bone. But he was off balance, his feet tangled up by an oil painting that had clattered to the floor. I slipped his next punch, felt another glance off my head, then got under his reach and hooked him just below the heart. He wasn't ready for it and I saw his mouth drop open and heard a sound like a dying animal's come from deep inside his chest.

People from the bar crowded through the entranceway

to watch. A waiter's loaded tray exploded on the floor and I saw a strobe light flare in the gloom and burn away all the shadows in the room. I hooked Val Chalons in the eye, then drove a right cross directly into his mouth, bursting his lips against his teeth. I knew it was time to back away, in the same way a fighter in the ring knows when he has taken his opponent's heart. A woman I had never seen was screaming incoherently and an elderly man was patting the air with his hands, as though his years had given him the power to impart wisdom and restraint to a dervish.

I started to step back, but Val Chalons tried to clench me, his mouth draining blood and spittle on my cheek and neck, the thickness of his phallus pressing against me. He forced us both against a table, his mouth as close to my ear as a lover's. 'My father screwed your wife, Robicheaux,' he said.

In my naïveté, I had believed the succubus that had governed my life for decades had been exorcised by the coming of old age. But it was still there, like a feral presence hiding in the subconscious, red-black in color, shiny with glandular fluids, waiting for the right moment to have its way. Some call it a chemical assault upon the brain. I can't say what it is. But the consequence for me was always the same: I committed acts as though I were watching them on film rather than participating in them. When it was over, I was not only filled with disgust and shame and self-loathing but genuinely frightened by the gargoyle that held sway over my soul.

In this case, that meant I genuinely invested myself in the deconstruction of Val Chalons. I buried my fist up to my wrist in his stomach and drove his head into the wall, clubbed him to the floor, and stomped his face when he was down. Then I felt Clete Purcel's huge arms lock around me, pinning my hands at my sides, dragging me backward through the tables and broken dishware and spilled food into the bar area, where someone pointed a camera strobe straight into my eyes.

Like a drowning man who has just popped to the surface of a vortex that has crushed his hearing, I saw Clete's lips moving without sound, then heard his words become audible in midsentence: '. . . took us upcountry into Shitsville, Streak. Why'd you have to load their gun? Why you'd do it, big mon?'

chapter twenty-four

Valentine Chalons was taken by ambulance to Iberia General and I was taken by five policemen to a holding cell at the city jail. Molly got me out at midnight, but I was to be arraigned the next morning and I had no doubt about the seriousness of the charges. At the top of the list was felony assault.

At the house, Molly filled a tin pan with ice cubes and water for me to soak my hands in. Through the window I could see the humid glow of sodium lamps across the bayou and hear Tripod running up and down the clothesline on his chain.

'Were you trying to kill him?' she asked.

'Maybe.' Then I thought about it. 'Yeah, I probably was.'

'Why?'

'He had it coming. He's a fraternity pissant and should have been blown out of his socks a long time ago.'

'You can't live with that kind of anger in you, Dave.'

'He threw his drink in my face. He dealt the play. He got his sticks broken. That's the way it flushes sometimes. Can we give it a rest?'

She was at the sink, the water running loudly. She turned off the faucet and stared at me. 'Why are you talking like this?'

'He said his old man screwed you.'

'Val Chalons said that?'

'I just told you.' I watched her face, my heart beating.

'Did you believe him?' she asked.

'Of course not.'

'Then why did you tear him apart?'

'Because that's what I'll do to any sonofabitch who insults my wife.'

In the silence I could hear the creak of the trees in the yard. Snuggs rubbed himself against my leg, his tail stiff, his head butting into my calf. I picked him up, my hands numb from the ice water in the pan. I flipped him on his back and scratched him under the chin. 'What do you think about it, Snuggs?' I said.

Molly took him from my lap and set him on the floor. Then she leaned over me and held my head tightly against her breasts, squeezing so hard it hurt, her mouth pressed into my hair. 'I love you, Dave Robicheaux,' she said.

I felt Bootsie step inside her skin.

At 8:00 a.m. the next day I went directly into Helen Soileau's office. The arrest report from the Iberia city police was already on her desk. 'I just can't believe this,' she said, picking up the typed pages and dropping them as though they were smeared with an obscene substance.

'Why not?' I said.

'You want to look at the photos of your handiwork? Val Chalons looks like he was chain-dragged behind a car.'

'He threw a glass of gin in my face. He made a filthy statement about my wife. I think he got off easy.'

'He set you up, bwana.'

'Am I on the desk?'

'Guess,' she said.

It was 8:16 a.m. My arraignment was at eleven. I knew my time as a viable member of the sheriff's department was running out. I picked up my desk phone and called Mack Bertrand at the crime lab. 'I got into some trouble last night,' I said.

'I heard about it,' he replied.

'I think I'm about to go on suspension. You remember those casts you made under my bedroom window?'

'Sure,' he said.

'Can you run some comparisons between them and the casts you made at the Chalons crime scene?'

'I already did. Your prowler wore workboots, size ten and a half. Our person of interest at the Chalons guesthouse probably had on rubber boots, around size eleven. No help there, Dave.'

'Why'd you make the comparison?'

'Probably for the same reason you wanted it done. We don't have one clue indicating who might have gone into the Chalons guesthouse and chopped that sad girl to death. Let me run something else by you a second.'

'Go ahead,' I said.

'Raphael Chalons has called me three times. But I'm not quite sure what he wants.'

'I'm not following you.'

'In one breath, he wants to know if there's any evidence the Baton Rouge serial killer murdered his daughter. When I tell him no, he seems relieved, then he gets upset again.'

'Why did you call Honoria Chalons a "sad girl"?'

'She attended our church for a while. I always had the feeling she'd been raped or molested. But I'm not an expert on those things.'

'Did she ever say anything on the subject?'

'No, she just seemed to be one of those people who always have reflections inside their eyes, like ghosts or memories no one else can touch. Maybe I watch too much late-night television.'

No, you don't, Mack, I said to myself.

I had spoken boldly to both Molly and Helen Soileau about wiping up the floor with Val Chalons. But my casual attitude was a poor disguise for my real feelings. It was ten minutes to nine now and my stomach was roiling, in the same way it does when an airplane drops unexpectedly through an air pocket. My scalp felt tight against my head and I could smell a vinegary odor rising from my body, like sweat that has been ironed into fabric. I bought a can of Dr Pepper in the department waiting room, ate two aspirin, and called Dana Magelli at NOPD.

'Do you have casts from the area where Holly Blankenship's body was dumped?' I asked.

'Yeah, there were footprints all over the place. Some homeless guys use it for a hobo jungle. What are you looking for?' he said.

'Size eleven rubber boots or ten-and-a-half workboots?'

'Why don't you call the task force in Baton Rouge?'

'My prints showed up at a crime scene they were investigating. They're not big fans.'

'Hang on a minute,' he said. He set the phone down, then picked it up again. 'Yeah, there was one set of footprints that could have been made by rubber boots, around size eleven or twelve. Wal-Mart sells them by the thousands. What was that about your prints at a crime scene?'

I started to tell Dana the whole story, but I had finally grown tired of revisiting my own bad behavior in order to publicly excoriate myself. So I simply said, 'Come on over and catch some green trout.'

'Thought you'd never ask,' he replied.

I wished I had come to appreciate the value of reticence earlier in life.

Molly and I met with my attorney outside the court at 10:45 a.m. He was a Tulane law graduate and a good-natured, intelligent man by the name of Porteus O'Malley. He was a student of the classics and liberal thought, and came from an old and distinguished family on the bayou, one known for its generosity and also its penchant for losing everything the family owned. Because our fathers had been friends, he seldom charged me a fee for the work he did on my behalf.

I was sweating in the shade of the oak where we stood, my eyes stinging with the humidity. Porteus placed his hand on my shoulder and looked into my face. He was larger than I and had to stoop slightly to be eye-level with me. 'You gonna make it?' he said.

'I'm fine,' I said.

But I could tell something else besides his client's anxiety was bothering him. When Molly went inside City Hall to use the restroom, he said, 'Ever hear of a woman by the name of Mabel Poche?'

'No, who is she?'

'She's hired an oilcan to sue you. The oilcan also happens to do legal grunt work for the Chalons family. She's also filing criminal charges.'

'For *what*?'

'She claims you took her four-year-old son into a restroom at Molly's place and molested him.' His eyes shifted off my face.

'It's a lie,' I said.

'Of course it is. But that's how Val Chalons and his friends operate. Screw with them and they'll make a speed bump out of you.'

Judge Cecil Gautreaux was an ill-tempered, vituperative man, disliked and feared by prosecutors and defense lawyers alike. He was also a moralist who liked to bait the ACLU by making references to Scripture while handing down severe sentences. A wrongheaded remark by a defense attorney could make his face tremble with quiet rage. He lectured rape victims and showed contempt for the collection of indigent drunks who were brought daily into morning court on a long wrist chain. Huey Long once said that if fascism ever came to the United States, it would come in the name of anticommunism. I had always believed that Huey had the likes of Judge Gautreaux in mind when he made his remark, and that Judge Gautreaux, given the opportunity, could make the ovens sing.

'You're entering a plea of not guilty?' he said.

'Yes, Your Honor,' I replied.

He rubbed his little, round chin. His eyes were sky-blue, the size of dimes, and they stayed riveted on mine. His facial skin was soft, translucent, with nests of green veins at the temples, his nostrils thin, as though the air he breathed contained an offensive odor. 'Just to satisfy my own curiosity, can you tell me why you had to destroy a man's place of business in order to satisfy a personal grudge?'

Porteus O'Malley started to speak.

'You be silent, Counselor. I'm talking to your client. Would you please answer my question, Mr. Robicheaux?' the judge said.

'It's a bit complicated, Your Honor,' I said.

'Why don't you enlighten me?'

'I guess there are some occasions when words are not quite adequate, Your Honor. I guess there are occasions when you just have to say, "Fuck it,"' I replied.

'I don't think you're a wise man, Mr. Robicheaux. Bail is set at fifty thousand dollars,' the judge said. He snapped his gavel down on a wood block.

I put up my house as a property bond and was back at the department at 1:00 p.m. Helen was waiting by my office door. I started to recount my experience in court, but she held up a hand to stop me.

'I've already heard about it. You'd better pray Cecil Gautreaux doesn't preside over your trial,' she said.

I waited for her to go on. Instead, she looked into space, a sad light in her eyes.

'Come on, Helen. Say it.'

'I tried to get you modified duty. Suspension without pay was as good as I could do. The D.A. and others want you canned.'

'Without an I.A. review?'

'The problem isn't just the beef at Clementine's. It's you, Dave. You don't like rules and you hate authority. You wage a personal war against guys like Val Chalons and take the rest of us down with you. No amount of pleading with you works. People are tired of following you around with a dustpan and broom.'

My face felt small and tight, my throat constricted, as though a chicken bone were caught in it. Helen snuffed down in her nose and touched at one nostril, her jawbone flexing.

'I'll clean out my desk,' I said.

'I got a call from a TV producer who does exposés on small cities,' she said. 'They're doing one on New Iberia and you're the centerpiece. They've got you on tape at Clementine's. I also got the feeling your wife is going to be portrayed as a bleeding-heart nun pumping it with a rogue cop.'

'We've always wanted film careers,' I said.

'You force your friends to hurt you, Dave. I think that's a sickness. But you act like it's funny,' she said.

'My lawyer says I'm about to be charged with child molestation. I'm also going to be sued. The lawyer for the plaintiff is a stooge for Val Chalons.'

'Shit,' she said. She walked away, her fists on her hips, breathing through her nose. Then she walked back toward me, her expression set. 'I'm not going to be party to this. You're on the desk, full pay, until I say otherwise.'

'I don't think you should –'

She pressed her finger against my lips. 'You got that?' she said.

'Yes, ma'am,' I said.

'Good,' she said.

Two hours later a woman detective who worked sex crimes notified me that Mrs. Mabel Poche had filed molestation charges against me. The location of the alleged crime was the restroom inside Molly's administrative offices. The date was the day Molly's agency had sponsored a hot dog roast and a race of hundreds of plastic ducks down Bayou Teche. An incident I hardly remembered – a lost child about to wet his pants, needing someone to take him into the restroom – was now aimed at my breast like a crossbow. The woman detective scheduled an interview with me for Friday morning. The *Daily Iberian* had already picked up the story.

I signed out of the office early and drove to Molly's agency. She was under the pole shed, a gunnysack in one hand, picking up chicken heads that had been lopped off on a butcher stump.

'Who's the ax murderer?' I said.

'We're going to have a chicken fry tomorrow night. I think one of the kids hijacked my weed cutter. Look at that.' She nodded at a machete that lay across the stump, its blade matted with blood and feathers.

'You remember a white woman by the name of Mabel Poche?' I asked.

'I haven't seen her in a while. I think she stopped coming around.'

'She says I molested her child in your office building. She's filing criminal charges as well as a civil suit.'

'It's been quite a day, huh?' she said.

'I suspect she'll sue your agency as well.'

'Oh, yes indeed. You can count on Mrs. Poche.'

'Helen Soileau stood up for me. I've still got my job. Things could be worse.'

She picked up the machete and knocked it clean of bloody feathers against the stump. 'You want to go out for dinner tonight and maybe fool around later?' She tossed a strand of hair out of her eye and waited for my reply.

Saturday morning my lawyer, Porteus O'Malley, called the house. 'A couple of lowlifes came by my office yesterday,' he said. 'They claim they were at Clementine's when you remodeled Val Chalons's head. They're willing to testify Chalons tried to pick up a steak knife from a table.'

'Who are these guys?' I said.

He told me their names. 'They say they're from around here, but they sound like they grew up in New Orleans,' he said.

'They used to peel safes with Stevie Giacano. Both of them have bonds with Nig Rosewater and Wee Willie Bimstine.'

He paused. 'Is Clete Purcel behind this?'

'His heart is in the right place,' I said.

'It's called subornation of perjury. How bad do you want to do time in Angola, Dave?'

The cable show whose intention supposedly was to expose the underside of our little town on the Teche aired that night. It had probably been in the can for weeks, but the producers had managed to bleed in footage of me destroying Val Chalons's face and half of Clementine's Restaurant. Actually, I had to give them credit. The show's juxtaposition of photography was splendidly done. The documentary began with aerial footage of the Louisiana wetlands, serpentine bayous shadowed by cypress and live oak trees, and huge tracts of young sugar cane bending in the wind, followed by land-based, wide-angle shots of plantation homes, street festivals, and sugar refineries shrouded at night inside clouds of electrified steam.

Then a camera obviously mounted on the window of a moving vehicle, as though the subject material had suddenly become a source of danger to the journalists, panned across New Iberia's inner-city slum, showing black dope dealers and white crack whores working the trade on Hopkins Avenue. A moment later the scene shifted to my house and Doogie Dugas and several uniformed cops going through the front entrance, while a woman identified as a Catholic nun stood half-undressed in the bedroom doorway, clutching a shirt against her breasts.

Clete Purcel watched the show in a blue-collar bar on the west end of town, made a call on a pay phone, then drove to my house and threw a pecan hard against my front window.

'What's up, Cletus?' I said, stepping out on the gallery.

'You see the molestation story in the morning paper?'

'Nope.'

'You see yourself on television tonight?' he said.

'Yep.'

'Stop waiting for Chalons to fall in his own shit. It's time to take this lying cocksucker off at the neck. I've got a call in to Jericho Johnny Wineburger.'

I walked into the yard. The wind in the trees caused shadows to slide across Clete's face, like water running down a window glass. He was wearing his porkpie hat and a wilted tropical shirt and gray slacks, and I could smell weed and beer-sweat trapped in his clothes.

'You're kidding, aren't you?' I said.

'You think you can beat these guys playing by the rules? Wake up. They own the ballpark. We're just the humps who carry out the garbage.'

'Been toking on a little Mexican gage tonight?'

'No, what I've been doing is wrapping a "drop" in black tape and filing off a few serial numbers.'

'Come on in and eat something.'

'I'm going to take Chalons down. Nobody is calling my partner a perve. You see Jericho Johnny around town, pretend you don't.'

He climbed in his pink Cadillac and roared off, a tape deck blasting out Bob Seeger's 'The Horizontal Bop,' leaves blowing from under the wire wheels.

Would Clete actually try to pop Val Chalons? Or was that just a mixture of weed and beer talking? I thought about it. Clete's Caddy swerved at the corner in front of the Shadows, flattening a garbage can into a building.

chapter twenty-five

The 911 call from a fisherman out by Lake Dautrieve came in at 5:43 Monday morning. 'She don't have no clothes on. I t'ought maybe it was some kind of accident. Like maybe she fallen out of a tree or somet'ing,' he said.

'Sir, calm down. Is the person injured?' the female dispatcher said.

'Injured? What you talkin' about?' the caller replied.

Helen picked me up in my front yard. The sun was just striking the brick buildings on Main as we crossed the drawbridge and headed up Loreauville Road toward the lake.

'I thought I was on the desk,' I said.

'This cruiser is your desk, so shut up,' she said.

We arrived at the crime scene just behind the coroner's van. Uniformed sheriff's deputies from both Iberia and St. Martin parishes were already there, stringing yellow tape through scrub oaks and gum and willow trees on the edge of the lake. The shallows were carpeted with hyacinths, and I could see the black heads of moccasins between the lily pads, barely breaking the water. High up on the windstream, turkey buzzards circled like ragged-edged oriental kites. I watched Koko Hebert stoop under the tape and walk toward a forked oak tree with the plodding ennui of a man who has long given up on the world.

Helen took a call on a hand-held radio, then tossed it on the seat of the cruiser. 'The boys from Baton Rouge are on their way,' she said.

'They think it's the Baton Rouge guy?' I said.

'A tattoo on the vic is the same as on a woman who was abducted by LSU Sunday afternoon,' she replied.

The abduction had taken place in a middle-income neighborhood a few blocks off Highland Road. The victim, Barbara Trajan, was the mother of two children, an aerobics instructor at a health club, and the wife of a high school football coach. She had a tattoo of an orange and purple butterfly on her abdomen, just below her navel. The previous afternoon, she had been working in her flower bed, one that paralleled the driveway. Her husband had taken the children to a church softball game. When they returned home, Barbara Trajan had disappeared. Her gardening trowel and one cotton glove lay on the concrete.

I looked across the lake at the sun. It was molten and watery, wrapped in vapor, just above the tree line. The previous night had been hot and dry, the clouds crackling with thunder that gave no rain. Now, a breeze suddenly sprang up in the south and riffled across the lake. A gray, salty odor that had been trapped inside the woods struck my face. Helen cleared her throat and spit to the side. 'Oh boy,' she said.

We pulled on latex gloves and went inside the tape. The ground was leaf strewn and soft, torn with drag marks, gouged by boots or heavy shoes, as though a man had been pulling a weight that resisted his grasp. The victim was nude, her chin fitted at an upward angle in the fork of a tree. Her wrists were bound behind her with plastic cuffs, her eyes open, as though they had been poached by a vision of human behavior she had never imagined. A white cotton work glove protruded from her mouth.

Koko Hebert stood behind the dead woman, wiping

mosquitoes out of his face. I saw him stoop over, reach out with his latex-gloved hand, then rise up again and jot something on a notepad. A moment later he walked past me, without speaking, his shoulders humped, his face flushed and oily in the heat. He ducked under the crime scene tape and went out by the lake, by himself, into the breeze. I followed him down by the lakeside. He was still writing on his notepad.

'Wait for the postmortem and I'll be able to speak with more specificity,' he said.

'I'm on a short tether. I'm not sure how much time I have left with the department,' I said.

'Entrance through the rear. Bite marks on the shoulders. Death by strangulation. With a chain of some kind. With tiny links in it.' He looked at me.

'Like the little piece of chain Fontaine Belloc hid on her person before she died?'

'That'd be my bet,' he said.

'How do you read this guy? Don't give me your cynical runaround, either, Koko. You're an intelligent man.'

'He's a classic psychopath, which means we don't have a clue about what goes on inside his head. But if you ask me, I think he's trying to lead the hunt away from Baton Rouge. I don't think he's from around here.'

'Why not?'

'He's transported two vics eighty miles into Iberia Parish. Both were alive during the trip. That means he incurred risks he didn't have to. It was for a reason. My guess is he lives not far from Baton Rouge, maybe around Port Allen or Denham Springs. He's squeezing his big-boy every time he sees us scratching our heads on TV.'

'Maybe he had another reason,' I said.

Koko lit a cigarette and studied the lake, either lost in his own thoughts or out of indifference to anything I had to say. Twenty feet out from the bank, I saw the gnarled, green-black tail of a gator roil the lily pads. Koko exhaled his cigarette smoke into the wind. 'Yeah?' he said.

'What if dropping the vic here is a "fuck-you" card for people he knows?' I said.

Koko continued to puff on his cigarette, his eyes veiled. I walked back toward the cruiser, then heard him laboring his way up the slope behind me.

'Know anything about anthropology, primitive man's behavior, that kind of crap?' he said.

'No,' I replied.

'Sometimes serial killers mark their territory, particularly when it has some kind of personal meaning to them. It looks like there're piss stripes on a tree back there. There were also piss stripes on a tree by the pond where we found the Belloc woman. I didn't pay much attention to it at the time because we had the semen on the vic.

'I've read through all the forensics on the Baton Rouge crime scenes. None of them makes mention of the perpetrator marking the area with urine. I think our guy is telling us something.'

'Why didn't he disfigure this one?' I asked.

'He did. Inside. I told you to wait on the post, but you don't listen. If you ever get this demented fuck in your sights, ask God to look the other way.'

It was not a morning to think about what I had seen.

Any inner-city street cop, homicide investigator, or member of a sex crimes unit carries images in his head that never go away, not unless he wants to burn them out of his skull with booze or yellow jackets or black speed. But what if the problem is not him or even the job? What if the problem is the simple fact that there is something bestial and cruel at work in the human race? What if his perception as a police officer is not a jaded but an accurate one?

When I was on loan to Miami P.D. I saw a black

mob in Liberty City drag three Cuban kids from a car and crush their heads into pulp with curbstones. I also saw five uniformed cops in Opa Locka beat a black motorcyclist to death with batons. Clete and I cut a corpse dancing with maggots out of a brick wall and had our unmarked car Molotoved in the same night. I've worked child abuse cases I will never discuss with anyone.

But the expression on the face of the Trajan woman, her neck and head trapped helplessly in the fork of a tree, contained a suggestion about the human condition I couldn't get out of my mind. I suspected she was a brave woman and fought her attacker to the end. I also suspected she was not undone by either her fear or the pain and sexual humiliation he visited upon her. But what I had seen in her eyes was worse. 'Loss' is not the right word for it. It was a realization that she was alone and powerless, and that beyond the perimeter of her vision a sadist was about to steal everything of value she owned – her dignity, her self-respect, her husband, her children, her career as an aerobics instructor, the quiet home she returned to daily, and finally her life. All to satisfy the libidinous pleasure of a deviate to whom she had as much importance as a stick of chewing gum.

What sociological factors could produce a man like this?

I felt almost as though I could see his face, like a figure moving around on the edge of a dream. Maybe I had seen him the night Honoria Chalons was murdered. Maybe I had processed him into jail, held each of his fingers in mine and rolled them on an ink pad, pressing the whorls in his skin onto paper, as though I were creating a dermatological artwork. Maybe the oil in his skin was transferred to mine.

But I knew with certainty that he was not far away, and that he would strike again soon, perhaps much closer to home, and that his intention was to deliver as much injury as possible to our community. I knew this in a way that was not demonstrable, not even to myself. But I knew it just the same, perhaps because I could not deny the cathartic, hard-pounding rush that violence had always brought me, one that was as pure and bright as a glass of ninety-proof whiskey flung onto a fire.

I went into Helen's office. She was gazing out the window at the cemetery, her hands in her back pockets, her breasts as firm as grapefruit against her shirt. 'How's it rockin', Pops?' she said.

'The serial guy is somebody we know.'

'Like down at the Kiwanis?'

'He broke his pattern when he murdered the teenage street hooker in New Orleans. It's not coincidence she talked to Clete and me a few hours before she died.'

'I know all this, Dave. It's not helpful.'

'Answer me this: With all the power and influence that Val Chalons has, why would he waste his time trying to ruin my reputation instead of finding his sister's killer?'

'He thinks you did it?'

'No, he doesn't. He's covering his own butt.'

I could see the fatigue in her eyes and I felt like a fool. What was she supposed to do? Take me off the desk because I had an unprovable intuition? Then I realized she wasn't thinking about our conversation at all.

'Raphael Chalons just got the paddles at Iberia General. He may not make it,' she said.

'What happened?' I said.

'He was visiting his son and had a stroke.'

I collected my mail from my box and went back to my office, dazed, unable to explain my feelings to myself about a man I had always thought of as corrupt and vaguely sinister. I found myself staring at the envelopes and memos in my hand without the words on them registering. I sat down at my desk and called the hospital. An intern in the intensive-care unit told me Raphael Chalons was alive but paralyzed down one side and unable to speak.

'Is he going to pull through?' I said.

'You say you're with the sheriff's department?' he asked.

'Yes, sir.'

'He's been in bad health for some time,' he said.

A half hour later Mack Bertrand called from the lab. 'I don't know if this is good news or bad news,' he said. 'The casts I made out at the Trajan crime scene this morning? I'm reasonably sure we've got a match with the casts I made under your bedroom window.'

'You say "reasonably sure"?'

'You ever watch this TV show where guys are always examining used Q-tips or a Kleenex some gal wiped her lipstick on?'

'I'm lost,' I said.

'None of this stuff is nuclear science. We're talking about muddy boots,' he said.

I called Molly at her agency and told her the voyeur at our house may have been the Baton Rouge serial killer.

'Well, he'd better not come around again,' she said. 'I'm going to pick up some steaks on the way home. Is there anything else you want from the store?'

You want a stand-up woman in your life? Marry a nun.

I bought flowers at the Winn-Dixie and took them to the nurse's station in the intensive-care unit at Iberia General. 'They're for Mr. Raphael,' I said.

'He can't have flowers in his room now. But I can keep them here at the station and put them in his room when he's moved,' she said. She was a pleasant-looking older woman, with soft pink skin and blue-tinted white hair.

'That would be fine,' I said. 'Can I talk to him?'

'No, I'm afraid not,' she replied. 'Who did you say you are?'

'Detective Dave Robicheaux, with the Iberia Sheriff's Department.'

'Are you the one who –'

'Mr. Chalons's son insulted my wife and I tore him up. I'm the one.'

'I see.' She had set my flowers on a shelf under the counter. She retrieved them and pushed them toward me. 'You need to talk to the resident about these,' she said, holding her eyes on mine. 'Sometimes the water in the container forms bacteria and creates problems for us.'

I walked off and left the flowers where they were. Through a partially opened door I saw the comatose face of Raphael Chalons, his head sunk deep in the pillow, his leaded eyes and hooked nose strangely suggestive of a carrion bird's.

That evening, while Snuggs and Tripod watched Molly flip a pair of sirloin steaks on the grill in the backyard, I called Jimmie at his apartment and asked for the address and phone number of the home on Lake Pontchartrain where Ida Durbin was staying with Jimmie's friends.

'What for?' he asked.

'I'm being hung out to dry by her son. That might have something to do with it.'

'Why blame her?'

'I'm not. So lose the attitude.'

'She's not in New Orleans.'

'*Jimmie –*'

'She's in Lafayette. Out on Pinhook Road. So is Lou Kale. Stay away from Kale. He's a real shithead.'

'You figured that out?'

After I hung up the phone, I joined Molly at our picnic table in the backyard and we ate supper under the trees with Tripod and Snuggs, who had their own bowls at the end of the table. Then she and I walked downtown and had ice cream, as couples do on a late-summer evening, and I said nothing about Ida Durbin or the Baton Rouge serial killer.

At sunup the next day I drove to Lafayette.

chapter twenty-six

I don't know what I expected. My experience with age is that it instills a degree of patience in some, leaves the virtuous spiritually unchanged, feeds the character defects in others, and brings little wisdom to any of us. Perhaps I'm wrong. I wanted to be wrong when I met Ida Durbin. I also wanted to believe I would not act on an old resentment should I have the bad luck to run into her estranged husband, Lou Kale.

They were staying in separate rooms in a lovely old motel built of historic brick on a part of Pinhook Road that had not been blighted by urban development and was still shrouded by spreading live oaks. It was not yet 7:00 a.m. when I showed my badge at the desk and asked for the room number of Ms. Connie Coyne. I had not called in advance.

'We don't have anyone by that name staying here,' the clerk said.

'Look again,' I said.

'No one by that name is staying here, sir,' he repeated, looking past me at someone waiting to check out.

'Don't tell me that. She's here. So is her husband. His name is Lou Coyne.'

'Oh, yes. They're both registered under his name. I just saw her go into the dining room,' the clerk said.

'Thank you,' I said.

According to Jimmie, Ida and her husband kept separate homes in Miami and obviously separate accommodations when they traveled. But the fact they were both registered at the motel under his name, indicating the charges were probably billed to the same credit card, made me wonder how separate in reality Ida's life was from her husband's.

Few people were in the dining room and it wasn't hard to pick out Ida from the other motel guests eating breakfast by the French doors, not far from the buffet table. Her hair still had its natural reddish tone and the years had not taken away her height or the thin, well-defined features of her face. The dramatic change was in her complexion. Perhaps it was an optical illusion, but in the broken light from the terrace her skin seemed etiolated, the freckles drained of color.

She was nibbling on a piece of dry toast while she read from a hardbound book. The only food on her plate consisted of a few melon slices, a half dozen grapes, and a piece of Swiss cheese. Her cup was filled with hot tea. She wore a flowered sundress that I suspected came from an expensive shop on Biscayne Boulevard.

She glanced up at me only when my shadow fell across her reading page. 'Why, Dave,' she said. 'I never could get over how much you and Jimmie looked alike.'

'How's the life, Ida?' I said.

'Oh, I hope that's not meant to injure. It's not, is it?'

I sat down without being asked. 'Why didn't you write and tell us you were okay, Ida?'

'Because I wasn't okay. Because I was a kid. Because I told myself Jimmie would be fine without me. Pick one you like.'

'A guy named Troy Bordelon went to the grave thinking he was partly responsible for your death,' I said.

'I never heard of this person. I didn't choose the life I've lived, Dave. It was chosen for me. But others may see it differently.'

'I happen to be in the latter category, Ida. Val Chalons is trying to frame me on a child molestation charge. He also defamed my wife. That's why he's in Iberia General Hospital. I stomped the shit out of him. If I had it to do over again, I'd rip up his whole ticket. The only regret I have is that his father may have had a seizure because of the damage I did to his son.'

If she took any offense at my remarks, it disappeared inside her face. 'You seem to be handling the pressures of life well enough,' she said, gazing at the terrace and the moss that was lifting in the oak trees by the pool.

I said earlier that in my view age is not a magic agency in our lives. But perhaps Ida was the exception after all. The country girl who had paddled an inner tube far out from shore and saved Jimmie and me from sharks was gone; the woman who had replaced her possessed the timeless and inured hauteur of a successful medieval courtesan. Jimmie had said she had wanted to see her son, Valentine. But where had she been all those years? Raphael Chalons had raised him, not she. Had Mr. Raphael excluded her from her son's life? I doubted it.

'Lost in thought?' she said.

'Why has your son done so much to harm me and my wife? Is he that fearful people will discover who his mother is? Is he that cowardly and insecure?'

She drank from her teacup, then set it back down in the saucer. The freckles on her shoulders seemed to disappear in the glaze of sunlight through the French doors. 'It was good seeing you, Dave. I hope things work out for you and your wife,' she said.

'Next time you want to wish me well, Ida, put it on a postcard and drop it in a mailbox,' I said.

'You're a bitter man,' she said.

'Just a realistic one,' I replied.

But my failed effort at reconciliation with Ida Durbin and the past was not over. On my way out of the lobby into the porte cochere, I almost knocked down a man dressed in a blazer, an open-collar print shirt, knife-creased slacks, and oxblood loafers. He was a muscularly compact man, his skin deeply tanned, his iron-gray hair slick with gel. When I collided with him, he had been holding an unlit cigarette in one hand and a gold lighter in the other. He apologized, lit his cigarette in an expansive fashion, and started to walk around me.

'You pointed a gun at me in a Galveston motel in 1958, Mr. Kale,' I said. 'You really scared me. You called yourself the butter and egg man.'

'Some people are walking memory banks. Me? I can't remember what I ate for supper last night,' he said.

'You guys are here to do business, aren't you? Your visit doesn't have anything to do with Val Chalons.'

'We need to dial it down, my man. I need to get inside, too, if you'll step aside.'

'I'm a sheriff's detective, Mr. Kale. You're a pimp. You want a trip down to the bag, that can be arranged. But regardless of what happens here, you keep your ass out of New Iberia, and you keep a lot of gone between you and Clete Purcel. You reading me on this, Mr. Kale?'

He removed his cigarette from his mouth and tipped his ashes away from his person so they didn't blow back on his coat. 'The name is Coyne, Lou Coyne. And you got the wrong dude, buddy.'

He went through the revolving door into the motel. It had rained that morning, and the breeze under the porte cochere smelled of wet flowers and leaves and the lichen that was crusted on the massive limbs of the live oaks. I didn't want to get any deeper into the world of Ida Durbin and Lou Kale, no more than you want to immerse yourself in the effluent that backs up from a sewage pipe. But I knew a predator when I saw one. Lou Kale and Ida

Durbin were no longer symbols or milestones out of Jimmie's and my adolescent experience. Nor were they simply foils to the innocence of the postwar era in which we had grown up. They may have been upgraded from their origins and elevated by economic circumstance into a larger world, but Ida Durbin and Lou Kale were the emissaries of organized crime, no matter what they called themselves. They were real and they were *here*.

Want to find out who the closet boozers are in your neighborhood? Ask the garbage man. Want to check out the local politics? Talk with the barber. Want to find out what your neighbors are *really* like? Ask a kid. Want to find out who's washing money at the track, fencing stolen property, running dope, greasing the zoning board, providing hookers for conventioneers, or selling gang-bangers Tech-nines modified with hell triggers? Forget news media and police pencil pushers and official sources of all kinds. Ask a beat cop who hasn't slept since 1965 or a street junkie whose head glows in the dark.

During the morning I talked with a retired DEA agent while he drove golf balls on a practice range; an ex-Air American pilot who flew nine years inside the Golden Triangle; an old-time Washington, D.C., hooker who operated a bar in North Lafayette; and a pharmaceutically addicted city Vice cop who had done two tours in Vietnam with the 173rd Airborne Brigade. They all shared one commonality – they had been witnesses to events of historical importance that few people knew about and they had seen forms of human behavior about which they never spoke. The latter quality alone, to my mind, made them exceptional human beings.

For generations all the vice in Louisiana had been run by a few individuals in New Orleans. Even when I was a beat cop, no one opened a brothel, set up a slot machine, or sold one lid of Afghan skunk without first kissing the ring of Didoni Giacano. But Didi Gee was pushing up mushrooms, gambling was a state-sponsored industry, and narcotics had become part of the culture. Louisiana, once a closed fiefdom operated by the appointees of Frank Costello, was now wide open to the entrepreneurial spirit. Drug mules hammered down Interstate 10, from both Houston and Miami, loaded with weed, meth, and coke. Pimps had their pick of crack whores, whose managerial costs were minimal.

But none of my friends had ever heard of Lou Kale or Ida Durbin. Nor had they heard of anyone going by the names of Connie and Lou Coyne. I began to wonder if I had been too hard on Ida. She may have saved Clete Purcel's life, I told myself, and according to Clete's account, even Lou Kale had seemed a reluctant participant in his interrogation and beating.

Or was I being romantic and foolish about people who had invested their lives in the use of others?

I drove back to New Iberia, unable to think straight. Helen had left a Post-it on my door. SEE ME, it said.

'Where have you been?' she asked, looking up from her desk.

'I took some personal time in Lafayette. I called Wally before eight,' I replied.

'What kind of "personal time"?'

'I saw Ida Durbin.'

'I have to meet this woman.'

'What is it, Helen?'

'Raphael Chalons wants to see you.'

'Why?'

'You got me. Unless he thinks you're a priest.' She looked at her watch. 'It sounded to me like he was already on the bus.'

I have heard both hospice personnel and psychologists maintain that human beings lose body weight at the moment of death, that the dimensions of the skeleton and the tissue visibly shrink before the eye, as though the escape of the soul leaves behind a cavity swirling with atoms. Raphael Chalons was not dead when I reached Iberia General, but his stricken face and hollow eyes and the sag of his flesh on his bones made me wonder if the Angel of Death was not deliberately casting a slow shadow on the haunted man who stared back at me from the hospital bed.

'I tried to bring you flowers earlier, Mr. Raphael. But the nurse felt my visit wasn't an appropriate one,' I said.

My words and their banality were obviously of no interest to him. His eyes were as black as a raven's wing, his facial skin oily, spiked with whiskers, furrowed around the mouth. One hand lay palm-up on top of the sheet. He crooked his fingers at me.

I did not want to approach him. I did not want to inhale his breath. I did not want his words to put talons in my breast. I did not want to be held captive by another dying man.

But I leaned over him just the same. His fingers rose up and tapped my chest, as though he could convey meaning through my skin to compensate for the failure of his vocal cords. His lips moved, but his words were only pinpricks of spittle on my face.

'I can't understand you, sir,' I said.

A flame burned in his cheeks and his eyes rolled up at mine, as a dependent lover's might. A clot broke in his throat. 'Not his fault,' he said.

'Sir?' I said.

His fingers tore a button on my shirt. His breath was dank, earth-smelling, like dirt spaded from a tree-covered grave. 'The fault is mine. All my fault. Everything,' he whispered. 'Please stop my son.'

'From doing what, Mr. Raphael?'

But his hand released my shirt and his gaze receded

from mine, as though he were sinking into a black well and I was now only a marginal figure on its perimeter.

The nurse came in and closed the blinds. It was only then I noticed that my flowers were on the windowsill. 'Don't worry, he's only sleeping,' she said. 'He has bursts of energy, then he falls asleep. He liked your flowers.'

'Has he talked about his son?' I asked.

'No, not at all,' she replied. She nodded toward the door, indicating she wanted to finish the conversation in the corridor. 'May I be frank? I was very disturbed by something I saw take place here. It was very distressing.'

'Go ahead,' I said.

'Mr. Val came into the room with two lawyers. They tried to get Mr. Raphael to dictate a will. But he wouldn't do it. Mr. Val was quite upset. No, the better term is irate.'

'Thank you for telling me this,' I said.

'You and Mr. Raphael must be very close.'

'Why do you think that?'

'He only asked to see one other person. Someone named Ida. Fortunately, she showed up here about an hour ago. I saw her stroking his hair on the pillow. She seemed a very elegant person. Do you know her, Detective Robicheaux?'

At three that afternoon a nurse's aide found Raphael Chalons half out of his bed, his sightless eyes staring out of his head as though he had looked into a camera's flash. The blanket and sheet had cascaded over his shoulders, like the mantle a medieval lord might wear as he walked toward a blade of light on the earth's rim.

chapter twenty-seven

Wednesday evening Molly and I towed my boat to Henderson Swamp and fished at sunset inside a grove of flooded cypress trees. In the distance we could see car headlights flowing across the elevated highway that traverses a chain of bays and canals inside the center of the Atchafalaya Basin. The air was breathless, the moon rising above the cypress into a magenta sky, the water so still you could hear the hyacinths popping open back in the trees.

We kept two largemouth bass that we caught on plugs and headed across a long bay toward the boat landing. In the dusk I could see cows standing on a green levee and lights inside the baitshop and restaurant at the landing. We winched the boat onto our trailer, then drove up the concrete ramp and went inside the baitshop for a cold drink. Through the window I saw a man on the gallery pouring a bag of crushed ice into his cooler, rearranging the fish inside. He put the plastic wrapper in a trash can and drank from a bottle of beer while he admired the sunset.

'Wait here a minute,' I said to Molly.

'Somebody you know?' she said.

'I hope not,' I said.

I approached the man on the gallery. The wind had come up, and I could see the leaves of the cypress trees lifting like green lace out on the water. The man felt my weight on the plank he was standing on. He lowered the bottle from his mouth without drinking from it and turned toward me. 'Yeah, I remember you used to talk about fishing over here,' he said.

'Always a pleasure to see you, Johnny,' I said.

He nodded, as though a personal greeting did not require any other response.

'How's your mother?' I asked.

'When you're that old and you smell the grave, you're thankful for little things. She don't complain.'

He slid another bottle of beer out of his cooler and twisted off the cap. The fish in the cooler were stiff and cold-looking and speckled with blood and ice under the overhead light. Jericho Johnny's shirt puffed open in a gust of wind across the water. He turned his face toward the horizon, as though a fresh scent had invaded his environment. As he stood framed against a washed-out sky, his eyes devoid of any humanity that I could detect, his nose wrinkling slightly, I wondered if he wasn't in fact the liege lord of Charon, his destroyed voice box whispering in the blue-collar dialect of the Irish Channel while he eased his victims quietly across the Styx.

I leaned on the railing, my arm only inches from his. 'You can't do business in Iberia Parish, Johnny,' I said.

He raised his beer bottle to his mouth and took a small sip off it. He glanced over his shoulder at Molly, who sat at a table in the baitshop, reading a magazine. 'That your lady?' he said.

'Look at me,' I said. 'Val Chalons is off limits. I don't care what kind of deal you cut with Clete Purcel.'

He closed the lid on his cooler and latched it. 'Purcel don't have anything to do with me, Robicheaux. You were nice to my mother. I was nice to you. In fact, twice I was nice to you. That means I go where I want. I do what I want,' he said.

He placed his unfinished beer on the railing and walked toward his car, his cooler balanced on his shoulder, ice water draining down his shirtback as though his skin possessed no sensation.

I went to Clete Purcel's office on Main Street during lunchtime the next day. His office had been a sports parlor during the 1940s, then had been gutted by a fire and turned into a drugstore that went bankrupt after the Wal-Mart store was built south of town. In the last week an interior decorator had hung the ancient brick walls with historical photographs of New Iberia and antique firearms encrusted with rust that had been found in a pickle barrel under a nineteenth-century warehouse on the bayou. The new ambiance was stunning. So was the clientele going in and out of the office. Clete was now starting up his own bail bond service, and the utilitarian furniture in the front of the office was draped with people whose idea of a good day was the freedom to watch trash television without interruption.

I walked through the litter and cigarette smoke and out the back door to the canvas-shaded brick patio where Clete often ate his lunch. He had planted palms and banana trees on the edge of the bricks, and had set up a huge electric fan by a spool table and sway-backed straw chair that served as his dining area. He was hunched over a crab burger, reading the *Times-Picayune*, the wind flapping the canvas over his head, when he heard me behind him.

'What's the gen, noble mon?' he said.

'You heard about Raphael Chalons's death?' I said.

'Yeah, tragic loss.'

'I saw him just before he died. He asked me to stop his son.'

'From doing what?'

'He didn't get a chance to say.'

Clete set down his food and wiped his mouth. He gazed out at the whiteness of the sun on the bayou. 'You're saying Val Chalons is a serial killer, maybe?'

'You tell me.'

'He's a punk who thinks he can wipe his ass on other people. He made you out a perve and that's why I –'

'What?'

'Called up Jericho Johnny Wineburger after I'd been toking on some substances I should have left alone.'

'That's the second reason I'm here. I saw him last night at Henderson Swamp.'

Clete twisted in his chair, the straw weave creaking under his weight. 'You saw Wineburger? Here?'

'I told him he wasn't going to do business in Iberia Parish. He told me to go screw myself.'

'Dave, I called this guy back. I said I shouldn't have bothered him, that I was wired, that we didn't need his help, that Chalons is not worthy of his talents. We had an understanding.'

'I didn't get that impression.'

'Look, here's how it went down. Originally I told Johnny we didn't need Val Chalons as a factor in our lives right now. Don't look at me like that. Johnny owes twenty grand to a couple of shylocks. The vig is a point and a half a week. If he doesn't get his act together, he's going to lose his saloon. I told him the shylocks owe me a favor and I could get them to give him two free months on the vig if he could get the principal together. But I called him back when I was sober and told him it was hands-off on Chalons. I told him the deal with the shylocks was still solid – no vig for two months. But he doesn't hurt Chalons. That was absolutely clear.'

'Maybe his pride won't let him take a free ride.'

'Wineburger? That's like a toilet bowl worrying about bad breath.'

'Then what is he doing here?' I said.

'With a guy like that —' Clete blew air up into his face and gave me a blank look. 'Don't let me roll any more Mexican imports, will you?'

A thunderstorm pounded through town that afternoon, then disappeared as quickly as it had arrived. When I got home from work, the lawn was scattered with wet leaves and the birdhouse Molly had nailed in the fork of a live oak had split across the nail holes and cracked apart on the ground, spilling all the birdseed in a yellow pile. I gathered up the broken pieces, dropped them in the garbage can, and found the listing for Andre Bergeron in the Jeanerette section of our local telephone directory.

'This is Dave Robicheaux,' I said when he picked up the receiver. 'I'd like to buy one of your birdhouses.'

'You called at the right time. I got a sale on. One for twenty-five dol'ars or two for forty-nine ninety-five.'

'I think I'll stick with one.'

'Installation is free.'

'Don't worry about it. Just drop it off at Molly's office and I'll send you a check.'

'No, suh, I give door-to-door complete service. That's what you got to do to make a bidness a success today. Me and Tee Bleu got to go to the Wal-Mart. You gonna be home?'

Twenty minutes later he was at the house, balancing on a stepladder while he wired the birdhouse to an oak limb. His son, Tee Bleu, was throwing pecans into the bayou. I wrote a check for Andre on the back steps.

'Miss Molly at home?' he said.

'No, she's at the grocery store. What's up?'

'Nothing. I just heard some people talking at the agency. Stuff they didn't have no right to say.'

His eyes fixed on me, then he began to look innocuously around the yard, his whole head turning from spot to

298

spot, as though it were attached to a metal rod.

'Spit it out,' I said.

'A couple of ladies was saying they ain't bringing their children to the agency no mo' 'cause of what happened.'

'You talking about the child molestation charge filed against me?'

'Mr. Val behind that, suh. It ain't right. No, suh. Ain't right.'

'You know much about Mr. Val?'

'Know as much as I need to.'

'You're a mysterious man, Andre.' I tore the check out of my checkbook and handed it to him.

His half-moon eyebrows could have been snipped out of black felt and pasted on his forehead. He studied his little boy playing down by the bayou, and shook his shirt on his chest to cool his skin. Through the trees we could see a dredge barge passing on the bayou, its hull low in the water, its decks loaded with piles of mud.

'When I was a li'l boy about that size, I seen a gator come out of the bayou after a baby. Baby was in diapers, toddling along on the edge of the water. His mama was hanging wash up by the trees, probably t'inking about the worthless man who put that baby in her belly. Gator got the baby by his li'l leg and started dragging him toward the water. Wasn't nothing nobody could do about it. That gator was long as your truck and two feet 'cross the head. The mother and the old folks was running 'round screaming, hitting at it wit' buckets and crab nets and cane poles, but that gator just kept on moving down to the water, wit' the baby hanging out its mouth, just like they was hitting on it with pieces of string.

'Then Mr. Raphael run down from the big house wit' a butcher knife and cut the gator's t'roat. He drove the baby to Charity Hospital in Lafayette and saved his life. People couldn't talk about nothing else for a year except how Mr. Raphael save that po' child's life.'

Andre stopped his story and looked down the slope at his son. The late sun was a burnt orange through the trees, and blue jays were clattering in the canopy.

'I'm not sure I get the point, Andre,' I said.

'People loved Mr. Raphael. But they ain't knowed him. Not like I knowed him. Not like I know Mr. Val. My li'l boy growing up in different times from the ones I growed up in. I'm real happy for that. That's the only point I was making, Mr. Dave. I got birdseed out in my car. You want me to fill up your birdhouse?'

'I have some in the shed. Thanks, anyway,' I said.

On his way out, he helped Molly carry in her groceries from her car, his face jolly and full of cheer as he set the bags down heavily, one after another, on the kitchen table.

After he was gone, I went inside and helped her put away the groceries. 'Andre told me some ladies at your agency won't bring their children there anymore,' I said.

'He shouldn't have done that,' she said.

'Man's just reporting what he heard.'

'I know who I married. That's all I care about.'

'You're a pretty good gal to hang out with,' I said.

I poured a glass of iced tea for both of us and sat down at the kitchen table to drink it. She leaned over me and hugged me under the neck and kissed me behind the ear.

'What was that for?' I said.

'I felt like it,' she replied.

That night I dreamed of two brown pelicans sailing low and flat over an inland bay in late autumn, the pouches under their beaks plump with fish. In the dream they continued north in their flight, across miles of sawgrass stiff with frost and bays that looked like hammered copper. They passed over a cluster of shrimp boats tied up at the docks in a coastal town, then followed a winding bayou into the heart of the Teche country. The pelicans turned in a wide circle over a swamp thick with gum trees and cypress snags, and sailed right across the home where Jimmie and I grew up. Through the eyes of the birds I saw the purple rust on the tin roof of the house and the cypress boards that had turned the color of scorched iron from the dust and smoke of stubble fires in the cane fields. I saw my mother and father in the backyard, hoeing out their Victory garden during World War II. I saw Jimmie and me in tattered overalls, building a wood fire under the big iron pot in which we cooked hog cracklings after first frost.

Then all the people in the yard looked up at the sky, like flowers turning into the sun, and waved at the pelicans.

I woke up from the dream and went into the kitchen to make coffee. What did the dream mean? Bootsie had said that one day the brown pelicans would come back to the Teche. But I didn't need dreams to tell me there were no pelicans on Bayou Teche, and that my parents were as dead as the world in which I grew up.

'Up early?' I heard Molly say.

'It's a beautiful morning,' I said.

She went outside and came back with both Tripod and Snuggs and filled their pet bowls. 'There's a robin standing on top of the new birdhouse,' she said.

'Andre Bergeron told me a story yesterday about Mr. Raphael saving a baby from a gator. Except his story seemed to be about something else.'

'A baby?'

'Yeah, a black baby. A gator came after it. Bergeron said when he was a little boy he saw Mr. Raphael save the baby from the gator.'

'The baby was Andre. At least that's what I always heard. The old man saved his life. Andre has ugly scars all over one calf.'

'Funny guy,' I said.

'Andre is sweet,' she replied. She looked at the clock on

the counter. 'It's only five-thirty. You sure you don't want to take a nap before you go to work?' She pursed her lips and waited, her chest rising and falling in the soft blueness of the morning.

'You talked me into it,' I said.

I attended the Friday noon meeting of an AA bunch known as the Insanity Group. The meeting was held in a dilapidated house in a poor section of town, and was supposedly a nonsmoking one. But people lit up in both the front and back doorways and flooded the house's interior with amounts of smoke that few bars contain. The people in the Insanity Group had paid hard dues – in jails, detox units, car wrecks, and the kind of beer-glass brawls that quickly turn homicidal. Few of the men shaved more than once every five or six days. Many of the women, most of whom were tattooed, considered themselves fortunate to have a job in a carwash. Anybody there whose life didn't trail clouds of chaos possessed the spiritual eminence of St. Francis of Assisi.

But their honesty and courage in dealing with the lot life had dealt them had always been an example to me. Unfortunately for me, the subject of the meeting was the Fourth Step of Alcoholics Anonymous, namely, making a thorough and fearless inventory of one's own conscience. It was not a subject I cared to broach, at least not since my encounter with Jericho Johnny Wineburger at Henderson Swamp.

I made no contribution during the meeting, although the previous week I had admitted my slip to everyone there.

'You want to say something, Dave?' the group leader said just before closing.

'My name is Dave. I'm an alcoholic,' I said.

'Hello, Dave!' everyone shouted.

'I'm glad to be here and sober. Thanks,' I said.

After the 'Our Father,' I bagged out the door and

headed for the department before any overly helpful people decided to chat with me about the Fourth Step.

I buried myself in the baskets of paperwork that had been delegated to me since I had been put on the desk. But I could not get Jericho Johnny out of my head. Clete had cranked his engine. Now neither he nor I could shut it off. In the meantime, Val Chalons had no clue that he was potential sharkmeat.

I hated the thought of what I had to do and fought with myself about it the entire weekend.

By noon Monday I was worn out with it and picked up the phone and called Val Chalons's residential number. The voice that answered was unfamiliar. I could hear hammering in the background, an electric saw whining through wood.

'Where's Mr. Chalons?' I asked.

'Out on the bayou, popping skeets. Well, they ain't exactly skeets.'

'Who's this?' I said.

'The carpenter.'

'Would you ask Mr. Chalons to come to the phone? This is Detective Dave Robicheaux.'

'He said I ain't suppose to bot'er him. Ain't you the guy who beat him up?'

I drove in my pickup down the bayou to the Chalons home. Only Saturday, the old man's ashes had been interred at a secular funeral. The transformation in progress at the property was stunning. A lawn crew of at least a dozen men was weeding out the flower beds, cracking apart and air-vacuuming layers of compacted leaves, ripping vines from the sides of the house, and stacking and burning piles of dead tree limbs.

Roofers, carpenters, brickmasons, and painters were at work inside and outside the house. The oak trees were dark green and looked stiff and clean against the sky. Both the yard and the house were now columned with sunlight. The terrace next to the side porch was already abloom with freshly planted flowers.

I walked through the trees, down the grassy slope toward the bayou. The scene taking place below could have been snipped from a magazine depiction of upper-class life in Cuba or Nicaragua prior to an era of Marxist revolution. A group of people I didn't know were gathered in the shade of a candy-striped awning, eating strawberry cake and drinking champagne, while two shooters with double-barrel shotguns took turns firing at live pigeons that a black man released one by one from a wire cage.

A nice-looking man in seersucker slacks, his tie pulled loose because of the heat, his sports coat hooked on his thumb over his shoulder, passed me on the slope. 'How are you?' he said.

'Fine. How do you do, sir?'

'It's mighty hot.' But the negative content of his reply was countered by a boyish smile. His hair was closely clipped, the part razor-edged, his face youthful and sincere.

'I've seen you on television. You're Mr. Alridge,' I said.

'Yes, sir. I am. Colin Alridge,' he said, and extended his hand.

A shotgun popped dully inside the breeze. I saw a pigeon in flight crumple and plummet into the water.

The televangelical lobbyist named Colin Alridge cut his head. 'That's an ugly business down there. I thought it was time for me to go,' he said.

'It's nice meeting you, Mr. Alridge,' I said.

'Yes, sir, same here,' he replied.

I watched him walk to his car, a bit awed at our age-old propensity for vesting power over our lives in individuals who themselves are probably dumbfounded by the gift that we arbitrarily bestow upon them. But I had a feeling

Colin Alridge would rue the day he had chosen to front points for the Chalons family and their casino interests.

Val Chalons disengaged himself from the group under the awning and walked out in the sunlight, shading his eyes from the glare with his hand. 'You don't seem to have parameters of any kind,' he said.

'Looks like you're doing quite a restoration on your old man's place,' I said.

'I don't care to hear my father referred to in that fashion,' he said.

'No disrespect meant. I didn't admire the ethos your father represented, but I liked him personally. Please accept my sympathies.'

'You're unbelievable,' he said.

Val's face was heavily made up to hide the beating I had given him. But cosmetics couldn't disguise the blood clot in his eye and the stitches in his mouth. Actually I felt sorry for him and wondered again at the level of violence that still lived inside me.

'I've got a problem of conscience, Val.'

'Thanks for sharing that, but I couldn't care less. I'd appreciate your leaving now.'

I heard one of the shooters say, 'Pull.' Another pigeon broke into flight, its wings throbbing, only to be blown apart above the bayou.

'That's an unlawful activity,' I said.

'Not on my land it isn't.'

The sun was boiling overhead. The shotgun popped again, like a dull headache that wouldn't go away.

'A friend of mine inadvertently sent the wrong signal to a guy by the name of Jericho Johnny Wineburger. He's a button man who works out of New Orleans. He's now in our area. I think he might try to do you harm.'

I tried to hold his stare but I couldn't. I looked across the bayou at the dust blowing out of a cane field.

'Button man?' Val said.

'A contract killer, a guy who pushes the "off" button on people. Jericho Johnny is a mean motor scooter, Val. He and another dude took out Bugsy Siegel's cousin with a shotgun.'

'Bugsy Siegel? This gets better all the time. And you've come here as a police officer to tell me that a friend of yours has aimed this person at me?'

'Yeah, I guess that sums it up.'

'Have some strawberry cake, Dave. Maybe a glass of non-alcoholic champagne, too. Back at your AA meetings, are you?' he said.

I walked back up the slope to my truck and used my cell phone to make an animal cruelty report on Val Chalons to the St. Mary Parish Sheriff's Department. I waited for their cruiser to show up before I left, to ensure as best I could that Chalons and his friends would kill no more pigeons that day. But more disturbing than his cruelty was his apparent indifference to the fact that a man like Johnny Wineburger might be in town to break his wheels. That one definitely would not slide down the pipe.

I got back to the office by 1:30 p.m., drinking a Coca-Cola packed with ice and lime slices, my heart rate up, my shirt peppered with sweat. Even in the air-conditioning, I couldn't stop perspiring. I washed my face in the lavatory and went up front for my mail. 'Been running up and down the stairs?' Wally said from the dispatcher's cage.

'How'd you know?' I replied.

But it wasn't funny. I could feel the blood veins tightening in the side of my head again and unconsciously I kept pushing at my scalp with my fingers, like a man who fears his brains are seeping out of his skull. Therapists call it psycho-neurotic anxiety. The manifestation is obvious but the cause is not, because the cause keeps itself armor-plated somewhere in the bottom of the id. I know of only one other experience that compares with the syndrome. Your combat tour is almost over. You're 'short,' counting days until you catch the big freedom bird home. Except your private calendar doesn't change the fact you're on a night trail in a Third World shithole, wrapped in your own stink, your skin crawling with insects, your toes mushy with trench foot, and out there in the jungle you're convinced Bedcheck Charlie is writing your name on an AK-47 round or a trip-wired 105 dud.

At 1:47 p.m. my Vice cop friend at Lafayette P.D. called. His name was Joe Dupree. Joe had worked Homicide for years before he had gone over to Vice, claiming he had burnt out on blood-splattered DOAs. But some said Joe simply wanted to be closer to a cheap source of narcotics. Sometimes I saw him at AA meetings. Other times I saw him wasted in a baitshop or by himself in his boat, out at Whiskey Bay, doing his own kind of time inside his own head.

'I busted a couple of lowlifes in North Lafayette last night. They say the word on the street is a husband-wife team out of Florida are setting up a new escort service,' he said.

'Lou and Connie Coyne?'

'That's who it sounds like.'

'Why now?' I asked.

'Oil is supposed to hit fifty dollars a barrel this year. You know a better local aphrodisiac?' he replied.

So much for the altruism of Ida Durbin, I thought.

Another half hour went by. I went into Helen's office. 'I've got to get off the desk,' I said.

She pulled on an earlobe. 'Really?' she said.

'Chalons is about to make a move. Against me or Molly or Clete. I saw this televangelical character Alridge out at his place. Jericho Johnny Wineburger is around, too. I can't figure any of it out.'

I thought she would be angry or at least irritated and dismissing. I knew I looked and sounded like a man waving his arms on the street, prophesying doom to anyone who would listen. Instead, she stood up and, just for something to do, arranged a floating flower in a glass bowl on her desk. 'The D.A. is going ahead with felony assault charges against you, Dave. Also, there's that molestation issue. Maybe we ought to count our blessings.'

'Roust Wineburger. I think he's got a contract on somebody. But I don't know who.'

'Give me an address,' she said, picking up a pen.

'I saw him fishing at Henderson Swamp.'

She clicked the button on her pen several times, staring wanly into space, afraid to speak lest she hurt me in ways she couldn't repair.

I went back to my office and tried to think. But long ago I had learned that my best thinking usually got me drunk. Through the window I saw a truck sideswipe a car at the train crossing, smashing it into a telephone pole, and was glad for the diversion. I dumped my incoming baskets of accident and domestic dispute reports and payroll requests and time sheets into a large paper sack, stapled it at the top, and dropped it in a corner like a load of bagged-up Kitty Litter.

Then my phone rang. 'I just had lunch with Ida,' Jimmie's voice said. 'There's something real weird going on with Valentine Chalons.'

'He wouldn't see Ida?' I said.

'No, she visited him at Iberia General. He was overjoyed. They were supposed to have supper in Lafayette last night. Lou Kale dropped her off under the porte cochere at the restaurant. But Chalons takes one look at her, turns to stone, and has the valet bring up his car. Ida was pretty shook up. What a prick.'

'Did Kale try to come in with her?'

'No, he just drove her there.'

'Did Chalons see him?'

'I guess. Why?'

'Get away from them.'

'What's going on?'

'Val Chalons is behind everything that's been happening. The old man wasn't even an adverb.'

'Behind *what?*' he said. 'Are you drinking again?'

But I had no moral authority on the subject of the Chalons family and I didn't try to answer Jimmie's question. At quitting time, I called Molly and told her I'd be late for supper and drove to Clete Purcel's motor court.

'You're saying Valentine Chalons is the son of Lou Kale?' Clete said.

'That's been the engine the whole time,' I said.

'No, the engine's money. It's always money, no matter what they say.'

'Same thing,' I said. 'Val Chalons has spent his whole life lying about who he is. What happens to his credibility as a TV broadcaster if he admits he's always known his real father is a pimp? Imagine Lou Kale showing up at Chalons's country club.'

Clete studied my face. 'You want to salt the mine shaft?' he said.

'You doing anything else?' I asked.

The two of us sat down at Clete's old Smith-Corona portable and composed the following letter. Actually, most of it was Clete's work and in my estimation a masterpiece Ring Lardner would have tipped his hat to.

Dear Mr. Chalons,

A hooker I happened to know by the name of Big Tit Flora Mazaroni just gave me some interesting information about a pimp who is now in Lafayette, one Lou Coyne, a.k.a. Lou Kale. After packing too much flake up his nose, he told Flora he's got an illegitimate son in Jeanerette, a famous TV guy who just inherited between eighty and one hundred million dollars. Guess who this famous TV guy is?

Guess what else? Kale says this TV guy is not only a liar and a phony but also a horny sex freak who is so hard up he had to bop his space-o sister. Flora says Kale is going to milk this particular TV dude for every cent he's got.

I happen to be in the P.I. business. I got a personal score to settle with Kale, but I can also protect your interests if the above material seems to describe anyone in your acquaintance. If you need references, call Nig Rosewater at Bimstine's Bonds in New Orleans. Nig will vouch for my confidentiality and total professionalism.

Have a nice day,
Clete Purcel

But masterpiece or not, Clete and I decided we should not neglect Lou Kale. Clete rolled another sheet of paper into the Smith-Corona and started typing, his porkpie hat cocked at an angle, his stomach hanging over a pair of boxer shorts that were printed with sets of blue dice.

Lou –

You are probably surprised to hear from me after you set me up and your two hired bean-rollers tried to put out my lights. But business is business. Valentine Chalons does not want you and your wife hustling cooze in this area. I get the sense there's a family fight of some kind going on here, but I couldn't care less on the subject and I'm not pursuing it. The point is Chalons is inheriting eighty to one hundred million dollars and indicates he does not need his life and reputation queered by a lot of baggage from a Galveston whorehouse.

The short version is the guy's seriously pissed off and he's hired me to take care of the problem. He says you're a gutless douche bag and you'll squirm back under the rocks with the first shot across your bow. True or not, I'd like to hear a counteroffer.

In my opinion, this guy is not normal and the cops should have taken a lot harder look at him for his sister's murder. This is not a guy who shares the bucks. For some reason he seems to think you and your old lady got a sniff of his money and are going to lay claims on it. Believe me when I tell you his feelings about you are real strong. Did you hurt this guy when he was a kid or something?

Keep a smiley face.

Sincerely,

Clete Purcel, Private Investigator

Clete folded the letters, placed them in envelopes, and addressed each of them. Twenty minutes later one of his bonded-out clients, a habitual alligator poacher, picked up the envelopes for delivery in Lafayette and Jeanerette.

'Beautiful work, Cletus,' I said.

'Not bad. There's only one problem,' he said.

'What?'

'What if Val Chalons is not Lou Kale's kid?'

But other events that evening, involving an anachronistic New Orleans player, would soon take our minds off the letters we had just composed.

chapter twenty-eight

Johnny Wineburger had erotic dreams, but not of a kind that he understood. Sometimes he woke throbbing and hard in the morning, and briefly recalled a fleeting glimpse of an undressed woman, a pale, black-haired creature wrapped in mist, but the dream never contained a face or a name. In some instances, the figure kissed his hands, then put his fingers in her mouth. In some instances, she bit down on them, hard, her eyes veiled by a skein of shiny hair. The pain he felt was not entirely an unpleasant one.

Johnny did not know what the dream meant. A friend of his in the life, a kid named Jimmy Figorelli or Jimmy Fig or sometimes Jimmy Fingers, who had been with the First Cav at Khe Sanh, told Johnny to talk to a psychiatrist.

'Why?' Johnny asked.

'It means you got repressed desires to be a bone smoker,' the Fig said.

'How you know that?'

''Cause that's what the shrink told me,' the Fig replied.

But in truth Jericho Johnny didn't really care what the dream meant. Women were interesting on occasion but not terribly necessary in his life. In fact, if asked what *was* important in his life, he would not have had a ready answer. He had graduated from a Catholic high school and his parents had gone to temple, but he himself never took religion seriously. Nor had he ever understood people's apparent worries about moral issues. If there were any mysteries to life or human behavior, he failed to recognize them. You were born, you hung around a while, then you died. You had to read books to find that out?

At age nineteen he carried a union card with both the Teamsters and the Operating Engineers. That's when he met the Calucci brothers and picked up a cool five hundred bucks for popping the snitch who sent Tommy Fig's old lady to the women's prison at St. Gabriel.

He'd always heard the first hit was the hard one. Not so. It was a breeze. The guy was in his car at the Fair Grounds, eating a chili dog with melted cheese on it. Johnny walked up to the open window, put a Ruger behind the guy's ear, and pulled the trigger three times. The guy still had the plastic fork sticking out of his mouth when Johnny drove off with a young friend he helped throw a newspaper route.

If Johnny had an ethos, what some would call a worldview, it was one that operated in his head like shards of light and sometimes sound. His second hit wasn't on a dirtbag at a racetrack parking lot. The target was the cousin of Bugsy Siegel, a guy who, like Bugsy, had made his bones with Murder, Incorporated. This dude was a stone killer – smart, armed, and with no mercy for the poor schmucks he took out.

Johnny and his partner had gotten on the train at Jacksonville, headed south along the Florida coast, their sawed-off double-barrel shotguns broken down inside their suitcases. The evening sky was pink and blue, the ocean sliding in long fingers up empty beaches, miles and miles of orange groves slipping past the Pullman's windows. It was the most beautiful evening of Johnny Wineburger's life.

Just outside of West Palm, the sun went down in the 'Glades and a black shade fell across the land. Johnny and his partner fitted the pieces of their shotguns together, plopping twelve-gauge shells packed with double-aught bucks into the open breeches. When their train passed another train headed in the opposite direction, Johnny and his pal kicked open the door to the bedroom occupied by Siegel's cousin.

Then one of the most peculiar moments in Johnny's life occurred. In the jittering light and roar of noise created by the trains passing each other, amid the flashes of gunfire and explosions of wadding and pellets inside the closed room, all the color drained out of the world. The entire earth reduced itself to a black-and-white ink wash that was like the reductive nature of his dreams. Life was simpler than he had ever thought. You pulled the trigger and the target exploded. In this instance, the target was holding a pitcher of martinis and was dressed in a robe with a fur collar, as a king might be. In fact, the shower of gin and broken glass sparkled like a crown in the dead man's hair. But the power he had represented was now Johnny's, just as if the dead man's testosterone had been injected into his own.

On his second hit he had found the secret few button men shared: clipping a rat or a dirtbag was scut work for pay; clipping a king was both an acquisition and a high that had no equal.

But times had changed. The Giacano family had crashed and burned with the death of Didi Gee, and Asians and black street pukes had flooded the projects with crack and turned New Orleans into a septic tank. Punks the Italians would have thrown off a roof now jackrolled family people and sometimes shot them to death just for fun. There was no honor in the life anymore. There was no money in it, either.

The pukes ran the dope and did drive-bys on school

vards. The government not only legalized lotteries and casinos but encouraged addiction in its citizenry. The income for a fence or good house creep was chump change compared to the amounts corporate CEOs scammed off their investors through stock options.

But a guy still had to pay the bills. The twenty grand Jericho Johnny had borrowed from the shylocks, at a point and a half a week, was eating him alive. So push came to shove and he took this gig out here in Bumfuck. Why not? He didn't invent the world's problems. Almost everyone he popped had it coming. Some he wasn't sure about, but that was their grief, not his. Everybody got to the boneyard. Which was better, catching a big one in the ear or dying a day at a time with tubes up your nose and a catheter clamped on your joint?

It was dark when he parked his car in a turnrow between two sugar cane fields and began walking up Bayou Teche toward the ancient plantation home that was legendary for the strange people who lived inside it and the overgrown trees and plants that seemed intent on pulling the house back into the earth. The moon was down, the sky black with rain clouds. Through the oaks in the yard he could see lights in the windows, a gas lamp burning in the driveway. Jericho Johnny stopped on the edge of the cane and felt the breeze blow against his skin and realized he was sweating.

A candy-striped awning swelled with the breeze off the bayou. There were white feathers scattered on the grass and the crumpled bodies of pigeons floating among the lily pads along the bayou's bank. What kind of geek shoots pigeons in his yard? Johnny wondered. Talk about no class. Somebody should ship the guy's whole family to Iraq, he told himself.

He was starting to feel uncomfortable about the job. Maybe he was over the hill for it. No, it was something else. He was fooling around with guys who thought real men hit golf balls. Their wives were all neurotic, talked constantly in hush-puppy accents, and treated their husbands like dildos. So their men whocked golf balls like they wanted to kill the tee, got their ashes hauled in Miami, then went back home and pretended they weren' cooze-whipped dipshits. Another bunch that should be humping a pack in a sandstorm, Johnny thought.

But his cynicism and bitter humor provided no relief for the quickening of heart that he felt, the dryness in his mouth, and the loops of sweat under his armpits. What was wrong?

He pulled back the receiver on his silenced Ruger and checked to see if a .22 long round was seated in the chamber. Up ahead he saw fireflies in the trees and smelled an autumnal odor of dead leaves and gas on the wind. Time to get it over with, pop the dude, and get back to New Orleans, he thought. In his mind's eye, he saw himself back in his saloon, eating a small white bowl of gumbo, the rain falling on the elephant ears and banana trees outside his back windows.

He moved along the edge of the trees at the back of the Chalonses' property, past the back porch, the lighted kitchen, the porte cochere that glowed an off-yellow from a bug lamp. Then he stopped under a cedar tree and gazed at the shotgun house down by the bayou. It was paintless and gray, made of very old cedar, with a tin roof and a brick chimney that reminded him of a decayed tooth. The wind puffed off the bayou and Jericho Johnny heard a solitary pecan *ping* hard against the roof and roll loudly down the metal.

In the light of the gallery, he could see a little boy playing in the yard. *Bad news,* Johnny thought. Nobody said anything about a kid being around. Bad karma, bad options. That's what happened when you messed with amateurs. No class at all.

He went up the slope toward the main house, into trees

lack with shadow, his face pointed at the ground so no ght would reflect off it. Then he made an arc that took im back down toward the water, past the yard where the hild was playing.

He moved quickly along the grassy slope, through a egetable garden and over a half-collapsed rick fence. Through a side window of the shotgun house he could see fat black woman rolling pie dough on top of a table.

Nobody had said anything about a woman being ome. This gig was starting to suck worse and worse. Maybe he should just blow it off, he thought. But the hought of continuing to pay a point and a half a week on wenty large didn't sit well with him, either.

Then he saw a man get up from his chair and step out n the gallery and speak to the little boy. The little boy egan picking up his toys from the yard and putting them n a wagon. Johnny waited in the darkness, the lint from he cane field itching inside his shirt like lines of ants. Why would anybody want to click the switch on a black guy like this, anyway? Twenty large for a guy who probably worked for collard greens and neck bones?

Because Johnny was supposed to do the woman and he kid, too, he thought. Well, screw that. The deal was or the man. What was that joke Jimmy Fig used to make about the door gunner in 'Nam? How can you shoot women and children? It's easy, man, you just don't lead hem as much.

Yeah, screw that twice.

The front screen slammed, but Johnny could still see he kid in the yard. Was the man still out front? Again, ohnny smelled an odor that was like sewer gas and humus and leaves that have turned yellow and spotted nside pools of rainwater. It was a pleasant smell, like late all, except it was still summer and too early for the ireflies that were weaving their smoky circles inside the cedar trees.

Time to boogie, he thought. Pay the vig and find a new gig. Messing with law-abiding people genuinely blew.

He turned to retrace his steps back to his vehicle. Just as he did, he thought he saw a woman moving toward him through the live oaks on the slope. She was barefoot, her dress little more than gauze, her skin glowing, her hair a black skein across her face. He stood transfixed, dumbfounded by the presence of a figure who had escaped from his dreams and who seemed to be approaching him in slow motion, as though until this moment she had not been allowed to be a full participant in his life.

Johnny felt his ankle sink in a depression and the tendon twist against the bone. He bit down on the pain and righted himself, momentarily losing sight of the woman in the trees. Behind him, he thought he heard leaves blowing across the ground or wind rustling in a canebrake. When he turned toward the bayou, a figure stepped out from behind an abandoned privy and swung a short cutting instrument out of the sky, whipping it down with such force that the blow exploded inside his skull like an electrical flash.

He did not remember striking the ground, or the blow that landed on the back of his neck or the one that cut deep into his shoulder. A black man stood above him, cocking his head one way, then another, a hatchet hanging from his right hand. The black man had big half-moon eyebrows and an innocuous pieface; his erratic, jerky motions reminded Johnny of an owl sitting on a branch in a tree.

Taken out by Uncle Remus. What a laugh, he thought.

'Wasn't going to hurt your boy or woman,' Johnny said.

The black man leaned over him. 'Say again?' he said.

I whack kings. I took out Benny Siegel's cousin, Johnny said somewhere deep inside himself.

Then the barefoot woman who wore only white gauze approached him from the trees, parting the veil of hair on her face with her fingers. She knelt beside him, cupping her hands behind his head, lifting his face to hers. When she put her mouth on his it was cold and dry, as hollow as the grave. Then he felt her tongue slide past his teeth and probe deep inside him, stirring a heat in his genitals he had never experienced before. In the distance he heard a train, one that rattled with light and roared with sound, and he now realized what it was he had always wanted.

The homicide investigation was conducted by the St. Mary Parish Sheriff's Department, and it wasn't until the next morning that Helen Soileau and I went out to the home of Andre Bergeron and interviewed him in the warm shade of a pecan tree. Out in the sunlight I could see the depression and blood splatter in the grass where Jericho Johnny had spent the last few minutes of his life.

'You hit him three times with the hatchet?' I said.

'I ain't counted. Man had a pistol in his hand,' Andre replied. 'Say, I done tole all this to them others.'

'But not to us,' Helen said.

'I ain't meaning no disrespect, but ain't y'all just suppose to work inside Iberia Parish?'

'We take a lot of interest in anything that happens on Mr. Val's property, Andre. We'd really appreciate your helping us out, that is, if you'd consent to talk with us,' I said.

'I seen the gun in his hand. My wife and li'l boy was in the house. So I done what I had to. His words to me was he wasn't gonna hurt my son or my woman. That's what the man said. Then he died.'

'Why do you think he would say that to you?' I asked.

''Cause he didn't come here to kill nobody but me. Or maybe he was sent here to kill all of us but he couldn't do it. You tell me.'

'You seem like a smart man. Why would a professiona hit man be here to kill you or your family?' Helen said.

'It don't make no sense to me, either,' he replied.

'Nice spot you have here,' I said.

'It ain't bad,' he said.

'How'd you get the drop on this dude? I'd say that wa: pretty slick,' I said.

'Seen him out of the corner of my eye. Circled 'rounc the house, got my tool off the po'ch, and you know the rest.'

'I knew this guy, Andre. He worked for money and nc other reason. He was the best in the business and chargec accordingly. You make somebody mad at you, somebody so mad he'd pay an uptown guy like Jericho Johnny Wine- burger to kill you and your family?' I said.

'What I know, me?'

'You don't think he was after Mr. Val?' I said.

'Ax Mr. Val,' he replied.

'Thanks for your time, partner,' I said, and handed him one of our business cards. 'Mr. Val is a man of mystery isn't he? You know where he might be now?'

'He had an argument wit' a man in the front yard this morning. Man wit' real li'l ears. He flipped the man's tie in his face and told him not to come 'round here no more. Then he went off by hisself.'

'By the way, where's the hatchet?' I said.

'Cops took it. I got to get to my chores. Anyt'ing else?'

Helen and I got back in the cruiser and drove down the driveway, past the carpenters repairing the house and the tree surgeons pruning the oaks. Then, for no apparent reason, Helen braked the cruiser and rested her arms across the top of the wheel. Her shirt was stretched tight across her shoulders, the fingers of her right hand flicking at the air, as though she were trying to pick thoughts out of it. The sunlight through the pruned trees was so bright she had put on shades and I couldn't read her expression.

'You feel jerked around?' she said.

'Yep.'

'Like he was pointing the finger at Val Chalons but pretending not to?'

'That's what it sounded like to me.'

She took her foot off the brake and let the idle carry the cruiser toward the highway, the pea gravel ticking under the tires. 'Why would Chalons pay to have his handyman hit?' she said.

'Money.'

'Money?'

'Money,' I said.

'Like Bergeron might have a claim on the estate?'

'You got it.'

'Try to make that one stick,' she said, easing her foot back on the gas.

As soon as we got back to the department, I found a note in my mailbox asking me to call Jimmie at his apartment.

'Lou Kale was here about thirty minutes ago. He seems a little irrational,' Jimmie said.

'Oh?'

'Yeah, he thinks I'm involved in some kind of scam with Clete Purcel. He says Purcel is trying to blackmail either him or Val Chalons. What's the deal?'

'Clete sent letters simultaneously to both Kale and Chalons.'

'He deliberately stoked up this guy?'

'I helped a little.'

'A police officer?'

'I think Val Chalons's real parents are Lou Kale and Ida Durbin. I think Old Man Chalons died without leaving a will. That means Val has no familial claim on the Chalons fortune. I think the handyman, Andre Bergeron, may be the heir to a hundred million dollars. So Val Chalons hired Jericho Johnny Wineburger to kill the handyman and maybe his wife and child, too.'

'You're making some of this up?'

'Nope.'

'And Kale thinks I'm involved in a plot to blackmail him or his son, with that kind of money at stake?'

'Seems like it.'

'I don't believe this.'

'I'll have a talk with Kale.'

'Let it slide. Rest up and try not to think. You and Purcel, both. No matter what happens, don't think,' he said, then quietly hung up the phone.

In the morning I walked downtown to Koko Hebert's office and waited for him to get off the telephone. Outside, the wind was blowing in the trees on Main Street and the air was still cool and damp-smelling in the shade, but inside Koko's office the atmosphere was stifling, the odor of nicotine wrapped like cellophane on every surface in the room.

'What is it?' he said.

'Did you get the post on Johnny Wineburger from the forensic pathologist in St. Mary?' I said.

'What about it?'

'We're on the same side, Koko. Can't you speak civilly to people?'

'No, you're on your own side, Robicheaux. That said, what do you want?'

I gave up. 'Could the wounds on Johnny Wineburger have been made by the same instrument that killed Honoria Chalons?'

'No.'

'You're sure?'

'She was cut by an instrument that was honed like a barber's razor. The hatchet Wineburger was killed with must have been used to chop bricks. You trying to make the black guy for Honoria Chalons's death?'

'It occurred to me.'

He swiveled himself around in his chair and stared out a side window at a brick wall. From the back, he looked like a sad elephant humped on a circus stool. He drew in on his cigarette, then released a thick ball of white smoke from his mouth. 'You're not going to win,' he said.

'Excuse me?'

'You think you're going to bring down Val Chalons. But he and his people are just getting started. When they're finished with you, your name won't be worth warm spit on the sidewalk. You and your wife will be picking flypaper off your skin the rest of your lives.'

'That's the breaks,' I said.

'I hate talking to you,' he said.

That night a hurricane watch was in effect from Pensacola, Florida, to Morgan City, Louisiana. But in New Iberia the air was dead, superheated, stained with the smell of dead water beetles, the trees traced with the wisplike patterns of fireflies. Along East Main the windows sparkled like ice with condensation. Just before 11:00 p.m. Dana Magelli called from New Orleans.

'Better turn on CNN,' he said. In the background I could hear laughter, music, bottles or drink glasses tinkling.

'Where are you?' I said.

'In the Quarter. Half the Second District is here. We got him.'

I had already hit the button on the remote TV control. 'You've got the Baton Rouge serial killer?' I said.

'The DNA won't be in for a day or so. But he's the guy. Fibers on the clothes of Holly Blankenship match a shirt in his closet. He got stopped in his Popsicle truck at a DWI check.'

On the television screen I saw a New Orleans police official talking on camera, a dilapidated house and weed-infested yard in the background.

'The guy started acting hinky at the check,' Dana said. 'So we got a warrant on his house. He had a fifteen-year-old hooker tied up in there.'

'He's from New Orleans?' I said.

'You sound disappointed,' Dana said.

'No, it's just late. Congratulations.'

'Yeah. Thought you'd like to know,' he replied.

After I hung up, Molly sat down next to me on the couch. Our air-conditioning had broken down and the attic fan was on, the curtains on the living-room window churning in the air. 'What was all that about?' she said.

'Dana Magelli says NOPD nailed the Baton Rouge serial killer,' I said.

She studied my face. 'You have doubts?' she said.

'The guy in custody is from New Orleans. Why would he drive from Baton Rouge to Iberia Parish to dump his victims?'

'It's late. Come to bed,' she said.

'I'm going to bring Tripod and Snuggs inside.'

'It's not supposed to rain until tomorrow.'

'Both those guys need to come inside,' I said.

chapter twenty-nine

The next morning the sky was the gray-black of gun cotton, the dried-out palm fronds in my neighbor's yard stiffening in the wind. The air was full of leaves, and smelled like iodine or ship's brass on a hot day out on the salt. Helen called me into the office as soon as I got to the department. 'I want you to go to New Orleans with me and question the guy they've got in custody,' she said.

'Why not wait on the DNA report?' I asked.

'It's a media circus there. Iberia Parish is going to get shuffled out of the deck. We're going to be left with two unsolved homicides.'

'I'm not understanding you,' I said.

'The Baton Rouge serial killer dropped two DOAs on our doorstep. The guy in custody had a Popsicle route in the Garden District and Baton Rouge. You brought up the question first – why would he drive eighty miles to leave his victims in our parish?'

'So he's not the guy. Wait on the DNA,' I said.

'This from you?'

'Why not?'

She paused, her eyes dissecting my face. 'You don't want your wife left alone?'

'I've made some serious mistakes in the past and other people had to pay for them.'

I saw the impatience go out of her face. 'What if we're dealing with two serial killers, not one? Two shitbags working together?' she said.

'It's a possibility,' I said.

'I'm taking you off the desk. The D.A.'s office can go play with itself. Sign out a cruiser, bwana. We'll be back by five,' she said.

The wind shook the cruiser all the way down the four-lane to New Orleans. When we crossed the bridge at Des Allemands I could see boats rocking in their slips, leaves starting to strip from the trees by the water. In the south, lightning was striking on a bay, quivering in the clouds like pieces of white thread.

The suspect had already been processed into central lockup. His name was Ernest T. Fogel, a man whose race was hard to determine. He had uncut wiry hair, deeply pitted cheeks, and skin that looked chemically tanned. His jacket was not extensive: a molestation complaint that was dropped and two arrests for battery against prostitutes across the river in Algiers. Both victims had worked out of bars a few blocks from his rented room. Inside his file was a social worker's recommendation to the court that Ernest Fogel be kept away from children and pornography. A guard opened Fogel's cell and let me, Helen, and Dana Magelli inside.

Dana was a trim, dark-haired man, a sharp dresser whose style often belied his emotional disposition. He introduced us to Fogel with the strange formality that characterizes relationships between criminals and law enforcement personnel inside the system. The protocol exists less for reasons of professionalism than the fact it allows guards and cops and prosecutors to insulate themselves from certain individuals who are dramatically different from the rest of us. I didn't know if Fogel was one of these or not.

He sat on a cot, unshaved, dressed in jailhouse orange, a metal tray of half-eaten food beside him. According to Dana, Fogel maintained he was innocent of any crime whatsoever. He claimed the fifteen-year-old hooker tied up inside his house was a niece by a former marriage and that he was trying to save her from a life as a crack whore. Simultaneously he kept offering pieces of information that seemed to indicate an enormous knowledge about the killings in the Baton Rouge area. So far he had not asked for a lawyer. I had the sense Ernest T. Fogel was having a grand time.

'Fibers from your clothing were on the body of a girl by the name of Holly Blankenship, Mr. Fogel. How do you account for that?' I said.

'Was that her name?' he said, looking up at me.

'It was the name of a runaway somebody killed and threw in a garbage dump,' I said.

'Me and my wife busted up. I ain't proud of everything I've did since then. That's just the way it is,' he said.

'The way what is?' Helen said.

'When you're a single man, that's the way it is. There's women for hire. I ain't put them on the street,' he replied.

'She was murdered the same day a friend of mine and I interviewed her,' I said. 'Then fibers from your shirt show up on her body. Then you get busted with a girl tied up in your home. That's a lot for coincidence, isn't it?'

'I don't know about no interview or what that's got to do wit' me. But say what you want.' He was looking straight ahead now, seemingly indifferent to his legal jeopardy.

'I think you're a player in this, Mr. Fogel. But I think you're the weak sister in the script,' I said.

His eyes clicked up at mine. 'I'm what?'

'Serial killers often work in pairs. One guy is the orchestrator, the other guy does the scut work. Between the two of them, they form a third personality that commits deeds neither man could do on his own. You with me so far?'

'No,' he said.

But he was lying. I saw the insult take hold in his face, a resentful light glimmer inside his eyelashes.

'It's an easy concept,' I said. 'One guy is the brains. The other guy is a sock puppet. You want to ride the needle for some dude who's probably having a nice lunch right now, maybe knocking back a cold beer, while you take his weight?'

Ernest Fogel made no reply.

'Do you know where you are? This is central lockup,' Helen said. 'Ever had the midnight express up your ass?'

He looked into space for a long time. Down the corridor a cop dragged his baton along the bars of a cell door.

'How about it, buddy? Why not get your side of things out on the table? Maybe your situation isn't as bad as you think,' Dana said.

'I need a razor and some decent soap. I need a hairbrush, too, maybe some aftershave,' Fogel said.

'That can be arranged,' Dana said. 'You want to make a statement?'

'No, there's gonna be press at my arraignment. I ain't going there looking like a street person. I'd better talk to a lawyer now. Y'all got a good one? I don't mean nobody's cousin in the public defender's office, either.'

Helen, Dana, and I looked at one another. The only sound in the cell was the reverberation of a flushing toilet farther down the corridor. Dana's handsome face was pinched with anger and frustration.

'You ever hurt children? You ever do that, Ernest?' he asked, his hands folding and unfolding by his sides.

Fogel stirred the tip of his finger in a small jelly container on his food tray, then licked his finger clean, the back of his head turned to us so we could not see his face.

*

A tractor-trailer rig had spun out on the bridge at Des Allemands, backing up westbound traffic all the way through St. Charles Parish, so Helen and I headed up the interstate toward Baton Rouge, our flasher rippling. On the southwestern edge of Lake Pontchartrain I asked her to pull off on the shoulder a moment.

'What's up?' she said.

'I just want to look at the lake,' I said.

It was an odd request, I suspect, but Helen was a tolerant and decent person and had become a survivor because she had always accepted people for what they are. The lake was smoky green, dented with rain, blown with whitecaps. It looked exactly as the Gulf had looked on the day Jimmie and I had found ourselves trapped on the third sandbar off Galveston beach many years ago, the day Ida Durbin saved us from our own recklessness. The horizon was threaded with lightning, the air peppered with the smell of brine, the surf brown and frothy with sand sliding back from the beach. For just a moment it was 1958 again, and I thought perhaps if I turned my head fast enough I would see the glistening hard-candy surfaces of Chevy Bel Airs and chopped-down '32 and '39 Fords with Merc engines roaring down the highway, their Hollywood mufflers throbbing off the asphalt in the rain.

But it was not 1958 and I was a fool to keep holding on to memories about it. For good or bad, the present and the future lay right up the Mississippi River – a ninety-mile corridor called Toxic Alley. Its smokestacks and settling ponds told their own story. And maybe I had seen the reality of my own future back at central lockup. I had been inches away from a deviant who was arguably a child molester, an appellation that had now been attached to my name. I got back in the cruiser and shut the door.

'Ready to rock?' Helen said.

'Pour it on,' I said.

But I got no peace the rest of the day. Back in New

Iberia, the rain swept in sheets across the town and filled the gutters on Main with rivers of black water and dead insects. Molly and I ate supper in the kitchen while our window shutters rattled against their latches and the bayou rose above its banks into the trees.

'Want to go to the movies?' she said.

'Not this evening,' I replied.

'I thought I'd take Miss Ellen. She doesn't get out much.'

'That's fine. I'll read a bit.'

'Did something happen today?'

'No, not at all. Just be a little careful.'

'About what?'

'I can't put my hand on it. It's like the war. It's like seeing a guy out there in the elephant grass, then not seeing him,' I said.

She squeezed my hand. 'Don't scare me, Dave,' she said.

After Molly picked up the elderly lady from next door and headed for the movie theater, I realized what it was that had bothered me all day. It wasn't the fact that a serial killer was in our midst or that I couldn't return to the year 1958 or the fact that Valentine Chalons had bested me at every turn. It was none of those things, even though they laid a certain degree of claim on me. The real problem was my last conversation with Koko Hebert. How had Koko put it? Something to the effect that when Val Chalons and his minions were finished with me, my name wouldn't be worth warm spit on the sidewalk. Then he had added, 'You and your wife will be picking flypaper off your skin the rest of your lives.'

That was it. The damage Val Chalons could do was endless. His kind planted lies in the popular mind, smeared people's names, destroyed lives, and floated above the fray while others did their dirty work for them. As their victim, you never got the opportunity to confront your accusers. You didn't get to walk out on a dirt street in nineteenth-century Arizona and empty a double-barrel twelve gauge into the Clanton gang. Instead, you and your family picked flypaper off your skin.

In the meantime, the predators would continue hunting on the game reserve. They'd transport crack, brown skag, and crystal meth down I-49 and across I-10 and peddle it in the projects and on inner-city basketball courts and street corners, where teenage kids carried beepers and nine-Mikes and looked you straight in the eye when they explained why they *had* to do a drive-by on their own classmates.

The by-product was the whores. Sexual liberation and herpes and AIDS be damned, the demand was still there, as big as ever. But depressed times didn't produce the whores anymore. The dope did.

And guys like Lou Kale were there to help in any way they could.

Yes indeed, I thought, Lou Kale, now living regally in Lafayette, about to open an escort service.

Years ago, many street cops used to keep a second weapon they called a 'drop' or a 'throw-down.' It was usually junk, foreign-made, pitted with rust, the grips cracked, sometimes without grips at all. The important element was the filed-off or acid-burned serial numbers. When the scene went south and a fleeing suspect turned out to be unarmed, the 'throw-down' had a way of ending up under the body of a dead man.

Mine was an old .38 I took off a Murphy artist and part-time drug mule who used to work out of a bar two blocks from the Desire Welfare Project. The barrel and sight had been hacksawed off an inch from the cylinder. The grips were wrapped with electrician's tape. But the previous owner's carelessness and neglect had not affected his weapon's mechanical integrity. The cylinder still locked firmly in place when the hammer snapped down on the firing pin and didn't shave lead on the back end of the barrel.

I put on my raincoat and hat, dropped the revolver in my pocket, and drove to Lou Kale's motel in Lafayette.

It was still raining hard when I parked under a spreading oak and showed my badge to a young woman at the desk. 'Lou Kale,' I said.

She was probably a college kid. Her face was plain, earnest, eager to please, totally removed for any implication my presence might have. 'He's in one-nineteen. Would you like me to ring his room?' she said.

'That's all right. Would you let me have a key, please?'

'I'm not sure I'm supposed to do that,' she said.

'It's fine. This is part of a police investigation,' I said.

'Well, I guess it's all right, then,' she said, programming a card for me.

I walked down the corridor, past soft drink and candy machines, and entered an annex that paralleled the swimming pool. I didn't feel good about what I had just done. The girl at the desk was probably a good person and I had taken advantage of her trust and deceived her. In my mind's eye I saw myself somehow making it up to her, and I knew at that moment that the script for the next few minutes was already written in my head and the final act was one that I must not allow myself to see. I stuck the electronic key into the door of Room 119 and pulled it out quickly. When the tiny green light flashed at me, I twisted the door handle and stepped inside, my right hand squeezed around the taped grips of the .38.

Lou Kale was asleep on his side, bare-chested, a pair of pajama bottoms notched into his love handles. The room was dark, but the swimming pool lights were on outside and the surface of the water glowed with a misty green luminosity in the rain. When I closed the curtain on the sliding door, Lou Kale's eyes opened as though he had been shaken violently awake.

'You know what a dry drunk is, Lou?' I said.

'Dry what?'

'It's a guy like me. That means you're shit out of luck.'

He lifted himself up on his arms. His abdominal muscles looked as hard as the rollers on a washtub, his chest and shoulders coated with soft strips of monkey fur. Even with the air-conditioning on, the room smelled like an animal's lair or unburied offal. By the bed was a service table, and in the middle of it a steak knife and ragged pink T-bone rested on a white plate marbled with gravy and blood.

'I got no beef with you, Jack,' he said.

'Remember when you woke me up in that motel in Galveston? You touched the muzzle of a nickel-plated automatic to the center of my forehead. You called me "hoss" and told me I had a lot of luck. I was twenty years old.'

'What are you doing with that gun, man?'

I had dumped all six shells from the cylinder into my palm. I inserted one of them into a random chamber and clicked the cylinder back into the revolver's frame. Then I put the hammer on half-cock, spun the chamber, and reset the hammer.

'I'm going to hand you this pistol, Lou. When I do, I want you to point it at me and squeeze the trigger. Maybe you'll punch my ticket. But if not, it will be my turn, and the odds for you will have shrunk appreciably. Are you processing this, Lou?'

'You need to fire your psychiatrist.'

'Take it,' I said.

'I don't want it.'

'This is as good as it's going to get, partner. I advise you to take it.'

But he kept his hands at his sides, his face jerking away

each time the barrel came close to him. 'Take it, you piece of shit,' I said.

'No!' he said, teeth clenched.

That's when I lost it. I hooked him in the face with my left, mashed my knee into his chest, and forced the revolver into his hands. 'Do it!' I said.

'No!'

'Do it, you motherfucker!'

The muzzle was pointed into my chest, inches from my sternum. I forced his thumb onto the trigger and pressed it back against the trigger guard. I heard the hammer snap on an empty chamber. His eyes were wide with disbelief as they stared up into mine.

'You're crazy,' he said, his voice seizing in his throat, like a child who has been crying uncontrollably.

'My turn,' I said, pulling the revolver from his hands.

'Just tell me what you want.'

'Val Chalons is your son, isn't he?'

'That's what this is about? Are you nuts? You make me pull the trigger on a cop over –'

I clenched my left hand on his throat and jammed the .38 into his mouth with my right, forcing the cylinder over his teeth. He gagged, spittle running from the corners of his mouth. I pulled the trigger and heard the hammer snap again on an empty chamber.

'Oh Jesus,' he said, trembling all over when I slid the barrel from his mouth.

'Is Val Chalons your –'

'Yeah, yeah, we found out when the old man needed a kidney donation. He had to get the kidney from the girl.'

'Honoria?'

He nodded, blotting the spittle and blood on his mouth with the bedsheet.

'Val put the contract on me?' I said.

'Figure it out. How many people want you snuffed?'

'I wouldn't be clever.'

334

'He don't consult with me. He's an educated man. People get in his face, he deals with it. *That* he gets from me.'

I looked at him a long time. There were other questions I could have asked him, but the surge of terror that had robbed him of his defenses was gone and I had no inclination to restore it. In fact, I wondered if the moral insanity that characterizes terminal alcoholism had not taken up presence in my own life. I wiped the .38 clean on a towel and opened the curtain on the sliding glass door. Hailstones were bouncing on the St. Augustine grass and the cement by the pool.

'I can't force you out of the area, Lou, but I'm going to make life as uncomfortable for you as I can,' I said.

'You did a switcherroo on that gun, didn't you? You palmed the shell?'

I flipped open the cylinder on the .38 and shucked out the cartridge I had loaded earlier. It had been one chamber removed from rotating under the firing pin.

'You got a lot of luck, Lou. Wear this on your key chain,' I said, and bounced the cartridge off his chest.

As I turned to walk out, I heard him scrape the steak knife off his dinner plate and charge at my back. I drove my elbow into his face and left him on the carpet, holding his nose with both hands.

A moment later I stopped at the desk in the lobby. 'I owe you an apology, Miss,' I said.

'What for?' the girl behind the desk said, smiling.

'One day I'll tell you. Here are a couple of gift certificates for a dinner at the Patio in New Iberia. The owner gave them to me, so it's no big deal.'

'You don't have to do that,' she said.

'Yeah, I do.'

'Thank you,' she said.

'Good night,' I said.

'Good night,' she replied.

I got in my truck and drove out from under the spreading oak where I had parked. A blue and pink neon sign in the shape of a martini glass and a reclining nude inside it was stenciled against the sky. I floored the truck through a broken chain of puddles and swerved out onto the old two-lane to New Iberia, the road ahead black with rain.

chapter thirty

At 8:01 a.m. Friday I called Koko Hebert at his office. 'Was Honoria Chalons a kidney donor?' I said.

He put down the receiver, then scraped it up a moment later. 'Neither a donor nor a recipient,' he said. 'Why?'

'Val Chalons was asked to be a kidney donor for his father. It turned out they weren't related. Supposedly Honoria bailed out the old man.'

'Honoria took all her parts into the grave.'

'You know how to say it, Koko.'

'Anything else?'

'Where do we start a search on a kidney transplant for Raphael Chalons?'

'No, where do *you* start a search,' he corrected, and hung up.

Outside, the rain was twisting in sheets, cars inching along in water up to the doors. The phone on my desk rang in less than thirty seconds after Koko had broken the connection. 'What are you trying to tell me?' he said.

'Val is not the son of Raphael Chalons. The old man didn't leave a will. The Chalons estate is probably up for grabs.'

'He sliced up his sister?'

'I wouldn't put it past him. But I doubt it.'

'Why?'

'He doesn't have the guts.'

'How does this figure into anything, except the fact you hate Valentine Chalons?'

'He tried to have me killed. I'm getting tired of your social outrage, partner.'

For the first time I could remember, Koko Hebert had nothing acerbic to say.

'The old man always went to Houston for his serious medical work. We need to get the judge involved,' he said. 'In the meantime, I'll process some stuff on the computer. Organ transplants involve lots of agencies. Maybe I can take a shortcut. I used to know the Chalons family physician in Lafayette. But I think he might be dead,' he said.

'I appreciate it,' I said.

'No, you're like all drunks, Dave. You just want your way,' he replied.

He was probably right, but at that point I didn't care. I attended the noon meeting of the Insanity Group, then drove back to the department through streets where the storm sewers had backed up and cars had flooded out and been left abandoned by their owners. At the noon meeting I made no allusion to the fact that the previous night I had forced a terrified man to point a revolver into my chest and pull the trigger and that I in turn had jammed the weapon down his throat and done the same to him. I began to wonder if in fact there were some deeds you confessed only to God, because no one else would believe them.

At 1:36 p.m. Dana Magelli called from NOPD. 'There's no DNA match on Ernest Fogel,' he said. 'We've got him on the abduction of the fifteen-year-old, but that's it. You got anything at your end?'

'Nothing I haven't already told you,' I replied.

'You remember the story about the abduction and murder of John Walsh's kid?' he said.

'Yeah, sure.'

'The partner of that serial killer in Texas, Henry Lucas? He might have murdered Walsh's boy. But we'll never know. The guy died of AIDS in the Broward County Stockade.'

I wasn't quite sure what his point was and in truth I was afraid to ask. The story he had alluded to was one of the saddest I had ever encountered as a law officer.

'I think Ernest Fogel is like that guy in the Broward County Stockade. We'll never know the extent of his crimes,' Dana said. 'He'll be out in a few years and keep killing people, maybe children, and it won't stop until mortality catches up with him. My wife says that's why I don't sleep at night. How about you? You get a full night's sleep?'

The radio said the hurricane churning out in the Gulf might make landfall between New Orleans and Mobile. Down in Plaquemines Parish, whose narrow extremities dangle like a severed umbilical cord far out in the salt, most reasonable people had already begun heading up Highway 1 toward Red Cross shelters in New Orleans. But by midafternoon the wind and rain had stopped in New Iberia and a dripping stillness had descended upon the town. Molly had said she was going to stop at the grocery store after work, but I thought it might be a fine evening to go out for dinner. Before leaving the office for the day, I called Molly at her agency and got the message machine.

When I parked in the driveway, Snuggs was waiting for me on the gallery railing, his paws tucked under his chest, his thick, short-haired tail flipping and curling and uncurling in the air like a magician's rope.

'How's it hangin', Snuggs?' I said, picking him up.

He rested on his back against the crook of my arm, purring, tightening his feet against me for extra purchase.

The two of us went inside. Molly was still not home. I called again at the agency. This time the message machine did not pick up.

I fed Snuggs and Tripod, then walked down to the bayou. The water had risen into the trees along the bank and was swollen with mud and cluttered with broken tree limbs and floating islands of green hyacinths that had torn loose from their root systems and were now blooming incongruently with yellow flowers. In the middle of the bayou an upside-down pirogue spun in an eddy, its hull shining dully in the overcast. The air was as cool and clean and fresh-smelling as spring, the trees dripping chains of rain rings into the bayou. Out of nowhere, two brown pelicans sailed past me and landed on the water not thirty feet from me.

I heard Tripod waddling down the bank behind me. I scooped him up and folded his tail down and rested his seat on my palm so he could have a good overview of the bayou. 'Check it out, Tripod,' I said. 'The pelicans are back on the Teche, just like Bootsie said they would be. You happen to know these two guys?'

If he did, he wasn't saying.

The pelicans floated past me, their feathers necklaced with raindrops, their long beaks pulled into their breasts. I flipped Tripod up on my shoulder and walked back toward the house, an unexpected sense of serenity singing in my soul.

Squirrels were chasing one another around the tree trunks and robins and mockingbirds were picking insects out of the new leaves on the ground. The birdhouse I had bought from Andre Bergeron hung suspended on a wire over my head, canting slightly in the breeze, its perch empty. I remembered I had still not poured birdseed in it. 'Time to fill her up, huh, Tripod?' I said, setting him down.

I got a sack of seed and a stepladder from the shed, and

climbed up to the birdhouse. I pulled the beveled plug from the roof and began pouring seed down into the feeder compartment inside. The plug swung back and forth on a tiny brass chain that was affixed to the plug's bottom and pinned inside the roof, so that the chain didn't dangle outside the hole and impair the clean structural lines of the wood. The birdhouse, with its pegs and hand-notched joints and sanded surfaces stained with vegetable oil, was a fine example of craftsmanship and obviously the work of someone who had an aesthetic eye.

But my attention was diverted away from my activity when I happened to glance back through my kitchen window. Inside, I could see the red light flashing on my message machine. Molly must have called when I had been watching the pelicans with Tripod, I thought. I climbed down from the ladder and went through the back door.

I pushed the 'play' button on the machine. 'I might be late. I'll pick up some frozen gumbo for supper at the Winn-Dixie on the way home, but first I need to take care of a problem,' Molly's voice said. Then after a pause, as though she were trying to restrain a vexation she didn't want to vent, she added, 'I'm disappointed in someone. He borrowed my tools again without asking. I need to straighten this guy out. Some people, huh, troop?'

I called the agency, but no one answered and the machine was still off. I tried her cell phone but got her voice-mail recording. The time was 5:43 p.m.

Straighten which guy out?

I stared out the kitchen window at the birdhouse suspended on a wire above my stepladder, the plug from the feeder hole dangling from its tiny chain.

Good God, I thought, and shut my eyes at my own stupidity.

I looked up Koko Hebert's phone number in the directory and punched it in on my cell phone as I headed out the door. 'Koko, can you go to the evidence locker and find the piece of chain that was on the body of Fontaine Belloc?'

I heard him sigh. 'How about tomorrow?'

'I bought a birdhouse from Andre Bergeron. Inside the construction is a length of brass chain that looks like the piece you found on the Belloc woman . . . You there?'

'Why don't you take care of it?'

'Because I think Bergeron may be with my wife now,' I replied.

I got in my truck and began backing up into the East Main. But a pearly limo with charcoal-tinted windows pulled to the curb and blocked my way. Someone in the backseat rolled a window down on its electrical motor.

'Get out of the driveway, Val,' I said.

He sat on the rolled white leather seat, dressed in pleated beige slacks and a golfing shirt, a bottle of Cold Duck balanced on his knee. On the far side of him was a woman I didn't know. Her face was stiff with makeup, her blouse unbuttoned on the tops of her breasts. I saw her take the last hit on a roach and drop it out of the top of her window onto the street.

'Your wife shouldn't make remarks about Andre,' Val said. 'Big mistake.'

'Say that again.'

'Somebody told Andre how your wife made fun of him. Not good, Davey boy. No, no, not at all good,' he said.

'You move your fucking car before I pull your teeth out,' I said.

He laughed, spoke to his chauffeur, then rolled up his window while handing the bottle of Cold Duck to the woman, as though the world beyond the boundaries of his limo no longer existed.

I backed into the street, cars swerving and blowing around me, then ran the red light down by the Shadows and headed for Molly's agency.

On the way I punched in a 911 on my cell phone and asked the dispatcher to send a cruiser to the agency and one to Andre Bergeron's house in Jeanerette.

'What's the nature of the emergency, sir?' she asked.

'My wife's life could be in danger. Who is this?' I said.

She gave me her name. She was new on the job and obviously swamped with calls reporting traffic accidents and power outages. 'Two of the bridges have been hit by boats and are closed,' she said. 'The bridge at Nelson's Canal might be open in a few minutes. But we can't be certain.'

'Call Jeanerette. Ask them to send a city car to the Chalons property. Tell them to place the black man, Andre Bergeron, in custody.'

'Sir, I can't do that without an explanation,' she said.

'He's the Baton Rouge serial killer.'

'Sir, I have to have verification of who you are,' she replied.

I dropped the cell phone on the seat and steered around a truck from the electric company and a repair crew that was working on a downed power line. Up ahead, I could see the turnbridge at the confluence of Nelson's Canal and Bayou Teche. Evidently the huge sprockets on the bridge had jammed when it was partially opened, and now traffic had backed up for hundreds of yards on both sides of the bayou.

There was only one thing for it. I abandoned my truck and began running by the side of the road toward the bridge, my hand tight on my holstered .45. But even as I was running past the line of idling cars and the faces of the curious and the bemused, the image of Val Chalons seated in the back of his limo would not go out of my head. No, it was not his imperious or insulting manner that bothered me, or that he seemed to be embracing and flaunting the meretricious world represented by his mother and Lou Kale. It went beyond that, something that was raw, designing, inhuman, genuinely evil.

But what?

You're being set up again, I told myself.

But sometimes your only option is to play out the hand, no matter what the consequences. Sometimes when you're deep in Indian country, the only speeds available are full throttle and fuck it.

The bridge's rotary system had locked against itself when the steel grid was only five feet from the asphalt. I backed off, then jumped into space and landed upright with a loud *ping* on the metal. People were starting to get out of their cars and stare. I raced to the other end of the bridge and jumped again, this time skinning my elbow and tearing the knee of my trousers on the road surface.

I got up and started running toward the rear of the traffic jam. A fat man wearing a silver suit and a Stetson short-brim was getting out of a huge purple Cadillac. The factory hood ornament on the Cadillac had been replaced with a pair of needlepointed brass cattle horns. 'What the hell is going on?' the fat man said.

'How much gas is in your car?' I said.

'Gas?'

'This is an emergency situation,' I said, opening my badge holder in his face. 'I'm taking your vehicle.'

'Not my car, you're not. I've got to be at the Oil Center in Lafayette in thirty minutes.'

'In about thirty seconds you're going to be on the ground in cuffs,' I said.

I got behind the wheel, and with the driver's door still open I backed straight down the two-lane to the next intersection, cut the wheel, then floored the accelerator down Old Jeanerette Road toward Molly's agency, slamming the door as the cement raced by me.

I ran a stop sign at eighty, clipped a mailbox and a garbage can, passed a tractor-drawn cane wagon, and forced an oncoming truck into a rain ditch. Water oaks along the road and collapsed barbed-wire fences and shacks and single-wide trailers with broken windows sped by me, then I saw Molly's compound up ahead.

The grounds were empty, the blinds drawn in the administration building, the St. Augustine grass green and stiff with the rain, an inch higher since yesterday. I pulled into the entrance, my heart hammering, sweat breaking on my forehead. I saw no sign of Molly's car, nor any other vehicle.

Think, I told myself. Would Molly have gone to Andre Bergeron's house to confront him about the unauthorized use of her farm tools? No, she did things in a measured way and was not a compulsive person. Normally, she would have telephoned a person who had wronged her, asked him to explain himself, perhaps invited him to come by and have coffee and talk with her. That was Molly Boyle's way.

But Molly's recorded telephone message had mentioned that she was 'disappointed' and the fact that someone had borrowed her tools without permission 'again.' She may not have been an obsessive person, but she had a low level of tolerance for people who lied or violated the trust of others, which she always referred to as an act of spiritual theft.

I parked by the administration building and rattled the doors, then walked next door to the cypress cottage which Molly used to share with a nun who had returned to the Midwest to care for her mother. The nun's car was parked under a pecan tree, covered by a clear plastic tarp fogged with humidity and pooled with wet leaves and bird droppings.

I wiped my face with my shirt. The air stank of stagnant mud, raw sewage backed up from the treatment plant, the bloated body of a drowned cow that gars were feeding on in the shallows. I could hear bottle flies buzzing inside the plastic tarp on the nun's car.

When the sun broke through a cloud, the tops of the cypress trees along the bayou lit up as though they had been touched with a flame. I saw an aluminum boat snugged inside a clump of flooded willows, its motor pulled out of the water, an anchor consisting of a cinder block threaded by a rope thrown up on the bank.

Forty yards downstream, Molly's car was parked behind the barn, wedged between the back wall and the remains of a disease-eaten mulberry tree that had been uprooted by the storm. Both the driver and passenger doors hung open.

I felt a wave of nausea and fear wash through my system. I ran back to the tarp-covered vehicle of Molly's friend, a pressure band like a strip of metal tightening against the side of my head. I meshed the plastic in both hands and ripped it free of the roof, showering myself with water and birdshit. A cloud of beetles and greenflies and a stench of rats rose into my face. But there was no one inside the car and no footprints around the trunk area.

I flung the tarp down and headed for the barn.

Chickens were pecking under the pole shed and the live oak that arched high over the barn roof. I started to go down by the bayou and circle behind the barn and come up on the other side, but I remembered there was a window in back that gave a clear view down to the water. I removed my .45 from my holster and pulled back the receiver and slipped a hollow-point forward into the chamber.

A rooster came out from under the tractor, its wings spread wide, its throat warbling, scattering hens across the apron of dirt that extended out to the drip line of the oak tree. I pressed myself against the front of the barn, the .45 pointed upward, the pressure band on the right side of my head squeezing tighter. The barn door was ajar. From inside I heard a hissing sound and smelled an odor like scorched metal.

I ripped the door open and went inside, pointing the .45 into the gloom with both hands.

Molly's wrists were locked with plastic cuffs behind a chair, her head enclosed in a burlap bag that Andre Bergeron had cinched around her neck with his belt. An acetylene torch lay on the workbench, a concentrated blue flame knifing from its nozzle. Bergeron held the sharpened edge of a machete under Molly's chin. He was bare-chested, his skin glistening, a bandanna wrapped around his head to keep the sweat out of his eyes.

'T'row the gun down or I take her head off,' he said.

I now realized how Valentine Chalons had played me. 'Chalons set us both up, Andre. I'm supposed to pop you so he can inherit Mr. Raphael's estate.'

'Don't matter. T'row down the gun. Both of us know you ain't gonna shoot it.'

'That's a bad bet,' I said.

'You t'ink? One more don't mean nothing to me,' he said.

My eyes had adjusted to the poor light and I could see him clearly now. He was standing on the opposite side of Molly, much of his body protected by hers. His skin was powdered with dust and bits of hay, his chest running with sweat, the top of his beltless trousers soaked with it. He tightened the machete against Molly's throat, lifting her chin upwards, the burlap stretching against her face.

'Okay, we'll work it out,' I said, and began to lower my weapon.

I saw his lips part over the whiteness of his teeth. 'That's more like it. Yes, suh, it gonna go smooth now,' he said.

His back was slightly stooped, his arm probably stressed by the unnatural way he had to hold the machete under Molly's chin. He straightened up slightly, shifting a crick out of his back.

I locked my sights on the top of his sternum and pulled

the trigger. The round hit him at an angle and spun him against the side of a stall. The round had cored through his back and blown a white swatch out of the wood. He lay on the floor, his head against the stall, his fingers spidered across the entry wound. Like most people who are the gunshot victims of a weapon like a .45 auto, his face could not register the amount of damage his body had just incurred. His mouth hung open, his stomach went soft and trembled like a bowl of Jell-O, his eyes fluttered and rolled as he went into shock.

Then he turned on his side and curled into an embryonic ball. Beneath one of his love handles was a half-moon incision, as thick as a night crawler, where he had given up a kidney for the father who had relegated him to a shack on the back of the family property.

But I didn't care about the fate of Andre Bergeron or the perverted genes or social injustices that had produced him. In fact, I didn't even care enough about him to hate him or deliver another round into his body, which I could have done and gotten away with. I uncinched the belt from Molly's neck and pulled the burlap bag from her head. I held her face against me and kissed the sweat in her hair and touched her eyes and mouth. I opened my pocketknife and sliced the plastic cuffs on her wrists and stroked her shoulders and arms and wiped the hair out of her eyes and lifted her to her feet, my hands shaking so badly she had to hold them tightly in hers.

In the distance I could hear a siren coming hard down Old Jeanerette Road.

Molly placed her forehead on my chest, and the two of us stood there a long time like that, not speaking, listening to the wind blow through the open door and out the back window, the green-gold splendor of the outside world beckoning like an old friend on the edges of our vision.

epilogue

Capitalists are hanged by the rope they sell their enemies. Mystics who help formulate great religious movements writhe in sexual torment over impure thoughts a shoe salesman leaves behind with adolescence. A Crusader knight in search of the True Cross returns to Marseilles from Palestine with a trunkful of Saracen robes, inside of which is a plague-infested mouse.

My experience had been, like George Orwell's, that human beings are possessed of much more courage and self-sacrifice than we give them credit for, and when the final test comes, they usually go down with the decks awash and the guns blazing. Our moral failure lies in the frailty of our vision and not in our hearts. Our undoing is in our collective willingness to trust those whom we shouldn't, those who invariably used our best instincts against us. But as a police officer I also learned long ago that justice finds us in its own time and of its own accord, and in ways we never, and I mean absolutely never, anticipate.

I would like to say I tacked up Valentine Chalons with a nail gun. But I didn't. Not even close. Val's denouement began and ended with his own peers and his own machinations. First, there were rumors he was the son of a pimp, then suspicion spread that out of fear for his own reputation he had concealed his intuitions that Andre Bergeron was the Baton Rouge serial killer, allowing Bergeron to continue murdering innocent women, including Val's own sister, with whom some said Val had conducted an affair.

The woman who had filed molestation charges against me admitted she was paid by one of Val's employees. The photographer who had stuck a camera in my face after I gave Val a beating in Clementine's told an alternative news magazine he had been personally assigned by Val Chalons to take my life apart with vise grips.

Val tried to immerse himself in charity drives and the activities of a scholar who was above the fray. He hired a young woman named Thelma Lou Rooney to do research on his ancestors who had ridden with the White League and the Knights of the White Camellia during Reconstruction. Evidently Val had long been possessed of a secret ambition to become a historical writer, an ambition that ironically he could have fulfilled without any help from anyone else. But Val was one of those who defined himself in terms of the control he exerted over others rather than in terms of what he accomplished as an individual.

Thelma Lou was pretty, blond, and extremely bright. She claimed a double degree in history and anthropology from the University of North Carolina, plus three summer sessions at the Sorbonne. She was a miracle worker when it came to extracting arcane information from decaying courthouse records. She was also an amazing filter for the Chalonses' participation in the activities of the White League, particularly the murder of blacks during the Colfax Massacre of 1873. Whatever information she dug up on the Chalons family either sanitized their roles or indicated that somehow they were victims themselves, or, as Val would say, 'forced to take extreme measures in extreme times.' The staff at Val's television stations loved her. So did Val.

In fact, Val and Thelma Lou were soon in the sack. He flew with her to Dallas and New York and bought her clothes that were arguably the most beautiful on any woman in our area. Unfortunately for Val, Thelma Lou Rooney was a pathological liar and con artist who could sell ice cubes to Eskimos.

Her real name was Thelma Lou Watkins, the seventeen-year-old daughter of a bovine, peroxide-headed woman who operated a mail-order quilt company out of Jellico, Kentucky. Her mother showed up out of nowhere with a birth certificate and filed statutory rape charges against Val, followed one week later by a civil suit asking for millions in damages.

Val compounded his problem by denying on the air any knowledge of the girl's age, then apologizing for any emotional injury he may have caused her. He was repentant, paternal, and dignified. On camera he looked like the patrician he had always aspired to be. But the next day Thelma Lou caught him at a restaurant frequented by Chamber of Commerce and media people and let go with a dish-throwing tirade that had the waiters backed against the walls. Then Thelma Lou's mother produced a taped telephone conversation between her daughter and Val that was so lascivious only one Lafayette broadcaster, a scurrilous late-night shock jock, had the temerity to air it.

When Val thought his problems couldn't get any worse, the woman I had seen toking on a roach in the back of his limo sold a video to a cable channel of herself and Val going at it on a water bed.

The same people whom he had enlisted in his attempt to destroy Molly and me homed in on him like piranha on a drowning water buffalo.

The day Val died, his gardens were abloom with chrysanthemums, the air golden, the oaks in his yard sculpted against a hard blue sky. But inside the guesthouse, where he had continued to live, the floors and counters and tables were cluttered with fast-food containers, the bathroom pungent with mildew, the trash baskets overflowing. For days he had not changed out of his pajamas or bathed or shaved. Evidently he rose early on the last morning of his life and dissolved a bottle of Seconal in a glass of bourbon, then sat down to listen to a CD on his stereo. The body of the man who had been the friend of the powerful, surrounded by sycophants, was not found for five days, when a meter reader reported an unusual odor to the city police department.

The song that had played on the stereo over and over again was 'It Wasn't God Who Made Honky-Tonk Angels,' sung by his mother, Ida Durbin.

The probate court that decided the disposition of the Chalons estate put its worth at nearly ninety-six million dollars. Attorneys whose only professional recommendation was the fact they were legally qualified to practice law under the Napoleonic Code appeared out of the woodwork from Shreveport to New Orleans. DNA testing proved that Andre Bergeron was the son of Raphael Chalons and that Val was not. Bergeron was convicted on three counts of capital murder and sentenced to death by injection, but this did not stop his wife from retaining a half dozen lawyers on contingency to represent her claim and her son Tee Bleu's. In the meantime, Lou Kale and Ida Durbin hired a private investigative group that, surprise, produced a last will and testament signed by Raphael Chalons, leaving his wealth to Honoria and Val.

The problem was the attorney who had notarized it was Sookie Motrie, a man so notorious for his various scams that an association of Louisiana trial lawyers introduced a bill in the legislature specifically designed to prevent Sookie from taking the state bar exam.

No matter, though. Sookie and his associates linked

arms with Ida Durbin and Lou Kale, claiming that Ida and Lou were the parents of the only legal claimant to the estate, Valentine Chalons, now deceased.

The upshot was a settlement that awarded half of the estate to Mrs. Bergeron and Tee Bleu and the other half to Lou and Ida.

Guess who's living today in the big white house on the Teche but no longer singing the blues in B flat?

Jimmie finished reconstructing our birthplace south of town and spends weekends there, sometimes with friends from New Orleans. He invites Molly and me to his barbecues and lawn parties, but I find excuses not to attend. It has been my experience that age brings few gifts, but one of them is the acceptance that the past is the past, for good or bad, and if you are fortunate enough to have lived in an era that was truly exceptional, characterized by music, chopped-down Fords with chrome-plated engines roaring full out against purple sunsets, and drive-in restaurants where kids jitterbugged and did the dirty bop and knew they would never die, then those moments are forever inviolate, never to be shared or explained, and, like images on a Grecian urn, never subject to time and decay. Why make them less by trying to re-create them?

I attend meetings at the Insanity Group and still have not learned how to sleep through the night. Every Sunday, Clete picks me up in his Caddie and we fish for speckled trout out on West Cote Blanche Bay. Molly, Snuggs, Tripod, and I live on Bayou Teche and in the early-morning hours often see two pelicans sailing low over the water, their extended wings touched by the sunrise. For me, these are gifts enough.